MINDLINE

MINDLINE
BOOK 2 OF THE DREAMHEALERS

M. C. A. HOGARTH

STUDIO
MCAH

Mindline
Book 2 of The Dreamhealers
First edition, copyright 2013 by M.C.A. Hogarth

M. Hogarth
PMB 109
4522 West Village Dr.
Tampa, FL 33624

ISBN-13: 978-1494771317
ISBN-10: 1494771314

Cover art by MCA Hogarth

Designed & typeset by Catspaw DTP Services
http://www.catspawdtp.com/

TABLE OF CONTENTS

CHAPTER 1

 T WOULD BE JUST HIS LUCK to begin his residency by reporting to the hospital as a patient. Jahir Seni Galare, nascent xeno-therapist, Eldritch noble and apparently complete lightweight, sat on a bench just outside the Pad nexus that had delivered him to the surface of the planet Selnor. He had his carry-on in his lap and was trying to be unobtrusive about using it as a bolster until the dizziness stopped. When he'd left his homeworld for the excitement and multicultural adventure that was the Alliance, he'd been unaware of how much gravity affected physiology until he'd begun suffering from Seersana's greater weight. While there he'd undertaken an acclimatization regimen . . . but apparently the capital world of the Alliance was even heavier than Seersana. Much more so, if his body was any indicator.

At least the dizziness gave him a reason to stop moving. He'd been traveling for the better part of six days now. Had he been inclined, he could have prevailed on his Queen to arrange direct transport from the world where he'd been studying to the world where the final phase of his education would commence, but he hadn't wanted to trade on his family connections. Instead he'd chosen to make the journey the way one of his . . . friends . . . would have, had they gone, by a series of vessels and shuttles.

He'd used the time to enjoy the culture—was that not why he'd left his world in the first place?—to see the varied aliens at their lives, so busy, so prosperous. And he was glad he'd had the chance to experience the Alliance's transportation system, because only now could he truly begin to understand just how vast the Alliance was. So many worlds. So many destinations. So many people. Compared to his homeworld, it was overwhelming. That he would have a good ten centuries to become inured to it did not lessen its impact now.

"Excuse me, alet," said a gentle but professional voice. "Do you need assistance?"

Jahir looked up and found two Pelted standing a polite distance in front of him. One was Tam-illee, humanoid with vulpine-influenced ears and tail and fur the color of champagne, dressed in the port's light gray and blue uniform. The other was a race he'd yet to meet, one of the winged Malarai, and it was she who'd spoken. She wore the same uniform, but with a sash over it, white banded in red, with a caduceus.

Jahir cleared his throat and said, "Thank you, aletsen. I should be fine, given some time."

The Malarai exchanged a glance with her companion, who flicked his ears sideways and backed away, leaving them alone. She was beautiful, with a human's face, almost devoid of fur save for streaks of felt leading back from her limpid eyes. There were felid ears hidden in her black hair, but one barely noticed them beside the wings that rose past them. The Malarai could not fly— could not walk well either without corrective surgery, if Jahir remembered his studies. Their wings had been engineered as decorations for the masters who'd wanted them as pets. His class on mental diseases of the Exodus had devoted an entire sub-chapter to the Malarai . . . but this woman seemed utterly at ease.

"A species rarer than mine," she said with a smile. "May I sit? On the edge of the bench. I won't come close enough to touch."

"Of course," he said.

She perched there, easy, one leg tucked under herself. "I'm Patience. I'm part of the port's medical response team. We keep

an eye out for passengers who might need help. You don't need
to discuss your situation with me, but would you be distressed if
I stayed here until you felt well enough to move on?"

"No," he said. "In truth, I have some notion of what ails me
and what must be done about it. And I am bound anyway for
Mercy Hospital, so I can discuss it with them there if necessary."

"Ohhh," she said, smiling. "Let's see, spring's just ended . . .
that means you must be a new resident, yes?"

"Yes," he said, startled.

She nodded. "Mercy takes its probationary residents at the
beginning of its slow season . . . for us in Heliocentrus, that's
summer, when the government moves to Terracentrus. A lot of
the city's transients go with it, which means less volume goes
through the medical system until the seat moves back here in the
northern hemisphere's winter." She smiled. "I went through the
Mercy residency myself."

"Did you?" he said. "Have you any advice, then?"

"Oh." She shook her head after a moment. "No. They're going
to work you within an inch of your life. Try to rest, eat, take care
of yourself in the moments you get." She glanced at him, canted
her head. "What's your specialty?"

"Xenopsychology."

"Ah," she said. And laughed. "An Eldritch therapist! There
must be only one of you in all the worlds."

"Very probably," he agreed. He studied her. "You went
through the program, but did not stay?"

"Oh no." Patience laughed again. Her wings shivered when
she moved; he found himself staring at them. "No, I wanted the
best education I could have, and that was it. But once I was done, I
wanted something a little less hectic." She lifted her chin, nodded
her head toward the passing stream of people. "This is good. I like
seeing so many people come and go. I love the bustle of the port.
The people aren't here because they're sick, they're here because
they're going somewhere. They're excited, or hurried, or rushed,
but even at their worst they're looking toward something. People
in a hospital are. . . ." She paused, then suggested a ball with her

hands and crushed it inward until her two fists met. "They're
. . . folded up into themselves, involved in their own healing or
sicknesses. It was a good place to learn but I didn't want to live
there." She smiled at him. "But we all have to make that choice.
Mercy can't take on all the people that want to work for it. It's a
big name, huge advances happening all the time. Very exciting
science. If that's what you want, it's one of the best places to be
in the Alliance."

"Then I should go about my way," he murmured. He thought
he could manage standing and the need to be done with traveling, to be somewhere instead of in transition, was powerfully in
him.

"If you're certain?" she asked.

"I am, and I thank you." He proved it by standing, and if he
remained weary at least he was no longer dizzy. "And for the talk,
also."

"My work," she said with a smile. "Good luck with the
residency."

Despite his best intentions, however, Jahir's first view of the
inside of Mercy Hospital was its walk-in clinic. He arrived listing
to one side, grateful to be upright at all and with no memory of
the journey from the port to his destination. He'd walked some
part of it, he thought, but. . . .

"Rough time, ah?" the Tam-illee nurse said while studying
his diagnostic read-outs.

"Something like."

The foxine nodded. "Wait here . . . the doctor will see you in
a moment."

"I assure you, I am not going anywhere."

The nurse chuckled. "No, I don't imagine you are. Just lie
back . . . on your side is better, it will keep you from feeling like
you're suffocating. There, that way. You're fine, all right? Nothing's going to happen to you here."

"Thank you," Jahir murmured, and did as he was told. It

would be ironic if he couldn't withstand the simple physical rigors of the residency when he'd agonized so over choosing it. All the factors he'd thought would deter him—the famed difficulty of the program, the stress of adapting to a new city and culture, the regret of leaving behind friends—had seemed far more obvious dangers than the one he hadn't even thought to evaluate. And which he should have, as Seersana had been heavier than his homeworld, and he'd had a problem like this before.

Jahir closed his eyes and strove not to sigh.

"Jahir Seni Galare. Did I say that correctly? No, don't get up."

He opened an eye and found an older woman studying her data tablet. Hinichi, he thought; there was a look to the wolfine race that differentiated them from the fox-like Tam-illee despite how often their animal attributes were limited to a set of ears and a tail. She looked at his bed's data, then at him and lifted her brows. "Well, then."

"Let me guess," he said. "I am the first Eldritch you've seen."

"That too," she said, and pulled up a stool. "I was more admiring your physique, which tells me close to everything I need to know. Just how light is the world you're from?"

"I confess I have not the first notion." Rousing himself, he added, "Seersana was heavier, however. That was my last place of residence."

"Ah? For how long?"

"Two years," he replied. "I am . . ." He stopped, then did sigh. "I am here for my residency."

"Here? At Mercy?" She shook her head. "You must be embarrassed."

"A touch."

She chuckled, but it was a kind one. "Don't let it bother you. Selnor's on the heavy side of the Mediger scale. You're not the first case of this we've seen. But if you were on Seersana for two years . . ." She glanced at the data tablet, thumbing through it. "Looks like you've had the adaptation regimen before?"

"How did you—"

"Know, since you don't appear to have any medical records?"

she asked with a wry smile and one sagging ear. She nodded toward his legs. "You've got unusual muscle for your frame. Not necessarily conclusive, but there's evidence of strain where it was pulling on your skeletal system before the bone density built to support it." She tilted her head. "Any reason you have no medical records?"

"None I can share," Jahir said.

"So I assume if I make notes on this case . . ." She stopped at his tiny head-shake. "And if I mark you in the system as having a medical condition, will that vanish as well?"

"I don't know," he admitted.

She wrinkled her nose. "All right. Better safe than sorry, then. I'll issue you an old-fashioned medical bracelet—you'll wear it, right?—so that people will know you have a condition that might need aid. Let's talk about treatment options, which have been somewhat complicated by your having had the regimen already." She set the tablet on the table and folded her hands on one knee, crossing her legs. "We could administer it to you again; that's your first option. That will solve the problem completely."

"And the issue with that option?" Jahir asked.

"That in a small but non-zero segment of the population, multiple courses of the adaptation regimen have a paradoxical reaction," she said. "The growth regulation mechanism self-sabotages and you start building muscle too fast for the metabolism to feed, including the heart muscle. The process will scavenge from every other available system, including your bones and visceral organs, to keep going, and you end up back on a bed again, except this time in one of our operating rooms where we rebuild you system by system. It's expensive and uncomfortable and you'll end up worse off than you started."

"How small is this small percentage?" Jahir asked, dismayed and, he hoped, hiding it.

"About six percent."

"And my other option?"

"You learn to live with this," she said. "And we put you on a medically supervised diet and exercise program. With some coaxing, your body will do the work it needs to do. But it will take time, and you'll have to keep to the program religiously. No cheating. That includes mechanical assistance, so no handy leg frames."

"Or—"

"Or you sabotage your own progress," the Hinichi finished. "Not as explosively as the adaptation regimen would if it failed, but you're going to feel every ounce of your extra weight every day. And if you're here as a resident, it's going to be up to you to manage the needs of the program with your work, and I won't lie—that'll be hard. You'll probably take two steps back for every step forward for a while."

He did not like feeling this weak. But the idea of trusting a medical system, no matter how advanced, with intervention during a catastrophic failure of his body when they had absolutely no medical literature, training or resources on Eldritch physiology . . . "If I try the latter, I can always fall back on the adaptation regimen if it fails, yes?"

"Of course."

"Then let us begin with less harm," he said, with a quirk of a smile. "And proceed to more if absolutely necessary."

"Wise of you," she said. "I'll go work up a schedule for you and get one of the bracelets. And by the way—" She smiled, brows lifted. "Welcome to Mercy."

⎯⎯ ∞∞∞ ⎯⎯

The nurse who discharged him gave him directions to the hospital housing, where he'd been assigned a room. His acceptance packet had included a map of the surrounding blocks and the apartments available there for those who wanted to live off the grounds, but he had not thought himself up to negotiating the Alliance's winter capital on his very first day . . . and that was before he'd discovered how much effort merely standing would be. The building he wanted was across a small park, but given its usual visitors it also included a slidewalk. He leaned against its rail and let it carry him, and there was a taste in the air like a storm: hot and wet as the breeze sifted his hair. He lifted his face to it and felt anchorless, a thing set adrift and yet unable to move.

He had wanted to know if he could handle a medical psychiatry career at its most difficult. Had in fact let Vasiht'h convince him of the wisdom of that course. He knew now that Heliocentrus would be all that it had promised. Two years of this and he would know, without doubt, whether he belonged here.

The thought of Vasiht'h clung to him as he checked into his new room. It was smaller than the apartment he'd shared with his Glaseahn roommate, but this one was his alone . . . was, in fact, the exact sort of room he'd been hoping for when he'd first arrived at Seersana University, wanting to preserve his solitude and his sanity by building a wall between his ability to read thoughts and feelings and the aliens he'd been so fascinated by, and so wary of.

Now that he'd spent two years living with one of those aliens, he felt the emptiness of this room too deeply. It reminded him of hollow places in his life, once filled by unexpected friends, now separated by several days of interstellar travel . . . and in one special case, by the veil of death, a death that would visit all of his alien companions centuries before it came for him.

Vasiht'h would have had one look at this place, declared it barren, and started making cookies. As a prelude, he'd say, to thinking about how to decorate it.

Jahir's smile faded quickly. He set his bags down and went to the too-clean desk to begin sorting through the orientation materials. Tomorrow morning he was expected for duty, and the day after that for a meeting, apparently, with his new personal trainer. At least they would keep him busy.

"You're leaving!" Kuriel asked, ears flattening. She twisted in his lap to look up at Vasiht'h. "You're leaving?"

"I'm leaving."

The two human girls sitting on the mat across from him

glanced at one another. Amaranth said, "It must be super important. You wouldn't go otherwise."

"What happened?" Persy added.

"Nothing's happened," Vasiht'h said. And then, more gravely, because he knew they would both understand and approve of the solemn confidence, "I'm going after Jahir."

"Yes!" Persy crowed, and bumped Amaranth in the shoulder with a fist. "I knew it!"

Amaranth grinned. "Yeah, but I agreed with you!"

"And how long have you known?" Vasiht'h asked, bemused.

"Since he left." Persy wiggled her toes. "Ever since he left, you've been . . . nervous."

"Antsy," Amaranth agreed. "Like someone with something on his mind."

"And we remembered what you told us when he fell asleep during that story—"

"—it was about the moth," Kuriel murmured against him. "The bright green moth who didn't look like the grey moths he lived with."

"Yeah, that one." Persy continued, "Anyway. You told us during that story how much it upset you that he was leaving, and you were so worried about him. I got to talking with Amaranth and we figured you weren't going to stay behind. You're going to be his best friend forever! Right?"

"Right," Vasiht'h said, firmly. The plan was perhaps a little more nebulous than they were assuming, but then again, did it really need any more granularity than that? As the Goddess Herself would say, the point was not to dictate the future, but to shape it. Friendship was a thing that shaped, if it was good. And what he'd had with Jahir had been too good to allow to pass out of his life.

"Will you write us?" Amaranth asked.

"Will you come back," Kuriel muttered.

Vasiht'h looked down at the Seersa in his lap. Her tail-tip and fingertips had been dyed bright pink since he'd seen her last week, no doubt in response to a flare-up of the disease that had seen her put in All Children's Hospital's permanent resident ward with the others. She'd confessed once that she feared she'd be the only one left in her room . . . and gentle little Nieve had died, and Kayla and Meekie had gone to Selnor into the care of a specialist. No doubt this felt like another step toward that fate. He squeezed her and said, "I don't know the future, Kuriel-arii. I'm going to Heliocentrus to help Jahir, but I don't know what that help will look like. I'd like to come back here, though." He looked at the two human girls watching him. "I'll certainly write you all, and Hea Berquist too."

"And you'll visit Meekie and Kayla?" Amaranth asked.

"We've had a letter," Persy added. "But knowing more is better!"

"If I'm allowed, I would love to see them," Vasiht'h said.

Persy leaned forward and tugged on Kuriel's tail lightly. "Aww, Kuri. Don't be sad. This is what Nieve was talking about when she kept saying there's magic in the world."

"What magic?" Kuriel said, ears flat. "All I see is that Nieve's dead, we're stuck in here and everyone's leaving. If there was magic, we'd all be healthy."

"If we'd been healthy we wouldn't have met one another," Amaranth said. She crawled over to sit in front of Kuriel, to one side of Vasiht'h's forelegs. "Then you wouldn't know to miss us. Would you like that better?"

Kuriel looked away, shoulders slumping. "No."

"I'll tell you what's magic," Persy said. "Magic is deciding to help your friends. Magic is deciding we're going to get better. Magic is deciding we'll stick together afterward and do something for other kids like us, when we get older."

"We are?" Kuriel asked.

"We are?" Amaranth added, looking over at Persy.

"Sure. Don't you think it would be nice? No one else has a Prince Jahir and Vasiht'h-Manylegs, and we only found them by accident, because they found us that day in the parking lot." Persy squared her shoulders. "Think of all the other kids like us who don't have someone like that. And we'd have gone through what they were going through. We could tell them it was going to work out okay."

"Even when you die?" Kuriel said.

"Nieve died happy," Amaranth said, quiet. "I don't know how she did that, but maybe we could help other people figure out how."

"There's school for that, you know." His voice didn't tremble, though he didn't know how when he felt such a soaring pride in them. "For becoming a helpmeet to children like you. They'd prepare you for the job you're talking about."

"Can you imagine us with degrees?" Kuriel said, distracted from her fears. "Like adults."

"I never really imagine getting older," Amaranth confessed. "I kind of just believe we'll always be here, you know?"

"Well, we won't," Persy said. "Either we'll die or we'll grow up, but either way we have to decide what to do with ourselves." She looked pleased with herself. "Right, Vasiht'h-alet?"

"Exactly right," Vasiht'h said.

"And what you have to do is leave," Amaranth said. She glanced at him. "Because you love him."

Vasiht'h hesitated.

"Do you?" Kuriel asked, curious. She looked up, ears flipping forward for the first time since his announcement.

He started to speak, then closed his mouth. All three girls were waiting on him, though, and pinned by their artless attention he couldn't stay silent. "I do, yes. You can love friends enough to cross the worlds for them."

Kuriel considered him a few moments longer, then dropped her gaze and petted his foreleg once. "Maybe there is magic in the world."

He hugged her, and the others too when they tumbled into his lap. He was glad he had the extra limbs for it.

Outside the room, Jill Berquist was waiting for him—for once standing, rather than sitting at her station with the cup of coffee their visits gave her the opportunity to savor. The human tilted her head. "How'd they take it?"

"Surprisingly well," Vasiht'h said, and sighed. "Better than I'm taking it, honestly." His smile was rueful as he looked up at her. "Seersana was my first foreign destination, and as cosmopolitan as it is, I'm not sure how I feel about navigating Selnor."

"You'll do fine," Jill said. "You Pelted, you're used to it. The melting pot of species, the multiculturalism, the busyness of it all. It'll be Seersana writ large, but you've got the Alliance in your bones. You'll find your feet. You've got a couple extra, it should help."

He chuckled. "I hope so." Sobering, he said, "I never got to tell you how much I appreciated the chance to volunteer here. Thanks for letting us do it."

She shook her head. "God, Vasiht'h. You did so much for them. I should be thanking you." She leaned down and wrapped her arms around him, squeezed. Surprised, he hugged her back, resting his nose against her shoulder, smelling antiseptic and coffee and some faint hint of lavender.

Stepping back, Jill said, "Good luck, arii. Take care of him for us."

"I will," Vasiht'h said, bemused.

He didn't wonder, padding back to the apartment, how everyone could accept so easily that he'd become Jahir's keeper. He only wondered how everyone could have known before him. Including Jahir.

It had been two weeks since his roommate's departure. Preparing for his own had taken much longer than he'd hoped. While he was glad it had given him time to say proper goodbyes to everyone, he was fretful at the delay. The trip to Selnor was going to take him longer than it had taken Jahir, who had found some lucky confluence of vessels, schedules and fares; another two weeks would elapse before he set foot on the capital world, and Goddess knew what could happen in that month.

There was no help for it, though. Vasiht'h looked up into the summer sky, inhaled, and went home to finish his preparations.

"You didn't have to do this," he said later to Luci.

"Don't be ridiculous," the Harat-Shar said. "Of course I did." She stared at the short red vest and then folded it into a neat square. "Besides, it's not like packing for you is difficult. You barely have any clothes."

"I don't mean the packing for me," Vasiht'h said, tucking his grooming kit into the bag. "I mean packing the apartment."

Luci shook her head. "Don't bother yourself over it, arii. I'll get the quadmates to help me. We'll bring food, make a party of it. The four of us will be able to do it in far less time than you could alone, and you need to get going." She glanced at him. "Any idea how you're going to handle everything once you arrive?"

"A little," Vasiht'h said. "I'll still be enrolled here, but I'll be taking classes remotely. Professor Palland arranged that for me. But they've extended that offer for one semester only because the classes are mostly lectures; I'll be taking the business electives on running a practice, so I don't actually have to be here." He drew in a deep breath, started folding his sari. The fabric shimmered as it slid over his fingers. "After this semester, they're going to evaluate whether it's working out and either give me another extension, or I'll have to transfer to one of Selnor's schools."

"Where are you going to stay while doing all this?" Luci asked.

"Goddess, I hope with Jahir," Vasiht'h said. "Because my budget is a little too modest to live alone. I'll figure something out, even if I have to borrow money from my parents."

"Have you told them yet?" she asked, sitting on the couch to watch him finish.

"My parents?" He shook his head. "I figured I'd call them once everything was settled. They'll worry less that way. It's not like their calls won't find me just because I'm in transit." His sister, though, he'd have to talk to first, or she might never forgive him.

Luci studied him with dark eyes in her boldly striped face. She flicked her ears out and said, "Worried about what they'll say?"

"No," Vasiht'h answered, sighed. "Not in the way you're thinking, anyway." He closed his carry-on. "Tea?"

"Chocolate if you have it."

He went to the kitchen and set out two cups. "This is going to sound ridiculous."

Luci twisted to loop her arm over the back of the couch and look at him. "Try me anyway."

"I'm a little afraid that if I talk about it to them, I might . . . make it come apart." Vasiht'h measured out the shaved chocolate for her cup, brown flakes tumbling into ivory ceramic. "Like it's not real yet. And delicate, and if I point too many people at it, it might never be realized." He glanced at her. "Does that sound as silly as it does in my head?"

"You're the therapist," Luci said. "What would you tell yourself?"

"That it doesn't matter if I'm right or not, if I make myself feel a certain way because of my beliefs," Vasiht'h said slowly. He put a pan of cream to warm for both their drinks. "I guess I'm just afraid."

"That you won't be able to make it work?"

"That I'll get there and he'll wonder why I came," Vasiht'h said, his ears flattening.

Luci snorted. "That's the one thing that *won't* happen. Trust me, arii. You show up at the door? He'll let you in."

"I hope you're right," he murmured.

⸺◦◦◦◦⸺

That night, he curled up in his room on the bolsters and pillows that served as his bed. Months ago he'd had cause to give thanks to the Goddess and had folded a paper effigy of her that he'd decided to keep. He'd placed it on a pillow at eye-level before settling for the night.

"This is it," he told Her. "My last night. I can't turn back now."

She said nothing—it wasn't Her way—but he thought the way the starlight fell on Her face made Her look like She was smiling.

CHAPTER 2

JAHIR'S NEW SUPERVISOR WAS human, male, and vibrated with a tension even a non-esper could have felt from the threshold of the room. His agitation was powerful enough to give Jahir pause, and that after the arduous walk from his new residence to the sixth floor of the hospital, where the orientation was being conducted in a conference room. That walk had acquainted him with the size of Mercy, and it had staggered him to realize that the only building that could have rivaled it on his homeworld was Ontine, the royal palace. He'd been familiar with Seersana's All Children's and General Hospitals, but they had to be half the size of Mercy, if he was any judge . . . maybe even smaller.

His entrance caused the only other person in the room to turn and look at him—an Asanii, one of the more humanoid felid races—and her movement caught the attention of the man. "You're not late," was the first thing he said. "But you're not early either."

"My apologies," Jahir said. "I'll endeavor to be earlier in the future."

"Sit." The man pointed to a chair with his stylus. "You look like you need it. You up too late seeing the sights or are you—" He stopped abruptly, frowning. "You sick?"

"No," Jahir said, and took one of the empty chairs, glad of it. His heart was racing; it made him feel uncomfortably fragile. "I am merely not acclimated to the gravity here."

"Oh hell. How bad is it?" The man raked him from foot to face with a glance. "Bad, from your build."

The woman was looking at him with interest, white ears pricked toward him. He ignored her and said, "I am under the care of Healer Gillespie."

"Already? Good. Glad you were proactive about that instead of trying to keep it hidden. We don't have time for that kind of thing. We're going to ask for everything—our patients need it— but it's your responsibility to tell us when you don't have it to give. Got that?" At Jahir's slight nod, the man continued, "I'm Griffin Jiron. Yes, that's really my name. I'm one of the advanced practice nursing team in the psychiatric department here, and you two have been generously assigned to me for the length of your stays. While you're here, you report to me. I set your schedules, I do your evaluations, I sign off on your stipends. You have trouble of any kind, or any questions, you come to me." He paused. "Questions so far?"

"How many times have you given this speech?" the Asanii asked with a grin.

Jiron snorted. "Not as often as it must sound. Which is something you'll have to learn while you're here: you have to think on your feet. Anything else?" He glanced at Jahir, accepted the silence and went on. "All right. Let's talk about Mercy. This is the biggest hospital on the planet. The planet that's also the capital world for the entire Alliance. There's no other facility to rival us for general practice in the Core and probably out of it. Before you ask—" Glancing at the woman, who'd opened her mouth, "No, not even in the summer capital. That would be because Fleet bases most of its ground offices in Terracentrus, including their medical center. They get a lot more Fleet people in residence over there, so a good part of their population reports to the military hospital. Terracentrus's largest hospital doesn't serve as big a percentage of the city's residents. So. Back to us?"

He paused until she nodded, ears perked, and continued, "Five thousand beds. Nearly forty thousand permanent staff and any number of transients. And before the year is out we'll see almost six million visits, of which about six hundred thousand will be to our crisis care center."

The numbers beggared the imagination. Jahir remembered his incredulity at reading that Seersana University's student population hovered between fifty and sixty thousand people a year; for someone whose homeworld probably barely supported enough people to fill one small Alliance city, the thought of so many people in one place had been beyond his ability to imagine. Finding himself working at a hospital with a staff the size of that student body . . .

Jiron was continuing. "Psychiatry is Mercy's smallest department because we don't do dedicated psychiatric care. That's a cultural thing locally. Most people here prefer to handle psychiatric issues through religious ministries, community support or other species-specific outlets. We do see some dedicated cases, but most of our work involves supporting the rest of the hospital with patients who need someone but don't want to avail themselves of the on-site volunteer corps. Miss Valani, you did a specialty in physiological support of psychological health, so we'll put you to work in the nutrition, exercise and health support group under Healer Parkenfields." He paused. "That name's not a joke either."

"Lot of that going around," the Asanii observed, grinning.

"You have no idea," Jiron said. "Mister Jahir, you have a chemistry specialty, so we'll be assigning you to Doctor Levine. Her group handles the urgent crashes—what we call people coming into the crisis care system or coming out of operations."

"Understood."

"As one of the advanced nursing team, I rotate through all the groups within psychiatry," Jiron said. "I'll be starting out in yours, Valani-alet, before moving to crisis care." He glanced at Jahir. "Gillespie presumably set you up with a treatment program?"

"She did, though I am not to meet with the physical therapist until tomorrow."

"All right. Valani-alet, think you're up to finding your group on your own?"

"I have my data tablet and a map, sir, I think I can manage."

Jiron tapped the name badge on his loose, shapeless shirt. "It's Griffin. If you need to be formal, Griffin-alet."

"Griffin," she said.

"But call the doctors Doctor or Healer, depending on how they introduce themselves," Jiron said. "And in front of patients, Jiron-alet or Nurse Jiron is fine. I am Nurse, not Hea; I didn't go through healer-assist training in the Alliance. I don't know how strict they were about that in your graduate programs, but enough people here will be irritated if you get it wrong, so get it right."

"Yes, Griffin!"

He laughed. "All right. Go. If you have any trouble, ping me. And tell Healer Parkenfields to set you up with the hospital hardware and uniform."

"Got it," she said, and added to Jahir on the way out, "Nice to meet you, and hope we have a chance to talk more soon."

"Likewise," he said, bemused at her energy level. When he looked away from the door he found his supervisor studying him. The human's agitation had become a laser-like focus that might have been unsettling had Jahir simply not had the physical energy to feel nervous. In that state of calm, he saw the spark of compassion in Jiron's dark eyes he might otherwise have missed.

"How bad is it?"

Jahir said, "Not enough for me to leave, if that is the real question you're asking."

"That's part of why I'm asking, yes," Jiron said, sitting back. "But not all."

"Then may I ask what motivated the question?"

That bought him another few moments of the human's regard, which he weathered in weary silence.

"You came very highly recommended, Mister Galare."

"Jahir," he murmured, because while he did not expect most non-Eldritch to understand how to use his name, he could not continue to listen to this particular mangling of it.

"Jahir-alet." Jiron reached for his tablet and swiped through it before pausing. "You had no less than nine letters. Did you know that?"

"Nine?" Jahir said, startled.

"Nine," Jiron said. "Very glowing ones." He thumbed down one and said with the air of someone quoting, "'It may be that the isolation of his species has given him the opportunity to develop a perspective external to the Alliance's multicultural-ism, one that allows him to observe it more clearly than those of us within it. He does not waste that advantage, and his insights are often as uncanny as they are fresh.' A Professor Sheldan." He looked up. "Fan of yours, I'm guessing."

"I would never have imagined him to write anything of the sort," Jahir said, startled, for he and Sheldan had had a less than amicable relationship.

"Let's say the list of your admirers is pretty long, even for someone good enough to get into our student residency program," Jiron said. "What I want to know is whether you really are that good . . . because otherwise, someone with your physical health problems—or at least, the ones you seem to be having—would probably wash out within three or four weeks."

Jahir had never thought of himself as a stubborn personal-ity. Certainly he'd had his moments of intransigence, but for the most part, he tried to remain flexible. Hearing his fate set out so cavalierly by a man who was probably a tenth his age, though, made him want, very passionately, to prove him wrong.

"You seem very certain of that," he said at last.

"What's your normal resting heart rate?" Jiron asked. He lifted his brows, then flipped his data tablet to display the pulse rate racing on it, a series of flashes above a number. "Because this would be an aerobic ceiling for someone humanoid, and that's what the sensors are reporting from you."

"Your tablet's sensors can detect medical data with useful

specificity without access to a halo-arch?" Jahir said, unable to hide his interest.

"Yours will too when we issue you one." Jiron pointed at the number. "How far off from normal is this?"

Jahir glanced at it. "Far enough."

The human sighed. "You know we can't cut you any slack."

"With five thousand beds to manage, I can't imagine so, no."

"And you're still determined to go through with this."

Jahir met his eyes. "You will have my best effort."

"And if that's not good enough?"

"Then," Jahir said, quiet, "you will do what you must, for the good of the hospital's patients. I would not expect anything less."

That earned him another long look, and then a lifted brow. "All right. I'll talk to Gillespie and get your schedule to you tonight. We brought you in. We might as well see if we can make it work."

"Thank you."

"And now, let's go introduce you to Doctor Levine. She'll show you around, give you a sense of the work."

———⚬✖✖⚬———

As her Terran title suggested, Grace Levine was another human, fair-skinned to Jiron's tawny. She had champagne-colored hair swept back in a chignon and a remarkable demeanor: professional while also seeming approachable, and alert without crossing the line into agitation. His first sight of her was of her white-coated back, bent over a desk to look over the shoulder of a Karaka'An felid in the shapeless scrubs Jiron wore. From that angle, she reminded him of Jill Berquist, the healer-assist from All Children's.

That impression was swept away when Jiron called her name and she looked up at them, and just . . . halted. Berquist had found him unusual, but she would never have been so stunned at the sight of him. For several very long moments, Levine said nothing, and Jahir wondered if she would have continued to say nothing had Jiron not said, "I'm sorry to interrupt . . . is this a bad time?"

"No," she said, straightening. "I was just discussing some of the oncology patients with Sera." Her professional facade reassembled as she spoke, and by now the gaze she turned on him was distant enough to be polite, and friendly enough to inspire confidence. "You must be one of the new residents we got this session."

"Jahir," he said. "I'm pleased to make your acquaintance."

"Likewise."

"May I leave him with you, Doctor? I have to make some arrangements for his schedule."

"Something I should know?" She glanced at him speculatively.

"I am having some difficulties with the gravity," Jahir said for what he hoped would be the last time.

She frowned. "You're going to undergo the acclimatization regimen?"

"I fear I already have," Jahir said. "Healer Gillespie has me under her care."

"Which is where I'm off to now," Jiron said. "If you'll excuse me?"

"Go ahead, Griffin. Thanks." She waved Jahir to one of the spare stools, watching him sit. "Looks bad."

"I will weather it," Jahir said, because the only other choice was to fail, and then what would he do? Something, but he would prefer not to contemplate it unless absolutely necessary.

"All right. I'll accept that for now. We've never had an Eldritch at Mercy. Unless I'm mistaken, and I doubt I am, not even as a patient. Anything we should know?"

He hesitated, then said, "You are aware of our talents?"

She nodded. "Do you use them on patients?"

"Not in the sense of intervening," he said. He thought of what he had done for Luci and the children, and of the research Vasiht'h had done. But he had been very careful not to affect the patients on his rounds that way. He'd never questioned that decision either, and wondered now why he'd made it. Not that it mattered—he strongly suspected the reason he'd been capable of that much psychic touch had been the stabilizing influence of Vasiht'h's presence, and he was absent that now. "It is unavoidable in the course of treating patients that I become aware of their emotions, however, and I do use that information to help tailor my responses."

"All right. I assume Griffin told you a little about our section?"

"That you handle those in worst need?" Jahir said. "A little."

"That's right." Levine leaned against the table. "We're the ones they call to help calm down the people who show up alone, bleeding their guts out, right as they're being rushed into emergency surgery. That means we get the gruesome accidents and the victims of violence . . . and when we're done with that, they send us in to see people who've been told they have almost no chance of living, or that their next surgery's going to be their only chance. And we see to the dying who have chosen—or who have no choice but to die here." She lifted her brows. "This is the deep end of the pool. Think you can handle it?"

"I am here to find out," he said.

"Fair answer." She grinned. "I'll tell you a secret, alet: I think this is the best place to work. There's not a day that goes by that we don't do something important, something productive. We're indispensable to the staff here, to the patients. It's grueling and heart-breaking, but we make a difference. I wouldn't trade it for something easier." She straightened. "So, pep talk done. Anything you want to ask?"

"Not so far," he said.

"All right. Down to the nuts and bolts. Wait, where'd you come from?"

"Seersana."

"All right. We've got a slightly longer day than they do, if I remember right, but not by much. We work a three-shift day, each shift about eight and a quarter hours: day, evening and night. We also have two rotations, acute care and high-risk. We'd like to start new people gently but we recently lost someone to family leave, so unless Griffin comes back with an issue you'll be working his slot, which is probably the roughest one we've got."

"Crisis care, night shift," Jahir guessed.

"Almost right." She grinned. "Evening shift. On the bright side, if you survive it? You're gold for anything we could throw at you. You won't be alone either, since we have two people on each shift in each area, plus one advanced practice nurse or healer-assist assigned to each shift. That will give you a total of four people to ask for help if you need it. My schedule floats on a three-month rotation. This month I'm available for the night shift, but I'm on call for emergencies the remainder of the time. Griffin's your residency supervisor, so he'll be coordinating everything for you, but while you're on duty you'll look to the AP nurse for anything you need to send up the chain. Clear?"

"Yes," he said.

"Good. I'll send you the bios for your shiftmates. They're fine people, so don't worry on that account . . . and God knows they'll be thrilled to see you. They've been covering for Jiraled for three weeks now and they're feeling it. Ordinarily we'd have hired someone to take over, but we'd already discussed bringing in psychiatry residents this time around, so we held off on that until you two arrived." She rested her eyes on him. "I'd say you start tonight, but I'm guessing that you're going to need at least one session with Gillespie's physical therapists before you start. Are you allowed to use any mechanical aids?"

"She suggested it would set my progress back."

"All right. Let's go find you your standard issue then, and we can meet Griffin here when he gets back."

He rose to follow her, grateful for the respite the interview had provided. Thankfully the hospital had a sufficiency of patients with mobility issues that allowances had been built into it; otherwise, the thought of climbing stairs would have daunted him. He'd preferred it on Seersana, since so few people used the stairwells; he was remembering the sunlit steps when someone heading into the room bumped him on the way past—

—sudden flashes of halo-arch readings and patient records, frustration and anxiety and exhaustion—

He didn't realize he was listing until Levine grabbed him,

and then he truly lost everything. He managed to say before he went down, "Don't touch—" and then gave in to the smothering weight of the mindtouch.

⟶∞⟵

When Jahir woke he was on the ground, against the wall . . . had he grabbed for the door jamb on the way down? Perhaps he was acquiring an instinct for preservation through these episodes. Levine and Jiron were crouched in front of him, with a nervous Seersa female hovering behind.

"You with us?" Jiron asked.

"I am, yes. Thank you." He sat up gingerly, mindful of the headache. Wrapping a loose arm around his knees he sank into his physical fatigue and let it serve as the ground for his scattered thoughts.

"Was it the gravity?" Levine asked. "I didn't even see you go down."

Her voice stitched together with the thoughts she'd injected into him with all the inevitability of a syringe, and he didn't like knowing, suddenly, that she found him attractive. He forced himself to look up at her anyway. "I'm afraid I sometimes react poorly to being touched."

Jiron made the connection first. "Is this the esper thing? I've heard about it, but I didn't think it was debilitating."

"It isn't always," Jahir said. He let his head fall, eyes narrowing against the headache. "But it can be . . . very disorienting."

The two humans exchanged glances, so quickly he shouldn't have noticed it with his gaze lowered. He could almost hear their thoughts: how frail was their newest employee, and how much coddling would he need? And was it going to be worth it, or should they pack him up now and send him back?

"Well," Levine said at last. "We'll just have to make it clear to the staff that they shouldn't casually touch you."

"That would be best," Jahir said, and forced himself to roll onto his knees, and from there, to climb the jamb to his feet. When they moved to help him, he held out a hand. "I'm fine. Just a bit out of sorts."

"Right."

Behind them, the fretful Seersa said, "I'm so sorry. I didn't mean to knock you down."

"Really, it's of no import. An accident." Though he now knew details about her she probably would not have shared with a stranger, and details about her patients she might have been appalled to have divulged. He smiled to ease her, and was relieved to see her ears lose their anxious tremor.

"If you're sure," she said. "I'm not usually so clumsy."

That made him laugh. Just a little, but it was something. "Nor am I."

Her ears splayed and then she grinned, and her worry became sheepishness. "I guess we all have bad days."

"Things can only go up from the floor."

"Keren?" Levine said. "You checking in, I assume?"

"Yes, ma'am! Sorry." The Seersa trotted into the room, tail and shoulders relaxed.

"Well," Levine said, studying him. "You *are* good."

"Pardon me?"

She twitched her head toward one shoulder in the direction of the Seersa. "I expected her to lose her fluster, but not to go from hovering to laughing."

"Ah." He folded his hands behind his back. "I have had some practice."

"At falling down and accepting apologies?"

"At my work," Jahir said. And, in case that had been too curt, "and also at falling down and accepting apologies."

She laughed. "All right, alet. Fine. Let's go get your data tablet and your clothes."

He fell into step behind her, but not before noticing Jiron's quiet . . . but as he passed the nurse he saw Jiron wasn't looking at him, but at Levine.

So then. Problems with the planet itself. Problems with the doctor charged with his section. Problems with the patients, who were supposedly the most difficult in the entire hospital. Not the

most auspicious beginning to his endeavor. But as he'd told the
Seersa, from the floor it was hard to go anywhere but up.

———oooo———

Vasiht'h was on the short-hop liner from one of Seersana's
orbital facilities to the station at the edge of the solar system that
served the big passenger liners when his data tablet pinged him
with a call and tagged it with his sister Sehvi's code. It floated the
local time-of-day for her too, which he found worrisome; she was
on Tam-ley, working through her reproductive medicine degree,
and she was usually asleep by the hour she was calling. Goddess
preserve him from whatever emergency had inspired her to stay
up. He accepted the call and watched her image fill the tablet
screen. She was, in fact, leaning toward him with a scowl, and
the audio picked up halfway through her sentence. ". . . had *better*
answer me this time because if you don't—VASIHT'H! Where
have you *been!*"

. . . and that would handily explain the emergency. He counted
backwards from the last time they were supposed to have talked
and then flattened his feathered ears. "Oh, Sehvi, I'm so sorry, I
didn't mean to miss our call—"

"I don't care about missing the call. I care about you not
answering all the messages I've left since! You had me worried
halfway into my grave!"

He winced. "I haven't had time to check messages. I'm . . . I
am sorry, ariishir."

Her eyes had narrowed, and were no longer focused on him
but on the area behind his shoulders, scanning the foreign cushions, the strange backdrop. "Where are you, anyway?"

"On a shuttle heading for Double Welcome." He sucked in a
breath and finished, "I'm going to Selnor."

She stared at him, mouth open, and then shocked him
by squealing and throwing up her arms. "Thank the Mother
Goddess! You can be taught!"

He couldn't help it: he started laughing. If it was at least half
at his own expense, well . . . Jahir had taught him that laughing

at oneself wasn't a bad thing, now and then. "Yes. Yes, fine, you were right. I was in the wrong track. And I let him go and should never have. Are you happy now?"

"Yes!" she exclaimed, and patted her palms together, eyes glowing. "So, what's the plan? Does he know you're coming?"

"No-o-o . . ."

Her brows lifted. "Intentional on your part, or are you just not sure what to say so you're not saying anything?"

"Maybe a little of both?" he tried. "He can't object if I don't give him the choice."

"You think he will?"

Vasiht'h thought back to the last meal they'd taken together, to the embrace the Eldritch—the Eldritch!—had offered, and the hints the brief raveling of the mindline had suggested at their touch. "No. I don't think he will, as long as he knows I'm sure. That's what would make him refuse. If he thought I was doing it because I felt obliged, or because I thought it was what he wanted."

"He's so cute," Sehvi said, gleeful. "You sure you don't want to take him to mate?"

Vasiht'h snorted. "You need to stop taking counsel from people with more sex hormones than we have."

"See, you're even starting to sound like him!"

Ignoring that, he said, "Anyway, the reason I didn't notice your messages was that I was figuring out how to handle school and packing and saying a lot of goodbyes. I have things worked out for a semester or so . . . after that I'm going to have to figure out what the long-term plan is."

"Do you know where you're staying?"

"I'm hoping he has a floor I can sleep on," Vasiht'h said. "Because all the money I can save I'll need."

She tilted her head. "Why haven't you asked Dami and Tapa for help? You know they would, in an out-breath."

"I know," Vasiht'h said. "I know, but I want to see if I can figure this out for myself." He rubbed the end of his muzzle, briefly allowing himself to feel the nervous tension that made it impossible for him to relax. Even his claws kept trying to ease out of their sheaths. "I keep thinking that this is it, you know? I went off to school. I patted myself on the back for that, for being independent enough to leave home and get along in a whole new place. But I really did choose the safest way to leave—"

"Well, no," Sehvi said. "The safest way would have been to stay somewhere on Anseahla. Maybe on the other side of the world, but still on the world, a Pad away from home."

"That would have been cheating." He managed a lopsided smile. "What I mean is, I left home but straight into school, and how is school challenging for us? What with Dami's work, and us always being in and out of classrooms even before we were old enough for them? We grew up steeped in academia, ari-ishir. I might have left Anseahla, but the school setting might as well have been home. It just had different scenery outside the windows."

"Okay, I'll give you that," she said. "For now. I'm not sure I agree, but go on."

He snorted. "Thanks, Sehvi."

"You're welcome, ariihir."

"Anyway." He drew in a breath and said, "I haven't really stretched myself yet. Really taken any risks. This . . . this is a risk. Following someone who doesn't even know I'm coming, trusting myself to figure out where to sleep, how to pay my way, how to manage school. I want to see if I can do it without help."

She cocked her head. "You don't think your Eldritch is going to be help?"

"I'm hoping he is," Vasiht'h said.

"And that doesn't count because—"

"Because if this works out . . ." He trailed off, allowed himself to glimpse the terrifying uncertainty of the future. He met her eyes and finished, "Then we're going to be there for one another for the rest of my life."

She sobered. "And if you're wrong?"

"If I'm wrong, then I'll learn how to land on my feet. And how to make new plans out of the ruins of the old ones." He suppressed his shiver. "But I'm praying I'm not wrong."

Quieter, she said, "Me too. How long until you get there?"

"He's been gone two weeks by Seersana's clock. And it's going to take me a little under two to get there," Vasiht'h said. "After that . . ."

She nodded. "Call me, okay?"

"I will, ariishir." He smiled. "I've got a few hours before this thing docks. Tell me how things are going, if you aren't too sleepy."

"After this news?" She blew her forelock off her brow. "There's no way I'm getting back to sleep. So, sure, let me tell you about my latest lab adventures."

He settled in to listen.

CHAPTER 3

JAHIR WOKE TO THE REALIZATION that sleeping was never going to be as restful as it had been at home, or even on Seersana; lying on his newly issued bed, which was only barely long enough for him, feeling the dragging ache in his limbs and the too-swift coursing of his heart, he drew in a long breath and couldn't even fill his lungs. It would have panicked him to wake feeling so ill had he not been living adjacent to one of the Alliance's premier hospitals. As it was, he resigned himself to the challenge, and did his best to ignore his distress as he painstakingly prepared for his first day. The uniform assigned to him was used the Core over with few modifications for everyone in the medical profession. Called by at least three different names by the people issuing them to him, it consisted of loose and shapeless pants and short sleeved shirt that sealed near the throat; he chose to wear a long-sleeved shirt beneath the latter, since it was cold in the hospital. The gloves were his choice, to help ameliorate the effect of accidental touches, and he removed his family ring for the first time since showing it to the children on Seersana, stringing it on a chain and tucking it beneath the collar of the shirt. With it hidden, his only ornamentation was the plain gray metal of the bracelet Gillespie had issued him.

His hair he braided back, something recommended to him by one of his practicum teachers, for hygiene purposes. Moving his fingers through the motions brought back childhood memories. When he'd graduated from the nursery and to his own room, gaining his own permanent servants, he'd also been permitted—required—to grow his hair, as was customary for the nobility: it was a sign of wealth, and for males in particular, an arrogance that suggested they owned too much power to ever be challenged to a duel, during which long hair would be a handicap. But a year into his newly-minted young adulthood, he had decided it was wrong to make himself into a doll requiring the time of some servant who no doubt had better things to do . . . so he'd chopped it all off at his shoulders.

His mother had taken him gently aside and explained that without the nobility to employ him, the servant would have neither room nor board; that the servant's family had served theirs for generations and that the Seni Galare had a responsibility to employ them at some task, no matter how trivial; and that by no means should he reduce the dignity of the men and women in his service by suggesting their tasks were beneath them, when they did them with diligence and skill. Ashamed, he had agreed to submit to the care of his body-servant, and apologized to him in private. The man, several centuries older than his young master, had graciously accepted the apology . . . and then asked if perhaps some length somewhat further down the back would please the youth while still keeping with custom.

Looking at himself in the cheap, simple clothes, with his hair pulled back in a servant's tail and his ring tucked out of sight, Jahir wondered what his mother—his whole household—would think of him now. He smiled a little before heading for his appointment.

———✴———

The exhaustion dogged Jahir all the way to the hospital's physical therapy facility. He passed the gymnasium used both by patients and staff until he arrived at the office indicated on his tablet.

It was next to a pool. For a long moment he looked at the
waters, gleaming in the brassy yellow sunlight let in by the
skylights. Then he shook himself and tapped on the jamb for
entrance, since the door was already open, attracting the attention of an Asanii woman in a plain blue tracksuit. Her ears
perked. "Ah, you're my eight-mark-thirty?"

"Jahir Seni Galare," he said. "I go by my first name."

"Pleased to meet you, alet. Will you sit? Unless it's more
trouble for you to rise again, then you can remain standing."

"Sitting is fine," he said, and took the chair across from her
desk, which was less a piece of furniture and more a sweep of
shelf that hugged the wall and then curled out to offer a place
to set tablets and mugs. Her computer was flush to the wall,
and she used it while standing—or with one foot on a ball she
was idly rolling as she clasped the information projected solidi-
graphically and moved it physically out of the way. Two years of
exposure to the Alliance's interfaces had worn away his wonder
at their magic; now what intrigued him was how many different
styles there were. Data tablets were as ubiquitous as her device-
free set-up, and there were any number of variations in between.
That level of personalization suggested an industrial base he still
could not grasp, even now. How fortunate these people were, and
often did not know.

"All right, I have the note here," she said, scanning a file,
which floated in front of her thin and pale as tissue. "But it's just
a note . . . for some reason there's no medical file attached." She
glanced at him quizzically, but he said nothing. "Well, we don't
need it as long as you can answer some questions for me. Healer
Gillespie's given me a good sense of your problem and it looks like
she's already put together a diet to serve your nutritional needs.
We can start from there—" She paused and shook her head. "Ah,
and I haven't even told you my name. I'm Shellie Aralyn. I'm one
of Mercy's physical therapy team, and they've assigned your case
to me, which means we'll be working together for quite a while.
If at any time you'd like to be re-assigned, please tell Healer Gillespie. I know some people have sex or species preferences . . . ?"

"Do they?" he asked, curious.

"Sure," the Asanii said, leaning against the wall and folding her arms. "Physical therapy is rough on people. You're vulnerable, you make mistakes, you break down. It's hard enough without making someone feel self-conscious about other factors. We'd . . . ah . . . have a problem supplying you with a same-species therapist, but within reason we can accommodate anything else."

"I'm fine," he said. "I want to be more capable in this environment, and am willing to accept any help to do so."

"Any help?" she asked, with a strange tone in her voice. Testing, he thought.

"I am here to work," he answered. "I can't work well compromised this way, alet."

"All right, good." She nodded. "Down the hall and to the right there's a locker room. Check in and ask the genie for something you can swim in."

"Swim!" he exclaimed, so surprised he let it show.

"Swim," she confirmed. "For what we want to accomplish, it's hard to beat. I take it you don't know how?"

"Not in the slightest!"

"Then you're about to learn," Aralyn said.

⁘

The locker room down the hall did in fact have a genie; the apartment in Seersana had had one, and while he'd rarely used it he did know how to operate it. Like that one, this one had limited settings, and seemed only to produce clothing, accessories, towels, the materials one might need in a gymnasium. He thumbed through the swim-gear, wondering if he'd find anything suitable, and was surprised to find full body suits. Rather appallingly revealing, he thought, but better that than to leave himself open to casual touch. It was hard enough on clothed skin without exposing himself completely. He selected one, watched the flash that evaluated his body's size and dimensions, and changed into the result it produced before putting his clothes away and letting the room lock it to his biosigns.

All this would have astounded him two years ago. It still did, and yet he watched his own hands go through the motions of manipulating the environment with unwavering confidence. That those two feelings could live together so seamlessly—the acceptance with the wonder—he no longer questioned. And he found, suddenly and unexpectedly, that he missed Vasiht'h, who would have commented on it.

Shaking himself, he stepped into the hall and did not see Aralyn by her office, so he headed for the glimpse of the water at its end.

By now, the scale at which the Alliance typically built should not have shocked him, and yet it did. The size of the pool, the skylights not so much windows as an entire glassed-in ceiling, the separate little hot tubs clustered along one edge like a series of tide pools, frothing water that spilled into the main tank . . .

Aralyn waved to him. "This way? I'd like you to meet my co-instructor."

"Your co-instructor?" he asked politely, and then started when a head breached the waters and turned his way. "Oh," he said, soft.

"You haven't met a Naysha yet, I'm guessing?" Aralyn said with a grin.

"No," Jahir admitted. He crouched at the pool's edge, then thought better of it at the protest in his joints and sat. "I am sorry if I stare," he said to the male in the pool, who grinned, lips peeling back from sharp teeth. "And I fear I don't know how to sign."

"I'll translate since I'm here," Aralyn said as the Naysha drifted closer.

Jahir had studied the Naysha along with the other species of the Alliance. Like the first generation Pelted, they'd been engineered on Earth; unlike those species, they were as alien as any of the natural-born aliens the Alliance had since discovered in its explorations. Somehow, the human scientists had managed to create something otherworldly with the Naysha. Jahir no longer remembered how many species had contributed to the DNA that

made them up, but the results looked a little like a sleek humanoid torso that flowed into the strong lower body of a cetacean,
more dolphin than fish. The face was some hairless amalgama-
tion of human and animal, with eyes half the size of Jahir's fist:
luminous eyes, a nearly fluorescent green, so large he could see
the striations in the irises.

The Naysha was studying Jahir with as much interest as
Jahir was studying him. The alien's grin pushed up the lower lids
of his eyes, sudden and merry, and he lifted webbed hands to run
them through a set of motions that flickered like schools of fish
turning in sunlight.

"He says you're the first Eldritch he's seen so closely, and
that everyone's wrong, only an idiot could mistake one of you for
human," Aralyn said with a laugh.

"Ah?" Jahir glanced at the Naysha. "May I ask why?"

Another stream of signs, one that ended with a slap on the
water.

Aralyn sighed. "Really, Paga?" When he pointed at the water,
she laughed. "All right, fine. Give me all the hard things to translate." To Jahir, "You know sea creatures sometimes have different
senses than we do?"

"I have heard," he said. The Naysha was still staring at him, so
he felt at ease doing the same.

"He says you have a completely different electrical field from
a human. Where 'electrical field' is a gross under-translation
of something far more complicated that I have no context for
explaining any better."

"Fascinating," Jahir murmured. The urge to touch the Naysha
was almost overpowering, to get a sense for that alien mind. He
shook himself a little and said, "Ah, I do apologize for staring.
And as much as possible, please teach me some of the basics of
the signing?"

"Of course," she said, and started stripping off her tracksuit. "We have a pod of Naysha here. They help maintain the
pool, serve as lifeguards, and, as in Paga's case, also have various
degrees that let them work with patients. We don't get a lot of

aquatic cases, but when we do they're in charge. I'd like him to help with you because when we landfolk teach first-time swimmers, we often get too focused on the mechanics. Part of the therapeutic value of water is that if you let it get to you, it really gets into you." She glanced at the Naysha. "There's a rhythm to water, and once you hear it, you never lose that. The Naysha are better at helping people tune into that." She smiled. "So I'll teach you how to swim. Paga will teach you how to *be*. If that makes sense?"

"I hope it will," he said.

She nodded, folding her jacket. "All right. Slide into the water, then."

He glanced at the shimmering surface, feeling a curious inertia. Swimming was not something Eldritch learned to do. The waters of their world weren't any more treacherous than other planets', but the Eldritch themselves had not evolved there, had little sense for the dangers that something natural to the world might have implicitly understood. So no one swam.

But he was here to expose himself to new experiences. And on Selnor particularly to push himself. So he sucked in a breath and shoved himself off the side of the pool and into the water . . .

. . . where he floated. And for the first time since arriving— not only to Selnor, but to the Alliance, where gravity was heavier by default even in controlled environments—did not feel the sucking ache of the gravity.

It was a testament to his self-control that he didn't moan, but he did close his eyes until he could master himself. When he opened them, Paga was floating across from him, large eyes even wider than usual. Aralyn was staring at him too.

The Naysha's hands flickered, and Jahir said, "What did he say?"

She laughed. "That you might not need much help from him after all."

He closed his eyes, felt the warm water lapping at his sides, the caress of it along his ribs, the liquescence of it like a long breeze over a field as he stretched his senses out, relaxed. He cleared his throat and said, looking at her again, "I am always willing to learn more."

Her smile was kind. "Well, we're here to teach. Let's get started."

⟋∞⟍

Jahir carried the glow from that session with him into his first shift at Mercy Hospital, and it was well that he did, for no one had understated the challenge. The senior healer-assist for the afternoon shift was a Harat-Shariin pardine, gray with large ragged spots; Jahir's fellow healer-assist was a Karaka'An woman, also gray but with narrow black stripes that bled onto her white throat. He met with them half an hour before the previous shift released in the combination lounge/office where he'd made Levine's acquaintance.

"All right," the pardine said. "We've got our newbie today, finally." He smiled at Jahir. "I'm Radimir, train Yulij, and this is Paige Nettlesdown. Paige, same volunteer corps as yesterday. I need you attached to triage for the first half of the shift. We're going to ease Jahir-alet here in slowly—"

"As slowly as possible!" she said with a chuckle. To Jahir, "We have the busiest shift of the three, most days. Right before dinner?" She shook her head. "Every case of indigestion's a coronary." To Radimir, "I'll go get the run-down on my patients from the people leaving and head there now, catch the turn-over."

"All right, thanks." The Harat-Shar turned to Jahir. "The emergency room is considered part of the crisis care system. We detach one assist there to help triage keep people calm. Otherwise, you get patients as triage decides we're needed. Patients assigned to you during your shift are yours until they leave the section; you hand them off when your shift is over, but their overall care is your responsibility. You'll also be overseeing the patients being left behind by the outgoing personnel. When we put you in triage halfway through the shift, you'll have to snatch time between incoming patients to keep a hand on the ones you've already got. We also have a rotating set of volunteers, and today it's Baird Ghardhoff, a Hinichi priest, and Shelvi, who's a laywoman in the Harat-Shariin pantheistic sect. Plus one human social worker, Jared Weldt, he's secular. If anyone asks for religious counsel, they're there, make use of them." He paused. "It's a lot to take in, but you'll get the feel for it. Good?"

"Good," Jahir said, because there was no other answer.

"Excellent," Radimir said, and lifted a hand as if to touch him on the shoulder before thinking better of it. He grinned, sheepish. "Habit."

"I appreciate the sentiment."

The Harat-Shar chuckled. "All right. I float between triage and assignment all shift, so call me if you need me." A soft ping interrupted them, and Jahir looked down at the pocket tablet he'd been assigned. "Looks like you're up. Get moving, alet. And welcome to Mercy."

"Thank you," Jahir said, and went, as quickly as his taxed physiology permitted.

The first four and a half hours of his shift passed with alarming rapidity. Four patients were assigned to him, including a rather difficult pair, a tearful mother who'd weathered an aircar crash better than the son who'd been admitted to one of the crisis care's extended stay beds. Of the other two, one was an emergency depression case, another a trauma patient who had needed nearly an hour's worth of attention to keep from panicking over the sudden loss of both her feet—the Alliance could attach new ones, but it had been an overwhelming experience. He also oversaw the patients left by the day shift, most of which needed little care save occasional check-ins. When he could, he sat to save his strength, and it seemed to help, though not as much as he wished.

Halfway through the shift, Paige found him. "Time to switch places," she said, and handed him a tray.

"What's this?" he asked, accepting it because he no longer had the energy to protest.

"Dinner," she said. "I noticed you had a hang-tag there and I don't know what you can and can't eat, so I just put a little of everything on it and brought it. There's a genie in our lounge but for the first six months I forgot to use it, and it's no use trying to do this work without fuel. So eat, then go report to triage."

"All right," he said, startled. And added, "Thank you, alet."

She smiled. "It's nothing. We have to look out for one another, and don't let anyone tell you differently."

After eating, he reported to triage, where he was given a stool in a corner of the room, and the four hours he spent there were among the most hectic and the most fascinating he'd had yet; all the people entering the crisis care system went through that room, where the healer-assist took their patient history and their vitals and assigned them treatment priority levels. He saw everything run through that room, from catastrophic injuries to people with hesitant, low coughs. And he'd expected to remain mostly unused, but every case that went through inspired the healer-assist to ask his opinion—quickly. He learned to keep his answers brief, and halfway through his tenure had become accustomed to the rhythm of the speech there, a staccato dense with data and stripped bare of every other ornament.

In one of the spaces between patients, the healer-assist, a woman barely recognizable as Tam-illee by the ears, for she was human in almost every other way, said, "You're doing well."

"Thank you," he said. "Is it always like this?"

"No. Sometimes it's worse." At his expression she laughed and wiped her face with the side of an arm. "But sometimes it's better. Sorry, I couldn't resist. We all end up with a ghoulish sense of humor after a while."

The work continued. He assessed the incoming with her, recommended some for psychological support and let the others pass. The last patient he received was unresponsive, and his tablet flagged him for immediate care. He frowned at it.

The Tam-illee glanced at him. "Something up? Did someone tell you we always assign unresponsives to you all for at least one follow-up?"

"Ah, yes, I was told." Quickly, as he recalled, by Radimir in the hall. "It's a scheduling issue, is all. Paige-alet's full up. I'll go back with him myself."

"All right."

After leaving the room, he paused to lean against the wall. He'd developed a painfully insistent headache and his chest ached from his battle to breathe enough to make his recalcitrant body move its increased weight . . . but he'd made it through the day, and hopefully—hopefully—each day that followed would be easier. He forced himself after the final stretcher. While waiting on the physical trauma attendants, he assigned this final patient to himself and then joined the others inside. As they worked over him, his gaze traveled the length of the limbs: human, male, and something about him nagged. Jahir had seen something like the presentation before. When the others exited, he hesitated . . . then ran a hand over the patient's chest, felt the faintest wash of an aura, dense and flat. He frowned and pulled his hand back, then made himself leave.

Back in the lounge, Radimir said, "You made it! Good for you. Ready to do it again tomorrow?"

"God and Lady willing," Jahir said.

The pardine grinned. "Go give the run-down to the people coming in. And remember to eat a bedtime snack."

"Bedtime snack . . . ?"

"It's full night out, alet," the pardine said, brows lifted.

"I had forgotten," Jahir murmured.

"You'll get the rhythm of it."

He nodded and logged himself out, heading wearily for the exit. The staff had its own set of elevators, and he let himself lean on the inside wall of one of them as it began its descent. His eyes drifted closed; it took the floor shivering beneath his feet to jar him alert, and when it did he found the buttons in front of him.

One of them said 'roof.'

So he hit it.

At the top of Mercy's acute care tower, Jahir let himself out of a tiny lobby and onto a terrace overlooking Heliocentrus's skyline. He walked to the edge of the balcony and rested his hands carefully on its rail, looking out. A wind cooled his face, made him aware that he'd been sweating, that some of his hair had escaped the braid he'd pulled it into.

The city was too large for him to hold in his heart or his eyes. He had to turn and turn to see it all, and even then he couldn't encompass it.

He had come from a place where to light a building required candles and lamps filled with oil, and servants to tend them, and it was costly and so it was rarely done. Looking outside his family home at night he'd seen the gossamer of the galaxy against the night's blue breast, and the moon, had heard nothing but a profound silence that seemed to bleed into the dark and isolate everyone in their separate shells of warmth and light.

Here—

So many colors against the dark. The lights smeared in his vision, though the wind dried his lashes as quickly as blinking wet them. There was no isolation here, no silence, no looking out into the night only to be denied. Here was all the connection he'd been longing for without ever having a name for what he was missing.

Standing on the roof so high above the city, he had never felt so alone, and so exhausted, and so alive. His skin pebbled at the touch of the warm breeze, at the salt tang of the foreign air, at the glitter of the lights.

The trudge back to his apartment felt eternal. By the time he reached it, he had to lean on the wall to stay upright and he almost stumbled into the door before it read his biosign and let him in. The last thing he wanted to do was eat, but Gillespie's warnings about his fate did he not increase his caloric intake moved him to the tiny genie in his kitchenette. He drank a sourly-flavored meal replacement and fell into his bed, and immediately passed into unconsciousness.

CHAPTER 4

"WHAT DO YOU MEAN, late?" Vasiht'h asked, trying to keep his claws from inching out of his toes.

"We've had an issue with our docking facility in Starbase Alpha. Your flight is one of several that has been affected," the woman behind the counter said.

"If I miss this flight, I'll miss all my connections!"

"And we'll do our best to accommodate you, alet," she said, trying to keep her own ears forward as she scanned the listings. "We're going to have to re-route you anyway, since our estimated time to repair for the starbase dock won't permit us to send you through Alpha today."

This sounded far more serious a mess than he thought. He wondered just how many passengers the spaceflight attendants were going to have to shuffle and felt a pang of sympathy for her, even if that didn't have any effect on the state of his stomach as he contemplated the delay. He'd chosen the economical way to go in-Core to the capital, a flight plan that required five connections across the sector. He was only on his second leg of the journey, and if all of them had substantial delays. . . .

"How long before I can get on the next flight?" he asked.

She was drawing multiple routes he could see in reverse on

the solidigraph floating between them. "It looks like your best path puts you on the shuttle leaving at mark twenty for Starbase Veta."

"Mark twenty! That's after dinner! I'll miss my connections—"

"We'll do everything we can to make sure you arrive at your final destination as close to your original arrival time as possible," she said. "But mark eight is the earliest I can send you out, alet. Shall I put you down?"

What could he do? "Yes, please." And added, "Thanks. I know this must be stressful for you."

She managed a smile. "A little. But not as bad as it must be for you. I really am sorry."

"I know," he said.

"I've put you on Flight 02-20018, departing mark twenty for Starbase Veta," she continued, flicking through her interface and dropping his name in the right place. "Looks like I can re-route you from Veta to Selnor Welcome Station with two days layover. We'll pay your hotel stay. The good news is that Veta's actually closer to Selnor than Starbase Alpha, so that part of the trip won't take as long. Flight 01-06212 to Selnor Orbital One will get you there within three days of your original time." She looked up. "That's the best I can do, alet. Unless you want to take a direct flight to Selnor . . . ?"

Even knowing the price tag on a nonstop flight, Vasiht'h considered it for a heartbeat before he remembered he was not that well-heeled. "No. This will do."

"We're processing a refund now for your last four flights," she continued. "And I've flagged you for priority treatment for the remainder of your trip. I hope that helps a little."

"That's very nice of you," he said. "Thanks."

"All right." She glanced at him. "You're re-booked, alet Vasiht'h. Please be back at the gate half an hour prior to departure."

Three days! Vasiht'h resettled his bag over his shoulder and went for a wander, ignoring the crowds of people streaming past. Not that it mattered; he was weeks behind Jahir as it was, so what was three more days? And yet he felt the urgency of it like an itch he couldn't reach to scratch. He stopped at one of the walls. Like most in the Alliance, the double world system that hosted the Seersa and the Karaka'A maintained a station near the edge of the heliosphere to accept incoming traffic and route it to the inhabited worlds, the research stations or any of the industrial habitats that might be making use of any asteroid belts or uninhabitable planets. This one had been tethered around the most distant planet, a world no better than a giant rock, and one rarely glanced down when using the windows . . . because the walls that stretched several stories up in the terminal were giant panes of flexglass and they looked out on a stunning amount of interstellar traffic. Enormous freighters shared mooring with sleek, single-person cutters, and in the distance one could see the gleaming lights of Fleet ships passing through on their patrols. In real space terms, most of the ships were too far to be seen unaided, but the datafilm on the glass not only magnified them for the aesthetic pleasure of those sight-seeing, but also hung their registries and—in the case of commercial liners—flight schedules as small tags beside them.

Vasiht'h had been off-world before, of course; had gone to Seersana from his home on Anseahla, and made the return trip several times for visits. But those journeys had been nowhere near so thorny, from a logistical perspective. His parents had paid his way, and he'd stepped over a Pad onto one of Seersana's orbital stations, and from there had gone nonstop home.

He'd never really felt out on his own. Not like this. It was scary . . . and exhilarating, that too.

Had he had the fin, he would have taken a direct flight to Selnor and saved himself the hassle. Even now, he was more stressed than moved by the glory outside the windows. But some part of him remained aware that had Jahir been with him, his friend would have spent all six hours of the layover sitting in front of one of these windows, watching the ships go by. Which was one of the reasons he was making this trip: because he craved that reminder, the sense of awe that only a stranger to the

Alliance could really feel, experiencing it.

Over a small lunch of clear mushroom soup and crackers, which was all his fretful stomach could handle, Vasiht'h went through his mail. Palland had left him some instructions on remote registration for fall semester, along with recommendations of classes best left for in-person sessions. His grandmother and two of his brothers had written him long rambling notes that he queued for later consumption; he was too nervous to give them his undivided attention. There were updates from friends, former classmates, former patients, even, sending him letters after the conclusion of his research studies.

The one person he wanted to hear from hadn't sent him anything.

There were any number of reasons for that, he thought while wandering the shops clustering the center of the station. Foremost being that Jahir was probably busy. It was also possible that his former roommate didn't want to talk to him, but somehow Vasiht'h couldn't take that idea seriously. He could still feel the warmth of Jahir's shoulder under his cheek in the embrace they'd shared before the Eldritch had left, and he knew with all the certainty of an esper that Jahir cared about him.

No, the possibility that distressed him most was that his friend was not just busy, but overwhelmed. And that made him too agitated to enjoy what he would normally have found comforting: the bustle of people, the hum of their conversation, the evidence of the Alliance's wealth and variety.

Three days. Goddess hear him, but surely another three days wouldn't matter.

———oøøo———

"Has he woken up yet?" Jahir asked as he washed his hands.

Behind him, the day shift assist he was taking over from shook her head. "No. They think they've made some progress by putting him on fluids, though, so you might get lucky today." He glanced over his shoulder at her and she finished, "If they don't wake up within a couple of days, they generally don't. Not here, anyway."

"Right," Jahir said, drawing in a measured breath. "Thank you, alet."

"Don't mention it. And keep out of Healer Jonsen's way, he's in a mood."

He lifted his brows. "Thank you for the warning."

"You don't need anyone taking any more stripes out of your hide than the gravity's doing," she said, and headed out, leaving him to stare after her. He hadn't recalled discussing his problem with anyone but his direct superiors, and yet within twenty-five hours—and twelve minutes, that being the length of Selnor's day by some clock he had not yet had explained to him—it seemed as if everyone knew. It wasn't in his medical files; he knew because he'd checked himself and found them empty, as he'd come to expect from the censors that dealt with the requirements of the treaty between the Eldritch and the Alliance. He glanced at the metal bracelet framing his wrist as he reached for his gloves. The narrow plaque said "Mediger's Syndrome" but the letters were too small to be read from a distance, or so he assumed. Or perhaps he didn't notice how close people came to read it? He found such things far from mind while working.

Paige, passing him on the way out, said, "You got triage first today. It's not too bad yet, though, you should have time to check on your patients."

"Understood."

Triage was quiet enough for him to do a quick round; as reported, his unresponsive remained so. The mother and son from the accident were doing better physically, but the mother was ready for discharge that afternoon and was anxious about leaving her child behind. His acute depression case was sleeping, and the woman without legs had acquired them overnight, in a feat of magic so astonishing that he stared at them when he came in.

"I know," she said. "Me too. But look!" She wiggled her toes for him. "They work!"

"You must be relieved," he said.

"You can't imagine." She sighed, then smiled up at him.

"Thanks for the help yesterday."

"I was glad to be of service," he replied. And then, because he knew it would make her smile again, "Show me the toes once more?"

She did one better and laughed.

He returned to triage, still smiling, and found yesterday's Tam-illee there, reading a data tablet and having a cup of coffee.

"Quiet afternoon," he observed.

She chuckled. "Enjoy it while you can." Lifting her mug, she said, "Catching up on paperwork. There's coffee in the break room."

"Later," he said, and sat on his stool to consult his own tablet. The pocket-sized one the hospital had issued him did indeed come with medical-grade sensor equipment, and was linked into the hospital's secure network. But he could use it for the more traditional uses of a tablet, which was how he realized he had a backlog of personal mail he'd been too tired to read. A great deal of it, including a missive from his mother. He started organizing them by priority and reached the end before he found—or rather didn't find—the one message he'd hoped he'd have received by now. Not seeing it made him wonder if he'd done the right thing, coming to Selnor.

Perhaps he simply needed friends here. In the past, he would have questioned the need for friendships, particularly with short-lived aliens who would never pace him through his life. Vasiht'h had taught him otherwise—

—the door opened for a healer-assist helping a very pregnant Tam-illee hobble in, half bent over her belly. Her leg as she extended it to walk was sodden, and revealed a brutal fragrance, like blood and the line between birth and death.

"This is Eleyna," the front-desk assist said. "Her obstetrician is on her way as soon as she's done with the delivery she's assisting at New Chaganall. We need to get Eleyna here to a bed as soon as possible."

Jahir's partner in the triage room had gone from alert to incredibly tense. Reacting to some cue he didn't have time to quantify, he said, "Why don't you log her in and get the stretcher?"

"Right," she said, and fled.

To the front desk assist, he said, "We can take care of it, thank you." Then, before the patient could panic, he held out his gloved hands. "Come, sit here."

"I'll get it messy," she answered, breathless.

Jahir smiled. "We've seen worse."

She grasped his hand—petrifying fear! And an overwhelming ferocity, both despair and determination. He flinched, and as brief as the movement was, still she caught it and looked up at him once . . . and then twice, startled, ears splaying. "You're—oh, should I . . . wait—"

He held up his free hand. "I'm fine, I promise. Please, sit."

She did, staring at him, wide-eyed. Only when she tried to find a comfortable position for her legs did she begin to breathe too quickly again. He drew her attention back by saying, "Can I help?"

"I . . . I'm just . . . I'm afraid," she finished, ears drooping. "I've made it so far! What if . . . what if something goes wrong after all these months?"

"You are in the hospital," he said. "And your physician will be here shortly. You'll have the best of care until she arrives. And even if they must do an emergency delivery now, you are far enough along for the baby to survive." He leaned forward. "Have faith, alet."

She swallowed and nodded. And added, with a whisper of curiosity, "You're an Eldritch. Working here?"

"So I am. Admittedly, this is not my specialty." At her attentive look, he said, "Psychology."

"Oh!" she said. "I guess that makes sense."

"It did to me," he said, smiling.

The triage assist showed up with the stretcher. He rose and said, "Your ride, alet. Let me help you—" Another touch, this time more determination than despair. The fear remained, but subordinated. "You're doing fine."

"You think so?" she asked.

"Just fine," he said, and set her hand on her belly, where he felt the unexpected impression of something somnolent, more curious than alarmed. "Both of you."

And then he was alone with his companion, who was standing at the door watching their patient recede. He studied her, waited for her to turn away and see him before he canted his head a little, inviting the confidence.

"My sister's lost two kids," she said, ears slicking back. "I just . . . it's the one thing that unnerves me. I know how much better it's gotten for us as Tam-illee in the years since the Exodus. And I know living someplace like this where you get the real advances in medical care years ahead of, say, the frontier, or even the Alliance suburbs. But I still . . . I just . . ." She shuddered. Then rubbed her eyes and said, "It bothers me."

"It would bother me too," he offered.

She looked up at him sharply.

"We all have something, alet." Jahir found the stool and lowered himself onto it, trying not to react to the ache in his hips and shoulders. "Most of us have several." He spotted the chair vacated by the pregnant Tam-illee, now soiled, and started to rise, but she waved him down.

"I'll take care of it. Save the wear on your joints." As she went for the chair, she added, "Thanks for handling it when I couldn't."

"You could have, and you would have, had you been alone," he said, allowing himself to lean against the wall. "But you are not alone, and there is no reason for you to face everything as if you were."

She glanced at him. And then she laughed. "Therapists!"

He lifted his brows, amused. "I fear I am guilty of the charge."

"You do well," she said, quieter. "And you really helped her back there."

"More by being a radical distraction from her own woes than anything else," Jahir said, rueful. "Two years of training, and none of it as useful as something I was born with."

"In this business, if you have any advantage, you use it." She reseated the cleaning wand in its charger and said, "Maya. Maya

FirstOnSite."

"FirstOnSite," he mused. "There is a story there."

"I could tell it to you," she said, smiling, and then stopped as their alerts went off. "But not quite yet."

The first four hours of his shift passed in a blur, then, as the late evening traffic picked up. He passed the triage watch to Paige and did rounds on the newly assigned patients and the ones from yesterday. Healer Jonsen was, in fact, disgruntled and he was glad of the warning to treat him carefully.

At some point—he could not have said when—he discovered he was sitting on the floor with his back to the wall, and could not remember how he got there. Dismayed, he rose, bracing himself, and had only just gained his feet when Radimir popped his head around the corner. "Need help?"

"No," he said. "I apologize—"

"Don't," Radimir said. "You've only been there ten minutes, and Paige and I have been keeping an eye on you."

"Ten minutes!"

"And everything's under control," Radimir said. The Harat-Shar smiled. "Alet, we're psychiatry in a crisis care setting. As important as we all know the mind is to the body's health, we are very much a support function here. The ER healers-assist and doctors . . . they have to get where they're going immediately. Most of the time we have to wait on them to do our job. So if you need to sit for a while to catch your breath, you can. No one's going to die because you were late." He paused, then splayed his ears. "All right, I suppose there are maybe a few times that might not be true. But they're going to be vanishingly small and there are three of us working the shift. One of us can get there in time. All right?"

Jahir drew in a breath, tried not to be alarmed at how raw his throat felt, and how much his chest hurt. "All right."

"Good. Now if you could check on Bed Twelve, they've asked for some counseling support there."

Having stumbled onto a solar system with two habitable planets, the Pelted had settled the Seersana-Karaka'A system first before continuing on and spreading out to found the other homeworlds that would become the Alliance Core; that made it an old and busy system, thick with settlements stretching from the interior worlds out to the welcome station near the heliopause. Vasiht'h had traveled to Seersana from a less settled part of the Core and thought the process had inured him to the scale at which the Alliance operated, and like most Pelted he took that scale for granted.

The first time he saw an Alliance starbase, he stopped short and sat so abruptly he kinked his tail under his hind end.

One of the flight attendants paused beside him and said, "First time?"

"Yes," Vasiht'h managed. "Are you sure that's not a planet?"

The man smiled. "Absolutely. It's no trouble to program the smart paint, so they give every starbase a unique exterior pattern as a navigation aid. All of us come in on computer-guided courses, but having multiple checks is always good."

"It's so big," Vasiht'h murmured. "And so busy."

"Just wait until we get closer." The man grinned. "We're still about three hours out. We won't recall everyone to their seats until we're only fifteen minutes from docking. Enjoy the show, alet."

"I will." And he meant it. From the tags hanging off the starbase it was roughly the size of a moon, and it was dotted with the bright shells of habitats, green and blue and brown and white under glass, like gemstones, the colors crisp against the vacuum. The surrounding paint had been streaked out with multiple lines and colors, leading to other habitats and facilities. In addition, several thick lines, gold or diamond-like, ran the length of the base. It was frankly beautiful, and it was surrounded in ships. Not just the commercial liners Vasiht'h had become accustomed to seeing on his own brief journeys in and out of Seersana-Karaka'A, but merchant and trade vessels of every size from single-person concerns to vast bulk freighters. Luxury ships for the wealthy shared space with pleasure cruisers, some small enough to mount solar sails. And cutting in and out of this constant traffic were the sleek ships of the Alliance's naval Fleet, and not just the little couriers that might dip in and out of a system like Seersana-Karaka'A . . . but the dark broad shadows of battle- and warcruisers, sliding into and out of the base for refueling and maintenance.

For almost three hours, Vasiht'h sat in front of that window wall, watching the starbase swell until it filled the glass from end to end. The tags on the coating popped into and out of view as new ships and features became visible, and there seemed to be no end to it.

And this . . . this was his home. His birthright, if all he'd been told growing up was to be believed. Humanity may have engineered the first Pelted . . . but the Pelted had left them and made the Alliance, and all this infrastructure had been largely in place by the time humanity returned to space and found their creations had outstripped them in technology, in numbers, and in vision.

Vasiht'h had always known all this in his head. He prided himself on being someone who lived mostly there, where the storms of passion that afflicted other species might leave him untouched. It had taken one very rare alien to show him that he could feel things as strongly as any other person, that this was not necessarily something to be avoided.

And the sight of Starbase Veta overwhelmed him emotionally in a way he would never have predicted. He felt the Goddess's hand in it, in just how much the Pelted had overcome to evolve into the people who could do something like this.

When at last he returned to his seat and strapped down for the final approach, he had wet eyes. Was it ridiculous that he could feel pride in the accomplishments of his own people? That a mound of metal could make him cry? And yet, he knew what Jahir would say. Jahir would probably have found the sight of Veta as riveting as he had.

Vasiht'h used the last fifteen minutes of the journey to start reading about starbases in general and Veta in particular. He'd anticipated spending the entirety of his layover fretting about the delay. To discover he was looking forward to it was a pleasing surprise.

Chapter 5

W HEN THE ALARM WOKE him, Jahir found himself on the couch with no memory of returning from his shift. He stared groggily at the data tablet on the coffee table and then forced himself upright enough to shut it off. Had he eaten? He couldn't recall. He'd gone to the roof of the hospital again to look at the lights; that much he remembered. But staggering back to the residence was the limit of his recollections. He rubbed his face and wondered how long it would take for the acclimatization to begin working . . . and then, resigned, he went to shower, change, and report for the physical therapy and then his shift.

On his arrival, Radimir peered at him and said, "You're on the beds first today."

"I am more present than I look," Jahir said. "I pledge it."

"Mmm. Well, you should have some coffee anyway. Paige brought in a bottle of it from one of the local roasters. Oh, and Griffin'll be by later to check in with you." He lifted a brow. "You've been keeping him updated, I hope?"

"Ah—I admit I have been busy settling in."

Radimir snorted. "Don't make that mistake twice."

"No," Jahir said, chagrined. "And I shall apply myself to Paige's offering, and thank her at first opportunity."

"You do that, alet."

The coffee was in fact, ambrosial, from its earthy, complex scent to the subtlety of its flavors and aftertastes. He neither sweetened nor adulterated it with the slim silver pitcher of cream beside it before heading into his rounds. He was not yet accustomed to the pace of the crisis care setting; many of his patients were gone, either discharged or whisked to other departments for further care, and he remained on call for those but practically his role was subordinated to the healers-assist in those departments—something for which he was profoundly grateful, as it saved him the trouble of frequent—and long—walks to other buildings.

In their place, he had new patients, and he tended to the newcomers before reaching the one who hadn't yet left. He entered the room with the human male and found him in much the same position, face still slack. Glancing at the halo-arch's monitors brought him precious little information, so Jahir reached a hand for the man's arm. He hesitated, questioning the impulse, and then closed the distance, expecting to be assailed, and instead . . . instead there was nothing. Just a sepulchral stillness that felt incredibly wrong from a living person. If he concentrated, he could sense a sludge beneath it, with the occasional flicker, like the dying embers of a fire. But the impression was so distant he had to work for it, and when he rose out of the trance he was not alone.

"Did you feel anything?" Healer Jonsen asked. Whatever pique had afflicted the healer the previous day was notably absent; today the Hinichi looked tense, but not aggressive. Hopeful, Jahir thought.

"I wish I could give you any news at all," Jahir said. "But I fear I see no cause for optimism."

"Neither do we," Jonsen said. "We've been unable to locate a next of kin from anything he had on him, and treaty stipulations with humanity prevent us from doing a DNA look-up without record of permission. I'm afraid he's going to die here, and no one will ever know why, or what happened to him."

"Is there nothing more to be done?"

"Oh, there's plenty that could be done." Jonsen looked down at the patient, and his ears flipped back. "Our first course with this is to support the return of the physical body to health and then see if the mind comes back with it. If that doesn't work, we can try more invasive techniques. But honestly, the body doesn't like us messing with its own treatment plan."

"I had a teacher so tell me once," Jahir murmured, remembering KindlesFlame's lecture on the subject.

"If we had a next of kin to consult, the choice would be easier. For us, anyway, because it would be up to them. Or if they had a preference on file. Since neither of those apply, we'll have to make the decision ourselves."

"Could he not be moved upstairs?" Jahir asked.

"Oh, he could. The question is whether we can afford it." Jonsen's smile was wry. "The beds don't come free. And if we keep him, we might displace someone with an active family, waiting for their return." He looked down at the man. "No, we'll keep him as long as we can, and then we'll have to either ship him to a different facility—where it's far more likely he'll expire—or try invasive measures. Given that the worst outcome in either case remains the same, we'll probably try something on him. Later today, I'm guessing, after the healers get together for their daily patient care conferences." He glanced at Jahir. "At which point we will either need you immediately . . . or not at all."

"I will do my best on his behalf," Jahir said.

Jonsen nodded. "But if you sense anything . . ."

"I'll be sure to communicate it."

"Good," the wolfine said, and left.

Jahir stayed a moment longer, willing himself to touch the skin of the limp wrist lying beside the patient's hip, and could not force himself to the task. Even now, the feel of that cold seemed to cling to his fingertips, tacky as the soil in a graveyard. He backed away, watching the monitors, and then went to attend to his coffee mug, left outside the room. If he used it more for the warmth than for drinking, it was still good coffee, and he was glad of it.

---∽∾∽---

"I didn't know you drank coffee," Paige said when they met at the bottle. She was refilling her own cup. "I mean, you drink coffee because we all take stimulants. I didn't know you liked this stimulant in particular."

"I love coffee," Jahir said. "Also tea. Hot chocolate now and then. Kerinne, perhaps not as often."

"Kerinne's not a stimulant, though," Paige said. She held out her hand for his cup and he passed it to her, careful of her fingers. He was feeling somewhat bruised and did not want to abrade himself further. "If you like this stuff, I can bring an order more often? This shop does hot buttered coffee, if you've ever had that."

"I have not," Jahir said. "It sounds deadly."

She laughed. "Only if you're not used to a lot of fat." She glanced at him, one ear up. "I bet if you check your list of okay foods, you'll find it on there."

"Will I?" He took the cup from her, surprised. "It seems a strangely specific thing."

"Oh, the lists aren't made like that." She waved a hand. "Your healer put in specifications—nutritional targets you need to meet and compounds you're supposed to avoid—and the database will generate the list dynamically. Who'd have the time to do it otherwise?"

"I had no idea," he murmured. Then added, "Perhaps you might answer me a question, alet? How does everyone know about me?" He lifted his braceleted hand and shook it. "I was under the impression this was the only evidence accessible to those who would have wanted to know."

"And all it takes is one person who's close enough to read it," Paige said with a chuckle. "After that, the break room takes care of the rest." At his quizzical expression, she added, "People talk."

"Ah," he said, quieter.

"Don't take it that way," the Karaka'An said. "It's because we take care of one another. We like to know how we can help, if we're going to need to."

This was, he thought, another extension of the Pelted cultural attitude toward privacy, particularly in regards to health and safety. They found privacy disturbing, reminiscent of the days when they were secrets guarded by humanity who wanted to keep them for their own purposes. Berquist had explained it to him briefly on Seersana, how the privacy laws for Pelted were radically different from those for humans. And neither of them were anywhere near as fanatic about it as the Eldritch.

"I appreciate being accepted into the community," he said, because it was truth. As much as he preferred the privacy of his own kind, he was not among them anymore . . . and the only help he was apt to receive while out on his own was limited to the help the people around him were willing to extend a stranger.

"It was a little quicker than usual with you," Paige admitted. She smiled. "Because you're unusual. And because you're obviously fighting so hard just to be functional. We can all respect that. So if you ever need anything—"

Like a nap on the floor? He thought of Radimir and withheld his sigh. "I am grateful. And hope to be worth the effort."

She grinned at him. "So far, so good."

Two hours later, the unresponsive patient died.

Jahir was in triage when the alert went off; by the time he arrived, the emergency team had surrounded a body that had gone from limp to spastic. The Eldritch stopped abruptly in the door; the sounds from the halo-arch melded into the sounds of flesh jerking against fabric, and none of that mattered because he could sense the chaos of the man's aura from across the room. He'd always been vaguely aware of people's emotional states, but he'd never been able to feel them with such clarity without touch. And it gave him an immediate headache; colors streaked in front of his eyes, breathless and nonsensical, and he leaned against the door frame until he could marshal himself.

As he stepped closer, the emissions collapsed, and so did the man. The halo-arch began to whine, a high-pitched noise that only exacerbated the headache.

By then, it was over, and all that was left was the paperwork.

Once one of the healers-assist left, Jahir came close enough to look at the man's face. He'd seen the dead before; among his own kind with their lack of most medical knowledge, it came frequently. His own father had been one of those dead, even. And little Nieve had died in his arms on Seersana, and the memory of that lingered, a reminder that even in the Alliance, people died. But the contrast between the man's aura while he lay comatose and the state he'd projected so powerfully just before dying struck Jahir as ominous. He found his tongue with difficulty. "What do you suppose . . . ?"

"Killed him?" One of the healers-assist shook his head. "We have no idea. Sometimes bad things happen."

His coworker snorted. "Yeah, like dying. Dying happens sometimes."

"But only sometimes," the first said with a grin as he began retracting the halo-arch and preparing the patient for his trip out of the crisis care facility. Glancing at Jahir, he said, "Never happened on your watch before?"

Nieve counted, he thought. "Yes." He glanced at the now quiescent readings from the halo-arch. "No idea at all?"

"Not that we know of. You can ask Jonsen, though, he was the attending."

"I may, at that," Jahir murmured.

❧

The rest of his shift passed quickly, punctuated only by the sort of strange occurrences Maya assured him were normal, as in the patient who brought a bag of live fish with her; having been afflicted with gut pains halfway home from the store where she'd bought them, she detoured to Mercy without stopping to drop them off. There were the expected series of accidents, some gruesome and some merely messy—one man with a cut he couldn't keep from bleeding who left the triage room looking as if something had been butchered in it. And there were the wondrous periods of quiet where he could rest against the wall and listen to Maya sipping from her mug and swiping pages on her data tablet.

He was grateful to hand off his work to the night shift and was contemplating whether he had the energy for a trip to the roof when Doctor Levine startled him. Not just by arriving early enough in the shift to intercept him, but by blocking his way.

"Doctor?" he asked, fighting his fatigue. "Is there something I might help you with?"

"If you have a moment?" She beckoned him after her, and resigned, he followed her to the small room in the back of the lounge that served as the shift supervisor's office. He wished Radimir was in it, but with evening handing off to the night shift, the pardine was talking with his own replacement.

"I hear you lost someone today," Levine said, eyes somber. She leaned against the wall with her arms crossed, creasing her coat.

"I would not go so far in claiming jurisdiction," he answered, his weariness making him more curt than he would have preferred. "The team lost him, I would say."

She nodded. "That's a good way of framing it. I encourage you to hold on to that. But if you have any issues later . . . talk to me about it. Or Griffin, if you're more comfortable with him. Losing a patient is hard. I don't want you to soldier on in stoic silence if you need help."

It was growing progressively more difficult not to stare at her. He did not question her compassion, or her ardor in presenting her case, but he couldn't help but wonder why she was so adamantly insisting that he needed help. Particularly—

—ah. *Her* help.

And yet, this was not her shift. How had she found out? God and Lady preserve him if she was actively monitoring his progress. Could he dare to believe she was doing the same with the other resident? He hoped so.

"Thank you, Doctor. I'll be sure to talk to someone if I feel it necessary."

"Good," she said. "Because I remember the first person who died on my watch . . ." She drifted off, eyes losing their focus, and he suppressed the urge to beg off before she could keep him any longer. More than anything he wanted to be off his feet and she was keeping him from his bed. She was talking again. ". . . and it was hard to convince myself I couldn't have done more. But there are some people it's not your destiny to heal or fix, alet. If you can't learn that lesson, you'll never make it in this profession." She lifted her brows. "And . . . you are falling asleep on me, aren't you."

"Not . . . precisely."

She chuckled. "Well, I won't keep you with maundering stories. It's just my habit to show up for the first bad trauma one of our newbies experiences. I find it helps head off the kind of heroics I attempted as a shiny new physician."

"I had wondered why you were here," he admitted.

"And now you know." Levine smiled. "So keep my offer in mind."

"I shall," he said. "Thank you. And good night, Doctor."

"Good night, alet."

It was reassuring to know he wasn't the first person to earn Levine's personal attention following a major event. And yet, as much as he wanted to believe that comprised her entire motivation, he felt as if she was staring at him as he walked away.

CHAPTER 6

STARBASES, VASIHT'H CONCLUDED after only a few hours on one, were glorious. He'd thought Seersana cosmopolitan, and it was. But it was also the Seersa's homeworld, and any population on it was bound to be weighted heavily toward the world's native race.

Starbase Veta did not have that handicap. Walking through the port to reach one of its Pad stations, Vasiht'h saw more variety in species than he had in a year at Seersana University. Possibly two. Or all four. Nor was that the only difference; there most of the people he'd been exposed to were academics, and the general population was skewed toward young adults. Here he found people in every stage of their lives, and in every seeming profession, including the Fleet personnel he'd rarely had cause to encounter though he knew, intellectually, that Fleet comprised a significant percentage of the workforce. He'd had a retired Fleet roommate once, who'd explained that to him—something about it being less a military organization and more the Alliance's exploratory, ambassadorial and emergency response team—but he'd never cared to learn more.

Now . . . now he was curious.

His hotel was in the major civilian settlement on Veta, which surprised him again by not being a welcome station writ large. He'd been expecting metal corridors and exposed ducting, like something out of a 3deo space opera. Instead, he walked off the Pad into the middle of a plaza beneath a sky as brilliantly blue as any planet's, complete with a breeze that brought him the smell of flowering plants, a perfume strong enough to make him sneeze.

"New here?" someone said behind him. He turned and found a middle-aged Hinichi woman regarding him, wolf-like ears cocked forward.

"Was it my flabbergasted expression that gave me away?" Vasiht'h said, smiling.

"Let's just say I've seen it before." She grinned. "Will you take some advice from an old hand?"

"Absolutely!"

"Have a walk through the city," she said. "And if you're staying for long enough, book yourself one of the tourist train rides. The base is worth seeing in its entirety."

"I'll do that," Vasiht'h said, grateful.

After checking into his hotel, he spent an hour wandering through the market district. He had no idea what was supplying the sun on his shoulders or the breeze through his fur, but it was all believable; he found himself forgetting he was in an artificial environment at all. Sitting at an outdoor café over a cup of kerinne and a pastry, he brought up a map and studied the results. If this was correct, the starbase's wall bisected the city, separating its port and commercial docks from the living area. The Fleet base ran the length of the starbase through its interior, and if the u-bank entry was correct, it should be visible in the "sky"—Vasiht'h looked up, squinting into the light, and saw a faint white arch traced against the blue, like a distant cloud. Except clouds were rarely so regular, nor did they hold so still.

The tourist train rides, he read, actually traveled the breadth of the starbase, running through tunnels in its skin. There were multiple options, from single-destination excursions to farming and resort habitats to grand tours spanning multiple days. His fingers hovered over those, but regretfully he chose one of the shorter options that passed two of the closest bubbles and permitted a one-way ticket. He could Pad back and make his connection to Selnor.

While heading for the rail station, he wrestled with a brief sense of guilt that he could be having so much fun when who knew how hard Jahir was working; probably to the point of exhaustion, if his academic career on Seersana was any indication. But if the Eldritch had been here, he would have been the first to be out investigating the environment; knowing that, Vasiht'h went to his explorations with a light step. He would bring back stories . . . and surely there would be time for a vacation, and he could bring Jahir here in person.

The trip was breath-taking. The train's sides were floor-to-ceiling flexglass, and the tunnel it traveled in was transparent; it spent part of the journey hugging the external skin, affording an amazing view of the uncompromising beauty of space and the ships gliding through it. The other part it spent flush to the internal wall, showing either the staggering size of the hollow interior and its massive spindle clustered with Fleet warships, or the lush habitats for farming or vacations, one of which even included a body of water large enough that Vasiht'h couldn't see its edge. 'For farming aquacultural goods,' the flexglass's datafilm reported when he asked.

"Why is it so big?" he asked one of the train's employees when she came by with a drink cart.

"Oh, it's the supercolliders," she said. "Fleet builds these things as service depots and command posts for the ships in the sector. All their ships come here to refuel, and this is the smallest size they can make them to meet the requirements for the supercolliders." She smiled. "We have another tour that runs alongside the colliders. You can't see the reaction, of course, but they're covered in lights that signal their status and when something is happening. We call it the Dancing Lights trip." She offered him a tray and he picked out a cup of hot chocolate as she continued, "The Fleet leases out the merchant space, and of course no one can think of a safer place to do business than under the nose of one of their biggest presences in the sector. So wherever there's a starbase, all us civilians follow, to support the merchant traffic."

"It must be a very exciting place to live," Vasiht'h murmured.

"I wouldn't be anywhere else."

He glanced up at her, but she was already moving on.

———◦∞◦———

The next few days in the crisis care section were grueling, but the work . . . the work was compensation. When Jahir could stand back from it, the memories that spilled through him were lightning, had the suddenness of shock and joy. He was good at what he did, even crippled by the gravity, and despite a pace too hectic for him to truly relax into each case he could tell how vital his role was in the emergency setting. Somehow he made it to the end of the week, and Jiron and Radimir were awaiting him at the conclusion of his shift.

"Sit," the human said. "We know you're tired, so we'll keep this brief." He nodded at the Harat-Shar. "Raddie tells me you've settled in."

"I think I have the rhythm of it," Jahir said, and sat, though he very much feared that he would not be able to get up again without aid.

"Looks like you've had some ups and downs," Jiron continued. "Including some low-down downs?"

"Doctor Levine already discussed the death with me."

The looks the two exchanged—far too tense to also be so chagrined, and too quick to suggest comfort with the problem.

"Should she not have?" he asked.

"It's not that," Radimir began.

"And it's not important," Jiron said firmly, though more as admonition to the universe to conform to his command than statement of fact. "Do you need any counseling in that regard?"

"No," Jahir said. He drew in a breath, a slow one, knowing by now that he would manage it no other way. "It was distressing, but I have known worse."

"All right," Jiron said. "I'll take you at your word. Otherwise, you seem to be fitting in with the crew. They speak well of you. Tomorrow's your rest day—use it well, all right?"

"I plan to."

"Good." Jiron stood. "I'll check on you next week, same time."

After the human left, Radimir said, "Need help?"

"No." Jahir stood, carefully, paused to make sure there would be no dizziness. He added, rueful, "Though it is a near thing. Alet? Was there aught I should know?"

"Ah?" The pardine glanced at him, ears flicking forward.

"About Doctor Levine."

The Harat-Shar's ears sealed back. "Mmm. No. She's just . . . a very driven individual." He ran a hand over his head, fluffing up his hair and his ears on the way back toward his forehead. "A lot of the humans are when they come here. Like they have something to prove. It makes for culture issues."

"I see," Jahir said, though he didn't. It was not the explanation he'd been expecting, though he could sense the truth of it.

"Don't worry about it, alet," Radimir said. "Just concentrate on the work. That's all that matters anyway."

———⟢⟡⟣———

What Jahir wanted to do with his day off was catch up on his correspondence, see some part of the city that did not involve the hospital, and maybe pay someone else to make him a meal. What he ended up doing . . . was sleeping. He woke in early afternoon, and that only because the sun was on his cheek. Sitting up, he assessed himself, and the time, and thought better of going out.

But a swim, he thought . . . that might be salubrious. Particularly if he wasn't doing the exercises Aralyn was working him through every day. He found his gym bag and made his way there. The usual groups were at the pool; he'd noted various patients with their therapists on his visits. His own was nowhere to be found, which was fine with him. He changed in the dressing room and went out to the water, and there he floated and found some relief from the stress of holding himself up.

The rocking of the water around him warned him that he was not alone, and he opened his eyes to find Paga floating nearby. The lower half of the Naysha's eyes were submerged, and even knowing he had a clear eyelid, Jahir found it strange. But he smiled and said nothing.

Paga rose and clapped his hands in a pattern that drew the attention of some computer the Alliance had hidden God and Lady knew where. When he signed, a holographic translation floated itself alongside him.

/The water called you./

"Yes," he said, startled into responding. And added, "I had no idea something could translate for you without aid."

/Necessary. Not everyone reads sign. Many people come here. Do not like it. Lacks the nuance Shellie gives./ The Naysha wrinkled his nose. /Makes me sound like a robot./

Jahir laughed, then covered his mouth. "My apologies. That was inappropriate. It's just—"

/True./ The Naysha slapped the water for emphasis. He was smiling. /Good to see you here./

"I like it here," Jahir admitted. He tried to sort through his feelings, found them opaque—like the sea, he thought. Impressions, but only hints of something vast and deep and powerful beneath. He looked at the Naysha. "Not just because it helps me."

/Thought so. But you hold back./

Jahir frowned at the words as they faded, then looked at him. "I read that right?"

The Naysha sighed, and it was strange to hear a sound out of his mouth. He shook his head. /Lacks nuance. You love the water?/

Jahir touched the surface with a palm, felt the buoyancy of it like the descant of a hymn, lifting him with it. He exhaled, closing his eyes. "I think I must."

The tapping on the water drew his attention. /Go,/ Paga signed, pointing at one of the doors that lined the hall. /There. Number ten./

"Must I get out?"

/Go./ A smile. /Worth it. Promise./

"All right."

Leaving the water was a physical pain. His entire body protested, and the water that sheeted off him felt like a layer of clothing that sloughed off and left him naked. He paused for a moment, half afraid he would fall back into the pool, and then trudged to the room the Naysha had pointed out.

Inside, he found . . . another pool, if a smaller one. Perhaps the size of his bedroom in the new apartment. He was studying the bottom when Paga appeared in it, startling him. The Naysha grinned and clapped again to summon the computer.

/Has tunnel. Necessary. This is a consultation room./

"A . . . for you and a patient?"

/For private talks./ Paga pointed at the door. /You can lock. There is a monitor, but it is vital signs only./ The Naysha tapped his chest. /So to alert if something happens. If you lock, then no one can come in. Not even me. Only override is if computer senses you are having a health crisis./

"A private pool," Jahir murmured.

Paga tapped the water, a more gentle request for attention. /You,/ he signed. /May love the water in a way I understand. Maybe. I don't know. You don't know. You can't know, until you meet the water. Here, you can be alone with it./ He lifted his chin, alien eyes steady. /I come back in one hour./

And then the Naysha was gone. Jahir peered into the water, and the tunnel was now shut by a door the color of the pool's walls, but there was a green light glowing on it. He sat on the edge of the pool and looked up at the ceiling. "Computer?" he asked, hesitant. "What's my heart rate?"

"Current heart rate," a soft alto said, "is one hundred seventy two beats per minute."

He winced. Well, at least he knew it was monitoring him. "Lock the door, please?"

"Door now locked."

He glanced at the door; like the one in the pool, it had a light indicator, which now shone red. The one beneath the water did too.

Paga had brought him here . . . to be alone with the water. To meet the water. He wondered at the alien's motivations, and also didn't care enough to waste any time on them. He stripped the bodysuit off and went to the pool . . . and found it good. Better than anything he could remember feeling. The water was warm and buoyant and close without inflicting any emotional response on him at all—save his own, and it was relief and a recognition that welled forth from his cells, from something older than them.

His family, the Galare, were scattered along several estates, but the Seni Galare made their home inland. On reaching his majority he'd taken to traveling with his parents, and then his mother when his father had died, to the royal palace twice a year, for the formal courts . . . and Ontine was on the coast. But it perched on the edge of a sea cliff, and with the shore a day's journey down and around the worst of the crags, he had never had the time to go. But he had always found comfort in the sound of the sea. And of the rain, too, at that. Water, he thought. A great kindness, a companion, a friend. He rested his head on his folded arms on the side of the pool and thought only enough to instruct the computer to warn him when his hour was done, and then he was silent, and fell into the feel of the water on his skin.

When Paga returned, the doors were unlocked and Jahir was waiting on the side of the pool, fully dressed. The Naysha cocked his head and waited.

"Thank you," Jahir said, quietly to be so emphatic.

The alien smiled and signed one of the few things Jahir had learned: /You're welcome./

⁂

That happy hour was on his mind the following day when he found Healer Gillespie awaiting him at the pool with Shellie Aralyn and Paga floating.

"Healer," he said, coming to a halt across from them.

"Alet," Gillespie said, studying him. She squinted and folded her arms. "When Shellie told me, I didn't think it could be possible, but it's true. You aren't eating."

"I do," he began.

"But not enough." Though the Hinichi's ears remained canted forward he could just glimpse the annoyed twitch of her lupine tail. "You've shed four or five kilos if I'm not wrong."

He had no idea how much weight that represented, but from their expressions it was enough to be a significant concern. He certainly hadn't noticed any loss, but then the hospital's standard issue had been loose on him when he arrived, and from his observation it was designed that way on purpose. "I have perhaps been too tired to pay much attention to it."

"You're going to have to start paying attention to it," Gillespie said, "or we're going to run smack into the problem we're trying to avoid by failing to administer another course of the acclimatization regimen. Alet, it doesn't matter if you cannibalize your body because a drug set goes wrong, or because you don't eat enough to sustain your activity level . . . the result's going to be the same."

"I did not think it would be so serious," he said, startled. "I am eating more than I usually do—"

"Are you also usually training for an athletic competition while hauling once again your weight around?" Gillespie said tartly. "Because that's the effect being here has on your system. And I'm only slightly exaggerating." She held out her hand. "Give me the bracelet."

Mystified, he slid it off, and noticed then how easy it was to do so. Frowning, he dropped it onto her palm.

"I've been doing some experimentation and I can't make any medical record on you stick for longer than a few hours," Gillespie said. She shook the bracelet. "However, this can be programmed for patients without hitting the records database. And I am going to set it to alarm every few hours, at which point you will go to a genie, enter your metabolic disorder, which you will note is handily inscribed in the metal, and it will generate something for you that you will eat. And I can keep tabs on you by setting up a dummy record for an Anonymous patient with no species, and I will. By this time next week I want to see your cheeks filled out. Understood?"

"Yes, alet," he said, meek.

"Good," she said. "I'm going to go set this up—" She jingled the bracelet. "You stay put with your therapists."

After the Hinichi left, he touched his cheekbone with his fingertips.

"It really is that noticeable," Aralyn said, her voice regretful. "I'm sorry, but even if I hadn't said anything to her she would have noticed."

Paga patted the water and signed. Aralyn said, "And yes, Paga's right. It's her job to notice . . . and mine to say something. We're your team. We're supposed to be looking out for your health."

"I know," he said. And added, rueful, "I have made my own trouble, I fear."

"That's how it usually goes," she said. "Patients failing to follow instructions. It only helps a little to realize how often we do it when we're on the other side of the table . . ." She shook her head. "Anyway, go ahead and change for the session. We'll keep it mild today, or you'll burn up all the calories she's going to make you eat."

"I cannot imagine eating more," he murmured. Mostly because he couldn't imagine eating, with the schedule he was keeping.

"You'd better," was all Aralyn said, and Paga agreed.

Now hobbled with a bracelet Gillespie had sworn would force him to eat at the right intervals, Jahir reported to work and found it hectic.

"You're starting on triage today, if that's all right," Radimir said as the Eldritch washed his hands. "And we got another unresponsive overnight, we'll want to keep an eye on her. Asanii, though, not human."

"Same presentation?"

The Harat-Shar snorted. "Once they're comatose, alet, they all present alike." He shook himself. "But yes, same results on the tests. Damned strange, if you ask me. Two within a week? Kajentaral knows what that bodes."

"Perhaps the cases are related," Jahir mused.

"Maybe, but you know what they say about Texas."

"Ah?" Jahir looked up, perplexed. "About . . . what?"

"Texas," the pardine said. "As in 'if you hear hoofbeats, it's probably horses, not zebras.' Something we tell interns when they're eager to diagnose patients with exotic diseases because they've had their noses in textbooks for four years." He paused, then added, "No idea about the Texas part. Except that I think it's on Earth, and it must have a lot of horses."

Jahir hid a smile. "I imagine. I go, alet."

"Yes, you do."

From the moment Jahir stepped into the triage room, he was swamped. By law he wasn't allowed to make any triage decisions, lacking the training, but he knew from the harried looks on the faces of everyone involved that they sorely wished they could put him to work doing in-take in a separate room. He did what he could to spare Maya, filling out the forms for incoming as she worked up the patient currently in the room. The pace was far more hectic than he liked, but he put himself forth on behalf of the patients, trying to soothe them before handing them off.

He was comforting a distraught Seersa who couldn't draw in a full breath without coughing up blood when his bracelet started vibrating and emitted a high-pitched chirp. The patient flattened her ears, staring at it. "What was that?"

"My keeper," he said, rueful. Since the Seersa seemed interested—and anything that kept her attention off her condition was to be encouraged—he said, "The gravity here is too strong for me. I am supposed to eat more often."

"Oh!" she said. "I've had some experience with that. My kids when they had growth spurts—"

He listened, attentive, until he could pass her on to Maya,

then said, "I have to pause for a few minutes."

"Go on."

The genie gave him some sort of blended fruit and yogurt drink that he obediently sat on a chair and drank. It was hard to relax, knowing how much work he had left to do, and harder still to choke down the entirety of the cup, given how dense it was. It was one thing to need the calories; another to have a stomach prepared to deal with them after a lifetime of lighter meals. He did his best, left the rest behind, and returned to the chaos.

Four hours later, he relinquished triage to Paige and went to do rounds on the admitted patients. The usual collection of accidents, sudden acute crises and victims of violence. He'd always thought of the Alliance as a polity at peace, and for the most part it was; from his reading, there were no civil wars, no major conflicts. The borders were subject to pirate activity, but the Core was far from the border, and Selnor itself was one of the best protected systems in the entire Alliance. But that there was a sufficiency of petty violence had surprised him, even knowing that it was unavoidable in a city the size of Heliocentrus. Even his own people had such problems, and they were far, far fewer in number.

The unresponsive Asanii was in the last bed on the row. He stopped beside her and ran a hand over the air near her face; as with the human, he couldn't sense her aura without bringing his fingers close enough to brush one of her ears, had he been inclined. In all ways he could discern, she had the exact same mental profile as the male who'd preceded her a few days ago. Were all unresponsive patients so? Or was this a quality specific to these two, one that might suggest the cause of their unfortunate state?

He wondered.

His bracelet dragged him to the genie one more time during his shift, and he did his best with the second concoction. Paige found him in the break room with it and lifted her brows. "Yum, yum, appetizing?"

"I suppose it might be, if I was accustomed to consuming half a day's calories in one meal," Jahir said. "As it is, I find it rather overwhelming."

She poured a cup of coffee into a mug emblazoned with Mercy's emblem—a dove beneath the sickle moon and stars of the Alliance's flag, reversed to symbolize the winter capital—and said, "Here. Cut the fat a bit with a stimulant."

He eyed the mug. "I have to imagine that would only make my metabolism more voracious."

"Probably," she said. "But are you going to get through that shake without it?"

Jahir took a draught of the coffee and was glad of it, if only because it was liquid and hot and thin.

Paige sat across from him with her cup. "Radimir's got my back right now," she said. "What a mess it is today." She shook her head. "Must be something in the air."

"Storms come," Jahir murmured. "They pass again."

"Things have a rhythm," she said. She studied him. "So, how are you liking it so far?"

"Working the section?"

"Working at Mercy."

He paused, then said, "I think one week is too short to tell."

"Particularly while fighting the planet?" She smiled. "Fair enough. But tell us if things get hard. New people usually hit a bump in the first two weeks. If they can get past it, they're fine. So let us help, all right?"

The constant offers of aid were beginning to concern him. Was turnover so high that the community felt compelled to prevent it so aggressively? "I shall let you know."

"Good," Paige said. "It doesn't have to be me. It can be anyone, as long as you have somewhere to turn."

The rest of his shift blew by so quickly he barely remembered anything that happened, and yet when it was over he was as mentally exhausted as he was physically. He made the trip to Mercy's roof despite his fatigue because he needed it more than he needed food or sleep: the chance to be isolate, to let the warm wind blow his thoughts clean. Once there, the city receded from a hectic mélange of noises, faces and fears to a distant net of lights, spangling the city's many towers as they rose, black silhouettes against a sky a deep cobalt blue. It gave him the opportunity to step back and breathe—carefully, but deeply—and find the remove he needed to work without involvement.

It was not the same as having somewhere to turn, though. As he put his back to the city lights, he felt the lack of balance painfully. The exhaustion that closed in on him as he made his way to his apartment preyed on him precisely because he had no life outside his work. And yet, until he was healthier, he couldn't imagine how he might access anything else.

He let himself into his room and sat on the couch, knowing full well that if he didn't rise he would fall asleep on it again. He was contemplating the wisdom of forcing himself to retire to the bed when the door chime sounded. A delivery? Someone from the hospital perhaps. God and Lady knew; he didn't remember telling anyone where he lived, but the way the hospital community worked someone might have followed him home one day just to have the information to communicate to everyone else.

Weary, he pushed himself upright. The Alliance's doors could open themselves on voice command, but he had never broken the habit of going himself. "Open," he said, propping himself up with a hand on the jamb.

The door opened, allowing a swirl of warm air into the room, and there across from him was Vasiht'h. For a heartbeat—very close to the longest heartbeat Jahir could recall—he stared blankly at his friend, who was supposed to be half a sector away. A cloud of mindtouches surged toward him, pierced the fog of his fatigue with golden spangles, and he tasted cinnamon and smelled the metal-and-scrubbed-clean scent of shuttles. As the moment stretched impossibly long, he found no words, until Vasiht'h found them for them both.

"I was wrong to tell you to go. Or at least, wrong to let you go alone. But I'm here now . . . and I won't ever leave again, until one of us dies . . . or unless you tell me right now to go."

"No," Jahir managed, startled by the baldness of it, by the

truth of it. Hoarse, he said. "No, I would never think to tell you such a thing. And I would never want it."

His heart unpaused, and on its beat the mindline erupted, fusing between them with a strength that staggered him. He didn't remember falling to a knee, and he knew when Vasiht'h caught him that the Glaseah didn't remember doing it either. All that existed for them in that moment was the impossible power of a bond between two minds, made permanent by vow and intent. He felt a kindred soul in proximity to his, and it burned brighter than the sun off water, the sun held at arm's length. It came packaged with the pain of knowing their disparate lifespans, the poignancy of his having chosen the Alliance, and all the glory that decision freed him to embrace . . . and he did. He did.

CHAPTER 7

VASIHT'H RESTED HIS cheek against his friend's shoulder, eyes tightly closed, and welcomed the mindline as it fused, bringing with it the storm of sensory impressions he had no context for—yet—the smell of antiseptic and coffee, the feel of water on skin, the smear of city lights seen through watering eyes. When he'd accepted it all and let it fade into the background, all that was left was the real, solid presence of the friend he'd never thought to make . . . because such friends only came once in a lifetime, and only if you were lucky. And feeling it, truly feeling it in his heart, he knew he'd been right to come.

And then he said, startled and indignant, "Why can I feel your shoulder-blade through your *shirt*?"

"What?" Jahir asked, voice bleary. He lifted his head and said, "Perhaps because the uniform is thinner than the clothes I have preferred to wear."

"Oh no," Vasiht'h said, tasting something through the mindline that felt sour, like rue . . . and chalky, like something medical on the tongue. "No, you've lost weight." He leaned back to look at his friend's face and saw the shadows beneath the cheekbones. "You have! What's wrong? You've only been gone three weeks!"

"It is the gravity, I fear," Jahir said. He squinted. "You do not feel it?"

Vasiht'h flexed his toes. "Yes, I guess. But it's not quite as heavy as Anseahla? Reminds me a little of home."

Jahir stared at him, wide-eyed. And then cleared his throat and said, "I find it difficult. Enough that each day is an effort. I know you will ask me how I find the work. . . . Honestly I will have to tell you that I can't say, because merely moving through this environment is so taxing that it colors everything else I feel."

"So why stay?" Vasiht'h asked.

Jahir paused, and though his expression remained composed Vasiht'h could feel his consternation like something bitter and cold through the mindline. "You are not here to bring me back to Seersana with you. Are you?"

"No, no," Vasiht'h said. He shifted his paws and made a face. "You don't have to loom like that . . . ! I meant it when I said I was here to stay. I have remote courses lined up for the semester, so for the next few months I can go anywhere there's access. What I meant was—and don't answer this immediately, just think about it—why run the trial here, where you can't even tell if your response is to the environment or the work? Your goal is to find out if you love the medical track. How can you tell if you can't separate it from the physical endurance test of just living here?"

"One cannot part something from its context," the Eldritch said, but he was thoughtful, not defensive. "No matter where I go, arii, I will be contending with environmental factors."

"But they don't have to be so extreme they overwhelm the rest of it," Vasiht'h said. "Goddess, Jahir. You're so tired you're *still leaning on me.*"

Surprise, tart like a lemon. "So I am."

Vasiht'h licked his teeth. "That shouldn't have tasted so good."

A laugh, then, one that startled the Eldritch on its way out. "Ah, should I ask the flavor. . . ."

"Lemon, and go sit on the couch. I'm guessing you haven't eaten yet."

Jahir rose with an awkwardness Vasiht'h found painful to

watch. "I was in fact considering sleeping."

Vasiht'h eyed him.

"I work the evening shift," Jahir said. "From mark fifteen to twenty-three." He tilted his head. "In fact, I would not have expected you to come so late."

"I just got on-world and I had no other place to stay," Vasiht'h said. "Besides, I had a feeling I shouldn't wait. Now sit, and I'll make you dinner."

"If you—"

"Yes, I insist. Before you fall down."

Vasiht'h felt the relief before he heard the Eldritch reach the cushions; the mindline gave it to him, a visceral weight in every joint that made the fur on the back of his spine fluff. He shook himself, set his bags down and went to investigate the small kitchen. While he wasn't surprised to find it pristine, he found the evidence of Jahir's complete depletion disturbing.

"I am sorry," Jahir murmured, the words embroidered with falling arpeggios, dim light, chagrin and weariness. "I have not kept with our habits. I have not so much as baked a cookie since I arrived."

"That's what you have me for," Vasiht'h said firmly. He found no pots, no pans . . . not even a plate in the cupboard. "Though it looks like a real meal is going to have to wait until tomorrow. Have you really been using the genie for everything?"

"I'm afraid so."

"I'm surprised you have two fin to rub together if all your meals have been coming out of your energy budget." Vasiht'h shook his head. "It won't hurt anything if I add another to the total?"

"Oh . . . no, it's no worry."

Vasiht'h glanced past the kitchen island at his friend, saw only a spill of hair over the arm of the couch. The mindline floated him Jahir's lack of concern on the subject of money. He decided not to push and flipped through the available options. They were locked to a specialized menu—high calorie, nutritionally dense. He snorted. "Now I know you're tired."

"Ah?" Drowsy, threaded through with something soft and clean and white. Eyelet lace? A memory of it, anyway.

"Because there's ice cream on this menu and you haven't ordered it yet."

The mindline spiked with an interest so intense that Vasiht'h glanced over and found Jahir peering past the arm of the couch.

He laughed. "Right. But you have to eat this soup first."

"Soup . . . does not sound like the sort of food they've been forcing me to eat."

"This one will do it," Vasiht'h promised. He brought a tray to the couch and set it on the coffee table, then settled alongside it, paws tucked close and neat.

"What is that?" Jahir asked, bleary.

"Cream of quail and mushroom," Vasiht'h said. "It's on your menu."

"It sounds . . ."

"Heavy," Vasiht'h said. "Eat. Please?"

Jahir sighed and sat up, reaching for the bowl. The mindline rested between them, shimmering and pregnant, and yet it didn't communicate anything beyond a faint static. Vasiht'h remembered their cautious experiments with the mindtouches back on Seersana, so much more vivid than this, and tried to keep his dismay to himself at the state his friend had been reduced to.

"It's not quite as bad as it looks," Jahir said, quiet.

"I'm completely sure it's worse than it looks." Vasiht'h flexed his toes and then pressed them together to keep from chafing them. "So I'm going to suggest you do a little more than think about whether you want to do this somewhere else. I'm going to suggest that you set yourself a deadline."

"Go on."

That the Eldritch wasn't protesting more was all Vasiht'h needed to know. "Set a date by which point you'll make a decision whether to stay or go. And not in two years."

Jahir looked up at him over the bowl, his honey-yellow eyes rimmed in red. "What do you suggest?"

"Two months."

Jahir looked away, but the mindline carried his internal flinch so clearly Vasiht'h's flanks twitched in sympathy.

"Look," Vasiht'h said, quieter. "I know you don't want to renege on your word. I know you feel you have a duty to fulfill your entire residency term. But these things have options for early termination for a reason, and "medical disability" is definitely enough of one to back out. You're here for a reason, arii: to evaluate this career option. You can't do that fairly under these circumstances. It might get better, so give yourself some time. But promise me you won't stick it out just to be stubborn about doing what you think is the right thing, but is actually the wrong thing—for yourself, and for the patients who could be served better by someone who isn't fighting the world just to stay on his feet for them."

The mindline carried a hush in it, like a still morning just before dawn. Jahir was looking at him, without speaking . . . but did he have to? Wasn't that impression enough?

But at last, the Eldritch did speak. To say, "I have missed you, Vasiht'h."

He blushed brightly beneath his fur, and was devoutly glad it wasn't as obvious as it felt, until he realized that it was obvious— through the mindline. He wondered what his embarrassment felt like.

"Spines," Jahir offered. "But . . . not prickly ones. More like . . . spongy ones." He narrowed his eyes. "That is not my memory. What on the world is it, then?"

Vasiht'h laughed. "I had a toy. A ball with little spikes. Most of the time when you grabbed it, it was fun, but once in a while you put your hand on it wrong and it poked you. Usually in the fold of skin where your joints make your fingers bend?"

"Ah!" Jahir said. "Show me a picture?"

Vasiht'h obliged him, grinning, and was pleased to hear the Eldritch laugh . . . until he shuddered and pressed his hand to his side. "What?" A shaft of pain like a constricting band around his waist. "Is that just—"

"It is an exercise, breathing all day. If I exert myself to any extent, anyway." Jahir managed a wan smile. "Healer Gillespie assures me with time I will acclimate. I have only been on world a week and a half or so, however. That is not long enough."

"So how long did she say it would take?" Vasiht'h asked, flattening his ears.

"She wasn't sure." At Vasiht'h's expression, Jahir said, "I know. You need not say it."

"All right, then I won't." Vasiht'h got up. "Finish the soup. I'll bring dessert."

"Ice cream?" Jahir asked, hope blooming through their nascent bond like flowers opening.

Vasiht'h grinned. "Finish the soup."

"I apply myself directly."

Thumbing through the ice cream listing was . . . terrifying was a strong word, perhaps. But the styles approved for someone with Jahir's dietary needs were denser than anything Vasiht'h wanted to eat as dessert. He chose a cocoa-flavored one and stopped to cue some music, selecting at random a neo-Baroque stream that slowly rose in volume until he could just hear the soft trill of strings. Not his sort of music, and he began to turn from it and stopped, because he found, abruptly, that he liked it. Not just liked, but had strong memories of the taste of a floral biscuit and strong tea, the warmth of sunlight on his neck and cheek, the murmur of conversation and the close harmony of a string quartet.

He didn't just like this music, he really, really liked it. The suddenness of his change in opinion struck him as somehow humorous.

Jahir was watching him.

"You like this music," Vasiht'h said. "So I like it."

The Eldritch's brows lifted. "Is it supposed to work thus? The mindline?"

"Goddess knows, because I don't," Vasiht'h said with a chuckle. He brought the bowl and set it on the table. "There's a lot written about mindlines, but I never read about it in detail for the obvious reason that I didn't think I'd ever have one." He sat, folding his tail over his rear paws. "Besides, the literature we've written is about mindlines between two Glaseah. I've never heard of anything recorded about a mindline between two different species."

"Ah!" Jahir said. "We can be anomalous." He brought his spoon to his mouth and stopped at the flavor, eyes losing their focus.

"Is it bad?" Vasiht'h ventured, ears sagging.

"It is . . . bizarre."

"Bizarre?"

Jahir pushed the bowl over to him. Vasiht'h eyed him, and the Eldritch said, "We are sharing thoughts. Sharing spoons on occasion hardly seems noteworthy."

"Point." Vasiht'h took up the spoon and tried the ice cream and stopped, too. He licked his teeth. "That's . . . yours." He laughed and pushed it over.

"And this from the person who drinks more than one cup of kerinne!" Jahir exclaimed. But he continued eating it, with an expression of puzzlement that curled the Glaseah's tongue like the touch of sour candy. Vasiht'h hid his laugh until the Eldritch looked up and said, "Like champagne."

"What is?" he asked, muffling his amusement.

"Your laughter, between us. Tastes like champagne. I wonder if tastes will be the primary method we use to translate emotional data?" Jahir frowned, pursing his lips. "I suppose there is a paper in it—"

"For someone who isn't us, because we are very busy people," Vasiht'h said. "With me playing catch-up to finish up this degree and you trying to make it through your residency without breaking a bone."

Jahir winced. "Alas, a shot rather too close to the heart for humor." He looked down at his bowl. "I appear to be eating this."

"You seem to be halfway through it," Vasiht'h agreed.

"I blame you," Jahir said, and continued. "Though . . . it is too heavy for me. And yet I keep eating it."

"Food works that way sometimes, when your body wants

something your tastes might not." Vasiht'h looked around. "You haven't even unpacked . . . !"

"Enough to get by—"

Vasiht'h covered his face. He didn't need to lift it to feel Jahir's chagrin, strong enough to fluff the fur on his shoulders. "All right," he said, taking a deep breath and looking up. "You finish the ice cream. I'll unpack for us both. I'm assuming I can stay here . . ."

"I don't know that there is anything in my tenancy contract to prevent it," Jahir said. "They allow spouses and other family members, I believe."

"We'll assume that's a 'yes' unless they come tell us 'no,' then. You finish eating. I'll . . . ah . . ." He came to a halt, looking at the room. It was barely half the size of the living room they'd shared in the student apartment at the university, and it held the little kitchen, one sofa and coffee table (neither very large) and that was it. There was little room to walk from the door past the couch. "There's a bedroom?"

"There is," Jahir said. "I fear I have little memory of using it."

Vasiht'h investigated and grimaced. This room was not much larger, though the bed could sleep two, if he was going to be charitable about the size of the two people. One more door led to a single person bathroom just large enough for most of the common Alliance species to use. Vasiht'h could get into it, but he doubted someone like Merishiinal, their nine-foot-tall centauroid Ciracaana friend, could have navigated it.

"You are disturbed," Jahir said from the door to the living room.

"It's a very . . . efficient . . . apartment," Vasiht'h said.

". . . and you have no idea where you will sleep," Jahir finished.

Vasiht'h folded his arms. "I'm guessing against the couch; that's about all we've got."

But Jahir was already gone. When he returned, his arms were full of the throw pillows from the couch, which he dropped on the floor beside the bed.

"If I sleep next to you, you'll trip over me on the way to the bathroom in the morning," Vasiht'h protested.

"If I cannot step over you, then I should stay in bed." Jahir went back to the living room and returned with the final pillow. "There are not enough unless we denude the sofa in its entirety—"

"It's all right," Vasiht'h said. "I can go get a few more in town." He hesitated, then added, "You really want to sleep in the same room?"

A hesitance, touched with iridescent hope. Just a glimmer of it, like the hint of a hidden sunrise on water. "Would you prefer not to?"

Vasiht'h smiled and took the pillow from him. "Here's good."

"Good." Jahir hesitated, then added, "I would normally be asleep by now."

"Then go to bed," Vasiht'h said firmly. "I'm still worked up from the flight in—I'll have to tell you all about it later!—so I'll just make myself a cup of tea and come sleep when I'm ready."

"Very well." Jahir smiled, and there was an anxiety in it that Vasiht'h could feel easing out of him through the mindline. "I'll look forward to the tale."

Vasiht'h shooed him off and went to make the cup of tea. He snagged his data tablet from his bags and started making a shopping list while listening to the familiar sounds of his roommate moving through the apartment. If it was a smaller apartment than either of them was used to, well, that just made it cozier. Just being in the same place again was good enough for Vasiht'h.

Ten minutes later, all those noises ceased and the mindline abruptly lost an active hum Vasiht'h hadn't even realized it had until it was gone. He peeked in the bedroom and saw Jahir's back and a spill of pale hair against gray pillows. Had the Eldritch always fallen asleep that quickly? Or was it a reflection of just how much strain his body was under?

Vasiht'h sighed and sat with his tea. According to his data tablet, it was very much the wrong time to be calling Sehvi, much as he wanted to. He would have to talk to her tomorrow, maybe while investigating the local markets. He wasn't sure how much money Jahir had, but eating nothing but genie-produced food

was harsh on anyone's budget. Cooking would give him something relaxing and productive to do for them both, and buying
groceries would get him out of the apartment, especially important if he was doing all his schoolwork remotely.

He was here. He was really here. He had crossed the entire
sector on his guess that he'd be wanted, and he had been. And
now he was sitting on a mindline out of legend, linking him to a
member of a famously rare and secretive species . . . who cared
about Vasiht'h just as much as Vasiht'h cared about him.

Had he asked for a more thorough vindication of his nascent
skills in psychology, Vasiht'h doubted the Goddess would have
supplied one. Sipping the tea, he went to his bags and withdrew
a pouch where he'd kept the little paper effigy he'd made of Her
on Seersana. She was a little rumpled from the journey, but that
seemed appropriate somehow. They all changed, passing through
experiences, and a Goddess must be a master of such changes.
He set Her carefully on the coffee table, straightening Her folded
legs so She wouldn't list. Once he'd propped Her up to his satisfaction, he said to Her, "Thank you." And meant it with all his
heart.

The tisane settled him, and the prayer, and he crept into the
bedroom, wings tucked tightly against his second back. As nests
went, it was a little bare, but he'd fix that tomorrow. For now
he couldn't think of a finer place to sleep, and he congratulated
himself on reaching it so stealthily when a glimmer of light fell
like a star in the corner of his eye. When he glanced up at the bed,
Jahir was watching him, eyes barely open.

Answering the muzzy hope, cautious and uncertain, that he
felt on that gleam, he whispered, "I'm really here."

"All right," Jahir murmured. And added, after so long Vasiht'h
thought he had fallen back asleep: "Two months."

"Two months," Vasiht'h agreed, wondering if they'd make it
that long.

CHAPTER 8

JAHIR OPENED HIS EYES the following day, expecting the sodden exhaustion and finding it. What he did not expect was the relief that flooded him with the late morning's light on his face. He was no longer alone; had, in fact, the most incontrovertible proof possible that he was not, for he had not yet looked over the edge of the bed and yet he could sense the sleeping mind of the Glaseah, close and low, like night air and distant chimes. He inhaled, careful of his sore ribcage, and let the breath out before rising and stepping around Vasiht'h to wash up for the day.

Strange to realize he had no regrets. He had expected at least one or two. What he had . . . were fears. He splashed water on his face and looked himself in the mirror, saw their shadows in his eyes. Not fears that he would one day learn to regret wedding himself to the mind of an alien, but fears that he would lose that union too quickly. A grand symbol, he thought, of his relationship with the Alliance and its swift-lived people . . . and a demonstration of how he'd decided to embrace it.

But to pretend that he hadn't already lost his heart to this life and the people in it would be just that: pretense. He would be glad of what he had while he had it. Jahir resumed his ablutions, dressed in the hospital's loose uniform and left—after leaving a

note. The resumption of the routine interrupted by his departure from Seersana buoyed his spirits so measurably that when
he arrived at the gym both Aralyn and Paga stared at him.

"You feeling better?" the Asanii asked, cautious.

Jahir considered. "My body remains distressed. But I am
happy, and that makes its distress more bearable." He lifted his
brows. "I suppose I am enacting the therapeutic values I use on
my own patients."

Aralyn chuckled. "The mind does have a pretty big say over
the body. But it does work both ways, so get your body in the
water so we can continue retraining it."

His good mood lasted all the way to the break room,
where the departing shift was already hurrying out—early, he
thought?—and Paige was dashing to the triage room. Radimir
said, "Oh, good, you're here . . . they've had a rough time, so we
let them go ten minutes early. The hospital's considering calling
in the health corps reserve; apparently another batch of unresponsives have been reported into some of the local clinics, and
they're not sure whether to call it as a medical emergency in the
making or a possible law enforcement issue. If you see any police
wandering around, be polite and tell them what you know. You
shouldn't—they were here earlier—but you never know when
they're going to show up again with something new. Meanwhile,
you're wanted on rounds today and there's a tough one in bed
two, suicide watch. Tam-illee tod who lost his wife a few hours
ago. See what you can do for him first, please."

"Of course," Jahir said, startled at the barrage. And added, "A
medical emergency?"

"I doubt that's where they're going to go with it," Radimir
said. "But finding seven similar cases like this within a couple of
weeks is strange. It might be coincidence, but if it's not . . ." He
shrugged.

"Right," Jahir said. "I'll go see to the suicide watch."

"You do that. Don't worry too much about the legal stuff. It
probably won't affect us here."

Jahir read the notes on the case on the way down the hall.

There was not much there; the foxine's wife was an engineer employed by the city to do maintenance on its power infrastructure, and a freak accident had killed her on the job. Jahir tucked his tablet in his pocket and stopped at the door. Even had he not been an esper, the anguish radiating from the bent figure would have reached him. There was an empty chair facing the foxine where the day shift had probably sat to keep him company; the Pelted's history guaranteed a poor reaction to anyone suffering alone, and their therapy emphasized presence as treatment and comfort for the afflicted. In the rounds Jahir had done during his practicum he'd observed the occasional individual to prefer to be alone, but in general the Pelted reacted favorably to knowing they weren't being elided. For that matter, Jahir thought it a healthier response, though he couldn't think of an Eldritch who would have found it bearable, to be seen in an excess of emotion, with its implied lack of control.

He sat in the chair across from the foxine, who did not move, twitch, look up. No doubt he'd heard people enter and leave often enough to ignore the sound. But when Jahir stripped off his gloves, the sound of them peeling from his flesh made one of the conical ears twitch. The foxine looked up, just enough to see past his fingers.

Gravely, Jahir met those stricken, blood-shot eyes, and offered his hand. He didn't know if the Tam-illee realized what that offer implied and suspected it didn't matter. What did was that no one should be alone in his grief, and Jahir was the one who was here to be that helpmeet.

The foxine took his hand, and the world dropped out from under him, and yet there was nothing to fall into—just an absence, an amputation so abrupt and so severe it left behind nothing but shock and a scream of negation that never seemed to end. Echoes, he thought, and drew in a breath that shuddered. He licked his lips to clear them of salt and found enough distance to remain aware of the Tam-illee's hand in his, warm skin on the underside of the fingers, faint impression of fur on the tops. That he wept didn't surprise him, but that it tickled when his tears lengthened enough to run down his throat, that did.

When something changed in the feelings, it was subtle, so very subtle. A gleam in the murk. Not developed enough to be curiosity or interest, but a dull confusion. Jahir opened his eyes and found the foxine staring at him. At his cheeks, at the wet creases around his eyes.

The patient did not say 'you feel it too.' No thought that coherent ran through him. But seeing his grief on someone else's face closed a loop for him. Jahir waited until those new feelings—of not being alone, though his heart screamed that he was—settled. Then he rested his other hand over the one he was holding, and clasped the foxine's fingers gently.

One of his Pelted instructors would have told him to speak, but there was no speaking into that grief. Jahir trusted his instincts and held the man's hand . . . and at some point, the fingers eased in his and the sense of grief drained away, and when the Eldritch opened his eyes, the Tam-illee had fallen asleep.

When Jahir stood he wobbled. He managed not to lose his balance—or tug the foxine out of his chair—and set the limp hand on the patient's knee before leaving the room. One careful breath at the door and he continued on his rounds. The unresponsive patient remained unchanged; Jahir thought about touching her but his skin felt raw from the experience with the Tam-illee and he very much did not want to touch anyone until the throbbing faded. He moved on instead to the other patients, and when he'd stepped out of the last room Paige ambushed him with a cup. "Here. Drink this."

He smelled it: coffee, but rich. In color, a dark cream with a slight head: he sipped it and stopped short.

"That's the hot buttered coffee the place down the street makes," she said.

"It is . . . astonishing," he said truthfully, and looked down at her to find her scrutinizing him, her arms folded. "I am sorry, have I done something wrong?"

"Something right, more like it. You look happier."

"Do I?" he asked, startled.

She nodded, ears flipping forward. "Good news?"

"A friend came to see me," Jahir said, and paused. "That word is very imprecise in Universal, and yet I have never heard 'arii' used except as a form of address. Do I have that nuance right?"

"You do." She nodded. "And yes, friend is imprecise. The Seersa have a bunch of words for degrees of friendship but none of them crept into Universal. So I'm guessing this is a close friend?"

"My closest," Jahir agreed. He tried the coffee again and found it just as astonishing on the second sip. "This is not a drink, alet. This is food."

She laughed. "Good. Maybe it will put some meat on your bones."

"Which reminds me," he murmured. "I should eat before my alert rattles my wrist. While it's still slow."

"It's been a quiet night," she agreed. "Thank An. Let's hope it stays that way."

It did stay quiet. Jahir moved into triage halfway through his shift, but even there the night was slow. He and Maya processed a few people—one with a digestive problem that felt like cardiac trouble, one elderly woman who'd broken a femur, and an allergic reaction that they'd passed through immediately. Toward the end of the shift, Radimir appeared at the door and waved him out. He took his leave and stepped out of the triage room, wondering what had brought the shift supervisor to him, and so agitated.

"What did you do with that Tam-illee we had on suicide watch?"

Jahir supposed "do with" was slightly less ominous than "do to," and said cautiously, "I held his hand."

"That's it?" Radimir's ears splayed. "Just . . . held his hand?"

"Yes?"

"We've all been holding his hand," Radimir said. "Or holding his entire body. You're sure you didn't do something different?" He glanced at Jahir's fingers and added with a lopsided smile, "Is there something magical about your hands that might rub off on the rest of us?"

"Did something happen?" Jahir asked.

"He was deep in shock and now he's not." Radimir shook his head. "He's talking now. Not much, but given how little he was interfacing with reality that's an improvement of over a hundred percent. I was hoping you could tell us how you did it."

Jahir leaned against the wall to save his energy. "I'm afraid it was as simple as holding his hand, save perhaps that for me such an act is an intimacy." Radimir canted his head and Jahir finished, "Because it means I touch his mind."

The Harat-Shar winced. "That must have been harsh."

There didn't seem any value in hiding it, but none in agreeing either. "I think seeing his grief reflected on someone outside himself helped." Jahir rolled his lower lip beneath the upper, thinking. "In fact, it is a bad thing that his family isn't present. Where are they?"

"The registration people tell me he doesn't have any on-world."

"And the deceased's family?"

"On their way from one of the stations in the system."

Jahir nodded. "When they arrive . . . I think that will help. Until then, we should keep him here unless we can release him to the custody of a friend or community support group."

"Now that he's talking maybe we can get that information out of him," Radimir said. He grinned, tired. "Maybe we should sic you on all our unresponsives. Have any luck with the other one we've got?"

"None," Jahir admitted.

"Ah well. Guess the magic touch only works when they can tell you're there."

"Perhaps," he murmured.

With only twenty minutes left before he passed his responsibilities to the night shift, Jahir stopped again at the door to the Asanii's room. She remained just where she'd been left . . . had not so much as shifted. The halo-arch's array of colors and noises were subdued, indicating their function and her relative lack of it. Jahir drifted closer and looked down at her. So there were others? Was it some disease, as the possibility of a medical emergency suggested? Or some new violence more suited to the police's intervention? He wondered what that intervention would look like; at home, there had been constables, deputized by the lords and ladies to which a town owed allegiance, but there was nothing so formal as a police force. The Eldritch were not so numerous as to need one, and the custom of dueling had supplied an outlet for the aggrieved to seek redress personally—or to decide the insult was not sufficient to the threat of dying. It was not a perfect system, but he was beginning to think there was no such thing. Gently, he reached out and brushed his hand over her forehead . . . but if there was magic in his hands, it did not suffice to save her. He curled his fingers into a fist above her brow, feeling the leaden weight of her aura.

And then it exploded.

Color! Noise! Light! A terrible urgency, the urgency of a failing body. Images, some that made sense, entire scenes—and some that didn't, and some that did and then were shredded and became nonsense that overwhelmed him. Somewhere beside him a siren went off, but he had already leapt away, his back striking the wall. The physical distance saved him from feeling her die. When the attendant rushed in with his healers-assist at his flanks, they were already too late. Jahir managed to find his way out and then sat heavily on the floor outside the room, which is where Radimir and Paige found him. He held up a hand to stay them, when they might have reached out to touch him. "No, please."

"What happened?" Radimir said, crouching in front of him.

Paige was staring into the room. "Looks like our unresponsive didn't wake up."

"She is . . . not going to, no," Jahir said, hugging his knees. He felt raw from the unexpected assault on his senses, and the synesthesia clung to him, painting Radimir's concern in blue washes that smeared into the hallway. He put his head down and closed his eyes, hoping that would help.

"Were you in there?" Radimir's voice was soft.

"Yes."

Silence then, long enough that he wondered if they were gone. But then Paige said, "Did you . . . feel her?"

He couldn't answer that without starting to shake.

A few moments later, a blanket draped around his shoulders and he looked up. "I . . . I am sorry. Did I—?"

"No, you didn't pass out," Radimir said. "It's only been a couple of minutes. I sent Paige for the blanket, that's all."

"Do all people die like that?" Jahir found himself asking, even knowing that neither of them could tell him. How could a non-esper know whether dying always felt like such a trauma? And yet, Radimir did.

"No. Sometimes people go peacefully. Smiling, even. There's no firestorm of activity in their bodies just before they die. Things just . . . ease quietly away, and then they're gone. There's a sense of closure and rest, when people die the way they want to."

"This was not restful," Jahir said. "And there was no closure. And they are not dying the way they have wanted." He shuddered. "How many more of these did they find?"

"Four more, scattered across the city."

"God and Lady help them," Jahir said softly.

CHAPTER 9

ASIHT'H WOKE TO A NOTE, and if it was virtual rather than hand-written it was still enough like old times to make him smile. He perused the attached schedule—an hour of physical therapy and then eight hours at the hospital—and decided that gave him plenty of time for everything he wanted to accomplish before his roommate got home. But first things first. He checked the time on Tam-ley and put in a call while unpacking his bags. Sehvi answered as he was pulling out his small travel pillow. He'd borrowed the apartment's far better projection equipment to supplant the one he'd been using in his data tablet, and her image appeared in the room with him, flat but life-size and in vibrant colors that blocked out the wall behind her.

"Ariihir?" she said, then found him in the room and pointed. "Talk now!"

"I intend to!" He grinned at her over his shoulder. He wiggled his fingers. "Look, I made it!"

"Annnnnd?"

"And he was glad to see me, and he doesn't want me to leave, ever," Vasiht'h got out, hardly believing it as he said it.

His sister squinted. "Is that hyperbole or do you mean it the way it sounds?"

"I mean when he opened the door on me I blurted out that I wanted to stick around until one of us died, and he said he couldn't imagine ever sending me away," Vasiht'h said, ears sagging a little with chagrin. "And then the mindline snapped into place and . . . that's it, as far as we're concerned. Other than working out all the little annoying things, like who sleeps where and how I'm finishing my degree and whether he's finishing his residency and—"

She held up her hands. "Goddess, slow down!"

He stopped obediently, grinning at her, until she folded her arms and started to laugh.

"What?" he said, all innocence.

"I'm glad you're happy," she said, more serious. Her mouth started twitching. "Though you're enjoying teasing me a little too much for your little sister's comfort."

"After all the times you've teased me—"

"Yes, but you deserved it!"

"Ha!" He laughed. "All right. Go ahead and ask."

"I want to know about everything! Start with the mindline?" She sounded wistful. "Is it as wonderful as all the stories say?"

"Better," Vasiht'h said firmly. He reached for his sense of Jahir and felt it as a warm answer, like sunlight on his second back and shoulders. Nothing more distinct: would that change with time? Would the bond grow? He couldn't remember what the literature had said, and even then what had they ever said about a bond with an alien? "I . . . I don't know how to describe it. But it's better than I imagined. In a less showy way." At her look, he spread his hands and said, "I . . . I don't know. But you know you read the romances other species write, and it's all passion and fireworks and it sounds very . . ."

"Uncomfortable," Sehvi said dryly.

"Yes," he said. "This isn't like that. It's comfortable, like knowing someone's going to be with you forever and not having to rush over to make sure of it."

She sighed out. "You're sooooo lucky, ariihir."

"I know," Vasiht'h said, serious. "And I intend to do everything in my power to show the Goddess that I'm not going to take it for granted." He drew in a breath. "Anyway. It's good that I came because Selnor's just about as heavy as home, Sehvi, and wherever he's from it's lighter than Seersana, by far."

Sehvi grimaced. "That's no good. They putting him through the acclimatization?"

"They can't, he's already done it once." Vasiht'h continued excavating his bags. "I've asked him to consider relocating someplace less strenuous and he's agreed that if in two months he doesn't feel any better we'll go. There's no point to him having one of the most coveted residencies in xenopsychology if he's going to be completely flattened by the planet during it."

"I certainly wouldn't want to do it. But I can't imagine what it's like, either. There aren't too many worlds heavy enough to give us pause."

"So I have two months," Vasiht'h said. "I'm going to use it to try to make him as comfortable as I can. He's really exhausted, ariishir. And he's lost a lot of weight. The kind of food they want him eating is like chewing your way through bricks. It might taste good, but it's denser than a black hole. Getting through a whole serving of it takes real fortitude. He hasn't even unpacked, and I get the impression that all he's done once he gets back from work is fall over."

She wrinkled her nose. "Sounds like a fun life. I knew he was a workaholic but you can tell him your sister has it on good authority from the Tam-illee—who are super-disciplined about things—that everyone needs a life outside of work. Speaking of which, what's Heliocentrus like?"

"You know, I don't know?" Vasiht'h said. "I just got here last night. But I'm about to go shopping, so I'll tell you next time we talk."

The answer to that question was that Heliocentrus was amazing. Vasiht'h went out into a bright day washed by a cool breeze driven off the coast and found the city bigger than any he'd ever been in. Even Seersana's capital hadn't seemed this populous, and a quick check of his data tablet told him that it wasn't. He tucked the tablet into his saddlebags and gave up on it for the day. No doubt he could lose himself consulting it for corroboration of every guess; far better to wander, trusting his own feet and senses to bring him where he should go.

Like most cities built in the Core, Heliocentrus had been designed around walking distances, with aircars—sparrows and wrens mostly but the occasional kestrel or larger vehicle also—following traffic patterns midway up around the skyscrapers. The greenspaces were frequent and well maintained, though the vegetation was lusher and more vibrant than the flora had been on Seersana; it reminded Vasiht'h of his homeworld, in fact, which had tended toward lush rainforests. The tropical brightness of the flowers that grew up lattices edging the buildings comforted him, like old friends, even if their colors and patterns were novel: fluorescent oranges on fire in the sunlight, startling bright blues splotched with magenta and pink, coral petals that bled to bright red at their curling edges.

There were two markets within walking distance, doing a brisk business selling fresh food grown on the city's roof gardens and in its greenspaces. Vasiht'h joined the people browsing there and asked many questions about what he was buying. Some of the produce was recognizable, Earth imports brought with the Pelted during the original Exodus and rigorously maintained across the Alliance on all the worlds where the cultivars could be supported. Some of them were native to Selnor, though, tagged with species-safety information but otherwise mysterious. Unfortunately none of these exotics had any information on Eldritch safety, but if something was broadly tolerated by most of the Alliance's species, Vasiht'h bought it, deciding he could try it even if Jahir couldn't.

He saved the meat for last and paid to have it delivered, and from the market went searching for a store where he could buy housewares and particularly proper pillows. After tending to that, he bought incense from an outdoor vendor who was burning it, a fragrant curlique of smoke that led him to her table. She had a selection of religious and spiritual items for a truly bewildering assortment of cultures, and he lost half an hour studying tiny effigies of gods and goddesses from around the Alliance, as well as the DNA helix jewelry used by those who'd made a spiritual practice out of the Exodus events. He even found a statue of Holly, who'd been the mother of the Pelted fight for freedom on Earth . . . standing peacefully alongside a figurine of Mary, Mother of God. The human Christian Mary, not the Hinichi Christian one, since the latter was inevitably portrayed with a pawprint medallion or a wolf at her feet.

Heading back to the apartment, Vasiht'h reflected that he would have to tell Sehvi that Heliocentrus was exactly what he would have expected in the Alliance's winter capital: balmy, tropical, cosmopolitan, enormous and beautiful. But even as he admitted to that beauty, he knew he would never want to live anywhere so big. He didn't feel dwarfed by the city, or at least, not to the point of feeling insignificant . . . but he didn't like knowing he'd never really know any appreciable percentage of the people he shared a city with.

Strange how the starbase had also felt beautiful and cosmopolitan, while also seeming small enough to get his arms around. A community, rather than a city, though the civilian city had been large enough to be called one.

Back at the apartment, Vasiht'h queued some of the recorded lectures from the classes he was taking and started working on dinner while listening. The cultured tenor of the professor discussing business and legal considerations for a psychologist's practice blended with the bubbling of boiling water for soup and the sharp snickt of the knife moving through the vegetables on the new cutting board. Once he had the soup simmering, he took a cup of tea to the coffee table and started on the reading. Halfway through it he realized he'd replaced the audio of the lecture with the music from last night. He still liked and didn't like it, and smiled, shaking his head.

By the time the alert he'd set to warn him of his roommate's impending return went off, he'd finished making dinner, unpacked Jahir's bags and arranged both their things in the small space they had, and was contemplating making another batch of tea and reading about heavy gravity complications. That occupied him until the mindline began to whisper: fatigue, perplexity, anticipation. He looked up before the door opened.

"I don't know what's more astonishing," Jahir said. "That you are here, and not actually the product of a happy dream I had . . . or that the apartment smells like something."

"Hopefully something good," Vasiht'h said, trying to hide his delight at the comment and knowing he'd failed when the Eldritch flashed a look at him that anyone else would have read as somber; but Vasiht'h had known him long enough to read the sparkle in his eyes, and even if he hadn't he could taste the effervescence of his friend's pleasure over the weight of his exhaustion.

"Very good," Jahir said. "Like home."

Vasiht'h said, "Good. Now sit and I'll bring you tea. You can tell me about your day. Or you can hear about mine, if you prefer."

"Oh . . ." Jahir trailed off. He sat, using a hand on the arm of the couch to steady himself on the way down. "How strange. To have come into this again. I needed it, when I was doing rounds before." He looked up, yellow eyes, pale face, wisp of hair escaped from an otherwise tidy braid. Strange to see his face exposed that way; on Seersana he'd left the hair down, and it had obscured a jawline far more masculine than Vasiht'h had realized. The Glaseah wondered how many women and men were swooning over him so far. "Do you know that you kept me steady then?"

"Yes," Vasiht'h answered, subdued. He poured two cups of tea, watching the steam flare from the cups. "That's why I sent you away. I wanted you to figure out if you could do without the emotional support."

Jahir accepted the cup, head and shoulders bent. Vasiht'h didn't think he realized he was listing. "And the answer to that is 'I do better with it.' But how is that a surprise to either of us, given our studies?"

"You're right," Vasiht'h said. "We should have known better." He sat across from the Eldritch, watching him drink and disliking the deep lines traced beneath his eyes. "Was it a hard day?"

"Somewhat," Jahir said, drawing the words out. A deflection? No, the feel through the mindline was of someone gathering scattered flower petals. Strange image, but when the Eldritch had collected them, he continued, "There was a suicide watch, which was difficult. A Tam-illee who lost his wife." He looked up from his cup. "I held his hand."

Vasiht'h flattened his ears. "That . . . must have been very bad."

The Eldritch took a sip and sighed, the steam parting off the top of the cup. "But not as bad as the woman I felt die." He set the tea down and laced his fingers together between his knees, head hanging. "There have been several patients the past week who've shown up at the hospital, and now at several clinics, in an unresponsive state. No one knows what has befallen them, but they are thinking some form of violence, or perhaps a disease."

Vasiht'h frowned. "They haven't found any clues?"

"None," Jahir said. He ran a hand up his arm, bunching the sleeve, and the cold that stippled his skin made Vasiht'h's fur stand. "Her death was not a good one. And I had a hand on her when she passed into that storm."

"You *have* had a bad day," Vasiht'h said. He tried to send as comforting a sensation as he could think of, given his friend's pleasures, and came up with sunlight on his backs on a summer morning.

Jahir looked up with a bemused look.

"Not good?" Vasiht'h asked, anxious.

"No, no, it's quite good," Jahir said. "It's just . . . I've never had an extra half of a body."

Vasiht'h laughed. "I'll get dinner."

After eating, Jahir prepared for bed and Vasiht'h washed dishes, putting a pot on the stove to heat some milk while he worked. Once it had warmed, he mixed it with a few herbs and honey and left it to steep while he lit the incense beside his paper

Goddess and finished putting everything in order. Then he took the cup with him into the bedroom and found the Eldritch sitting on the edge of the bed. He offered the cup, which Jahir took with a bemusement that he answered by saying, "Warm milk. Something to help you sleep and stoke that metabolism that's overworking."

Jahir accepted it without protest and had a sip. "You've made everything so cozy," he said, quiet. "And so quickly."

"It's nothing," Vasiht'h said, padding to his pillows and settling in them. "I can move in this environment freely. If you could, you'd have done all this yourself."

"Maybe," Jahir said. "But not in the same way. And it would have been . . ." He stopped, searching for a word and finally settling on, "Sterile."

"That's a little harsh, isn't it?"

But Jahir shook his head. "No, it is exactly what I mean. Where there is no union of unlike minds, there are no fresh ideas. I might have gleaned some from my interactions with the culture, but you . . . you accelerate that process, and make it personal." A chill stole through the mindline. "I have seen a great deal of suffering in the past week and a half. Would it sound ridiculous if I said . . . 'life is short'?"

"It would sound surprising, maybe," Vasiht'h said. "But not ridiculous."

The Eldritch passed a hand over his face, pressed a thumb under the brow; Vasiht'h felt both the pressure and the dull ache it was relieving.

"You're tired," he said. "Finish the milk and rest, arii. I'll still be here tomorrow. No dream, promise."

Jahir smiled. "If you're certain."

"I am. I'm going to make myself a cup of tea and I'll be back once I've finished with it."

"All right. Good night, arii."

Vasiht'h padded out, lowering the lights on the way out, and poured himself the last of the tea. He settled down to read as the incense burnt itself out, its last plumes of smoke slowly falling.

When the last ember flickered out, Vasiht'h set his cup aside and stretched—

—and the mindline had not gone dormant, which surprised him into thinking, /*You're still awake.*/

More astonishingly, he got an immediate answer, too brittle-edged for someone as tired as his roommate should be: /*I fear I am, yes.*/

/*But why?*/ Vasiht'h asked.

A fleeting cacophony: noise, light, sound. Then, coalescing over it: /*I am having trouble not seeing/feeling things now that it's dark and there's nothing to distract me.*/

Vasiht'h put his cup down and returned to the bedroom. Jahir was lying on his side under the blanket, but the light from the other room gleamed on his eyes. The Glaseah sat down on the floor across from the Eldritch and said, voice low, "What was that?"

"The Asanii, before she died. Her mind . . . it was . . . disordered."

"Strange," Vasiht'h murmured, and the interest that sharpened in the mindline sounded like . . . a letter opener? Where had he gotten that association, and its connotation of anticipation?

"Ah—I suppose you don't open letters with letter openers," Jahir said, chagrined.

"I don't get many physical letters, no," Vasiht'h said, bemused. "So what has you so curious?"

"You seem convinced this is not normal," Jahir said.

"No?" Vasiht'h fluffed up a pillow and set his forelegs on it. "We have a large family, you know that. And a lot of friends with their own extended families. I've seen a couple of people pass away, and it doesn't feel like that."

"That's what Radimir said." A flash: Harat-Shariin, snow pard, too busy to do anything as stereotypical as leer. "My shift supervisor. But he was talking about the physical aspects, I thought."

"And what about our education makes you think those things can be separated?" Vasiht'h asked. He wrinkled his nose. "No, arii. It's not supposed to be that messy. That . . . chaotic."

"There was some sense in it, betimes," Jahir said. "Not much." He concentrated, found some impressions and shared them: music, some kind of Baroque rock. The smell of citrus oil burning in a carved stone holder. A shadowed street corner, and the feel of something in a thin paper envelope—

"Stop!" Vasiht'h exclaimed.

Jahir froze. Even his mind seized at the command.

"No, no, you didn't upset me," Vasiht'h hurried to say. "But . . . that last image. Are you sure about it?"

"Yes?" Jahir said, perplexed.

"Can you get any more of it? Was there any more to get?"

The frown this time was more felt than seen, a tension in the mindline. The image again, and more clearly the feel of paper, and something soft in it, almost powdery. It gave beneath the fingers.

"Oh Goddess," Vasiht'h whispered. "Your unresponsives aren't sick. They're on street drugs."

Chapter 10

"**I** BEG YOUR PARDON," Jahir said, his heart racing. "You have said what?"

"Those patients you've been getting," Vasiht'h said. "Their condition must be the side effect of an illegal drug. Because that was unquestionably the memory of buying one, and that makes a lot more sense than a bunch of people suddenly showing up in comas because someone's been trying to kill them with some new way of killing people. Particularly when all the old ways still work."

"But a disease," Jahir began, grappling for something less ominous, less . . . sordid.

"Possible," Vasiht'h said. "But how coincidental is it for her to have that memory and also have a mysterious and fatal disease?"

"But how . . ."

"Do I know how it's done?" Vasiht'h grimaced. "I keep forgetting you skipped the undergraduate level at the university. The highest risk population for street drugs is still in that age range, and it's a lot more common in multi-species environments and communities above a certain size. Like, say, college. We got subjected to a lot of material about the dangers of street drugs."

Jahir sorted through the discomfort in the mindline. "And

. . . you . . . knew someone who succumbed?"

"I knew someone who was affected by someone who succumbed," Vasiht'h corrected, and the mindline tasted now like
bitter gall. "And that was bad enough."

Jahir settled back into the bed, pulling the blanket closer
against the cold. "I did the reading on illegal drug use for the
aberrant class, but I did not think it was so . . ."

"Possible?"

"So prevalent, yes," he said at last.

Vasiht'h's mental shrug felt like lukewarm water, something
that helped with his chill. A little, anyway. "This is Heliocentrus,
arii. It's one of the biggest cities in the Alliance. Statistically, it's
going to be more common here. Plus, it's a city that has a lot
of traffic. It's easier to get things in and out of a place like this,
where there's so much activity anyway."

Jahir was silent for several long moments, tasting his companion's certitude through the mindline. He could tell that it
wasn't his, but it felt very real to him anyway. And if Vasiht'h
was right, the consequences of not acting on the knowledge were
frightening. "I will have to tell someone."

"I hope so," Vasiht'h answered, quieter.

"Tomorrow," Jahir murmured.

❦

"What?" Radimir said, staring at him.

"I said—"

"I heard what you said," the Harat-Shar said, holding up a
hand. He shook himself. "I heard it, but no one's reported any
visible signs of drug use on these patients. At least, not illegal
ones."

Jahir tilted his head. "Why do I hear an uncertainty in your
voice?"

"It's not uncertainty," Paige said from behind their shift
supervisor. She offered Jahir a cup of coffee, holding it by the
insulated bottom to leave the handle free for his fingers. "It's bel-
ligerence. Because what he's not telling you is that a lot of those

signs are invisible to everything but a thorough autopsy."

Jahir glanced at the Harat-Shar, who sighed and rubbed the bridge of his nose. "And that is a problem, because . . ."

"Because you can't get an autopsy of a Pelted patient without advance written consent of that patient. You can't get it retroactively from his or her family members either."

"That seems . . . strange?" Jahir said, frowning. "My impression of the cultural imperatives for the Pelted was that they were more open when it comes to privacy."

"Privacy, sure," Radimir said with a sigh. "Autopsies are another thing."

"It's because so many of us were used for medical experimentation before we escaped Earth," Paige said. She was warming her hands on her mug. "Letting people tell other people that you're sick is one thing. Letting people cut you open to record the results is a whole different category of thing." She smiled, a faint tug of one edge of her mouth. "Which means the patient who just died isn't going to be available for the procedure unless she's signed a specific legal document." Paige sipped from the cup. "Doesn't seem old enough to have thought that would be necessary, but we could be wrong."

"And the human?" Jahir asked. "Do the same laws obtain?"

"No," Radimir said. "But we'd either need permission from next-of-kin or an okay from a judge." He sighed. "And it's not our decision to make. This is something we'd have to pass up to the ethics committee. Which is a lot to ask on the strength of an impression." He looked up at Jahir. "Are you sure about this?"

"I am more sure of it than I am that it is a disease. And if it's a possibility, does it not merit exploration? If I am correct—"

"Then we're going to have to attack it differently," Radimir agreed, and sighed gustily. "All right. But I'm not guaranteeing anything, you understand?"

"Of course," Jahir said.

Paige watched the Harat-Shar walk away, then said, "Don't take it personally. He's just upset about the possibility that you're right. And I think you are."

"You do?"

She nodded. "A hunch."

"I would think a new disease requiring quarantine measures would be far more distressing," Jahir murmured.

Paige smiled, sadly this time, he thought. "Oh, I think they're both just about as bad. In different ways." She glanced up at him, ears sagging. "Did you really get images of her life before she died?"

He looked at the steam coming off the coffee in the mug he held. "I did, yes."

"That must have been . . ." She stopped. Then gathered herself and said, "At least someone was with her when she died."

Stunned, he looked up, but she was already walking away.

⸻ ❧ ⸻

The Tam-illee widower had not yet been released, but when Jahir stopped in his room, the foxine looked toward him, focused on him. There was awareness in his eyes that had been absent before, and Jahir paused, one hand resting on the door frame.

"You," the foxine said. "You were the one who cried for me."

Had he cried for him, or for his lost wife? But then, did it matter? He'd also done it for the foxine, so that he might know he was companioned. So he said, "No one should be alone with their grief."

The Tam-illee looked away. "They say our family's going to be here by tomorrow morning at the latest."

"So I heard," Jahir said, and since the foxine seemed disposed to talking, he entered and sat again on the room's extra chair.

"They're going to be crushed," he said, picking at his pants. "She was their only daughter." He drew in a shaky breath and opened his mouth to continue and couldn't.

"You don't have to talk," Jahir said, quiet.

"No, I want to. I think." He pressed a thumb to his chest. "I feel like it's wrong to be able to talk. Or think. Or move." He looked up at Jahir. "I know it must not be, but . . . it feels wrong."

"It will feel wrong for some time."

The foxine cast his head down. Then asked, soft, "Can I . . . would you—"

Jahir reached over and gathered the hand that was resting on the foxine's knee, and drew the anguish with it.

The Asanii was gone, of course. To her family, perhaps. Or to the morgue to await them. Jahir stopped at her room and felt the shape of its emptiness, remembering the synesthesia and the desperation of her death. Somewhere, in some other part of the city, there were others like her. Would they be alone when they died? He passed his hand over his brow and found he was shaking. Two months, he'd told Vasiht'h. He began to wonder if he could make it that long. Whether it was the physical weakness or an emotional one, he didn't know. But as much as he loved the work, it drained him.

That night he stopped by the roof before returning home to the smell of something fragrant: spices, and coconut milk. Vasiht'h was overseeing something simmering on the stove when he entered. There was a cup of tea on the counter, and he knew it was his before he reached it and took a judicious sip.

"You feel like something beautiful," Vasiht'h said, prodding what looked like the thigh of a game bird in the pan with a spatula.

"There is roof access at the hospital," Jahir said, looking into the cup. There was some sort of symbol on the bottom, just visible through the dark, clear infusion. "Sometimes I have gone up there, to clear my thoughts."

"You should do that more often, when you have the energy," Vasiht'h said. "It's good for you. Could you hand me those two bowls?"

Jahir leaned over the counter to fetch them over. "You are not hurt?"

That won him a puzzled look over his shoulder, one that felt like knotted yarn through the mindline. The sensation was so surprising they both laughed.

"You felt that," Jahir guessed.

"I did! But no, no. Why would I be hurt?"

"Because I . . . had some pleasing experience that I did not invite you to?" Jahir said, slowly, not entirely sure himself why he'd asked.

Vasiht'h snorted. "Arii, you're going to have a lot of pleasing experiences in your life that I not only won't be a part of, but won't want to be, either." He scooped a serving of the curry into one of the bowls. "There's no use being hurt about that. I'm going to be around for you, but that doesn't mean living in your pocket."

"I am glad you feel thus," Jahir said, taking the bowl. And then, despite his better judgment, "Many things you won't want to be part of?"

"I'm guessing that eventually you're going to want a lover," Vasiht'h said. "And trust me when I say I'm not at all interested."

"I—"

Vasiht'h looked up at him, and the mindline shivered between them, silent and waiting. Into that receptivity, into that space where he could not lie, Jahir said, "I imagine that one day I might, yes. But not soon."

And the rest of it hung between them: *Maybe not before you're gone.*

Vasiht'h said, gentle, "Go sit with your plate."

He went, which is how he realized there was no table in his apartment. Nor space for one. He frowned at the coffee table, and was still frowning at it when Vasiht'h put a glass of wine in front of him.

"I do not normally drink," he said.

"No, you don't," Vasiht'h agreed, and set a glass of his own down. "But you need the calories, and that knotty yarn feeling in you might respond well to it. Not that I'm going to make a habit of it. But you had a rough day yesterday." He sat at the coffee table and chuckled. "This arrangement makes me feel more like a poor student than our actual student apartment did."

"It does feel a bit . . . utilitarian."

Vasiht'h snorted. "That's one way of putting it. So, how did the day go? Did you tell them?"

"I did," Jahir said. "They told me they'd have to take it to the ethics committee because of the difficulties in obtaining an autopsy."

Vasiht'h winced. "I didn't think of that." He started cutting into the meal. "I just hope they get to making that decision before anything else goes wrong."

Jahir looked at him sharply.

"It could be nothing," Vasiht'h said without looking up. No doubt Jahir's reaction had traveled the mindline. "But if they don't know what it is, then it's something new. And who knows where it's coming from or how many people are getting into it."

The thought was so appalling that Jahir put his fork down, and that at last made his roommate look up at him.

"Eat," he said. "You did what you could."

"What if it's not enough?"

"What can you possibly do?" Vasiht'h asked. "You can't go raid the morgue, and even if you did, how would you know what to look for? You passed it on to the proper people. Now you have to let the system work."

"And if it doesn't?"

Vasiht'h shook his head. "Eat, arii."

He ate, but the worry that he had not done enough gnawed at him, and he knew Vasiht'h felt it too.

CHAPTER 11

"**D**ON'T LOOK NOW," Paige whispered, passing him on the way out of the break room. "But you've got the entire chain of command heading your way."

"I beg your pardon?" Jahir asked.

"I'd get a prop if I were you," the Karaka'An added, grinning. "Give you something to do with your hands so you don't fidget." And then she was gone, leaving him staring after her.

. . . and then Radimir, Jiron and Grace Levine entered together, barely clearing the door like a blood clot squeezing through a particularly narrow capillary. They advanced on him, Levine in the lead wearing a look as coldly focused as a scalpel's edge. Or, he thought, chilled by the memory, a sword dripping blood on bare earth.

"Mister Jahir," Levine said, and the clipped speed of her voice did nothing to dispel the imagery. "Radimir here tells me you have a theory about the unresponsives."

It was difficult not to react to the ridiculousness of the form of address. Jahir wished he'd had time to get that cup, and settled for folding his arms, even knowing that the posture usually reflected a defensive frame of mind. And since she hadn't asked any question, he waited.

"You do have one, yes?" she asked, looking up at him.

"Yes. I did share that theory with him, and I presume he shared it with you?"

"But how can you be sure?" Levine asked. She held up a hand. "This is not an idle question. We need to fix this now."

The curtness of her delivery, the bald questions, the tension in her shoulders and jaw . . . he glanced at Radimir, who said, "We got in two more of them last night."

Jiron was nodding. "The emergency response team found them in the same house. In the same room, even. Which suggests they knew one another. So either they have similar enough lives to have been exposed to the same disease, or—"

"Or you're right," Levine said. "But if it is a disease, it's spreading and we have no idea how because it hasn't affected anyone here yet and we had the first case almost two weeks ago now." She looked up at him. "We went ahead and okayed the autopsy of the human, but we didn't find anything conclusive except that whatever it was did this made a complete wreck of his brain. Like part of it was sludge. So I want to know—" She leaned up on her toes. "How sure are you?"

"God and Lady," he said, hushed. "I don't know."

"Then your task for today," Levine said, "And your only task, because everyone else can do without you, is to see if you can glean anything from the bodies we've got in the beds now. Before they become corpses. I don't know how this esper thing of yours works and on a better day I might even care. But today, all that matters is your ability's given us one of the few clues we've got, and unless the police come back with something conclusive it might be the only thing we get. The uniforms are working on that apartment. You work on this."

"As you say," Jahir answered. "I will go directly."

"Good," she said, and left.

Radimir added, "She was serious. We can get along without you, all right? See what you can find out."

"Of course," he replied, but his spirit sank. The single clue he'd found had involved an accident—one that had also required him to be present in the mind of someone dying a violent death. He did not look forward to standing vigil over two more bodies, hoping to catch them in similar extremis. And yet, if there truly was nothing else . . .

He looked at Jiron. "Was the autopsy truly inconclusive?"

"Other than the damage?" Jiron shook his head. "There wasn't anything they could use. Usually you'd see something. Damage to the digestive tract, enlargement of the veins, scarring or significant damage to the nasal tissue or the skin . . . the ways you can take a drug are pretty limited, even these days. We should have seen something unless this stuff works so fast there's no time for that kind of wear to build up. And if that's the case . . ."

"You believe me," Jahir said suddenly.

Jiron nodded. "I do. Levine and I are both from Earth, but I come from a less fancy part of town. I've seen more drug cases than she has, and the pattern has me on edge. All young adults, all in similar types of clothing, suggesting a similar socioeconomic status . . . I can see this as some new drug being passed around at a party. But it could be a disease they're sharing instead. So . . ." He shrugged. "We need more evidence. You're a long shot, but sometimes it's the long ones that pay off."

"I shall do my best."

And if there was nothing? He went to the first room and found a comatose young woman: another of the Asanii, calico-patched like the woman who'd served him gelato on Seersana week after week. A little more orange than black on her, but the resemblance disturbed him. He stretched his senses out and found her aura close and hard, like armor against his invasion, and wondered what he could hope to learn. They had sentenced him to a death vigil on these hapless innocents, and for what? For the slimmest hope that he might hear something from them in their minds' last frenzied exhalations?

His eyes strayed to her brow. Levine's description of the deceased's brain clung to him. Had it really been so gruesome? He had to imagine so; she didn't seem the sort to resort to hyperbole in a situation this grave.

Jahir sighed and folded his hands on his lap, closing his eyes and forcing himself to concentrate; to extend himself, even knowing what awaited him if he succeeded.

———❀———

It was, however, a very disappointing shift. He gathered nothing from the patients, and when at last he dragged himself from the stool and made his way carefully to the break room, he found Levine having an agitated discussion with Jiron while Radimir looked on. His entrance caused them all to fall silent, and then Levine said, "Well?"

"Nothing," he said. "I feel nothing when they are quiescent, so. It is only . . ." He drew in a breath and finished, "It is only as they are dying that I have an opportunity."

"Radclifte Clinic by the port has two other cases, and they're both more advanced," Levine said. "Maybe—"

"Doctor," Jiron growled, but she talked over him.

"—go see if they have anything for you—"

"You are not sending him across the city to play vulture there when he's just spent eight hours doing it here," Jiron exclaimed. "For God's sake, he's got Mediger Syndrome!"

"It's not like he'd have to walk there," Levine said, caustic.

Jiron looked at Radimir, who flattened his ears and said, "I can't support anything that would constitute a physical danger to someone I'm responsible for. He might be a student resident, Doctor, but the operative word there is 'student.'"

Levine met Jahir's eyes across the room and the force of her regard pinned him by the door. "Well? Ignore your nursemaids and make your own decision."

"I was not aware there was one to be made," Jahir said. "You have asked me to attempt to learn what there is to learn from our patients—"

"I asked you to help us get to the bottom of this," she said. "And you have a better chance of it if you keep trying."

"I fear I do no one any good if I collapse," he said, voice growing rough. He cleared his throat and said, "Doctor Levine. I will do everything in my power."

"See that you do," she said. She drew in a deep breath and closed her eyes, composing herself. Then said, "I apologize, alet. This is just . . . a very serious situation. Normally our department wouldn't be involved in anything like this, in fact. Except that . . ."

". . . I brought you information you might not have otherwise had," he finished.

"Yes," Levine said. "And there's some pressure from above for us to keep giving them something they can use. If you're tired, of course, go get some rest. Just . . . keep the gravity of the situation in mind."

"I assure you, Doctor, the gravity of the situation is the first thing on it."

She nodded and smiled at him, a look more frazzled than reassuring; he valued it for the genuine vulnerability in it anyway. "All right. I'll be by to talk to you tomorrow."

He watched her leave and was still staring after her when Jiron said behind him, "Don't worry. We'll run interference for you."

Jahir turned from the door to find the human watching him, arms folded and one hand clasping his elbow. "I beg your pardon?"

"I don't think even I got that one," Radimir said to Jiron. "And I know what you meant."

"She's right when she says we don't normally get dragged into things like this, at least, not this early in the process. They usually call us in to help manage the psychological aspects once they know what's going on and have a plan for dealing with it," Jiron said. "Having people beating down her door asking her to magic up more clues has made her nervy. But Radimir and I are here to oversee your education, and we're not going to forget our responsibility to your health and wellbeing. All right?"

"All right," Jahir said, subdued.

"Just remember the first duty of a healer," Radimir said.

"Do no harm?" Jahir asked.

"Don't become one of the casualties."

CHAPTER 12

$\mathcal{V}$ASIHT'H CHECKED HIS saddlebags one more time, then looked up at the narrow house facing one of the greens-paces. Heliocentrus was riddled with stair-step communities, houses that were built on terraces lining the edges of small parks. The topmost terraces usually bled onto concourses leading into marketplaces, businesses and high rises, sculpted around more of the greenspaces, so it was not unusual to be walking down a street and find oneself on a bridge overlooking a stadium-like arrangement of small houses. He had an invitation to this particular one, though, and rolled his shoulders once before jogging with determination to the front door and pressing the chime. A few moments later, a Tam-illee in an apron opened it, then called over her shoulder, "Girls! It's your friend from Seersana!"

Kayla and Meekie dashed through the door and into his arms before he could open his mouth to greet them. Grinning, he rested his head between theirs and gave them as big a squeeze as they could handle, which set them both to giggling wildly.

"If you'll give me a moment, alet," Meekie's mother said with a bright smile. "I'll go get the picnic basket."

"Of course," he said, and sat in front of the girls. They looked better . . . much better. "Look at you both. You're practically glowing!"

"We feel better too," Meekie said, serious. "Whatever the doctor's doing, it's helping a lot. He says we might be in remission within the year!"

"And then maybe we can go back home," Kayla added. "I miss everyone on Seersana."

"I have letters," Vasiht'h said. "They're in my bag. Maybe over lunch you can read them."

"Ooh, letters!" Meekie clapped her hands. "Yay!"

From in the house came a call: "Shoes, girls."

"Shoes!" Kayla said. "I always forget. I'll get yours, Meekie." She scampered back inside.

Meekie leaned into Vasiht'h's arm with a sound very like a purr. "It is nice to see you again, Manylegs. Except—" She pulled away to look at him. "I thought it was Prince Jahir who was coming to Selnor?"

"It was, and he did," Vasiht'h said as Kayla returned. "And it's a long story."

"I like long stories," Meekie said. "Especially about people I know."

"What's this?" Kayla asked.

"It's Prince Jahir. Vasiht'h-alet says he's here and it's a long story."

"Ooh, long stories! I love long stories!" Kayla exclaimed.

Vasiht'h started laughing. "I've missed you girls."

"We missed you too," Kayla said with a grin.

"All right," Meekie's mother said, reappearing without her apron and with a basket. "Lead the way, girls."

"Come on, Manylegs," Kayla said, grabbing his arm. "Just wait until you see the duck pond!"

They walked together down the grassy paths leading toward the park, the two girls on either side of Vasiht'h and Meekie's mother trailing. On the way, Vasiht'h explained how he'd decided to follow Jahir off-world after all, and the straits he'd found his friend in once he'd arrived.

"So he's sick," Meekie said, ears flat. "Like us."

"A little," Vasiht'h allowed. "If he leaves Selnor and goes somewhere easier on his body, he'll be back to normal, though."

"But he won't go because he promised to stay, and princes always keep their promises," Kayla said. "That's what Persy would have said, anyway. In the stories, princes have duties, and they have to do their duty or what's a prince for?"

Meekie nodded agreement. "It's about honor."

Vasiht'h looked from one to the other, brows lifted. "You think that's what it is, do you."

"Of course!" Meekie said. "But you should get him to come see us, and maybe rest a little."

"I want to try."

"Good," Meekie said. "Here, this is a nice place to eat."

Vasiht'h passed out the letters while Meekie's mother set out the food, and they shared sandwiches and news while the girls read bits of the letters out loud. Electronic correspondence was more typical than physical mail, which made such things a special treat. Afterwards, the elder Tam-illee went for a walk, leaving him with the two of them, and Kayla's frown. "So," he said while dipping an apple slice in some of the spiced honey. "What was in the letter that's made you make faces, arii?"

Kayla said, "Well . . . some of it is just . . . girl to girl stuff. You know."

He didn't, but he didn't want to point that out.

"But she also says that Kuriel's gotten a little weird since we've gone."

"She was afraid of being left behind," Meekie said. "But Persy and Amaranth stayed! Didn't they? They were still there when you left?"

"They were," Vasiht'h confirmed.

"I don't understand, then," Meekie said. "More people stayed than left. So she's not really alone. I mean, we miss her, but we're not lonely. . . ."

"We also get to play outside now," Kayla said. "We're not stuck in a hospital all the time. We can make new friends. They have to stay in the ward. And there were never any volunteers as much fun as Vasiht'h-alet and Prince Jahir."

"What can we do to help her?" Meekie murmured, frowning. She took the paper and smoothed it. "Other than call more often. That's what we can do, right, Vasiht'h-alet?"

"It is, yes," Vasiht'h said. "Just remember, ariisen. Sometimes when you're scared, bad things can seem more important, more immediate, than they really have to be."

"You mean you make them seem worse than they are because you're already upset," Meekie said, and nodded. "Dami tells me the same thing."

"We will write her, then," Kayla said. "Today. We can tell her that our parents hope to move back to Seersana once our treatment's done, and then maybe she will have something to look forward to." She glanced up at Vasiht'h. "What about you, Manylegs?"

"What about me?" Vasiht'h smiled at them both.

"Is Prince Jahir making things bigger than they really are because he's tired all the time?"

Thinking of the comatose patients, Vasiht'h said, "What I'm actually afraid of is that they're bigger than he thinks they might be."

A long pause. The two girls looked at one another, then Meekie said, "I hope not."

"Me too," Vasiht'h said.

"Enough sad things," Kayla declared. "Maybe you can play flying saucer, Manylegs?"

Surprised, he said, "Can the two of you?"

"Oh yes!" Kayla grinned and went through the picnic basket until she came up with a plastic disc. "We can run now. See? Meekie, fetch!" She threw the disc and Meekie sprang to her feet, laughing.

"I am not a pet dog!" she called as she ran after it. Leaping, she caught it and called, "Flying saucer!" And sent it back over the field. Kayla squealed and sprang after it.

For a pleasing half an hour, Vasiht'h played flying saucer

with two very much healthier girls. After that, Meekie's mother rejoined them for a ramble through the park, culminating at the duck pond, which had a bridge over it so people could stand over the water and watch the fish darting beneath the clear surface of the water. The ducks in question were far more exotic than anything Vasiht'h was accustomed to seeing on Seersana; more like Anseahla's avians, with plumage in startling rose pinks or bright oranges edged in black. He left when the afternoon started to wane with promises to return again soon and breathed out, feeling something settle in him. He hadn't really held any hope that their doctor's new treatment for their particularly virulent strain of Auregh-Rosen would be able to help. That it had, and so much!

On the way home, Vasiht'h detoured to investigate one of the siv'ts listed in the city directory. It was tucked into the corner of one of the high rises on the bottom floor, facing one of the grassy fields that extended into a courtyard between two other skyscrapers. Vasiht'h ducked into it and found himself in a low, small room, paneled in dark wood carved in arabesques to evoke the sacred exsufflation of the Goddess. There was a single altar in the front of the room, beneath a wooden relief of Aksivaht'h: full frontal, rather than in profile, which made this a shrine used by a priest or priestess. He hunted near the door and found their hours listed; he was between consultations, which suited him. He wasn't here for the services Glaseahn priests provided, anyway. Instead he went to the altar and took one of the sticks of incense from the box on the altar. Using the brush and cloth stored in the drawer at the foot of the altar, he cleaned the surface of waste ash and discarded the burnt down incense left by the last postulant. After tidying, he lit the fresh stick and wedged it into the slot, then sat in front of it and clasped his hands.

And didn't know what to say.

Thank you, for Jahir, of course. He'd said it to Her effigy in the apartment and had the feeling he would never be done with saying that. Thank you for Meekie and Kayla, for their health, and for how they'd grounded him in what had come before. A fervent prayer for whatever crisis was brewing in Mercy's crisis care beds to be resolved as quickly as possible. An even more fervent one that he might be up to the challenges that he was facing. In the end, he closed his eyes and let the peace of Her presence seep into him, and took strength from that. Then he stood, dropped a fin coin into the box by the door to help pay for the upkeep of the shrine, and went home.

He had enough time to start dinner and listen to another lecture, and was in the middle of making notes for his business practice course when Jahir let himself into the apartment, looking if possible even more haggard than he had when Vasiht'h had first arrived. The dread that flooded the mindline was enough to turn his stomach. He half-stood, wings spreading. "Arii?"

"I appear to have become a person of interest," Jahir said, tired.

Vasiht'h didn't like the sound of that, and knew Jahir could feel his wariness. He said instead, "Sit, all right? It can wait while I get you a cup of something warm. Tea, coffee?"

"No more coffee," Jahir said as he seated himself, then leaned on the arm of the sofa with his feet curled close. Without even stopping to shed his shoes. The sense of cold through the mindline was so distinct Vasiht'h smoothed down his fur. "Paige-alet brings coffee from someplace nearby? It's very good, but very heavy."

"What do they put in it?" Vasiht'h asked, going through the cupboard for the teapot.

"A stick of butter."

Vasiht'h looked up.

"Not a joke," Jahir said, wry. "And it's very good, but I am so tired of drinking calories. Something clear, I beg of you, arii."

As Vasiht'h made the tea, the oppression in the mindline only strengthened, until it felt so thick he was having a hard time breathing. "So, tell me what happened, before it chokes you."

"I'm—"

"Don't apologize!" Vasiht'h exclaimed, sensing the words before his roommate could articulate them, even in his own mind. "Don't. It's all right, really." He brought the teapot over, using the trip to sort through his own feelings and separate them from Jahir's. "It's guilt, isn't it? You feel guilt for making me feel your negative feelings."

"I . . ." Jahir trailed off, his gaze losing focus. Then he looked up sharply at Vasiht'h, eyes wide.

Vasiht'h nodded. "That's what I thought." He put the pot down. "Look, the bad comes with the good. It's like that in everything, right?"

"Yes," Jahir said, with a subdued sorrow that tasted like wine. That impression was unexpected enough that Vasiht'h paused before continuing.

"And I wouldn't trade the good for the absence of the bad," Vasiht'h said, when he was sure of his voice. "You might not have known what we were walking into when we started encouraging the mindtouches, but I did. I grew up with people who didn't think anything of falling in and out of each other's heads." He poured. "I know it's going to take a while for you to accept that I mean this, and to work past your own upbringing. Until then, I'll repeat it so you'll remember. It's all right. I don't mind the bad moments."

"There are like to be many bad moments," Jahir said, low.

"Before we get out of here?" Vasiht'h pushed the cup over to him. "Maybe. But maybe things will look up too. So tell me what has you so wound up, and then I'll share my day with you and cheer you up."

Jahir inhaled, eyes closing. "Apparently my suggestion has caused some consternation in the department. An autopsy revealed a desperate condition, and now everyone would very much like to know how I understood the problem to be related to illegal drugs rather than any of the other possibilities."

"So they did do the autopsy?" Vasiht'h said, ears flattening. "On . . ."

"The first patient to present with the condition," Jahir said. "A human male. He had some substantial deterioration of the brain."

Vasiht'h frowned, and he guessed his furious thinking communicated itself to Jahir because the Eldritch finished, "Doctor Levine said what they found was 'like sludge.' What are you thinking, arii?"

"That it's strange they didn't notice that until the autopsy," Vasiht'h said. "The halo-arch should have picked up some sign of deterioration long before it got to the point of . . . well, catastrophic meltdown like that."

"That seems reasonable," Jahir said. "But I admit, even a year of schooling and an internship at Seersana's General, I still am not familiar enough with medicine here to guess at why the halo-arch might have missed something. Alliance technology still seems magical to me. When there is magic, it is hard to guess what things are impossible." He warmed his fingers on the tea, rolling the cup between his hands. "Whatever the case, my shift supervisor, my residency supervisor, and now the department head are all very interested in what more I might learn from the two cases that arrived earlier. And the latter has suggested that if I do not divine anything from them, I might go check on the other cases in a clinic across the city."

"Which I hope you explained might be asking a little much?" Vasiht'h said. "You got the information you did by chance. The only way you could possibly duplicate your success is by sitting at the side of one of these people until she dies. And that's assuming that there will be anyone to sit by—if the autopsy showed there was some problem with their brains, I'm sure they've already got a neuro specialist just waiting for the chance to get his hands on one of them so they can find a way to cure them."

"I had not thought of that," Jahir said, and hope crept into the mindline like the suggestion of relief after pain.

"I wouldn't be surprised if they haven't already figured something out by the time you come in tomorrow," Vasiht'h said. "Just watch. Now. Ask me who I saw today?"

Obediently, Jahir said, "Who did you see?"

Vasiht'h let the images leak: the two girls playing flying saucer, squealing with laughter. Jahir sat up abruptly, tea forgotten.

"Oh, they are well!"

"Better than I expected," Vasiht'h said. "And they'd love to see you."

That brilliant joy became muted, so abruptly it felt like a cloud covering the sun.

"You're thinking that it's going to be hard for you to get away, given how you feel," Vasiht'h said. "And maybe it would be. But there's no reason you have to go all the way over to their house. We can meet somewhere closer, where you don't have to walk much or get up. You get one day a week off, yes?"

"Yes," Jahir said slowly.

"And it would be good to see some people you know," Vasiht'h said. "Especially the girls."

A sigh, and affirmation, warm and quiet and sure. "Yes."

"Let me arrange it?"

"Tentatively," Jahir said. "This situation with the hospital . . . I don't know how it will develop. Radimir and Jiron—my shift and residency supervisors, respectively—say that it's unusual for people in our specialty to end up involved in anything so urgent. If you're right, I should no longer be involved soon . . . so . . . tentatively."

"A few days," Vasiht'h said. "I'm sure it'll be in other people's hands by then. Don't forget how many people are working on this, arii. Not just your department, but now the surgical specialists, the emergency personnel, the city police, no doubt the city's public health officials . . . it's not all on your shoulders." He felt the ease creeping into the mindline. "Let's get you fed and into your bed, all right? I've got warm milk on the stove already. Drink it and sleep. Tomorrow things should be easier."

CHAPTER 13

"He SAYS," ARALYN reported, watching the Naysha sign, "that you shouldn't exercise today. Soaking only."

Jahir glanced at Paga. "Is there some reason . . . ?"

Paga glanced at Aralyn, enormous eyes unblinking. The Asanii sighed and sat on the edge of the pool, sliding her legs into the water and flexing her feet. "Look, you haven't told us what you've been up to at Mercy. But your stress level in the past week . . ." She shared a look with the Naysha and shook her head. "It's been tremendous. Neither of us need the vital sign monitors to notice it."

Jahir said, "It is not intentional, I assure you."

"I know. We both do. But there's only so far we can push you when your heart's already hammering at the speed of light." She smiled wryly. "I think having you keel over is not what Healer Gillespie has in mind for your treatment plan." Paga signed something and she added, "Yes. Contraindicated. Very much so."

"I would very much like to learn the sign for 'contraindicated,'" Jahir said, allowing himself to smile.

Paga snorted and pointed at one of the private chambers, then signed at length. Jahir caught some of it now: simple pronouns, words about water and rest. Aralyn waited until he was done and then frowned in concentration, swishing her legs in the water idly. "This is . . . a psychological thing," she said at last. "If you don't mind that."

"Not at all."

She nodded. "Paga has made the suggestion that we discuss throttling your exercise program back in favor of time in the water spent recuperating mentally. That normally we'd be trying to strengthen your body because someone in your position would be moving as little as possible during the day. But that's not true of you, is it?" She lifted her brows.

"I . . . don't know." Jahir sat on the steps leading into the pool, chest-deep, so that he could face them both without leaving the water. "I don't know how little is typical. But I do my work. It is why I came. It is not strenuous work under normal circumstances."

"But it involves staying on your feet for eight hours straight?" Aralyn asked.

Paga rolled his eyes, and that gesture in a Naysha, executed with those vast irises and coin-sized pupils, was dramatic. Jahir cleared his throat and offered, "Sometimes I sit?"

"Sometimes he sits," Aralyn muttered. To Paga, "I think you're entirely right." She sighed and pointed at Jahir. "You are a stubborn man, you know that?"

"I have been so accused, now and then," Jahir said, lowering his head.

She snorted. "I bet. Since we can take for granted that you're overworking yourself, I'm going to talk to Gillespie about formalizing the change. For now, though, I want you to come here and . . . rest. In the water. You can do one lap to practice your technique if you want, but only one lap, and I'm going to reset the heart rate monitor to something more aggressive. If you hear it go off, or if Paga signs for you to stop, you do that immediately, understood?"

"Yes, alet."

Aralyn clambered to her feet. "Good. Now float like a good patient. And get out when you're ready. And if you want to use the private pools, check yourself into one."

After she'd walked away, Paga tapped the water—a more gentle bid for attention than his open-palmed slaps—and then clapped the translation on. /You have questions, I think./

"How did you know?" Jahir lifted a hand, shook his head a little. "That I was overworking, not that I had questions."

/You give me much credit. Aralyn also noticed. She thinks it is the monitor that tells her, but she has good instincts. That is what she hears with./ The Naysha tilted his head on the stalk of his neck. /I know because I hear/taste it in the water./

"Oh," Jahir whispered. "How very much I would like to know how that feels to you . . . !"

/You could. Yes? I am not wrong in that understanding?/

"No, you're not," Jahir said. "And if that was an offer to share that sense with me, oh, how I would gladly accept—"

Paga's translucent eyelids narrowed, just a touch. /Except?/

"Except I am so raw," Jahir said, sliding his hands up his arms and leaning over them. That the admission came so easily was a surprise, but something about the Naysha elicited the confidence. Jahir could not imagine Paga breaking trust with him; water held too many secrets for someone immersed in it not to know how to keep them. "I'm not used to the amount of touching I'm doing lately, and there's only one influence to steady me in any of it."

/And this is part of what has your body so taxed./

"No doubt," Jahir murmured.

/Then you come to this water to be healed. Do you understand?/ Tapping the water for emphasis. /This remains therapeutic. But you and I know the truth. What you need from this is not strength. Not the strength of the body. The strength here./ Touching his breast. /This strength./

Jahir looked at him for a long moment. Then he said, "Yes."

/Go soak in the private pool. And, alet./ When Jahir looked up, Paga finished, /When you are no longer raw. When you have a center to move from. You come to me, and I will share what it is like. To taste/hear through the water./

A shiver ran the length of Jahir's spine, though he held himself tightly to keep from revealing it. "Ah, alet. You give me a reason to work toward my health."

The Naysha grinned. /I know. I am a therapist. My task, to find incentives. Yes?/

Jahir laughed. "And you do very well at it."

⸺∞⸺

Only one of the unresponsive patients remained in the ward when Jahir arrived.

"Taken away for surgery prep," Radimir told him as the Eldritch washed his hands and tucked the chain he'd hung his ring on beneath his collar. "They're going to try tomorrow. The surgeon they've tapped for it is the best in the city—one of ours, of course—but she's full up today and she wants time to study the autopsy results and the male's body before she goes in."

Jahir closed his eyes, and a feeling very like a prayer fell through him like a ray of sunlight. "I am very glad to hear it."

"So are we," Radimir said. "If it can be put back together, Septima can do it."

"Am I still—"

"On death watch for the last patient?" The Harat-Shar's smile was crooked. "I'm afraid so. Since there's only the one, though, I think you should do the usual rounds. We'll keep you off triage so you can be available if his status changes, but Levine was adamant. For once, the light is shining on our department and she doesn't want to fail. Particularly not with everyone watching."

"Understood," Jahir said. "I go."

"And alet?"

Jahir paused at the door.

"You're going above and beyond what we ask of people." Radimir's shoulders were tense and his tail flicked in agitation, and his eyes were clouded with a worry so distinct Jahir could feel it from across the room. "We ask a lot of our people; that's what we're known for, after all. But I know, and some of the rest of us know, that what you're doing is something none of us could do, and that none of us will really understand what it costs you. Just that it does." He grimaced. "I'm not saying this well. But I want you to know Griffin and I are serious about looking out for you."

For a moment, Jahir said nothing, in his astonishment, in his gratitude. Then he dipped his head and said, "Thank you."

"You're welcome. Remember to take your breaks."

For once the shopping was done early; Vasiht'h checked the status of the pantry—or what passed for one in the apartment's excuse for a kitchen—and the stasis unit and was satisfied. He had time to go wander, find a sunny place to catch up on his schoolwork and maybe read some of the correspondence from his family. He had letters from two cousins, one of his older sisters, three brothers and his grandmother to read, and while he wouldn't get through all of them today they would make a good reward for getting through his legal class lectures for the week. Vasiht'h packed and padded out, checking his data tablet for someplace to go. Several festivals and performances popped up on the city locator—tempting, but probably too distracting—but hadn't Jahir said something about a coffee shop? Any place that buttered its coffee had to be worth investigating. A quick search found him the likely culprit and he set off that way by foot, eschewing the Pad kiosks that might have brought him there more quickly. He didn't feel like waiting in line, no matter how quickly it was moving; this close to lunch, there were a lot of people eager to skip the travel time to their destinations.

There was an exhilarating freedom in not having to attend classes, he reflected as he passed beneath a trellis of riotous orange flowers and started down the walk past several high rises. He could get used to making his own schedule. And he supposed he'd have to, if he truly went into private practice. Vasiht'h frowned. Of course, he didn't know what his life would look like in the future. After his experiences last year he was committed to the clinical therapy track, which would see him graduated with a degree to practice xenotherapy as a private psychotherapist, either as part of an existing practice or head of a new one. Jahir, though, was still in the medical track. They'd have to find a hospital for him to work at. What would that be like? A little awkward, maybe, but they would figure it out, wouldn't they? That's what friends did. Or . . . partners, Vasiht'h guessed. They were more than friends now, and a side-step from lovers. Partners worked.

The coffee shop was tucked into the corner of a building several stories tall, but shorter than the skyscrapers around it; there were two footbridges above its roof, in fact, one close enough for Vasiht'h to see the buckles on people's shoes, and one far enough that he had trouble making out what species they were. The aroma wafting from the interior when the door opened was promising, and there was a small patio shaded with vines trained onto another trellis and potted trees.

Ten minutes later, he returned to the patio and settled at one of the low tables with a mug of something he wasn't entirely sure of: kerinne with a shot of espresso? But he thought it might be interesting, and he could well imagine Jahir being willing to try it. His tentative sip convinced him that it was drinkable, but he still couldn't make up his mind about it. As he rolled the taste over his tongue, he wondered . . . could he carry the sensation back to Jahir? Share the memory of it? Would the mindline work that way? Maybe only if his memories of it were good. He concentrated on it, closing his eyes and savoring it, trying to fix in mind the bitter complexity of the taste, the sweetness and spice of the cinnamon, the richness of the cream.

Strange to think that a memory could be a gift. A literal one, to be passed to someone else. Pleased, Vasiht'h drew his data tablet from his saddlebag and started on his legal coursework.

———⧜———

"They're all nervous as a Karaka'An in hell without a map," Paige said. "And you know we have twenty of them. Hells, I mean." She leaned against the door into triage. "Thank An for a quiet night. I think if we checked any more of those patients in Levine would have a coronary."

MCA Hogarth   137

"At least it would give us something to do," Maya said from in the room, where she was running routine diagnostics on the equipment.

Paige flipped her ears back, but didn't disagree. She said, "At least that Tam-illee widower's family came for him."

"I saw," Jahir said. "I hope they take good care of him."

"They will," Maya said. She set aside her data tablet and picked up her cup. "We're pretty good about that. We lose so many kids. . . . We build the support networks before we need them. Because we know we probably will." She managed a wintry smile. "I'm going to go get a refill, Paige. Watch the room for me?"

"Sure."

As she padded into the room, Jahir said, "I am sorry I have not been able to relieve you, alet."

She snorted. "Don't worry about it. I wouldn't want the job they saddled you with, believe me."

He was surprised that he agreed with her, though he kept it to himself. He'd assumed that any form of work would have its disagreeable chores; certainly that had been true at home, and the husbandry of an estate while it might have seemed glamorous most involved a great deal of tedium and hard work. But he loved so much of xenopsychology. To learn that there were parts of it he might not love at all was disconcerting, particularly when he'd been warned by everyone who cared about him that the medical psychology careers could be . . . wearing.

This certainly qualified as wearing.

Jahir returned to his vigil on the remaining patient, a Hinichi male. The only thing that leavened the oppression of his hours there was the knowledge that this patient's companion would be in surgery tomorrow. He knew the magic of Alliance medical technology could fail—had held the evidence of it in his own arms when it had—but he could not bring himself to believe that this puzzle would be beyond one of the best surgeons on the capital world.

A memory from Seersana drifted past: KindlesFlame across a coffee shop table with him, talking about the medical paradigm, and the dangers of falling too in love with it. A lecture about the autonomy of the body, and the need to intervene as little as possible to support the healing. And at the last, a warning that there was intensity to be found in an emergency room, even in the short time one had with the patients there. Jahir opened his eyes and focused on the quiescent body, watching the ribcage lift and fall beneath the thin hospital gown.

Radimir leaned into the room. "Nothing, ah?"

"No," Jahir said.

"Well, night shift's arriving. You should get off that stool before your joints freeze up."

Jahir nodded and rose. He rested a hand on the male's ankle, just a feather touch . . . and was shocked to feel a pale echo back.

"What?" Radimir said. When Jahir glanced at him, the Harat-Shar said, "You've stopped moving. What? Can you feel something?"

"A little. Yes." Jahir let his other hand rest on the other foot and stretched his senses out. A flame of hope lit: maybe one of them would survive. Maybe one of them would wake up.

Come! he called. *Come back!*

Another echo, like a flicker of light in a dark room.

That was all the warning he had before the world erupted.

The cup fell off the table and shattered, spraying the kerinne on the patio. Vasiht'h leaped to his feet so quickly his feet tangled and he stumbled, catching himself on the table's edge. Something was wrong. Oh Goddess, something was catastrophically wrong. The mindline was a howl in his head and all of it was urgency: COME NOW COME NOW BEFORE IT'S TOO LATE

He didn't remember running back. He remembered fear, mind-blinding, throat-burning, chest-constricting fear. He remembered how much his legs trembled as he darted through the afternoon crowds. Time smeared. The light on his shoulders and back flickering: shade, then sun, then shade again. The towers of Mercy Hospital, skidding into the emergency room. Somehow getting out to the person at the desk that he was here for one of the employees. Her polite attempts to calm him down. His desperation . . . the door that had opened for another patient, the one that allowed him to rush in.

Ignoring the startled people he left in his wake.

The calls that he couldn't make sense of, because the only thing that mattered was in front of him and needed him NOW.

The urgency of it, the mounting terror—

—and then crashing into a room and diving for the crumpled body at the foot of the bed, and vaulting after the spark he could barely feel in the mindline, dwindling.

Noise and sound and light—

No, Vasiht'h snarled into that maelstrom. *No, I did not just find him to lose him!* And dragged that spark back up through the screaming chaos, digging into it, feeling it slip away and refusing, refusing to let it fall. With everything in him, with every experience that had made him, with every breath he'd taken in comfort and safety, he drew back and pulled his best, his dearest friend with him, until the spark became a flame, and the flame became a light, and the light became the sun and flooded him, and Jahir welled back into his own body and fell forward into Vasiht'h's arms, gasping. The animal panic that accompanied him made both their hearts race, and that was fine for Vasiht'h but not good for an Eldritch already too taxed by the world. So he clutched Jahir close and said, "You're fine, you're fine. You're here, you're safe." Vasiht'h let his head sag forward to rest against the fine white hair. He could feel Jahir's fingers digging into his back. They were going to leave bruises. When had the Eldritch ever been so frightened? Frightened enough to show it?

Easier to concentrate on that than to let himself feel how scared he was, too.

"Who the hell—"

"Let us—"

"Stay *back,*" Vasiht'h growled before he even looked up to see the people trying to approach. He lifted his head, just enough to see them. A Harat-Shar and a Karaka'An in the uniform of healers-assist, both of them wide-eyed and fretful. He forced his fur to smooth back down while also shifting his lower body to keep as much of Jahir hidden from them as possible. "Stay back," he said, quieter. "Don't touch him, or you'll make it worse."

More people were showing up at the door now, and the threat of their entry, the probability that they'd accidentally brush against Jahir—or do it on purpose, trying to help—Vasiht'h's fur fluffed up again. "Who are you?"

"We were about to ask you that," the Harat-Shar said. "And these people need to get in here. The patient just . . ."

"Died," the Karaka'An said, ears flattening. "Like the others. Was he here again? Did he . . ."

"He was touching him." The Harat-Shar's tail was lashing. "He said he felt something. He was touching him and concentrating. . . ."

And when the patient died, he almost took the Eldritch with him. Vasiht'h's arms tightened around Jahir's. "This is one of the drug victims?"

One of the other strangers said, "That's yet to be determined."

"Temple."

Everyone in the room froze, including Vasiht'h. Jahir moved his head, trying to lift it and failing. He rested it against Vasiht'h's shoulder, eyes still closed, and said again, hoarse, "Temple. Injected at the temple. Or . . . into the carotid. With an AAP."

The Harat-Shar stared at him, mouth agape.

"Are you sure?" one of the others asked, intent.

A flicker of images, so vibrant Vasiht'h wobbled: the cold pressure of the metal against skin, the hiss, so close to the ear. The sudden rush—

—so good—

"Stop!" he hissed, digging his own fingers into Jahir's back. "Come back!"

Jahir shuddered and rasped, "I'm sure."

"I am too," Vasiht'h muttered, his skin crawling at the memory. He concentrated on the taste of the espresso-laced kerinne: the fatty cream, the nose-itching bite of the cinnamon, the earthy bass note of the coffee. He felt Jahir's frown against his shoulder: concentration. Interest. A whisper: *More.* Vasiht'h closed his eyes and dragged the rest of the memory back from before the spike of crisis: the sweetness: honey, not sugar, and a wildflower honey that tasted like the air smelled. A hint of something else . . . /*Nutmeg?*/ Yes, nutmeg. /*You've been learning your spices.*/

/*Because you taught me.*/

They both felt Jahir swallow, and the violence of his shaking began to subside.

A cleared throat drew Vasiht'h's attention from the very important task of making sure his friend didn't fall apart. "So . . . ah . . . you didn't say who you are?"

"And how the hells you got in here," a second voice said, irritated.

Vasiht'h looked up and found another man shadowing the Harat-Shar . . . human, this time. "I'm Vasiht'h," he said. "And I'm his partner. And you damn near killed him. And for what?"

"He's right." The healer bent over the body frowned, parting the fur at the male's temple. "You could have missed it. But there's a pump injection site here."

Everyone in the room looked at them. Vasiht'h's claws inched from his paws. "Great," he said. "Now you know. And you can stop asking him to throw himself off the tops of buildings."

"Va . . . Vasiht'h . . ."

Vasiht'h ignored Jahir. "And I am, in fact, taking him home. Now."

The Karaka'An woman said, "Makes sense to me. He's off shift. Right, Radimir-alet?"

"Well . . . yes . . . but they might have questions . . ."

The human, who'd been silent since the outburst that had heralded his arrival, said now, "I think they can wait. You— Vasiht'h, right?—can you get him up? I don't think he can stand without help. We could get a stretcher."

"We could put him in a room here?" Radimir said.

"No," Vasiht'h and the human said in unison. Vasiht'h

glanced at him warily, but the human shook his head. "No, Rad, he's got to get out of here. Get some real down-time. That's not going to happen if he stays." He looked at Vasiht'h. "So, can you get him up? Because if you're the only one who can touch him right now, it's going to be hard for us to help you."

"I can manage," Vasiht'h said. "I have before." He braced his feet beneath himself and turned his attention to Jahir. */You're listening./*

/. . . I am./

/Can you—/

/—I don't know. I . . . I don't know./

Vasiht'h didn't like the taste of the sendings, disjointed and brittle. *Hold on, then.* Sliding his arms under Jahir's, he started to rise, and was grateful when the Eldritch managed to stumble up with him.

"Are you sure you can make it?" the human said, assessing them once they'd stood.

"Jiron . . . alet." Jahir managed the words and nothing else.

"Get us a stretcher," Vasiht'h said, and ignored the tired denial in the mindline. He held Jahir up until it arrived and then helped arrange him on it . . . and the moment the Eldritch was prone he passed out. The snuffing of his consciousness in the mindline was so abrupt Vasiht'h panicked until he felt the reassuring weight of the Eldritch in the back of his mind. Not receding, not distant. Just exhausted. He sighed out, realized he was shaking.

"Can we get you anything?" the human, Jiron, said, his gaze somber. He rested a hand on Vasiht'h's shoulder.

"No. Yes. No. Just . . . oh Goddess. Tell me this is over."

Jiron looked at him, then at the Eldritch. "I hope to God it is."

That wasn't good enough, but it was also all he was going to get. Vasiht'h followed the stretcher out of the hospital.

CHAPTER 14

WHEN JAHIR WOKE, IT was to shock that he was awake, and fear at what it might bring . . . and then a hand snaked into his, squeezing the fingers, and the nightmares scattered. Jahir opened his eyes and found Vasiht'h sitting next to him on the floor by the bed. His bed, in the apartment.

For a very long moment he could say nothing. Had nothing to say. There was light on his face, pale morning sunlight. A blanket up over his shoulder, hiding the uniform.

He had socks on.

What he finally said, then, was, "You put socks on me."

"Our feet were cold," Vasiht'h answered. And then his head fell forward to rest against their joined hands, and while he didn't weep the mindline shook between them, a gleaming shimmy that suggested the strength of the will that was keeping his friend from overwhelming them both. Relief. Panic. Anger. A great deal of anger.

"I'm here now," Jahir offered, hoarse.

"You almost died!" Vasiht'h exclaimed. He looked up, eyes fierce. "That wasn't in the deal. It was forever until *I* die because I'm the one who has the shorter lifespan! You're not allowed to go circumventing that! At least, not less than two weeks after

I show up!"

Jahir winced and pressed his fingers against the Glaseah's. Four to his five; furred on the top and skin on the bottom. Complicated hands, so different . . . it kept him focused on reality, to concentrate on them. "I did not go courting my predicament, arii," he said, and the mindline made it apology.

"I know." Vasiht'h's shoulders slumped. "I know. I just . . . if I hadn't been there. . . ."

They were both silent then, dread congealing between them.

Even now, even feeling his complete depletion, the hollow aches that warned of a frailty as much mental as physical, Jahir found it difficult to believe that he'd almost died. That someone's mind could draw his after it and smother them both. He'd read about such things of course; there were even stories of people doing it a-purpose. Horror stories, naturally. Myths of terrible villainy. To discover those stories were true in a place as mundane as a hospital?

When he let his mind wander, the memories of the cacophony tried to crowd back in. He turned his face into the pillow, shoulders tightening.

"Computer," Vasiht'h said. "Put the baroque original channel back on."

Strings swelled into the silence, dispelling the ugliness. Jahir felt the tension flow out of his spine, and accepted that this was deeper trouble than he had been prepared to admit to.

"And this is going to end," Vasiht'h said, answering the thought. He shook their hands gently. "All right? They got what they needed. They have the proof. Now it's up to them. We're therapists, arii, we deal with people who can respond to us. We can't do a thing about people who need surgical intervention."

"Yes," Jahir said. Softer, "Vasiht'h . . . I did not mean to imperil myself. I am sorry."

A wash of remorse. "I know. I know, and I'm sorry I yelled at you. I was just . . . I still am . . . really upset. Scared." Vasiht'h ran his free hand over his face, from forelock to lips. He shook his head. "I was lashing out at an available target. I didn't mean it."

"I know," Jahir said. He tried, tentatively, to extend his own forgiveness through the mindline, felt it accepted with an embarrassment that felt like a faint tint of peach on pale skin. He made himself look toward the window. "Is it morning already? Really?"

"Yes," Vasiht'h said. "And don't you dare tell me you're thinking of going to work. You can call in sick."

"But who will replace me?"

"They have on-call healers-assist. All hospitals do. They can wake someone else up to take your place, and you will rest."

And he did feel weak. But lying in bed with nothing to keep the impressions of the dying mind from preying on him. . . . "I think I would prefer aught else. Something to fill me."

"Then you'll let me arrange for that," Vasiht'h said. "While you call in. Or I can do it for you . . . they know me by now."

"Do they?" Jahir paused, sorting through hazy memories. "You reproached them." A better memory: a snarl like a hunting cat's. "God and Lady, you yelled at them."

"I was a little upset," Vasiht'h mumbled.

A trickle of golden amusement snuck past the fear and exhaustion. Jahir said, "A little?"

"They were pushing you." The Glaseah's ears fanned back. "They were pushing, and they didn't have the slightest idea what they were asking of you. I know it seems funny, and maybe it is, a little, in retrospect, but this is important, arii: non-espers are never going to understand what they're asking of people like us when they ask us to perform for them. As far as those people know, what happened to you was the equivalent of someone taking a punch. They don't understand: you *were* a dying person. And if I hadn't been there to separate the two of you. . . ."

Jahir sat up, ignoring his anxiety. "And yet, where we have talents that are not otherwise available, we have decided it is our duty to use them. Is that not so?"

"And you have," Vasiht'h said, still gripping his hand. "And you did your duty. It's done. Over. It's their game now. Right?" When Jahir didn't answer, the Glaseah said, "Jahir. It's not your place to die for these people."

"There are some who would say to die to protect others is a great good."

"And what makes their life more important than yours?" Vasiht'h asked. Exasperation filled the mindline with burrs, prickly and close. "You're not a soldier. You're a healer-assist. Not even that yet, until you graduate. That gives you the duty to try to save your patients. Not to commit suicide."

That penetrated. Jahir winced.

"Jahir?"

He met his friend's eyes. Brown, earnest and far too somber.

"This noble sacrifice impulse . . . I understand it, and I understand you have it. But I also want you to know: you've already made it. By coming to the Alliance, by committing yourself to being willing to care about people who are going to die centuries before you do. By committing to *me*, to a mindline with me. All right? Please, don't go looking for more opportunities. The ones you've got are going to be hard enough on you."

"Do you really believe yourself to be a sacrifice?" Jahir asked, quiet.

"Not yet," Vasiht'h said. "But I'm not kidding myself that one day I will be, and neither should you." He paused, then added, ears flattening, "Unless you go get yourself killed. On the second week of your promise to me."

The pain in the mindline wanted more than words. Jahir brought their joined hands to his heart and pressed the back of Vasiht'h's hand to his chest, where the racing of his taxed heart could be felt as an undertow between them—psychically, if not physically. And that made his friend sigh and relax a little.

"Go on," the Glaseah said. "Call in. I'll take care of everything else."

"I hear and obey," Jahir said, to make him laugh, and it worked.

Vasiht'h waited until he heard Jahir's voice, talking in a low tenor murmur to his supervisor, before putting a pot on for tea and dragging his data tablet off the coffee table. He couldn't remember the last time he'd felt so taxed himself, but the night had been harrowing. The death impression kept trying to reassert itself in nightmare, and when it had, it had disrupted Jahir's sleep and jerked Vasiht'h awake to soothe it away again. It had only stopped when he'd thought to leave the music running, and that had given them both a coherent framework to cling to. But he hadn't slept well or much, and some part of him was still desperately trying not to realize just how close a thing it had been. If he'd arrived too much later . . .

He rubbed his face again. He didn't like feeling so raw. Some part of that was Jahir, though . . . and that he could fix. They both needed filling, with something so vast the events of the prior evening wouldn't find any purchase again. And it had to be something that wasn't too physically demanding. Vasiht'h paged through the tourist listings for Heliocentrus, feeling more than hearing the call in the other room end. His hearing was average for one of the Pelted, and it surprised him to hear the hiss of the shower so clearly until he identified its source in the mindline. Come to think of it, a shower sounded good to him too. He scratched at his pelt where it had matted against his side where he'd been leaning against the bed all night and made a face.

The good parts of the mindline were very good.

The bad parts were terrifying.

Vasiht'h stared at nothing for a while and then shook himself and returned to examining the listings. Museums, too much walking. Concerts . . . promising, but they'd done concerts before. He wanted something less expected. Tours of rooftop farms, an exotic flower festival, three or four art exhibits, including one touring the Alliance on artifacts from the Diaspora . . .

. . . when he found what he wanted, he grinned and made arrangements. If it bit hard into his funds, well, celebrating living through the previous day was worth it. That took care of the afternoon. If he timed it right—he made a quick call. By the time Jahir was stepping into the living room, he was ready with their lunch and tea.

"It is strange," Jahir said. "To be in normal clothes."

"Given that you've been falling asleep in uniform, I'm not surprised," Vasiht'h said. "I happen to like you this way." A hint of trepidation, cold and sour, seeped through the mindline, and Vasiht'h wrinkled his nose. "I don't mean it that way. I just think you should have more balance in your life. Working so much that you collapse in your clothes at night isn't balance, arii."

Jahir hesitated, then sighed. "No," he agreed, and sat on the couch. "No, you're right." He studied the omelet in front of him. "I suppose we should do something with the day?"

"We should," Vasiht'h agreed. "And I know just the thing."

⸎

One of the bad things about a mindline, Vasiht'h discovered, was how hard it made keeping secrets. He suspected as time passed they would find it more and more difficult to hide things from one another; lying was already impossible, and pushing each other out of the mindline felt incredibly wrong, even by accident. That he managed to keep their destination a mystery was mostly due to their lingering disorientation; in the future, Vasiht'h thought he'd have to resign himself to managing very few surprises, save perhaps by determinedly not thinking about them.

He was grateful to have succeeded this time, though, because it made Jahir's startlement when they exited the Pad station onto the marina all the more satisfying. Heliocentrus was a large enough city that most of it lay inland . . . but the site for the Alliance's winter capital had been chosen because of its climate, its beauty, and its proximity to some of the most gorgeous beaches in the southern hemisphere of the planet. Heliocentrus's citizens promptly capitalized on those assets, setting some of the coastline aside for swimmers and using part of it for small pleasure craft. The horizon before them glittered an unbelievable aquamarine blue, darkening toward the sky, and the native avians fluted their cries as they dipped close to the bright-crested waves.

"Oh, the sea," Jahir said softly.

"You haven't seen one?" Vasiht'h asked, standing beside him on the boardwalk.

"From space, briefly." Jahir turned his face into the breeze, eyes half-closed. Vasiht'h didn't think he realized he was tilting his head up to the sun . . . or that here and there, passersby stopped to stare at him. "But not at the shore, no. This is marvelous, arii."

"Good," Vasiht'h said firmly. "Because we're not done yet."

"Ah?"

"Come on," he said, and couldn't help a touch of mischief. "We're going to miss our ride."

Their ride was a sailboat, and after being issued their lifevests—two for Vasiht'h, since his much denser body wouldn't float without a second one around his lower half—they were given seats at the rail. Jahir's fascination broadened the mindline, filled it with a sizzling that made Vasiht'h stretch his paws and roll both sets of shoulders, and grin: grin, like everything was new. And then he started laughing.

"What?" Jahir asked, glancing at him with bright eyes.

"I was so busy setting up this adventure for you, to give you something to do you've never done before," Vasiht'h said as the ship slipped its moorage and began to glide into the turquoise waters. "And it didn't occur to me that *I've* never been on a sailboat!"

Jahir turned his laugh into his shoulder, muffling it, but it sparkled in the mindline like champagne bubbles.

The trip was amazing. They spent it with the sea breeze in their faces, shading their eyes in search of the acrobatic fliers that dove for fish, and pointing out the distant fins of the double-wings, some of whom drifted closer to investigate the ship: ray-shaped mammals with four wings set at right angles to one another. The creatures twirled them as they dove beneath the keel, vanishing with a slap of their forked tails on the water.

"I had no idea," Jahir said as the ship curved into the wind, making its long turn back toward the marina.

Vasiht'h sampled the mindline's ease, found it filled with

brine and a clean, humid wind he could taste in his mouth. He licked his teeth and smiled up at the Eldritch. "About what?"

"The worlds that could exist inside already alien worlds," Jahir said, looking back past the sails at the horizon. "What must it be like, do you wonder? To belong beneath the surface of the water?"

"I don't know," Vasiht'h said. Then added, a trifle wistfully, "A little bit like belonging to the sky, I guess."

Jahir glanced at him. "That feels like a child's pillow?"

"Like a happy dream, is what you mean," Vasiht'h said. He reached over and patted his stunted wings. "Even if these were big enough to work, we're not designed to fly. I don't think you can get less aerodynamic than a squat centaur. But I sometimes wonder what it must be like."

"I think it must be amazing," Jahir said, staring out over the water. The wind pulled some of his loose hair against his cheek. Vasiht'h thought it was good to see it down; he associated the braid with the hospital, and preferred this evidence that his friend was not working for a change. And he was so busy in that contemplation that the tickle of his friend's idea surfacing in the mindline caught him by surprise. "Perhaps we should visit some-place light enough for you to fly. Like the world of the Phoenix."

"What?" Vasiht'h shook himself, then chuckled. "I'm too heavy to fly, even on Phoenix-Nest. Though it would be a fasci-nating trip."

Jahir nodded, a small drop of his chin. Then added, "Does it distress you?"

"Not to be able to fly?" Vasiht'h frowned and looked up, fol-lowing the trail of a soaring sharp-winged Selnoran kite. "Not in the way I think you think. Not like someone who feels they should be able to, and can't. More like . . . someone who has no reason to believe they could, and would love to know what it's like anyway. Does that make sense?"

"It does, yes," Jahir said. Was that peach color in the mind-line shyness? It smelled ambrosial. "I like to swim. I have been learning as part of the physical therapy. Perhaps swimming is a little like flying."

Vasiht'h grinned, wiping his damp forelock out of his eyes. "I tell you a secret, arii." He felt the Eldritch's attention and said, "I like to swim too. And I tell you, if there's anything as awkward as a Glaseah in a pool, I haven't seen it yet."

Jahir pursed his lips. "Perhaps an Akubi in a pool."

That accompanied by an image of one of the giant dinosaur-like avians, floating with spread wings while caricatures of other swimmers dashed away in alarm. Vasiht'h laughed. "Okay, I'll grant that one."

There was a silence then, filled by the creak of the ropes and the sough of the wind, and the shimmer of the sun on the waves was reflected in the mindline and sent gooseflesh racing down Vasiht'h's sides. He sighed and smiled, found the Eldritch smiling back.

"This was wonderful. A revelation. Thank you."

"We're not done yet!"

"What could possibly be better than this!"

Vasiht'h grinned. "You'll see."

After their trip, Vasiht'h brought him back across the Pad to their part of town, and up to the coffee shop. Jahir stopped at the patio. "This is not the place Paige buys her concoctions—"

"It is," Vasiht'h said. "I have to pay for a cup I broke, so I figured I'd take care of a couple of things at once. Sit, I'll bring you a drink. What would you like?"

"Not hot buttered coffee!" Jahir exclaimed. "Otherwise . . ." He trailed off. "Surprise me."

Vasiht'h didn't bother to hide his grin or the glee that suffused the mindline between them. "I'm planning to."

He left the Eldritch sitting outside in the late afternoon sun, basking in the sense of repletion he could feel in the mindline as he ordered for them both: kerinne for himself, with that espresso again, and a clear coffee, a specialty varietal grown not far from Heliocentrus in the rain forests that thickened the nearby slopes.

If he timed it right . . .

He was just opening the door with the tray when Kayla's mother appeared, and both girls shot from her side and into Jahir's open arms, squealing their greetings. The rush from the tour on the sea was nothing to the incandescent joy that set fire to the mindline, so intense he flexed his fingers on the tray to keep from dropping it. Then he drew in a deep breath and went out to keep them company, and the look Jahir shot him over their heads could not have been paid for in all the treasure in the worlds.

"I'll go get some hot chocolate," Kayla's mother said, smiling.

The girls chorused their assents and then cuddled into their very favorite Eldritch prince. "We're not too heavy?" Meekie said.

"No. No, not at all."

"And we don't hurt you when we squeeze?" Kayla added.

"You can squeeze as hard as you like," Jahir said, and when they did, added, "And now, ariisen . . . tell me everything, everything."

∞∞∞

For once, Jahir sat on his bed and exhaustion felt good and right and proper—the result of a full and fulfilling day, and not of simple battle against something as mindless as a world's gravitational pull.

"That," Vasiht'h said, padding in from the bathroom, "was worth every fin."

"Was it very expensive?"

The mindline tightened, like a mouth puckering with disapproval. "You are not allowed to pay for it. I'm already staying with you. That's saving me a lot in rent." Vasiht'h plopped down amid his cushions, scattering several. He flexed his forelegs, claws winking at their tips and then sliding back into their sheaths. He added, "You can pay for the drinks, if you want."

Jahir laughed. "Leaving the expensive part of the day to me, I see."

Vasiht'h grinned and fluffed up his body pillow. "I've missed doing this with you."

"Which part of it?" Jahir asked. "The sight-seeing or—"

"The kids," Vasiht'h said. "We did good there. And we were good at it."

"We were, weren't we?" Jahir murmured.

Some of his thoughtfulness leaked, for the Glaseah asked, "And why do I taste tea now? Black tea?"

"Because that is what I was drinking with Healer Kindles-Flame when we were discussing job possibilities after the conferring of the degree," Jahir said. "I had mentioned you, in fact. He'd said he hoped you went clinical."

"Did he?" Vasiht'h sounded amused. Curious, also, which felt like the smell of lemons? No, pepper. No, both. Jahir paused, frowned. But his friend had continued, "What did he say?"

"That to find Glaseah outside research and education was rare, and that those who broke the rules typically went the farthest."

"Mm." Vasiht'h pleated the edge of his pillow. "It's funny. My sister also told me I should go clinical. She also said . . ." He looked up at Jahir from beneath his forelock, one brow lifted. ". . . that we'd do well together in practice."

Jahir hesitated, and could not find fault with the notion. "I think she'd be right." He settled on the bed, careful of his limbs. "What do you suppose we'll do when we are done with the schooling?"

"I don't know," Vasiht'h admitted. "I'm waiting to see what you're going to do, to be honest. I can set up a practice anywhere, or join an existing one. But it'll depend on where you end up working. Medical xenotherapists usually end up in big hospitals or clinics. They don't start their own businesses. You'd have to go where you could find a position."

"Not quite as pleasing a prospect as choosing someplace because one wants to live there, and then finding work," Jahir said.

"No, but where would you want to go?"

A good question. Where would he want to go, if he could go

anywhere? He had ties in the Alliance, but they were tenuous. So long as Vasiht'h went with him. . . .

"It seems an imposition," he said, tentative. "Forcing you to follow me."

"Maybe," Vasiht'h said. "But if that's how it's got to work, that's fine with me." His smile was a pale reflection of the calm that rippled through the mindline, like water trickling endlessly down the wall of a fountain. "I never in my life thought I'd come into a mindline, arii. I'm not going to give it up just because I'd have to let you choose where we lived." He wrinkled his nose. "I think the time to be concerned about you having that much impact on my life was long before I walked in this apartment door and said 'yes' to a permanent psychic bond."

Wryness was like cinnamon up the nose. Jahir wasn't sure whether to laugh or sneeze. He settled for smiling, resting his head on the pillow. "Well, there is time yet."

"So there is," Vasiht'h said, unconcerned. He curled up in his nest and yawned.

"Two months," Jahir added quietly, after they'd turned off the lights.

After a long pause: "Two months."

CHAPTER 15

 JAHIR WALKED OUT OF THE halcyon day into a crisis care center crazed with activity and poisoned by dread and hovering tension. As he halted at the break room door, a weary Jiron looked up and said, "Oh, you're back? Already?" He glanced at his data tablet and said, "Hell, when did it get to be evening shift?"

"Alet?" Jahir asked. "Why are you here?"

"Because everyone who can be pulled into this has been." The human pushed himself from the desk. "And you're just in time to get dragged back into it, I'm afraid. Go on, get ready. I can talk to your back."

Jahir walked past him and began washing. Behind him, Jiron continued. "So yesterday, Radclifte Clinic shipped us all their unresponsive cases, figuring our neuro team could fix it. That gives us nine of them—gave us nine of them—and today four of them are dead." Jahir jerked his head up and looked over his shoulder as the human finished, pinching the bridge of his nose. "And three of them died in surgery."

"How . . ."

"Is that possible? Damned if we know. They're not telling us anything down here except that the failures were catastrophic and no one understands the etiology of it, so how can they fix it?

The lab's been on every kind of screening, tissue sample and draw they can physically pull out of a body or read off a halo scan and they're coming up empty. If we didn't have your word for it being a drug—if we didn't have what looked like injection sites—then we'd be guessing it's something else because this doesn't match the profile of any street drug we know. Which means . . ."

"It's something new," Radimir said from the door, his voice sharp with fear. "Has Griffin told you about the police yet?"

"No," Jahir said.

"Try not to step on them," the Harat-Shar said. "Because they're getting underfoot with all the speed of roaches."

Jiron made a face. "Radimir . . ."

"They might want to ask you questions. Just answer them as best you can."

"Understood," Jahir said, subdued. "What are my duties for the shift?"

"You'll love this, I'm sure." Radimir's tail lashed. "But Levine's left you standing orders to keep hovering over the bodies. She's had someone doing that since the day that one died on you, so this isn't special treatment. Except it is special treatment, because unless they conferred my psychology degree on me yesterday, I'd say she's hoping that you're going to find some magical fix for this that everyone else is missing because they don't read minds."

"It's hard to blame her when reading minds is the only thing we've got left," Jiron muttered. At Radimir's hiss, he held up his hands. "Sorry. I'm just . . ."

"Exhausted," Radimir said. "Like the rest of us." He sighed.

"But surely the police," Jahir said. "Know the names of these victims, and can now speak to their families, their friends. That is how it's done, isn't it?"

"Sure. But that's assuming they're turning anything up, which they're not, yet. So until then . . ."

God and Lady only knew what Vasiht'h would say when he discovered Jahir had been put on death watch again. The thought made him say, "Jiron-alet?"

"Yes?"

"When I applied, I believe I did not give any—" Next of kin sounded dire, and a little too formal for the Alliance. What was the proper term? Ah. "Emergency contact names."

"That's right." The human eyed him and then his expression relaxed. "Oh, let me guess. That fierce bodyguard of yours that showed up, right?"

"Ah?"

Radimir was chuckling. "Oh yes. The one who dented the doors on the way in. Torqued all the ER intake people the hells off."

"Gave hospital security a few strokes too." Jiron smirked, then tried to rub the expression off his face. "God, only good part of the day. So, is that your emergency contact?"

Somewhat bemused, Jahir replied, "Yes, please. Vasiht'h. He is staying with me."

"He sure is, because I can't imagine him suffering anything else," Jiron said. "Is he always that ferocious?"

Jahir thought of claws inching from dark toes and how brown eyes could simmer with rage. Somehow he thought the incidents that had inspired Vasiht'h's wrath on Seersana would be kindling in compare to the events that might do so here. "When need arises."

"Hopefully need won't arise again anytime soon, then," Jiron said.

"I don't know . . ." Radimir groped for a mug and refilled it from the coffee bottle. "The distraction would be nice."

Jiron said, a joke obviously old enough to be carrying the humor despite his lack of energy. "Harat-Shar."

Radimir answered, in much the same fashion, "Bones to skin."

"Yeah, yeah. Form observed." Jiron nodded to Jahir. "You ready?"

"As much as I am able."

"Then go. If triage gets busy, Paige and Rad and I will cover it."

Which left him again to his silent, ugly vigils, in five rooms now, rather than the nine that should have held them. Jahir had witnessed at close hand the failures of Alliance medicine, knew at heart that even science had its limits. It was easier to accept for these slack-faced adults than it had been in bright young Nieve, too young to have gone to ash in a Seersana wind. But there was a surreality to his residency narrowing to a stool in a room, listening to the low beeps and clicks of the machinery monitoring a body that could not respond to all the therapy he'd spent two years learning to employ. This was not how he'd imagined his xenotherapy residency playing out, and he found the way it reduced all the Alliance's diversity to this one state unnerving. He needed little evidence to know that death unified everyone, from the most alien to the most similar. What he wanted—what he needed—was the living brightness of this world outside his stagnant own. Being here, in these rooms, was a little too much like a reflection of the stasis he'd fled his homeworld to escape.

He kept the vigils anyway, because that was where duty had brought him.

"He what?"

Calling Sehvi hadn't been the best idea, given her tendency to overreaction. But Vasiht'h had desperately wanted to talk to someone about the week, and damn the Well-pushed call charges and the possible drama. He also hadn't felt like going out, and it seemed ridiculous to put his head back down when he had no reason to be so tired. Still, staring at her horrified face, he wasn't sure this was the alternative he should have embraced. A nap was sounding better and better. "Why are you looking at me like that?"

"Because I don't want the next call I get from Selnor to be informing me of your death!" she exclaimed. "Goddess on high, ariihir! You have no idea how deep the waters are you're diving in!"

"Oh, I have some notion," Vasiht'h said with a hint of asperity, "given that I watched my best friend almost die."

"And it didn't occur to you that he could take you with him?" she answered, silencing him. She lifted her data tablet and pointed at it. "I've been reading up on the mindline while you've been off experiencing it. And this period right now, the first few months after it forms? Are a big deal. And while I don't at all object to you pushing the mindline to the point that it guarantees you a lifetime of deep, psychic communion with someone you obviously already care about, I do care about the whole 'in the first few months it's much harder to disengage' part that suggests if your Eldritch lordling is going to get himself killed, you're going to get dragged after him!"

Vasiht'h stared at her, his ears sagging.

"Didn't think of that, did you," she said, fur bristling.

"I didn't know," he said meekly.

"You didn't bother to learn," she said. And then threw up her hands. "Oh, hells. It's not like you needed to know. If the two of you were living a normal life it wouldn't matter. I just did the reading because I was curious and I wanted to be able to help, and now you call me and tell me you felt him vanishing into nothingness and . . ." She shuddered. "Now it feels far too real. And much too significant." She pointed at him abruptly, her finger occluding part of the viseo. "This is far too much stress for me!"

"It hasn't been all that fun for me either," Vasiht'h said.

"No . . ." She deflated. "No, it hasn't, has it. Just . . . don't do any more death-defying tricks, all right?"

"Trust me, it's the last plan on my list." He smiled weakly. "So, you really did read about the mindline? For me?"

"Yep." She settled back down again. "It says the first half year or so sets the character for the bond. Basically controls how deep it's likely to get."

"And this is something you control by . . ."

"I'm not sure you control it, really," Sehvi said. "At least, not consciously. The books say you can make the attempt, but it's more about how open you are to it."

"There are good parts of it, worth being open to," Vasiht'h said.

She canted her head. "And the bad parts?"

"Those too," Vasiht'h said, quieter. "Because it feels easier not to be alone?"

"Even when your partner's dying?"

He looked away, all the fur on his spine standing on end. Then met her eyes and said, "But he didn't. And all that's in other hands now." He managed a lopsided smile. "Because really, what are the chances that the fate of the known universe could rest on the shoulders of two student xenotherapists?"

She chuckled. "When you put it that way. But then, it's not the known universe, right? Just a handful of people in a hospital in Heliocentrus."

Vasiht'h glared at her. "Don't give the Goddess ideas."

"She doesn't need any," Sehvi said. "She already has them all."

Jahir didn't need to be told the name of the woman who entered one of the rooms while he was waiting alongside the patient. She was Harat-Shariin, some sort of pard like Radimir but golden-hued rather than gray, with short brown hair tied down with a handkerchief and the scrubs worn by personnel in operating rooms. She could have been a healer-assist or anesthesiologist or any number of people, but he knew better.

"It was not your fault," he said.

From her start she hadn't noticed him sitting beside the bed—or more likely, she'd taken him for a family member, no doubt having seen many similar scenes in a career that had lasted long enough for her to become one of the best in her field. Her eyes narrowed as she considered him. But if she found him worthy of commentary she kept it to herself, and said instead, "I don't have the first rhacking clue how to fix these people."

From her such an admission was probably rare. He treated it accordingly. "I've been told they are not presenting with symptoms of any known drug."

"That's a radical understatement." She folded her arms. "Whatever the hell it is, it bonds to every cell it touches and then

... what it does, no one knows. Except that when I try to remove it, it explodes like an angels-damned grenade and takes everything down with it. If I try to pussyfoot around it, I have until it decides to explode on its own, and once it detonates it's game over again. I have machines that can let me reach into someone's head and remove cells one by one, and all it gives me is a ringside seat to the inevitable meltdown when it fails." Her lips pulled back from her teeth, revealing carnassial fangs. "I was six hours into the last operation when the patient died. Six hours. I thought that one was going to pull through."

He waited, and was rewarded as she continued, "I'm the angels-damned best in the entire sector. And these people are dying on my watch. Under my fingers. And no one knows the hell what's wrong with them and it's rhacking me off."

So many things he could say, and yet what he did was, "It does me as well."

That snapped her out of her monologue with a sharp, surprised bark of laughter. "Does it?" She raked him with another of those looks: not the kind he associated with Harat-Shar, but a surgeon's assessment. "How long you been on world? Mediger's, yes?"

"Nearly four weeks, and yes. It is so obvious, I assume."

"To anyone with a brain." She paused, her ears sweeping back, and scowled at the patient. "You're the one who figured out what we were facing."

"Yes."

"No doubt any words of wisdom you might have conjured up, you would already have shared. You're ... what, xenopsych?" She snorted. "Hell of a thing, having a half-crippled esper shrink fall over the truth in a hospital full of people who should have seen it first."

"It has occurred to me as unlikely."

She laughed. "Humble. Didn't expect that. So, tell me truly, doc." A smile, hiding too much anger and anguish to fully use her mouth. "What do you think?"

"I think that I would very much not like to feel another one of these people die," Jahir murmured.

"You and me both." And then she paused. "Felt it, did you."

Jahir threaded his fingers together in his lap. "Intimately."

She was staring at him now, with that clinical gaze. "What was it like?"

Revisiting the impressions was not something he enjoyed doing, but because they were both fumbling toward the empty holes where the answers were supposed to be, he replied. "Like feeling everything you thought made sense . . . lose cohesion."

"Same for all the patients you touched?"

He looked at her sharply.

"Well?" She cocked a brow.

He forced himself to step back and examine the sensations . . . and then he compared them to what he'd felt when Nieve had died in his arms. But Nieve's mind had fallen out from beneath her when her body failed, and though her thoughts had scattered, the last few of them had carried a sense of her personality, her self. Neither of the two who'd died on Selnor had given him that, even when he'd received fragments of their memories. Memories alone did not convey a soul. Did neurons? God and Lady knew.

"There is something, isn't there," she said. "Tell me."

"I was just noticing," Jahir said, piecing the impressions together, "that . . . there was chaos on both occasions. A . . . shredding of the mind."

"Yes." She drew the word out, rubbing her nose with a finger as she stared at the readings on the halo-arch. "I can see that."

"Does it help you?" he asked.

"I don't know. But I'll take anything." She held up a hand. "No, don't talk. You're about to try to psychoanalyze me, or palliate my pain at having failed. Don't bother. I know I'm upset. I know why I'm upset. I don't need a fancy rare breed therapist fresh off the shuttle explaining it to me. I'll work through it in my own rhacking time."

"Will you?"

She stopped, eyes fixing on him. He held her gaze and lifted his brows, and drew from her an unwilling chuckle.

"All right," she said huskily. "Maybe I won't. But it's not your job right now to heal my pain, Long and Tall. Understood? We have jobs to do."

"So we do," he said and stood. He was due to move to the next patient anyway. And he was turning when he felt the first sparks, like the warning of nerve pain pricking up the pathways. He halted immediately and reached for the patient's wrist, knowing full well he shouldn't, and yet: he refused. Not this time. This time, when the cacophony came, he was full: full of the sea stretching to the horizon and the cry of kites and the joy of the children in his arms, bursting with the rapture of new experiences, spilling over with the strength of them, and this was the order he imposed on the chaos the mind tried to devolve into. No more noise, but music! No more blinding lights, but a soothing nightfall, pierced by the gemmed veil of stars and city lights. No more racing, screaming, flailing, no more no-sense, but sense and a heart beating, one note to the next, one breath to the next.

No, he told the unmaking force. He exerted himself on it, and used every ounce of his strength. *No. NOT THIS TIME.*

The last thing he heard before sliding to the ground was the scream of the halo arch's alarm switching off, and the resumption of its soft chimes and clicks.

CHAPTER 16

"**T**HIS TIME I CALLED HIM for you." Jiron's voice, sounding tinny and out of focus, but slowly swimming back into tune. "Not that it mattered, because he was on our doorstep by the time it went through."

Jahir blinked past crusted lashes and tried to sit up.

"Don't," Vasiht'h said just before the world began to spin. Jahir clutched at the edge of . . . a chair? No, he was on an unused bed in a dark room. Not only that, but there was a halo-arch above him; any further movement upward was going to be repelled by its force field.

"I'd say you have another ten minutes, maybe twenty to get yourself together before the entire organizational chart falls on you," Jiron continued. The mindline's hissing worry and warm support made the words seem distant, as if they were floating on water. "Pretty sure the only reason it's taken this long is because . . . well, you're in a bed. I've got Radimir over there watching the corner though, because I think you're about to have visitors. A lot of visitors."

"Why—"

"Because," Jiron said, and there was wonder and tension in his voice. "You kept one of the unresponsives from dying."

Silence. From everyone.

The human pushed himself upright. "I'll be right outside. When you hear noise, that's when your reprieve's over. And make sure you tell them the cost of what they'll be asking." A strange note in his voice then, but emphatic.

"Understood," Jahir managed, though he was puzzled, and then they were alone.

"So. What exactly was it you were doing?"

The mindline conveyed reluctance, and the pressure Vasiht'h had pushed through to speak without terror or anger: as if he was buried alive and suffocating, pressing against the earth. Jahir shuddered. "I didn't intend anything. But when he started dying, I . . . I refused. I refused it." He sought the Glaseah in the dark and found his gaze. "It was disorder and cruelty and a heinous way to go to one's death, so I . . . imposed myself on the disorder, and made it sensical again."

This silence was far more threatening. There were demons hiding in its darkness. Jahir groped through the dark until he found Vasiht'h's shoulder, and the touch yawed a world open around him, one where an aching void stood in for him because he was gone. His wordless apology spilled into that hole and strove to fill it, and failed for so long he thought the mindline would dump him back into his own head, alone . . . and then Vasiht'h covered his fingers with a hand.

"When I showed up, they'd hauled you onto this bed because you were having an arrhythmia." He cleared his throat. "A potentially fatal one."

"A what?" He sought some memory of this, had only a hazy one of tasting his pulse in his mouth, a flutter.

"I'm not sure how it worked," Vasiht'h said, and though his voice remained calm his hand on Jahir's was trembling. "Maybe it was that you overdid it physically and that triggered the episode because your body's already under too much strain. Or maybe some of this . . . disorder . . . devolved onto you through the mind link you had with the patient. Either way . . ." He trailed off again, and this time Jahir caught a flash of limbs flailing, the wail of a halo arch, the tense back-and-forth of Jiron and someone else. He swallowed.

"You need to do some serious thinking," Vasiht'h continued after a moment. "About the wisdom of throwing yourself into situations where you have no data on the dangers involved."

"That . . . is gently said," Jahir answered, quiet. "Since what I believe you should be telling me is 'Arii, what the hell did you think you were doing.'"

Vasiht'h met his eyes, and in them there was such grief. "Is that what I should be telling you or what I want to be?"

"Both?"

"Jahir—"

"Vasiht'h," he said. "I vow this to you now—I will not do these things again without you."

"That's making the assumption you're going to do them again!"

"I am making the promise I know I can keep," he said, with more urgency, for he heard voices in the corridor. "I am hoping I will be less involved, but I can't guarantee it. What I can is that I will no longer do it without help. If you'll help me."

"And if I say no?" Vasiht'h asked, and then they were no longer alone.

"Well," Grace Levine said, leaning on the door. "What the hell are we going to do with you, Mister Jahir."

"I beg your pardon?" he asked as behind her the Harat-Shar surgeon, two healers-assist and one male Hinichi in street clothes crowded close.

"Saving a life by throwing yourself into ventricular fibrillation is a little dramatic, don't you think?" the Harat-Shar said, looking past Levine. "How did you do it? Can you do it again?"

Beside him, Vasiht'h made a noise somewhere between growl and despair.

Levine cleared her throat. "I believe you know of Healer-surgeon Septima."

"We have met."

"This is Marron Celvef. He's an investigator with the local

police department."

The Hinichi inclined his head.

"And all of these people are necessary right now why?" Vasiht'h interrupted. "Given that it's only been maybe an hour since my partner collapsed and nearly died?"

"No one with the sense to have a VF in a hospital emergency room nearly dies," Septima interrupted. "He was fine the moment they put them under the halo-arch. This isn't some backwater frontier or bygone century." She pushed past Levine into the room. "So can you do it again? Because if you can keep some of these patients from collapsing I might have more time to do the surgery that fixes them."

"And if there are memories you might have of anything relevant to where these people might be buying these drugs. . . ."

Jahir looked at the Hinichi, who shrugged, a small motion of his shoulders. "Doctor Levine explained how you'd derived the first information. I don't pretend to understand it, but I'm willing to be educated."

"Later," Septima said. "We've got five people here who need your help now."

Through the mindline, Jahir could feel how badly Vasiht'h wanted to say 'no' for him. To urge him to say no, either in words or through the link they shared. But the Glaseah was sitting on that impulse with a discipline that felt like pain, like a heart racing to bursting and a diaphragm stitched through with burning from struggling to breathe.

"I don't know," he said, carefully. "How safe this is for me."

"Obviously not safe at all," Radimir said from behind the crowd. "Can I say something here?"

"You're going to anyway," Septima observed, dry.

The other Harat-Shar put his ears back. But he spoke. "It's obvious that by the time these people get to this stage, they're not coming back. I can see wasting Septima's time on finding a miraculous solution, but siccing the resident esper on them in the hopes of . . . what? Finding some clue? Why not talk to the bleeding people who are still alive? Why aren't you finding them?" He looked at the Hinichi, who flipped his ears back but remained composed. "Save the criminal investigation for the professionals who know how to do it. And the surgery to people who like it. This isn't our field. We're xenopsych. We deal with people who are awake!"

The comet that streaked through the mindline was Vasiht'h's, not his, and it shimmered against the words: *people who are awake, people who are awake*

/*I've done work with people who sleep. We both have.*/

Jahir glanced at him, met his eyes. /*You have changed your mind.*/

/*No,*/ Vasiht'h said, his words throwing off cold shadows and shivers. /*Yes. No. Just . . . we've done similar things before.*/

/*Sleeping people are not people in comas.*/

A silence between them, too taut, filled with all the things they were thinking and unable to articulate.

"I won't do anything else without Vasiht'h," Jahir said aloud, and wasn't sure if the keen in the mindline then was born of pain or the fierceness of a Pyrrhic triumph.

Levine eyed him. "This is your . . . friend? Do you have any credentials?"

The bristling of Vasiht'h's fur had a texture in the mindline, like the static electricity in the air before a storm. "I'm also a xenopsych student. We've worked together before."

"Two of you?" Radimir sounded interested. "Same specialty?"

"I was research before I went clinical," Vasiht'h said. "I studied the effects of dreams on mental states—"

"All of which is very fascinating but doesn't solve my problem, which happens to be these dying people's problem," Septima said.

"We will help you," Vasiht'h said. "But right now, all of you have to leave."

It was almost amusing, how complete the confusion in the room became.

"Excuse me?" Levine said.

"All of you," Vasiht'h repeated. "Out of here. Until the halo-arch releases him and he can sit up he's not doing another

Goddess-blessed thing. So go away."

Jahir added, quieter, "I would appreciate the time to recuperate. I can hardly help anyone when I cannot even sit up."

"First smart thing anyone's said in the past ten minutes," Jiron muttered. Louder, "You heard the Glaseah. Out."

———— ⬡ ————

Once they'd trooped out, Vasiht'h backed away from the bed and sat heavily, rubbing his face. "We need a plan."

Cautious optimism, like too much rain on tender flowers that bent beneath the strain. It was a pretty image, but it reminded Vasiht'h too much of his roommate's nightmares of gardens, back when they'd been on Seersana. Which seemed very long ago right now. "A plan?"

"Yes," Vasiht'h said. "If we're going to do this, we need a plan. One that gives us a way to back out gracefully before something else happens."

He waited, hoping for something from Jahir because Aksivaht'h knew he didn't have any thoughts. Unfortunately, if the empty weight hanging between them was any indication, the Eldritch was as short on ideas as he was. They met one another's eyes and acknowledged the implication of that quiet, and Vasiht'h looked away with a sigh.

"Arii," Jahir said. "You know it is not my intention to perish here."

"Are you sure?" Vasiht'h asked with asperity. And then held up his hands, embarrassed. "I'm sorry. I didn't mean to snap at you. I'm just . . . I don't . . . these past two days. . . ."

"I know," Jahir said, solemn.

It was that solemnity that pierced Vasiht'h's desperate fears. "You meant it," he said slowly. "About the promise."

"I did."

"Because I . . . I've never heard you promise anything unless you were going to do it," Vasiht'h continued, and frowned, searching the past two years of their friendship. "Come to think of it, I don't know if I can count on my hands the number of times you've ever said anything that could be construed as a promise."

Strange that he could feel the heat of someone else's blush in his own skin. Jahir cleared his throat and said, "It isn't done. Or shouldn't be, unless one is willing to make good on one's word."

"Then if I make you promise to back out if things get too bad. . . ."

"Without defining the conditions that meet that criterion, I am not sure you would be content with the words."

"Like dealing with a fairy king, is that what you're saying?" Vasiht'h asked, and started laughing at the look on Jahir's face. The taste in the mindline was even funnier: lemonade with not enough sugar.

"You have those stories?" Jahir asked.

"No, but the humans do, and we're all descendants," Vasiht'h said, grinning. He sobered when he remembered what they were joking about. "By my standards, the conditions are already bad enough."

"Then perhaps we should base the decision on aught else. Like, perhaps, success?"

"And if there is no success?" Vasiht'h asked. "What if we never figure out how to heal these people? What if there's no healing them? People die. Drugs certainly kill them. Even legal ones, given in the wrong combinations."

"Success might also be our helping the authorities find the purveyor of these drugs."

"We're not detectives, arii," Vasiht'h said, ears flattening. "Goddess, you don't even know how a society like this works, most of the time. You're a true-alien here." A twinge in the mindline—disagreement? He rode over it anyway. "Or are you saying we should be plucking clues out of their heads and handing them over?"

"We can," Jahir said, guarded.

"And we might not," Vasiht'h said. "So then, how do we define success? When you've had enough?" The pregnant silence then made him lean back. He prodded it gently with mental fingers and then pointed the physical one at the man lying on the bed, starting to object . . .

. . . and then he stopped. Because it really was the only answer. The only one he knew Jahir would accept, and so the only one he could. He folded his arms, hugging himself, and hung his head. Of all the jobs in the world the Goddess could have picked for him, the one where he had to sit back and let his best friend in all the worlds make such tremendous, potentially lethal mistakes and find his own way was . . .

. . . what he'd signed up for. Wasn't it?

Jahir himself had told him the opinions of good friends could help someone shape a decision. But that didn't give him the right to make that decision. Did it? Or did the mindline change all those things? Did that make it more like being married? A partnership implied that you looked out for one another. But his parents would be the first to tell him that marriage didn't mean you got to force your partner to do things your way. A series of compromises, they'd say. But they'd never given him any guidance on compromising when it was a matter of life or death.

—which led him to Sehvi, who was studying reproductive medicine on Tam-ley. The Tam-illee—and many other races of the Alliance—made such life or death decisions together all the time, when they chose to have children.

"You're asking a lot of me," is what he finally said.

"I think I know that I do," Jahir said, picking his words so carefully Vasiht'h could sense his concentration through the mindline. And then added, "Two months. Less now."

"Still?" Vasiht'h asked, looking up at him.

"As a final deadline," Jahir said. "There is not enough balance in this path, arii. I don't even know if I am beneath this halo-arch because my body gave way or my mind did. As I said, I am not planning to die here, with so much yet to learn."

Vasiht'h held that vow in his mind, and it was sharp as a sword, an image he knew had not come from his life experience. "Two months," he said finally. "Or until you've had enough."

"Yes."

"All right." He wouldn't say that he could live with it when he was only barely resigned to it, but he could give his friend that much.

"Go have some tea, arii. You're thirsty."

"I am?" He paused, wings flexing, and grimaced. "I am. How did you pick that out of all the rest of the things in my head?"

"I don't know?" A tendril of curiosity unfurling, tender as a new leaf and as eager for sunlight. "But your mouth is dry, and it is bothering you."

"It is." Vasiht'h eyed him. "Don't move."

"The halo-arch would not permit it anyway."

"Don't move your thoughts either. No reaching past this room for the minds of unconscious patients."

Jahir managed a laugh. "I don't think I could even do so when healthy. As I am now . . ."

Vasiht'h folded his arms.

"I promise," the Eldritch finished, and there was a sparkle in the mindline. Light on water, bright as mirth against the dark of what they'd been discussing.

"Good," Vasiht'h said. "I'll be right back."

Down the hall he found a break room with a coffee pot sitting alongside a bottle of coffee branded with the café's moniker. He ignored them both and searched the drawers until he found tea packets and poured himself a cup of boiling water in a mug with Mercy's dove and sigil. Settling in a corner, he looked out on the halls and tried to imagine working someplace like this every day, day after day. Tried to imagine Jahir doing it, and could just barely. But it didn't seem right to him, and he wondered if that was his own wishful thinking or one of Her suggestions. He was still wondering when the human who'd been helpful turned up at the door and paused at the sight of him.

"Jahir's friend," he said.

"Vasiht'h." He held out a hand palm up. "I got sent to take a break."

The human snorted, covered Vasiht'h's palm with his. "He's good at knowing when other people need them, at least. Griffin Jiron. Residency supervisor."

"He's mentioned you." Vasiht'h blew the steam off his tea. "You should find someone with the authority to issue me a pass, because Jahir's not coming to work without me anymore."

Jiron drew a chair out from one of the tables and sat, crossing his legs and resting his hands loosely on his calf. "This have something to do with how you know when he's about to fall over?"

"We have an esper's bond," Vasiht'h said. "Glaseah call it a mindline."

"That's how you keep pulling him back," Jiron said, quiet.

Vasiht'h nodded.

"Since I'm not eager to add 'dead resident' to my list of experiences at Mercy, I'll be sure you get your pass." He cocked his head. "How'd a Glaseah end up with a mindline with an Eldritch? If you don't mind my asking. That sounds like quite a story."

"I guess it is." Vasiht'h smiled a little. "I think the real story is 'how did an Eldritch end up off world.' You've never seen one, have you?"

"Not until your friend walked in the door to the conference room."

Vasiht'h nodded. "I think that's as much answer as I can give you. He's the rare event. Everything else just . . . accretes around him. Like gas around a star."

The human considered that for a long moment, then said, "Does gas accrete around stars?"

"Doesn't it? I thought that's how stars formed?"

"I don't know," Jiron admitted. "My astrophysics is a little rusty."

Vasiht'h laughed. "And mine was never very good in the first place." He flexed his hands on his mug. "Alet, thank you. For not giving us trouble about this. And for watching out for him."

"My job," Jiron said. "But you're welcome." He stood, stretching one arm against his chest. "Speaking of job . . ."

Vasiht'h saluted him with the mug.

⸎

"Do you mind if I come in?"

"As long as you do not mind that I don't rise," Jahir replied to the silhouette of the Hinichi investigator.

"No," Celvef said. "You've been through quite enough. And I'm not going to bother you with too many questions."

"Then by all means."

Did Vasiht'h know he was entertaining guests while he was supposed to be recuperating, Jahir had no doubt he would catch a lecture—deservedly so. But he did not think Celvef was going to tax him; the man carried himself with quiet confidence, and there was no eagerness in his mannerism, not in speech, nor in motion. He sat on the chair near the wall and said, "Doctor Levine told me you were responsible for discovering this was an illegal drug. From memories you saw in the minds of the victims?"

How one word could transform an entire situation. Not patients: victims. Jahir said, "That's right. Though it was my friend who understood what I was looking at. I have . . . very little experience with the Alliance."

The Hinichi nodded. "You won't mind if I ask you a few questions? They're going to sound strange, and it's fine if you don't remember clearly; I'd rather you admitted to not knowing than have you come up with something you're not sure of."

"Go ahead?" Jahir asked, mystified.

Celvef took out a data tablet. "This image you saw of the sale being made. What time of day was it?"

"It was dark, but the light source was yellow, and intense, and small."

The Hinichi glanced at him, hand still poised over the tablet. "Sure of that, are you."

"Yes," Jahir said, puzzled that he was. "It was a very vivid picture." He watched the man's hands scribing the words and said, "You are asking in the hopes of identifying where and when this happened."

"Exactly."

Jahir nodded. "Continue then. I shall answer as best I may."

Between them, they gathered much more from that single

memory than Jahir thought possible, though he had to demur on some of the responses. When they were done, the Hinichi leaned back. "Thank you. I know that doesn't seem like it will lead anywhere, but you never know where a clue will take you."

"Is there aught else I might do?" Jahir asked, though he really didn't want to hear a repetition of Levine's command that he hover over the beds of the dying.

Celvef shook his head. "No. Though if you catch anything else, I'd be glad to hear about it. We're going to find these people, alet. Your help might help, but even without it . . . we'll find them." He smiled faintly. "This isn't the first time we've had illegal drugs running through the port. If someone's going to get them on-planet, this is where they try it."

"I would think somewhere lower profile would be more prudent?"

"Somewhere lower profile won't have enough traffic to hide in," Celvef said. He tucked his data tablet back in his pocket. "Heliocentrus is huge, alet. There are a lot of ways to get lost in a port this size. And their only other choice is Terracentrus, and running drugs under Fleet's nose is just asking for trouble. This is where most of the commercial traffic comes, so this is where the thieves come, too." His smile was a predator's smile, and recalled the wolves from which some part of his DNA had been mined. "They don't learn, though. Heliocentrus's police department has one of the best drug trafficking groups in the Core. We'll find them, alet. And we'll find this product they're running." He stood. "Thank you for your time. Can I send you my call-code? In case you 'hear' anything else."

"Of course."

The Hinichi tipped him a salute and left.

Some time later, the halo-arch sang a rising arpeggio and withdrew, leaving him to gingerly push himself upright. The medical bracelet tinkled as it heaped itself on his hand and he stared at it while assessing his own condition and finding it woeful. His entire body ached; his ribcage in particular felt oddly uncertain, as if he wasn't sure whether he could draw in a full breath and was surprised that he could. And he had a dry mouth, a headache, and felt altogether too weak to walk out of the hospital, which is what he dearly wanted to do.

When Vasiht'h arrived bearing a cup of tea, Jahir said, "Tell me no one is hovering outside, waiting to ambush me?"

"You're safe," Vasiht'h said, handing him up the cup. "Though I can't guarantee that until we get out of here. Radimir told me you're off duty now, so what say we flee?"

"I would very much like that, though I may have to do so . . . rather slowly."

Vasiht'h snorted. "That's fine. And if anyone tries to stop you, they can explain themselves to me." He glanced at the halo-arch's readings. "Jiron told me you could go as long as all those tell-tales were green, and they are, and as long as you don't leave the hospital grounds. In case you have a relapse."

"That's fine," Jahir said. "The place I'd like to go is on the grounds."

"Not home?" Vasiht'h asked, canting his head.

Jahir sipped the tea, cautious of its heat, grateful for it. "No. But not far."

—⊗⊗⊗—

"This is Paga," Jahir said an hour later.

Extricating themselves from Mercy had taken more time than Vasiht'h had liked; even knowing they weren't going far, and that the halo-arch was reporting nothing that needed surveillance, the hospital had been nervous about discharging the Eldritch after he'd required serious intervention. But they'd released him before any of his coworkers could chase him down, and that had been all Vasiht'h had wanted. The trek to the gymnasium had piqued his curiosity, but he hadn't asked; he could sense his partner's fatigue through the mindline, a cold fog that had been burning clearer the closer they'd come to the facility. Now that they were here, there was no arguing with the relief Vasiht'h could taste as clearly as water after thirst.

The Naysha bobbing in the water was staring up at Vasiht'h

with interest. He returned the look as Jahir continued, "He is one of my physical therapists. Alet, is Aralyn in?"

Paga clapped, activating a holographic translation, and signed, /Off duty now. She works morning to afternoon shift./ Tapping the water lightly. /You look bad./

"I have had . . . a difficult day," Jahir said. "May I use one of the private pools?"

/Go on./

"Arii," Jahir said to him. "I shall be there, in that room. They monitor me . . . it is safe, I pledge you."

Another pledge, in less than a day. Goddess. Vasiht'h said, "I'll be here when you're done."

"Thank you." Words that sounded courteous aloud, but were accompanied by a fervor in the mindline. So much of his friend was like that, hiding under the surface. More water metaphors. Vasiht'h shook his head and sat by the pool's edge.

Paga drifted closer and ducked his head to get close enough to see Vasiht'h's face. Peering, he signed, /So here is the heart./

"Ah?"

/The heart. His. Yes? When you came. That was when he started lightening./

It had been a while since Vasiht'h had worked with anyone in sign, but he recalled the limitations of the translation and wished he'd been more diligent about gaining the skill. But then, he lacked Jahir's constraints. He offered the Naysha his hand and said, "Do you want to talk this way? It might help."

The Naysha's enormous eyes focused on his palm. /An interesting experience. I have not had it./ He set his webbed hand in Vasiht'h's: the palm was slick, like the skin on a dolphin.

/And now what do I—/ The Naysha paused, then grinned, showing teeth. /I see./ Another pause, his eyes losing their focus. /Oh, and I do see. How strange it is! So many legs! Legs at all!/

Vasiht'h laughed. "All right," he said, cradling the alien's hand in his. "Go ahead. Tell me what you meant."

/This,/ Paga said, and the sense then was of a tether against a maelstrom.

"Anchor," Vasiht'h offered. "Is that what you meant?"

/It is. But do not feel it like a four-footed land-bound feels it. Feel it like I feel it./

Vasiht'h closed his eyes and sank into the communion. He'd grown up playing in and out of the minds of his siblings, accepting embraces from his parents that extended into his psyche. Now and then he'd brushed minds with strangers or friends, usually by accident; while he didn't have Jahir's contact sensitivity, touch did make it easier to hear stray thoughts or feelings from other people. But he hadn't tried reaching this deeply since . . . well, home. And more importantly, since before the mindline.

The mindline changed everything.

/Ah ha!/ Paga's interest, sharp as a hunter's. */So it is the same for you too. You anchor one another./*

And they did. Nothing in his childhood had prepared him for how different it was to touch other minds while bonded to someone else. He'd always felt grounded, when reaching mentally for others, as if it was nearly impossible for anyone to knock him off his feet. But that same groundedness, he discovered, had prevented him from being able to reach deeply into someone else.

Jahir had pulled him free from the ground; he felt as if he was floating, in orbit around someone else's spirit. Still safe, captured in someone's pull, but . . . free, too.

/Something new for you too, ah?/ Paga asked.

"I had no idea," Vasiht'h admitted, wide-eyed.

As if sensing his need to re-evaluate, the Naysha let go of his hand and finned backward, casual. */As it should be. Yes? With the right people./*

"Yes," Vasiht'h said. He drew in a long breath and said. "Yes. Now if I can get him through the next month and a half or so, maybe we'll have the leisure to explore some of those new things."

Paga straightened. */This is new to me? Why this time?/*

"Because he's promised me if he can't acclimate to Selnor by then, we're going."

/Good./

Vasiht'h looked up sharply.

Paga wheezed—laugh? Snort? Amusement, Vasiht'h thought. The Naysha slapped the water. /You think I think this world is good for him? I do physical therapy. He should not be here./

"The acclimatization regimen—"

A head-shake. Paga signed, /I tell you something. You watch the story. Long ago—/ Another of those wheezes. /—when I was new. Schooling. Yes? Looking for new experiences. Like you, like him. And I think: I am a made creature. Long ago, in the long ago. Some scientist made my kind. So I should go and meet true-aliens. Water aliens, like me. I went to the world of the Platies./

"Ah?" Vasiht'h leaned forward. "What was it like?"

/Amazing./ The Naysha paused, petting the surface of the water with his palms. Then his fingers flew, flicking droplets in his ardor. /That world. So amazing. I cannot tell you. You are not a water-dweller. Maybe if you touch me, I could try. Give you the memories, but it would not be the same. Even for me, they fade. They were too different. The water was like . . ./ Another long pause. /Like I would think a womb. Warm and dense. Full of life and data. It was . . . it was alive, a living thing. I understood then. How aliens could come to be. In water. Rather than to have been made, like the Naysha. But I could not stay there./

Vasiht'h had been so entranced by the description of the ocean that the final sentence jerked him upright. "Wait. What?"

/I could not stay./ Paga's hands became more deliberate, forming the words in the air as if shaping his own feelings: ambivalence. Regret. But a peace, that too. /It was too hard for me there. To breathe: that water was too thick. To swim, too. A great effort. It was a living sea . . . for someone else./

"Ah," Vasiht'h said, quieter. "Yes. I see."

Paga nodded, a very humanoid motion on a face that looked very alien. /Yes. You do. Your friend, though. Does not yet. So I do not say anything./

Vasiht'h grimaced. "It would be easier if we could take advice from people when we needed it, instead of having to wait for the wisdom to accept it . . . which usually doesn't come until after you've made the mistake."

Paga grinned, gape-mouthed. /Yes./

"Well," Vasiht'h said with a sigh. "All I can do is wait."

/And be what you are to him./

"That too." Vasiht'h wiggled his toes in the water, then unbuckled his saddlebags. "And I might as well enjoy myself while I do it."

/Enjoy your—ah!/

Naysha interjections looked like splashes, Vasiht'h saw. He grinned and shook himself a little, wiping the water from his eyes. "Thank Aksivaht'h your pool isn't too deep, since I don't float."

/No! You very much do not! You stay. I find you an inflatable./

Vasiht'h waited, swaying in the water. He hadn't been lying when he'd told Jahir that he liked swimming. And dipping his paws in the water had made him feel how grimy and tired he was. The temptation had been a little too much for him.

Paga returned, towing the long, noodle-shaped float behind him. /Here. Better./

"Much," Vasiht'h agreed, using it to get his shoulders comfortably above the water. He curled his forelegs a little and extended his wings, using them to help him stabilize. "Look at me! A regular fish, I am."

/Strangest fish I ever see!/

"Ha!" Vasiht'h said. "Maybe I am heavier and slower than you, but that just means I make a better splash." He shoved his wing toward the Naysha, who whooped and dove. A few seconds later, someone tweaked his tail. "Now you're asking for it," he said with a grin. "Watch yourself, merman. I might be as graceful as a rock, but once I get moving I'm hard to stop—"

/Save me from the swimming rock!/

"You have no idea how big a wave I can make . . ."

—⊗⊗⊗—

Jahir rested his head in his arm on the side of the private pool and attempted to let his thoughts settle. He'd needed the solitude, wanted desperately to put a barrier between himself and the events of the past few hours, between himself and an awareness of a frailty he'd never accepted fully until he'd woken up under a halo-arch. It was one thing to faint and wake to the sight of fretful coworkers and a panicked friend who insisted that his psychic communion with someone in her dying moments had nearly killed him. It was another to have physical evidence of how close he'd come. That this physical evidence made it clear how near to his physiological limitations he was operating, just by being here, was equally unwelcome.

There was too much noise in his head. So he went to the water, and beseeched it to take the noise away, and after a time—too long a time—it did. His thoughts eased, bled to silence, and left him floating there with a warm sense of presence: Vasiht'h's proximity, made manifest as if the Glaseah was close enough for Jahir to feel his body heat. That too, was a comfort. More of one than he'd anticipated. He hadn't expected regrets over his decision, but he had anticipated more discomfort, more anxiety.

But he had none. Choosing the mindline was the one decision he'd made since leaving home that he accepted with all the ease of a child accepting the love of his parents, as if it was birthright. He could rest here, as vulnerable in spirit as his body was, naked in the pool, and be completely at peace: someone was guarding his back.

The first effervescent bubble that bobbed up through the link tickled. He opened his eyes, brow furrowing a touch, and waited to see if the sensation would repeat: again. Another tickle. And then a flood of it, dancing, quick as laughter. Jahir lifted his head, evaluating the sensations, and when they did not ebb he rose, careful of his weakness, and dressed, and went out of the private room to see what was occasioning such a mysterious amusement.

. . . and found Vasiht'h in the pool, having a water fight with Paga. He wasn't sure what astonished him more, the unlikeliness of a Glaseah in water, or how mighty a splash Vasiht'h could scrape up with those wings he rarely unfolded. Paga had just vanished beneath one of them when he reached the edge of the pool; though his back was turned, Vasiht'h noticed him first through his incredulity. Within a few moments both of them were facing him with airs of contrition that the mindline informed him quite ably were less than genuine.

"Playing like children," he said.

"Maybe a little," Vasiht'h said, and amended, "Like Naysha children, anyway. Glaseahn children don't usually go swimming for fun."

Paga signed, /Naysha children don't play like this either. You do not make waves. You make tsunami!/

"It's a gift," Vasiht'h said with a grin and lifted his wings, waggling the thumb claws. Paga cowered in mock horror.

"Oh, enough!" Jahir said, and they stopped instantly. He finished: "At least, not until I join you!"

Paga paused. /You should not be pushing water. That is true exertion./

"Excellent," Jahir replied. "I shall have diplomatic immunity from your warring. Consider me a neutral party. I will float at the edges and make wry commentary."

/You ask for trouble!/

"He's right. It's all the same water, you know. Neutrality's not going to keep you from catching our backsplash." Vasiht'h grinned.

Jahir lifted his brows, just a touch. "I can take it."

Paga drummed the water, laughing. /So proud!/ he signed to Vasiht'h. /We teach him the error of such pride./

"I'm afraid we will," Vasiht'h replied. "Come on in, arii. But don't think we'll spare you just because you can't fight back."

"It is the furthest thing from my mind."

They were more careful of him than that, and he won himself a scolding once or twice for flicking water back at them. But he laughed, sometimes aloud and sometimes in the mindline, where he felt his amusement reciprocated.

/Enough!/ Paga said. /I surrender. I have water up my ears! I can't remember the last time that happened./ He grinned. /Stay as long as you like. But not . . ./ He pointed at Jahir, the webbing stretching fine between its tip and his folded thumb. /. . . for longer than another hour. You are more tired than you think. Sleep is what you need./

"An hour or less," Jahir repeated.

"I'll make sure he does it," Vasiht'h added.

Paga grinned, more naturally this time. /A good pairing. I approve. You needed this Naysha's approval. Yes?/ He laughed and gently splashed them. /Good night, aletsen./

Vasiht'h's smile washed through the mindline like a warm tisane. "I like him. You had good luck, getting him as part of your team."

"This from the person who just spent an hour trouncing him in his own habitat?"

The Glaseah laughed. "I take my victories where I can get them, right? Especially where no one else expects them." He waded over to where Jahir sat perched on the steps leading out of the pool. "Anyway, I see why this is refuge for you. You feel much calmer now."

"I did not expect to find one here." Jahir looked out over the pool, quiet now; most of the physical therapy took place during the day, and only the occasional person came by to take advantage of the facilities at night. He'd come to expect a few, but not many. "But I was deeply grateful for it. Particularly before you arrived."

"It still helps you," Vasiht'h said. He dragged himself up the steps and stood on the edge of the pool, water pouring off him in thick streams.

"It does. And . . . that does not look at all comfortable."

Vasiht'h chuckled. "It's fine. There'll be a Pad drier around here. I'll find it before we leave and be good as new." He settled his bulk carefully, stretching his paws in front of him. "Paga's right about you needing to get back soon."

"Yes," Jahir said. He watched the reflection of the stars from the ceiling's skylights compete with the artificial lighting in the room. "Vasiht'h . . . I saved a life."

A hesitation, beneath which he sensed a deep-rock faith, unshakable. "It was in the Goddess's mind to allow that life to be saved. But . . . yes. You were the instrument." Vasiht'h added, wry, "Don't let it go to your head."

Jahir hid his smile, knew Vasiht'h felt it anyway. "I won't."

"Mmm. Well, let's dry off and get home. We have a long day tomorrow."

"I pray we don't," Jahir said. "But I'm afraid you're right."

CHAPTER 17

$\mathcal{I}$T WAS WITH TREPIDATION that Jahir returned for his shift the following day, but the first news he received while standing beside Vasiht'h was welcome.

"No one died."

Radimir was nursing a cup of hot chocolate in the break room, his tail curled around the stool's leg. Jiron was supervising the shift change behind him, watching the outgoing debrief the incoming. Paige had brought another bottle from the cafe and was breaking the seal on the spigot. She'd poured him a cup and given it to him, handle-first, before he could speak at all. He felt Vasiht'h's amusement, warm and a little tired.

"Did anyone new come in?" Jahir asked, though he didn't want to know the answer; that troubled him.

"No," Radimir said. "So there's a small blessing. And they're going to try something new this time."

"What's that?" Vasiht'h asked, sitting and tucking his tail over his paws.

Radimir nodded toward Jahir. "They've been doing some analysis of the halo-arch data on the patients that died, and on the one that you brought back, and they think the key might be depressing the neural activity when it starts overreacting.

They're going to have a healer-assist team floating around with a tranquilizer. See if they can reproduce your unexpected success."

"It may do nothing more than put them back into their original state," Jahir said.

"That's better than having them die." Radimir's tail flicked once. "The longer we can keep them alive, the longer we've got to figure out how to fix them." He looked up. "You're still wanted on the watch, though. Until all this is over . . ."

Paige, glancing at him on her way out, said, "Never thought you'd miss triage, did you."

His startled thought—/was it so obvious?/ bought him an equally surprising response, for he hadn't expected one.

/You do a thing with your eyes. It's subtle, but if you're watching for it, it's there./

Jahir glanced down at Vasiht'h. /What thing is this?/

Amusement again, fleeting, like a glimpse of a deer in sun-dappled woods. /A little crinkle of the lower lid./

/Does everyone stare at my face thus?/

/If the only way to figure out what you're feeling requires it, I think the people who like you do try./

Jahir considered that, then offered, dry, /Professor Sheldan would be disappointed./

/That his whole 'you put people off by not emoting enough' speech was wrong?/ Vasiht'h snorted aloud. /My heart bleeds for Sheldan./

When Jahir returned his attention to Radimir, he found the Harat-Shar staring at them. "Alet?"

"What . . . was that?" Radimir said, one ear sagging and his expression baffled.

"What was what?" Jahir asked.

"It was like watching an entire conversation. But I didn't hear anything." Radimir's eyes were round. "Did that really happen, or have I gone deaf?" He touched the sagging ear hesitantly.

In the back of Jahir's mind, Vasiht'h said, /We're going to have to work on that./

He laughed, and tried to muffle it. "Well. I am for the patient watch, then."

"So you are. You might get descended upon by Levine or Septima. If they pressure you too much, find one of us, all right?"

"I hope it won't be necessary. But thank you."

"And drink that," Radimir added. "She's bringing it to fatten you up."

Jahir looked into the cup, suppressed a sigh. Dutifully, he took a sip and said, "I will be making rounds."

"We'll call you if we need you. You do the same."

Out in the corridor, Vasiht'h said, "I didn't mean to surprise you."

"If you did, it was only to delight me," Jahir replied. "Do not apologize for it." He checked his data tablet. "We begin the rounds. I confess it is not very exciting."

"Sitting in a room with nothing to do until someone starts dying?" Vasiht'h grimaced. "I don't know. That sounds like more excitement than I can handle." A jingle of bells, more cheerful than the words. A joke, then.

"This should be harder," Jahir murmured.

"What, the mindline?" Vasiht'h blew his forelock off his brow with the force of his sigh. "Yes. I know what you mean."

The first patient was male and human, like the initial victim. Sitting on the stool in the room, Jahir wondered how the Hinichi investigator was faring, and if they would resolve the case soon enough to prevent any more fatalities.

"So," Vasiht'h said. "When you feel my feelings, do they feel like tastes and colors and textures?"

"Yes?" Jahir frowned. "Sometimes I can't identify them, however."

"So it works off my memories as well as yours?" Vasiht'h frowned. "Not always though. Most of the time, I recognize the things it's keying off of."

"But not always." Jahir glanced at him. "Will that change over time?"

"I don't know." Rue, sour as an unripe berry. "Sehvi's been doing more reading on it than I have. I haven't even been doing the reading I should be!"

"You have been somewhat distracted," Jahir said, exaggerating the tone until he could feel the trickle of golden effervescence returning through the mindline.

"Not fair!" Vasiht'h said, grinning. "You're already using the thing to tailor your comments to my reactions."

"If the tool is there . . ." Jahir smiled, then allowed the good humor to deflate as he watched the readings on the halo-arch. They never fluctuated. "It is for my own sake as much as yours, arii."

"I can see that," Vasiht'h replied, subdued.

"Perhaps you might catch up on your reading? It would give you something to do."

"And what will you do while I read?" Skepticism, sharp like a butter knife: not enough to cut, but enough to warn of truer weapons.

"Listen to your thoughts while you study," Jahir said.

Vasiht'h's ears prick. "Will that work?"

"I don't know. But the experiment will occupy us both."

"Works for me," Vasiht'h said, and dug in his saddlebag for his data tablet.

The time that passed then had a peculiar quality, with Vasiht'h's mind supplying a murmur in the back of his, like a distant trickling stream of facts and conjectures and graphs and the halo-arch overlaying it with the anxiety of its never-changing read outs and soft chirps and hums. Jahir sat on the stool and tried not to become too involved in either, lest the juxtaposition grow too discomfiting.

An hour into their vigil, a Seersan healer-assist glanced in the room. "Doing all right?"

"So far, no change," Jahir reported.

She nodded. "I'm Evie. I'm the specialist who dialed in the drugs for the new treatment they want to try."

"Pleased to make your acquaintance."

She chuckled. "Still polite after sitting here for this long?"

"He's always polite," Vasiht'h said without looking up from his data tablet.

That spread a grin over her demi-muzzle. "All right. Well I hope not to be needed, but we'll see. If anything happens, the halo-arches will dispense the medication automatically, but an alert will go off and I'll show up to see how it goes and adjust anything as needed. Hopefully, we'll take care of the problem."

"That would be ideal," Jahir said.

"We should all live in an ideal universe," she agreed, one ear twitching outward to go with her crooked smile. "Of course if we did, they wouldn't need us healers." She touched the side of her fingers to her brow in casual salute. "Carry on, gentles."

After she left, Vasiht'h sighed and stood, stretching. "We should move on, shouldn't we? I could use the walk."

"Yes, let us."

Leaving the room caused him to be ambushed: by Paige, with an alarming-looking cup. "Here. Drink this."

"Should I ask," Jahir said, and though he kept from sounding glum aloud, Vasiht'h started chuckling beside him. */Do you want that you should drink this for me in my stead?/*

/Oh no. It's all yours./

"It's a nutrition shake. It's mostly dairy but I got it coffee-flavored. That should help, right?" She grinned at him.

"I'm sure," he said, accepting it. "Thank you."

She chortled and padded off, leaving him staring at the cup.

"Everyone's looking out for you," Vasiht'h said, amused. "But I think she in particular just wants to fatten you up."

"I think this residency may ruin me for milk forever," Jahir said, and sipped it. He kept from wrinkling his nose with difficulty.

"Oh, it can't be that bad," Vasiht'h said, laughing.

Did the mindline permit? It did. Jahir shoved the taste and texture of it to his partner, who covered his mouth.

"Yes? Not so bad?"

Vasiht'h stuck out his tongue, licked his teeth. "Consider it incentive to start eating real food more often."

Jahir sighed and forced as much of it down as he could as they walked to the next room.

———∞∞∞———

While he would not have called that shift pleasant, having Vasiht'h with him was . . . more than comforting. Comfortable. Right. As the hours passed, he found that he felt less tired, though his body remained taxed and he still couldn't so much as walk briskly without elevating his heart rate to a point where his head started aching. But it was more than bearable.

"Have you made headway on your studies?" he asked as they prepared to head to the break room to pass the evening's information to the night shift.

"More than I expected," Vasiht'h said. "Thank the Goddess. I don't want to think about what my major professor would do to me if I didn't keep up on the schoolwork after getting him to approve my excursion across the sector." He tucked his data tablet back into his saddlebag and straightened—and then frowned and took Jahir's wrist so unexpectedly Jahir stumbled. "Stop. Do you feel that?"

They both looked toward the patient they were about to leave.

A hissing spark rising. The nauseated anxious feel of an overstimulated body.

Jahir reached out to touch the victim's wrist. Behind him he heard Vasiht'h yelling for Evie . . . but he wanted to be there, with the patient, to savor another of the Alliance's miracles. His fingers grazed flesh, brought him the shooting streams of disconnected thoughts, jangled, tangled, rising in an inchoate mire—

Somewhere very distant, he heard something hiss, a series of chimes, and then an alarm go off. Beneath his mental fingers, the patient's mind imploded.

He hit the ground so fast he didn't know he'd been struck until his shoulder smashed against the floor tiles. The link breaking felt like skin ripped off a wound, but it was nothing to what had been falling on him with the force of a planet, inexorable and terrifying. Vasiht'h had two forelegs over his waist and his upper body twisted off him, one arm around his chest. Above them, the

Seersa and her team were frantically at work but it was too late.

He could not even turn his face into Vasiht'h's hold. The nearness of the danger had shocked the will out of him . . . and Vasiht'h also, if the singing silence in the mindline was any indication.

After a very long moment, Vasiht'h took first one leg, than the other, off him, but left the arm. He moved it down in response to Jahir's difficulty breathing, and together they remained there, on the ground, lying alongside one another until someone above them called the time of death.

Less than a minute, Jahir thought. Probably? His sense of time had distorted. He shivered.

Jiron appeared, crouching alongside them, ignoring the bustle behind them of healers and doctors and assists and morgue attendants. When Jahir could focus on him, the human said, "Don't need a halo-arch this time, looks like."

He had to swallow to become capable of speech. When had his mouth grown so dry? "No. A near thing, but no. And God and Lady, no more tranquilizers."

"Not that one, no," Jiron said. "We have more than one. They all work differently."

Hazy memories of his pharmaceutical class on Seersana ghosted through his mind, but he was too rattled to grasp any of them. "You mean to try them all until one of them works?"

"What other choice do we have?" Jiron said. "It's the only lead we've got on something that could help. Unless you count Eldritch esper medical students, and as far as we know we've only got one of those in the Alliance."

"Very probably," Jahir agreed. Beside him, Vasiht'h lifted a head that ached clear into his own. The mindline made him feel raw.

"I don't think that you should be doing this anymore," Jiron continued. "I'm going to talk to Levine about it. You've given us enough to go on, alet. I was only barely comfortable with you doing this when you first started. Now that it's clear that doing it endangers you every single time you try it . . ." He shook his head.

"I can't condone it."

Jahir began to protest that he had volunteered, but the words died in his mouth. The reluctance he felt was not Vasiht'h's, but his.

"No objections?" Jiron's brows lifted. "Good. I expected to fight you about it, but it looks like you have some sense after all."

Vasiht'h struggled upright, rubbing his head. His lower body was partially curled around Jahir's in a pose that kinked his spine, but neither of them wanted to lose the contact. They were both listing. Toward one another, at least, which made it less likely they would fall down.

"You should be off shift in a few minutes," Jiron said. "I'll give your rundown to the night shift so you can get home early. Any comments?"

Jahir had intended to respond, but the words that spilled from him came from seeming nowhere with an urgency that brooked no interference. "Wet. The drug. They call it wet."

Jiron's pupils dilated visibly, though he didn't move.

"Tell them," Jahir said.

⁘

On the way home, Vasiht'h muttered, "Now you've done it."

"Perhaps," he answered, tired. "But surely that will give them enough to have done with all this."

"I wouldn't count on that."

CHAPTER 18

VASIHT'H WOKE BEFORE Jahir the following day, and not by intention. Their near miss with the sedated patient had left him feeling hung over, a gross injustice since he'd hated the feeling so much the only time he'd over-indulged that he'd spent the rest of his life being careful never to do so again. But he'd rolled onto a side that had put the light from the window right in his eyes, and he'd been unable to shrug off the irritation.

A cup of tea failed to settle his stomach, though he drank it slowly, measuring each sip and willing it to soothe his frayed nerves. The silence of the apartment felt too complete with Jahir sleeping so deeply. What were they doing here? Paga was right. They were both in the wrong place. He picked up the Goddess effigy, which was no longer quite so crisply folded; Her legs were getting curled from being set on the table with a little too much force, and one of Her wings wouldn't tuck all the way in anymore. "We've got half of it right," he told Her. "We just have to get the other half."

She didn't answer, of course; She never answered directly. It was, he thought suddenly, because of what Paga had told him, and his own mother, and that he had told Professor Palland: advice, no matter how sage, was rarely well received when it was needed.

The Goddess was too wise to give Her children the answers, when answers were too easy to dismiss without the experience that made them seem like good ideas.

What Vasiht'h really wanted was his own mother. He checked the data tablet for the time on Anseahla, which wasn't too far off from Selnor's, at least at this point; Goddess knew how long that would last with each planet rotating differently and who knew what celestial mechanics applied. He'd never been very good with those things. Should he write her a letter? He was contemplating it when the door chime rang.

Startled, Vasiht'h looked at the door. Had he heard that? But who would come calling? Who even knew to come calling?

When the chime sounded again, he stood and said, hesitant, "Come in."

The door opened for a Hinichi in the plainclothes of an investigator, and at his back, a woman Vasiht'h didn't recognize in a uniform he did, from viseos and newscasts and more recently from his wanders through Starbase Veta.

"Pardon me, alet," the Hinichi said. "We were told this was where we could find Mercy's Eldritch resident?"

"You're in the right place," Vasiht'h said. "But he's sleeping. We had a rough time yesterday."

"You've had a rough time for a few days now, if reports are accurate," the Hinichi said. "When do you think he'll be awake? It's important."

Vasiht'h looked from him to the woman and did not need his classes in clinical assessment of body language to read just how important it was. "If you'll wait here, I can wake him up. He's about due anyway."

"That would be very helpful, thank you."

Vasiht'h nodded and let himself into the bedroom. His roommate was sleeping with his back to the room, blanket close around his shoulders and his hair spilled away from his neck. The morning sun left pale lavender shadows beneath the vertebrae visible there, and Vasiht'h thought he was overreacting to how deep those shadows were, and how prominent the bones.

Probably. He hated to wake Jahir, but he crept closer and sank into the mindline.

/Arii?/

A vague sense of assent, too clear for a dreaming mind.

Vasiht'h blew out a breath in relief. /It's important./

Jahir rolled his head back, just enough to look over his shoulder. His eyes were bloodshot, and Vasiht'h suppressed his wince, hoping it didn't echo through the line. "There are people here," he said. "The police . . . and Fleet."

The words stung him awake. Jahir tried to sit up and paused to let his spinning head stop moving before he managed. "Here?"

"I'm afraid so. I didn't want to wake you but . . ."

"No," Jahir said. "It's well. Please tell them I'll be out in a few moments."

"All right."

Left to himself, Jahir gripped the edge of the bed and waited for the strength to stand. He'd fallen asleep without undoing his braid or setting his ring back on his finger, and it hung loose over his knees, swinging with every labored breath. On impulse, he touched the smooth metal and then set it over his finger; even still on the chain, it slid easily into place. How much flesh had he lost? God and Lady. If the two individuals waiting in his living room would accelerate the ending of this particular episode of his life, he would gladly eschew another hour in bed to help them do so.

Ten minutes later, he stepped out of the bedroom to find Vasiht'h sitting across from their guests. There were coffee cups and a plate of scones sitting on the coffee table. The male was Celvef, from the hospital; the woman was unfamiliar to him, a light brown Karaka'an feline with darker brown hair wrapped around her head in a neat coronet that would have suited an Eldritch noblewoman. She had eyes the bright green of a sunlight seen through a new leaf, and they lifted to him the moment he appeared, and then both his guests were rising.

"Please," he said. "It's not necessary. I am Jahir; my room-mate said you were seeking me?"

"Yes," Celvef said. "And thank you for seeing us. This is Commander Parker, a colleague of mine from Terracentrus. She works in Fleet's illegal drug agency."

"Commander," Jahir said.

"Sit, please," Vasiht'h muttered.

Celvef nodded. "Yes, please. I know you have issues with the gravity here. We're not going to take up too much of your time, and we'd like you to be comfortable."

So he sat and rested his hands on his knees, waiting for the two of them to settle. When they had, the Karaka'an spoke first. "Marron told me you'd heard something new from the latest victim."

"That's right," he said. "The identity of the illegal drug in question."

"And you're sure of it," she said, eyes resting on his, forth-right and far too grave.

He tasted it on his mouth with the eagerness with which it had been said by the man who'd died. The anticipation and the dread and the terrible, terrible yearning. "Wet."

Celvef and Parker exchanged looks.

"You're absolutely certain," Parker said.

"He didn't make it up," Vasiht'h said, toying with the handle of his cup. "I don't think either of us could have come up with something like that."

"I'm certain." Jahir met her eyes. "You know this drug, though the people at Mercy do not."

"Yes," she said. She exhaled, eyes fluttering closed. "Yes. Hell, yes, and we all hoped it wouldn't ever get this far in."

Vasiht'h tilted his head, his curiosity peppery, almost painful to feel, too associated with grief and fear for them both. "This sounds like there's a history?"

"Not a long one, but a bad one," Parker said. She took up her coffee cup, brushing her thumb against its wall. "We only started seeing wet in the past half year on the frontier. It's an exotic; from what we've been able to learn, it's not something that can be synthesized in a lab yet, so it's very expensive. We were hoping between that and the need for materials that aren't as easy to find in-Core, we wouldn't see wet incursion here for at least another few years. But all the money's in the Core, so that was probably naive."

"It was a reasonable thing to hope for," Celvef said, quiet. "Just not maybe practical."

"No." Her voice was harder. "So the bad news is one of the most dangerous illegal drugs we know of has made it all the way to the capital, which means it's likely it's spreading elsewhere also. The good news—what little we can offer—is that because it can't be manufactured artificially it has to go through the port somehow to reach the city. Marron called us in to help with that."

"That is good news!" Vasiht'h said.

"Yes," Celvef said. "We're hoping with Fleet helping us with the crack-down outside the orbitals, we'll be able to catch this one coming in. But I'm afraid we haven't communicated the worst of it."

Jahir rested his hands on his knees and tried not to grip them. "Which is?"

"We say it's one of the most dangerous illegal drugs on the market," Parker said. "There's nothing else to compare to it at all." She put her coffee mug down again without having taken a sip. "Two doses."

"Two . . . doses?" Vasiht'h repeated carefully. "To . . . addiction?"

"To dying," Parker said, voice clipped. "That's all you get. Sometimes not even that. The first hit can kill you."

"I beg your pardon?" Jahir said when he could speak.

"Two doses?" Vasiht'h added, incredulity throwing sparks through the mindline. "*Two*? Why in the name of the Goddess would anyone take that risk? What could possibly be so good?"

"They say it feels like being god of the universe," Parker said. "And it excites the people who think they can beat the odds. They're not going to be one of the ones who die from it. The drug effect helps with that: the euphoria they feel, the sense of power, it makes them sure it can't happen to them. So they do it once, and then they do it again, and that's it. We haven't run into anyone so far who's made it to a third dose."

"But how does that even make sense?" Vasiht'h asked. "How can you make a business out of a product that kills your repeat buyers the first time they come back for more?"

Celvef cleared his throat. "Wet is very, very expensive."

Parker added, "We think that might be why they're chancing distribution here, right under our noses: to get it into the most advanced medical systems. Because if you all can find a cure for it . . ."

Was it possible to feel so much horror without becoming physically ill? The only thing that kept Jahir upright was Vasiht'h's steadying presence at his side, and his partner's reciprocal shock and rejection.

"Needless to say, a drug that kills within one or two doses presents a challenge for law enforcement," Celvef said, drawing them back. "Our deadline for investigation gets far tighter if the victims can go from committing the crime to being dead within a day, if they're willing to take more than one dose that close together. So if you 'hear' anything more . . ."

"Of course," Jahir said, managing the words past his nausea . . .managing the promise. Because that's what it was.

"We aren't expecting miracles," Parker added. "Marron's told me the toll this takes on you and we want to make it clear that we're not asking you to do anything beyond what you might already be doing. Fleet's good at this, aletsen. Whether you intervene or not, we're going to be done with this episode within a few weeks, particularly now that we know we're dealing with a wet outbreak. Since you're sure, we'll go ahead and post a bulletin to the medical staff in the city so they can keep an eye out for what few signs there are of someone who's used. You're not the only ones working on this. All right?"

"Yes," Jahir said.

"Good." She nodded. "And thank you both, aletsen. You gave

Marron the clue that got my people involved. That was vital."

"You're welcome."

She nodded and rose, and let herself out. Celvef stood and added, "That goes for me too. I needed to know how short my timelines were. Now that I do . . . well. That will make a big difference. Thank you, aletsen."

"Any time we might serve," Jahir said.

"I'll see you out," Vasiht'h added, though in their laughably small apartment that amounted to little more than a formality. Once they were alone, the Glaseah's hindquarters slid down until he was sitting, wings half splayed.

"I know," Jahir murmured. He leaned back into the chair, resting the back of his head on it; felt more than heard Vasiht'h come closer, sit next to him. The scrape of the plate against the table, though . . . that he heard, and couldn't believe his roommate had any appetite for the remainder of the delicacies set out for their guests.

"I don't," Vasiht'h said. "Have an appetite. These are for you."

"You cannot be serious."

The plate came to rest on his knees. He opened his eyes and looked down at the pastry in disbelief. "Arii—"

"Like it or not," Vasiht'h said, subdued, "you're still on Selnor, arii. You've got to eat." He sighed, rubbing his arms. "We did good. We should focus on that."

"We have done nothing to save those who came to us seeking succor."

"We can't help people who've willingly chosen to gamble with their lives. Not with odds stacked that hard against them. Maybe if we'd known them before they got involved with this stuff. But you heard the commander. Once they get this far, it's over for them."

"Alliance medicine—"

"Isn't magic," Vasiht'h finished. He grimaced. "Don't mistake me: I hope to Aksivaht'h Herself that someone comes up with some miracle cure that will reverse the catastrophic effects of their mistake. But it really is a catastrophic effect, and even if they do find that miracle it won't come in time for everyone." He nudged the plate with a finger. "Try to eat."

Jahir stared at the light winking off the red cabochon of some nameless berry. "I would prefer broth."

"Broth won't put weight on your frame," Vasiht'h said. "I'll make you a clear tea if you'll eat that scone."

He almost said no, but the mindline brought him a taste, like apples and brown wheat and sunlight. His mouth watered.

"I'll take that for a yes."

Jahir sighed and broke off a piece of the scone. "I am not looking forward to the next few days."

"Me neither," Vasiht'h said. "But we'll get through it together. And hopefully it'll be over soon."

CHAPTER 19

"TELL ME IT HAS BEEN a gentle day," Jahir said when they found Paige in the break room the following afternoon.

"For the values of gentle that apply around here," Paige answered affably. "The usual assortment of broken bones, heart issues, sudden allergic reactions, that sort of thing."

"But no new drug victims," Vasiht'h said.

"No. And none of them have died since the last one either," Paige said. "The whole staff's unhappy, though."

/Can't blame them for that./ Which Jahir received with the weight of a rain on his back. Backs. The images could be confusing when the mindline delivered them directly, rather than allowing him to re-interpret them to suit his own experience. He savored the sensation of having a second spine and then focused on the present.

"Seems like some kind of bulletin came through on the situation," Paige was continuing. She lifted a mug and a brow.

"Is it buttered?" Jahir asked, trying not to sound as pained as he felt.

She chuckled and opened the spigot. Dark brown coffee spilled into the cup, steam flaring around the stream. "You can take it clear if you're that tired of it."

"Yes, please."

"Right. You too, alet? I didn't catch your name."

"Vasiht'h. And yes, that would be welcome, thanks."

She passed them the mugs and said, "Anyway, ever since it came through everyone's been moody. Really, really moody. I'm guessing it wasn't good news."

"No," Jahir said. "I imagine not. Thank you, alet."

"It's not a problem." She glanced at Vasiht'h with lively interest. "A Glaseah and an Eldritch . . ."

"Now you've seen everything?" Vasiht'h offered, smiling.

"I hope not," she said. "But if I have, then this is a pretty fantastic finisher."

Vasiht'h canted his head, his curiosity curling through the mindline like a plume of incense smoke. "Fantastic? Really?"

"Oh, yes," Paige said, vehement. Her eyes sparkled. "So completely unlike, and yet you stand together and exude this rightness. I love it. Being around it is so relaxing." She tapped her fingertips on her own mug's wall and said, "Like . . . if such a good friendship could happen between you two, who couldn't it happen for? Makes you feel good about the universe."

Jahir glanced at Vasiht'h for confirmation of the bemusement in the mindline, then said, "I am glad we had the power to make someone smile today."

"This is awful now," Paige said. "But it will pass. You'll see how it works. You can't work in a setting like this and let it all get to you, so you don't." She pushed off her stool. "Good luck with the drug patients."

"Thank you," Jahir answered, but it was a reflex; every other part of him was resonating as if struck. He felt Vasiht'h's solemn attention before the words came, and this time the incense smoke felt like gravity.

/Not what you wanted to hear about what you'd have to become to stay here?/

"No," Jahir said aloud. He centered himself. "But we are here now. For now."

‐⊶⊷‐

Levine and Septima's arrivals were not a surprise. He and Vasiht'h were in the second room, keeping their vigil while the Glaseah studied and Jahir wondered how he had become a silent witness to death after having studied in a profession that should have involved life, and struggle, and a great deal of talk. When the two women's shadows fell into the room, he glanced toward the door.

/Oh, great./

That irritation felt like rolling over and falling off a pile of cushions. Jahir suppressed a very inappropriate amusement, particularly since his feeling on the matter was more apprehension than frustration, and said, "Aletsen. Is there aught we can do for you?"

"Actually, we were wondering if we could have a talk with you outside," Levine said. As Vasiht'h started to rise, she added, "Your friend's not necessary. We're not going to be doing any dramatic interventions." She offered him a lopsided smile. "Just talk."

/I don't like it./

/They may have legitimate reasons for their request./

Vasiht'h's arch tone was peppery in the mouth. /Like what?/

/Perhaps they wish to discuss issues that may have legal ramifications for the hospital? You are not an employee, technically./

Vasiht'h's eyes narrowed.

Jahir allowed some of his unhappiness to bleed into the mindline, something that forced him to face that it existed. That he didn't want to be here. /It would get me out of this room, arii./

The Glaseah's sigh would have been inaudible had he not heard the echo of it soft between their minds. Jahir turned to the women and said, "As you please."

He followed the women to one of the unused conference rooms, noting how much had changed since yesterday. Septima walked like someone embattled, shoulders tight and hunched forward, ears flattened backward and tail low, tip twitching. Levine had her hands in her coat pockets as if she needed a place to keep them to prevent any fidgeting, and she had her head bowed as she waved them into the room. Jahir sat on one side, and the two of them sat on the other, and they studied one another for several moments. The women looked haggard. He could only imagine what he looked like.

"We all got a memo this morning," Levine said.

"I had heard," Jahir offered when she seemed to be searching for words. "The investigator informed me of his intent."

"So you know a little of what we're fighting here."

"Somewhat."

"And you know that we hope this will be the last round of it," Levine said. "And that these patients are going to be the final few we get before Fleet and the Heliocentrus police shut these criminals down."

"Yes," he said, wondering now where this was leading, and why Septima was being so quiet when she hadn't seemed disposed to quiet before.

"What we wanted to say is . . ."

"I don't think I can fix this," Septima said abruptly. "And while I'd like you to help me try, your two keepers are adamant on the subject. They don't want you involved."

Levine cleared her throat, cheeks flushing, but added nothing. He looked at her, then at the Harat-Shar, and lifted his brows. "My two keepers being . . . Jiron and Radimir, presumably?"

"Yes. They think this is killing you. Which is a touch hyperbolic on their part, but I'm not expecting exacting medical standards out of psychologists."

Levine's mouth tightened . . . but she didn't object either.

"And you," he said to her, "would like me to try."

"I," she said, pausing to pick her words carefully, "think that your presence in their final moments might be the only comfort they get before they die. But I'm not going to force you to do anything you can't do."

Jahir glanced at Septima. "And helping you would entail . . . what, precisely?"

"Come into surgery with me," she urged. "Do whatever magic

trick it is you do to keep these people from dying. Maybe then I'll have enough time to figure out how to fix them."

How astonishing to be accused of magic by the Alliance after years of his finding their technological magical. Truly, perspective—and ignorance—colored everything. "And if I collapse?"

"You'll already be in an operating room," Septima said. "We'll catch you. We're not going to let anything happen to you."

. . . Of course not, because they needed him. His sole expertise. He remembered Radimir's speech about nothing being so urgent in their field that it needed a quickness, or presumably, a uniqueness.

The worst of it was that he found it hard not to say yes. The chance to find a solution to the physical reduction of these people? If he could have a hand in that . . .

In his mind, Vasiht'h seemed to whisper, *At the cost of your life?*

And that was a question he could not answer, save perhaps that some part of him, some very miniscule part of him, but a real part none the less, deeply resented having been forced into the position of answering it. He closed his eyes, threading his hands together on his lap, and began to speak.

The piercing tone of an alert interrupted them. Levine fumbled for her tablet. "Yes?"

"We've got nine incoming, and they're all your drug victims, Doctor."

He and Levine met eyes across the table, and then they were out the door. He came to an abrupt halt a few steps down the hall and braced himself against it with an elbow, panting. The mindline flooded him with warmth as Vasiht'h's footfalls beat a double-drum against the floor. "Arii!"

"Something has gone very wrong," he said, and before the tide of anxiety could crest into real fear, "Not me. There are more coming. Too many more."

"How many is too many?" Vasiht'h asked, ears flattening.

"Nine."

"Nine!"

"And one of them is dying," Jahir finished, neither knowing nor caring how he knew. But he had his answer as he forced himself to run down the hall, ignoring Vasiht'h's distress. The stretcher passing him was the one he wanted, and he fell in alongside it, grabbed for a hand. The disorder was so vast. There was no imposing himself on it, when the days had depleted him of anything to use as framework.

So he took it into himself, instead, and found the answer to the question. He could no more stand by and let someone die if he could prevent it than he could have watched someone collapse in a street without attempting to help.

—⊗⊗⊗—

Vasiht'h's cry of dismay strangled in his throat as the mind-line stretched to breaking. He hauled on it as if it were a rope he could grasp in his hands but that didn't bring Jahir closer . . . so he went after him and it was like swimming into the grip of an undertow. Never in his life had he been so terrified. What would it be like to die this way? Horrible, torn to shreds, his last moments a panic . . .

No!

He pulled back, refusing chaos.

No!

Bit by bit, he clawed Jahir free of it until they both spilled into physical reality, tangled limbs, every nerve over-sensitized. Above them, the stunned healers-assist at the side of the stretcher were staring at the patient monitor. Vasiht'h didn't have to be told that his partner had committed another of his miracles. What mattered was getting said partner off the hall floor, and Jahir was resisting him.

"Need to . . . go . . . that way . . ."

"If this is about someone else dying," Vasiht'h began, lips pulling back from his teeth.

"No." Exhaustion so heavy it felt crushing. "Need to know . . . what's happening. Why so many?"

"If I go find out will you promise to sit in a chair and not dash off after anyone else?" Vasiht'h asked. "Because if you don't promise, I'm not moving."

"I'll stay." Jahir's slow, shallow breath strained his ribcage; Vasiht'h felt the lightning pain of it through his own torso. "Please, find out."

"As much as I can," Vasiht'h promised, and unconstrained by Selnor's gravity he ran until he found someone who could talk to him: Radimir, who like Jahir had finally sat down after assigning everyone to their new rooms. The Harat-Shar was deflated, hands limp in his lap and shoulders slumped.

"Alet?" Vasiht'h asked, cautious. "What happened?"

"This is just the beginning," Radimir said. "The beginning, and the ending." He ran a hand over his head, creasing one ear. "There were three separate parties with this stuff. This was the result of one of them."

"Three parties?" Vasiht'h asked, incredulous.

"We're hoping we get to the last two in time, but if we don't . . . they'll be coming here." Radimir looked up at him. "It's going to be a long night. That's the bad news."

"There's good news?"

"Oh yes." The Harat-Shar's smile was feral, humorless. "A victim here, a victim there . . . that's hard to trace. Three parties' worth of people, with contacts to buy this trash?" He shook his head. "The police couldn't ask for a better chance at finding out what's going on."

. . . but it was going to get worse before it got better. Some of that must have marred his expression because the Harat-Shar said, "You should take your Eldritch and go home, alet. These people are going to die and there's nothing either of you can do to prevent it. Now that we know that, there's no reason to make him watch."

"He would argue that there's a chance," Vasiht'h said. "Come to that, your Harat-Shariin surgeon would probably disagree with your assessment."

"She can disagree all she wants. It won't change facts." Radmir sighed and pushed himself up. "It's her job to try to solve the problem. That's what we're paying her for. The two of you? This isn't your fight. You're not trained for it. You don't have the tools. And frankly it's a waste. You don't put therapists in a room with a corpse."

"They're not corpses yet," Vasiht'h said automatically.

"Yet," Radimir agreed.

To the Harat-Shar's back, Vasiht'h said, "He won't go home. You and I both know it."

Radimir paused. Sighed gustily. "Then do what you have to do."

Fine wording, Vasiht'h thought, struggling with grumpiness. What you have to do. None of it had to be done. And he didn't want to be doing it at all. He returned to Jahir's side, and saw anew the fatigue that had become so habitual it had altered the posture that had seemed bred into his friend's bones: that easy, straight-backed grace, the finish to all the movements, and most importantly, their control so as not to intrude by accident or purpose into the space of people who might touch his mind.

Jahir lifted his head, waiting.

"It's a real, honest-to-Goddess outbreak," Vasiht'h said. "And this might be the opportunity the police have been praying for. But there are going to be a lot of bodies before it's over, and they're coming tonight." He controlled his anxiety as much as possible and said, "You know, instead of standing watch over them, we could put ourselves to work on their families. I'm sure they'll be arriving at some point. They'll need support."

"And they will have it," Jahir said. "From us, or from someone else." His breath ended in a small shudder. "We can bring them back."

"For what?" Vasiht'h asked. "So they can die a day later?"

"So their loved ones have time to say farewell," Jahir answered, quiet.

Vasiht'h covered his face. He couldn't bear to look up until a hand slipped into the crook of his elbow, tugged gently. When he looked past his fingers, his partner was looking through them.

/Arii. Beneath your fear, you could no more let them die this way

than I can./

/No,/ Vasiht'h admitted, because the mindline permitted no lies. Denial, perhaps. Delusion. But not outright lies.

"Then stay with me," Jahir said aloud, voice rusted with exhaustion. Another alert began singing down the hall, but the eruption of movement and noise seemed to stream around them, leaving them insulated in a quiet only they could pierce. Because it was a reciprocation of the question that Vasiht'h had sprung on him at the door when he first arrived. He had been the one asking for the Eldritch to commit to him. And now . . .

"Always," Vasiht'h said.

They didn't go home that night. Vasiht'h didn't argue it, but Jahir felt his agitation through the mindline. They acknowledged it there, in the rich space between them, and then kept moving. Four more failed in the hours that followed, and each time they did Jahir brought them back, fighting the screaming un-sense of their minds and counting on Vasiht'h to pull him back from that darkness. Each time he did so, it was harder to come back; he was surprised to find his clothes clinging to his skin and wondered when he'd begun sweating.

The next cluster came an hour into the night shift, six more and one of them died before they'd even passed him through triage. Jahir was aware of Septima diving in and out of rooms, attempting to learn something, anything she could use; all his attention remained focused on the unfortunates, and worse, the families that had begun arriving. He had not appreciated how completely the hospital staff had been insulating him from the families until they no longer could. Then their anguish cried out for intervention, and he had nothing left to give them . . . not so much as a listening ear. And that injustice gnawed at him, whispered something about imbalances that he had no time to consider. If Vasiht'h was aware of it, the Glaseah was soon too tired to comment.

The last group arrived several hours after midnight, and they

were accompanied by a figure Jahir recognized, though it took
him far too long to recognize what should have been an unmis-
takable silhouette: the Malari from the port, who jogged in
behind the eighth stretcher, wiping her cheeks with her shoulder
as she guided it down the hall.

"You know her?" Vasiht'h asked, bleary.

"In passing," Jahir said, but her suffering was so acute he
forced himself to rise and follow her to the room where she had
stopped moving, like a toy deprived of a hand to push it along.
She was staring at the face of the woman in the bed, tears dropping from her eyes onto the arms she had folded high over her
chest. Her spine was bent, wings so tightly tucked together they
trembled.

"Alet?" Jahir asked, gentle.

She shivered. "When I was new here, she took me in. And
she's been my best friend ever since." She looked past her shoulder at him. "Twelve years. For twelve years. And now this." She
dashed a hand against one eye, smearing her tears. "I've read the
bulletin. This is it for her. And for what!"

"We're sorry," Vasiht'h said.

In his voice, somehow, was all the grief of the past few days,
so obvious that it won her attention. She looked down at him,
shaken, then back at the body. And then she began sobbing.

Jahir slipped an arm around her shoulders, over the wing
joins, took like a blow the shock of her misery and felt Vasiht'h
brace him against it like a rock steady against the force of a wave.
The Malarai turned into him and let herself fall apart, and he
held her, smelling the musty warmth of the feathers near his face
as he rested his head on hers. She was so slight, as if she owned
a bird's hollow bones, and he could no more let go of her than he
could have let go of any of the people who'd been dying here. He
let his sorrow mingle with hers, settle like sediment, win him
breathing space.

They left her to the brutal vigil. Neither of them spoke.

Jahir brought seven victims back. Before the eighth could follow, one of the first began again. He rushed for that bedside and took up the hand and hit a wall so hard he thought he'd fallen—and then he had, in truth, beneath not just Vasiht'h but the entire healer-assist team, tearing him from the patient who'd careened to his ending.

"No," Maya said, eyes fierce. "You are not having another heart attack."

The anxious flutter in his chest relented. He looked up, dazed, could not rise. Had he?

"Yes, you almost did," Vasiht'h said, torn between a corrosive anger and a bleak and hyperactive fear. "Again. No more. These people don't get second chances."

"This patient might have been an anomaly—"

"*No*," Maya said, her voice hard. "I hate to say it, alet, but they had their chance outside this hospital, to do the right thing. They've landed here, fine. We're going to do everything we can. But they don't get second chances if it means you have to have a coronary to give it to them."

He couldn't argue with them. Not with Vasiht'h curled protectively around him, not with the entire team glaring down at him, so ferocious in his defense. The Glaseah gave their tacit intent words: You are already doing enough.

It didn't feel like enough. But he had no desire to die here. He relented, let them help him into a chair in the hall, wordlessly drank the concoction passed to him by a caring hand. Then he rose and returned to the fight.

———⚭———

He bought them time.

Time for devastated families and friends to arrive to whisper their last goodbyes. Time for Septima and the entire team of surgeons and specialists who descended on the floor in her wake to fight for some kind of palliative. No one hoped for a cure anymore, only for a chance to mitigate the damage. He caught bits of conversation in the halls, agitated and swift: ". . . never seen anything like this, what the hell asteroid did they get it off of," ". . . hope this is the only thing they find out there . . ." ". . . bad enough, but no idea what the rhacking mechanism of action is for this thing . . ." ". . . afraid to touch it with anything but an autoclave . . ."

The desperation and anger and heartbreak in the ward were crushing, so swift and thick he felt them as something to push against when he walked. He would not have been capable of fording those rapids without Vasiht'h at his side, and would not managed the work without Vasiht'h to draw him back from the storms when he went to them. He could push order onto disorder, could draw chaos out of a mind into himself, but he could not make it back, and when he thought himself lost the Glaseah's hand would be there, clutching hard enough that he expected bruises on his true flesh. Even more importantly, beneath his friend's terrified belief that this was insane and that he was pushing them both too hard, Jahir touched a core of faith and duty that matched his own. Vasiht'h would protest their course of action with every breath, but his heart was as fully committed as Jahir's. He could not countenance allowing these people to die alone either.

They managed, together. Jahir heard the undercurrent of Vasiht'h's fervent prayer for an ending and shared it.

Sometime close to dawn he stumbled into the break room to find something to drink while Vasiht'h parted from him for necessities. He was staring into an empty cabinet, seeking a clean mug, when Levine entered behind him. Her swift stride had degenerated into something closer to a shuffle, and he empathized powerfully with her fatigue. They were all working long past their proper shifts, in hopes that this flood-tide represented the last of the patients they would see before the police and Fleet shut down the channels completely.

Without preamble, Levine said, "You could go rest. Nothing's going to change."

"They will die," Jahir said, voice a husk. "That is change enough."

"And we're not going to be able to stop them." She came close, stared up at his hands, then shook herself and went for the cabinet under the sink. She brought up a mug and offered it to him. "So there's no reason to kill yourself over it."

"So everyone has been telling me over and over," Jahir said. "Yet no one else has gone home, Doctor." He slipped his fingers through the mug's handle. "We are keeping sacred vigil, each and every one of us. Do not deny me the privilege."

"You really think it's a privilege?" She moved closer, enough that momentum brushed her coat's hems against his legs. Nor, he noted blearily, had she released the mug into his grasp.

He marshaled himself and spoke the only truth the past hours had left him with. "To serve life is always a privilege."

In retrospect, he should have seen it coming. Should have seen it implied, as inevitable as dawn in a day, by the attraction she'd been unable to disguise despite her attempts when they were first introduced. It was his exhaustion that hobbled him, mind and body, and after she touched him, her desire, swamping his revulsion. In his several centuries, he had been endowed with many chaste kisses, awarded by family, by priests, even once by the Queen on his being named as heir to the Seni. He had not yet been the recipient of a passionate kiss, and would not have wanted this to be his first experience of it: dulled with the despair of too much death while being touched by someone who wanted him too much, and whom he very much did not want. That she knew it partway through and this epiphany flooded him with her unwanted humiliation and embarrassment only made it more painful, and that it brought with those emotions far too much insight into her character gave him an unwelcome responsibility.

Levine backed away, pressing the side of her hand to her mouth. "I . . . I'm sorry. I thought—" Her stammers chopped off as she flushed bright coral.

"Doctor," Jahir said, after he'd caught his breath. The memory of her tongue made his stomach clench. "A misunderstanding, only."

"Hell of a misunderstanding," she said. "I didn't mean to

impose. . . ." Her façade crumpled and she turned away quickly.

He made sure of their privacy and said, quieter, "You are lonely. It was natural to have hopes." Sorting through the vivid but unwanted impressions, he added, "It is not racism to harbor no attraction for your Pelted colleagues."

"Oh really?" she asked, caustic. "At what point would you say that line gets drawn? When is it just 'my taste' and when is it bigotry?"

"I don't know," he said, tired. "But consider that you have made an advance now on someone who is not the same species as you."

That made her bark a reluctant laugh. "Yes, but you look human. Just . . ." A long pause as she looked over her shoulder at him, with all her longing and regret in her light eyes. "More beautiful than any human has any right to be."

This was more trauma than he could heal . . . too old a scar for a night that had already stretched too long for his patience and endurance. He had not asked for the taste of her mouth on his, or the intimacy of her breath and the tensile length of her body on his, nor for the desire she'd forced him to feel through her skin. "I apologize, if I presented too great a temptation."

Her shoulders stiffened. "Oh . . . Oh, God, no. It wasn't your fault. It's mine and . . ." She covered her face. "And I'm tired, and you're half dead on your feet, and there was and will never be a good time for this conversation. Alet, I am sorry. I took liberties. If you feel you need to take action against me—"

He grimaced but she pushed on, "then I will own those consequences. What I did was wrong."

"It was a moment. You have repented of it. That is enough."

She studied his face, her own still flushed. Then she jerked her head in a nod and hurried from the break room.

Fortunately, he found a chair in time to sit, for his knees no longer consented to their duties. He rested his elbows on them and then put his face in his hands and waited for the trembling to pass. The taste of her remained but he could not bring himself to rise and fill the cup. It was not solely the unwanted touch that aggravated his nausea, but too much of everything combined with the sudden proof of life struggling to push past death and pain, of a very sentient need to fight fear with vitality and a connection with others that he found achingly difficult to sustain in the maelstrom of the situation he found himself in. He stood in the center of storms, and did not know how he had thought himself in love with the excitement of surviving them.

Vasiht'h found him thus and filled the cup for him, with coffee Jahir could smell through the Glaseah's more sensitive nose. The mindline loomed, more real than the world around him until his friend pushed the cup into his hand.

"What was it?"

Jahir cleared his throat and made himself take the offering in both hands. The heat stung his fingers and he flexed them. "Levine."

Vasiht'h scowled. "And?"

This was not a matter for accidental public disclosure. He gave reply through the mindline, feeling them raw and immediate without the insulation of spoken words and their ambiguous distances. /She mistook her own interest in me for mine./

The Glaseah took the cup back from him and drank from it quickly. "Ah, Goddess, her lipstick tastes like fake raspberries."

Jahir began laughing, accepted the cup that Vasiht'h nearly pushed up to his lips for him, washed the taste out of his own mouth too. Wiping it, he said, "That was not the response I was expecting, I admit."

"From me? From her? From yourself?"

"All of it?" He sighed and managed a wan smile. "All of it."

Vasiht'h glanced out the door, then said, low, "Nearly half of them are already dead, arii."

Jahir followed his gaze. Then, allowing the Glaseah to feel his resolve, he answered, "The other half are not."

Vasiht'h sighed and rose, and together they went out again.

It took three days for the last victim to expire and leave the crisis care ward emptied of everything but routine. Three days of what felt like nonstop movement to Vasiht'h, until his ankles ached and the pads on the bottom of his paws cracked and started oozing, and he hopped on three feet until he could find a first aid kit and seal them up. What little sleep he stole came to him only because he was forcing Jahir to rest, and the moment his partner was in a chair or leaning against a wall or stretched on an unused bed, his own head fell forward too. They inevitably woke within twenty minutes and returned to work, not just on the victims, but with their families, their friends, the staff when stress distorted their perspectives and drove them past their limits. With every interaction, the mindline flexed and broadened, something that ordinarily would have been pleasure and now felt like pain, like a stretch held past the point of comfort and into tearing. He was exhausted, footsore, and wanted nothing more than to go to a temple and collapse in a cloud of incense smoke and the implied presence of the Mother.

But he kept going, because Jahir needed him, because the patients needed them, and because the staff needed them.

There was a comfort to working in a team this big, even if he could watch the friction of the situation stripping the gears. To know that if one of them failed, someone else would be there to shore up the weakness. But none of that compensated for the stress of simply being here.

On that third day, after they'd watched the last body leave the ward, Jiron came to them. His eyes were a grimy red, his face sagging and lined and his hair a disheveled draggle stuck to his brow and the sides of his neck. "Go home," he said.

Vasiht'h found a particle of energy somewhere, enough to tense in anticipation of his roommate's defiance. But Jahir said simply, "All right," and staggered toward the door. Vasiht'h hurried after, his reflexes dulled by the long stretches of adrenaline-fueled vigilance, and put his shoulder up against the Eldritch's hip to keep him from falling. Together they stumbled back to the apartment, where Jahir did not pause to eat or change or even say good night, but fell into his bed and was unconscious before he struck the mattress.

Vasiht'h tottered after him and found himself leaning on the door. There was so much to do. Wasn't there? Schoolwork he'd been ignoring. Letters he should have been answering. Calls he wanted to make—Goddess, Sehvi, and his parents. He should cook something so they'd have something to eat when they woke, because no doubt they'd only wake to use the bathroom and then collapse again, and Jahir needed food so badly Vasiht'h could feel it in the hollows of his bones, an ache so deep it bypassed his stomach and became a cell-deep yearning. He should do all these things, and instead he managed the distance between door and his pillows and no more. His only nod to all that had happened was to fall asleep with his torso on the bed, where he could feel the warmth of the Eldritch's skin. His fingers crept out until they caught smooth metal, and he hooked his fingers in Jahir's medical bracelet, and then he lost the world and all the stunned grief, and his last thought before doing so was: *It was hell and it was harder than everything we've ever done but we made it.*

CHAPTER 20

VASIHT'H COULD NOT remember ever waking up so groggy. He blinked sleep-crusted eyes and licked dry teeth, stared at the thin sunlight falling through the edge of the window. His back had kinked in two places, and the only cure for that was hot water . . . and it was obvious he wasn't going to get back to sleep. He pushed back from the bed and glanced at its occupant, chanced a feather-soft touch, mind-to-mind and found only the dull blank of complete unconsciousness. That quiescence suited him; he wanted a respite from the noise, needed space.

In the silence of the apartment, he washed, made his room-mate a small meal and tea and left it in stasis, and then buckled his bags on and let himself out. The sunlight felt like a benison, and completely unreal, as if it had been years since he'd seen it rather than days. He stared up into the brilliance of Selnor's sky, squinting, and then went into the day. He had no specific des-tination; meandering, he went from one of the public parks to a plaza market and past it to a gallery district. The murmur of conversation, the normalcy of laughter and talk, the sight of chil-dren frisking alongside their parents or darting between trees . . . the pleasure of looking at fresh fruit and vegetables and thinking nothing more urgent than whether he wanted to eat it for dinner later . . . slowly these things began to work on his jangled nerves. By the time he reached the siv't he felt he could sit in front of the Goddess without twitching, and cleaned the altar for his incense with hands that no longer shook.

Settling there, he tucked his paws neatly beneath his body and let his wings ease open . . . and in him, something crumbled, and hot tears seeped from his eyes. He covered his face and let them come. The resin smoke implied Her embrace as it broke around him. He cried for the dead, for their families, for the waste. He cried for the staff, and for himself. Most of all, he cried for Jahir, for having needed to come here for the lesson only She knew he'd needed, because whatever She'd needed to teach him had required so much of him.

When all of it had drained from him, he breathed out and relaxed for the first time in days. Picking through his bag he found a wipe and cleaned his face. So many things he could say to Her. So many things in his heart, still. What he chose was, "Thank you."

Then he went back home, not rushing, enjoying the tropical breeze that stole between the buildings to ruffle his fur, the warmth of the sun. The apartment was still silent when he entered; Vasiht'h paused, listening with both ears and mind, and heard nothing. Relieved that Jahir hadn't shorted himself on the rest he so obviously needed, the Glaseah went to the kitchen and considered the ingredients he had left, and set to the meditation of cooking.

Once supper was in the oven, he sat with his data tablet. A few moments later, he stopped on the news feed's report of the wet crackdown. He read the précis but couldn't bring himself to continue on to the detail. It was still on his tablet when the door chime distracted him.

Surely not the police again? Vasiht'h closed the door to the bedroom to keep the noise from waking Jahir and then went to see who'd come.

Grace Levine was standing on their threshold.

Since 'what do you want' seemed unnecessarily rude, Vasiht'h stepped back and said, "If you're looking for Jahir, he's asleep."

"Good," she said. And then, embarrassed. "Ah, I mean . . . that's good. He needed the rest. May I . . ."

"Come in?" he said, frowning. "But—"

"You'll tell him," she said. "Whatever I say. Won't you?"

Vasiht'h folded his arms.

"Because that's all I need," she said. "And honestly, if I tell him, he'll probably argue with me." She grimaced, ran a hand along her temple as if discouraging a nascent headache. "In that way he has of politely not arguing with you, but you know he's disagreeing with you."

Curiosity pricked, Vasiht'h said, "All right."

The human entered, her discomfort making her awkward. She shoved her hands into her coat pockets, walking to the couch but remaining on her feet beside it. "You heard the news?"

"That they found the culprits? I saw, but I didn't read the full thing."

Levine nodded, a jerk of her chin. "It's worth reading. They did good work." She looked away, rolling her lower lip between her teeth.

"Just say it," Vasiht'h said, torn between pity for her obvious unease and irritation with her for being here, for intruding, and very definitely for how she'd made Jahir feel.

"We've ended your friend's residency contract," she said. "For health reasons."

Vasiht'h stared at her.

"I wrote his evaluation myself," she said. "I think he'll find it fair."

"You're sending him away?" Vasiht'h asked, incredulous.

"I think we have to. And before you ask, because I know you're going to . . . no, it's not about me not wanting him around to remind me of how acutely I humiliated myself." The wryness faded. "It's because we've talked and we honestly think . . . it's enough." When he didn't answer, she said, "Don't you?"

He looked away.

Nodding, Levine said. "Tell him, will you? He won't argue with you."

"Oh, he'll argue," Vasiht'h muttered. "But I'll win."

A hesitation. Tentatively, she said, "Is it as good as it seems from the outside?" At his quizzical glance, she said, "To be the one he chose."

Vasiht'h flicked his ears back.

"I know it's a personal question," she said. "I'm sorry. You don't have to answer."

Not so long ago, he could remember his own angst before he'd known whether Jahir wanted to be his friend or not. It gave him an unwilling sympathy for her disappointment, and to honor it, he said, quiet, "It is."

She sighed, head lowered. When she lifted her chin, she had found a smile that looked more natural: resigned, a little sad, but honest. It made him like her, all of a sudden. "I thought so. Anyway. Don't let him come back to work. He's done at Mercy." She paused. "Unless he wants to say goodbye, of course."

"Right," Vasiht'h said. "I'll tell him."

She nodded and headed for the door. As she reached it, she added, "The police say if he hadn't been here, it might have been months before they realized what was going on."

Vasiht'h tried to imagine what months' worth of penetration into the Heliocentrus market would have meant. He shuddered.

"Yeah," Levine said. "Me too." She inclined her head. "Thanks, alet. Thank you both."

For a very long time after she left, Vasiht'h stared at nothing, trying not to imagine the catastrophe they'd averted. Surely the police were overstating the matter. He shuddered again and forced himself to start moving.

Jahir did not wake until several hours after Vasiht'h had put dinner in stasis. The Eldritch appeared in the door, leaning on the frame with bowed head, braid falling in an untidy rope past a neck that had become too hollow, all tendon and sunken flesh. There was a query in the mindline, too diffuse for words, so indistinct Vasiht'h worried that he should still be in bed . . . and yet they both knew what had brought him from it, for the Glaseah felt the pangs in his own stomach.

"You smell dinner," Vasiht'h said, in response to the inarticulate query. "Stew tonight."

Jahir nodded slowly, and found words, though his tenor remained husky. "I should eat."

"You should. Come sit."

After the Eldritch groped his way into a chair, Vasiht'h said, "It's over. The police broke it open."

Jahir looked up at him sharply, the fog blown from his thoughts. Then he leaned back and some tension he'd been holding in his chest, in his legs, flowed from him and left him limp. "So it's over."

"In more ways than one," Vasiht'h said. Quieter, "Levine came by. They're ending your residency."

He expected something in response to that: dismay. Upset. The defiance Levine had predicted. Something. But the mindline echoed, carrying nothing but the receding sound of his own words, until they too faded.

Very softly, Jahir said, "Arii. Take me home."

Vasiht'h stared at him, quivering. Then nodded and rose to see to their dinner.

CHAPTER 21

AHIR'S PERSONAL ACCOUNT was backlogged with messages dating back to the moment he arrived on Selnor: friends at school, patients from his supervised clinical practicum on Seersana, his advisors, his mother, the children from the hospital, their healer-assist, even Nieve's grandmother, sending him well wishes on his new course. There were so many he set the data tablet back on the table and curled up on the bed. Vasiht'h was taking care of their travel arrangements; the Glaseah had not so informed him, but the hum in the back of his mind consisted of whispered flight numbers and memories of calls made to the university and to spaceliners. At some point, Jahir would offer to reimburse him for the money he was spending on his behalf, but not yet. Not yet.

He could not wrap his arms around the past days.

He could not move through any of it at all. The mindline kept him anchored, for which he was profoundly grateful. But he felt nothing at the realization that he had failed to complete a residency which was renowned the worlds over for its intensity and the treasure of the experience it offered. He felt numb from core to fingertips, and even his trips to the private pool did not break him free of that shell.

/You are exhausted,/ Paga signed, unconcerned. /Go, and you will find yourself again./

"I don't recall telling you I was leaving," Jahir said.

The Naysha smiled. /Write me./

Jahir thought of happier moments at the pool and said, "You promised me once . . . a touch. And I would have it—" His heart constricted, the first hint of emotional involvement he'd felt in what felt like ages. "—and I cannot."

The Naysha's smile grew softer. /Offer stands. Anytime. Come back. I will honor it./

It was harder to walk back into Mercy. To don the clothes of a student and not a member of its staff and to pass through its doors, accept the double-takes. He found Jiron in the break room and the man waved him back out of it and to an empty conference room.

"I would have stayed," Jahir said.

"We all know you would have stayed," Jiron said. "That's not the issue. You and I both know that."

"You have not sent away any of the others."

"On the contrary. We called in relief for everyone who worked those three days, and not just because they needed the rest. Septima's still on leave, in fact. She told us herself she'd come a little unhinged, needed some time to swing back to center before she came back."

"You are here," Jahir observed.

"I am. But I took a day off myself. Alet . . . sit, please."

It hurt to sit. Not just physically but in some interior space, where he felt frozen and movement threatened to break something entirely. Jahir clasped the edge of the chair with thin fingers and leaned forward a little, bracing himself with the toes of his boots. It was strange to wear them again.

Jiron walked around the table and pulled a chair over, turning it and straddling it, arms loose over the back. "But you are right, in that I haven't sent any of them away. But none of them, not a single one of them, was doing what you were doing, hour after hour. You admit that, right?"

Quietly, Jahir said, "Of course."

"Then appreciate it when I say that your talents . . . someone's got to make rules for them." Jiron exhaled, shoulders slumping. He rubbed his face. "Watching you and that Glaseah of yours near-kill yourselves here and not having the first clue how bad it was or how hard you were pushing yourselves or whether I needed to pull you back or not . . . it's like trying to tell a brain surgeon what to do when you don't know basic science."

This image clung to him, faint as a dandelion seed. "You are calling us . . . soul surgeons."

Jiron chuckled. "It suits." Shaking his head, he continued, "You need to develop a better understanding of these powers of yours, alet, because when you do, they're going to be an amazing asset in whatever you choose to do. But throwing you into the deep end of the medical pool like this isn't going to foster and develop those powers. It's going to shatter you. You have to have more respect for the hand that holds the tool."

Jahir jerked his head up, meeting the human's eyes. In them he saw compassion . . . and an utter certitude that lent weight to the blade-sharp pain of his last words.

To have respect for the hand that holds the tool. What had he been doing with himself? And why couldn't he stop? And at what point did duty become an excuse for self-harm?

"You're going to go far, alet," Jiron said. "Just don't cut yourself off at the ankles before you start the race."

"I . . . shall endeavor to avoid that," Jahir answered, still stunned.

Jiron nodded. "Now come on. We've got a little cake out there waiting for you. God knows you could use the calories."

It was a congenial gathering: Paige and Radimir, Maya and Jiron, the staff from the desk, some of the healers-assist from the emergency room, now too well acquainted with him from the past week. He accepted his serving of cake and with it the humbling evidence that he had made friendships here, in as short a time as he'd had: shallow in knowledge, perhaps, but fast in trust, forged in the crucible of their shared work.

The cake was lemon, with raspberry filling. He wondered what Vasiht'h would have made of it. His friend had not baked since arriving. Of Levine he saw nothing.

―――∞∞∞―――

"You're leaving?" Sehvi asked, one ear splaying and the other upright. "But you just got there!"

"I know," Vasiht'h said, rubbing his eyes. "But I can't even tell you what we've been through, ariishir. It's been . . . it's just . . . it's huge. I think we've lived two years' worth of time in the past week and that's it. We're going."

She narrowed her eyes and asked, thoughtful, "His idea or yours?"

Vasiht'h considered and said: "Ours."

She huffed softly. "I guess that's how it's supposed to work." She folded her arms and leaned back, and her expression gentled. "You look pretty awful, big brother."

"I feel awful," he said. "Mostly on the outside. I'm so tired. I can't remember the last time I was this tired."

"And on the inside?"

"I think I'm okay." He pressed the heel of his hand to his chest. "A little worried, maybe."

"About?"

"This was our decision, and it's the right decision," Vasiht'h said. "But he's still not . . . well . . . animated. Part of that is the physical toll, I know. I'm guessing he'll revive once we're off the planet. But I'm a little worried that part of it is still emotional."

"Hmm. What does the mindline say?"

A good question, and what sprang to mind in response was, "To wait."

She canted her head.

"To wait," Vasiht'h repeated, and sighed. "So that's what I'm doing. We're out of here in less than a week."

"Back to Seersana," she guessed.

"Back to Seersana."

"Are you happy?" she wondered.

Was he? "I'll let you know when I figure that out," he said.

———∞∞∞———

The last people they saw before leaving Selnor were Kayla and Meekie. The children came running to Jahir and stopped abruptly a few paces away. Kayla squinted up at him, then motioned him down. Obediently, he went to one knee in front of them, which brought him in range of their very grave faces. Kayla reached out, touched his cheekbone, brushed some of his hair back from it; through her fingertips he felt her sober recognition.

"You look like we used to, before we started getting better," Kayla said, and Meekie nodded.

"Like Nieve, actually," the latter said. "Worse than us."

"I have had . . ." He paused to clear his throat. "A very long few days, ariisen."

Meekie glanced at Vasiht'h, whom Jahir could feel at his back, still and patient. "You're going to do something about it?"

"Is it his to do?" Jahir asked.

"Well, you're not doing anything about it, obviously," Kayla said. "Manylegs?"

"We're leaving," Vasiht'h replied. "Tomorrow. Back to Seersana."

"Oh, yay!" Kayla exclaimed. "So you'll be there when we get there in a year?"

"Less than a year now," Meekie added.

Jahir thought of all the schooling he would have to retake, of the residency he had to begin anew. "We'll be there."

———∞∞∞———

Leaving the apartment, Jahir thought he should feel something, but he accepted that he didn't, and that this was perhaps not unexpected. He allowed Vasiht'h to help him pack, and to chivvy him to the port, and from there off the surface of Selnor and up to Heliocentrus's geosynchronous station to await their ride out of the system. Sitting on a chair beside one of the great windows looking out on Selnor's crowded orbitals, he breathed freely again for the first time in weeks, lifted a cup without effort, felt his heart slow to a pace he recognized. The physical relief was so acute he couldn't keep up his side of the conversation, and Vasiht'h let it lapse. The mindline lapped him with his companion's understanding, soft as a blanket. He accepted it and watched the ships go by, and wondered when the winter in him would thaw.

CHAPTER 22

THE JOURNEY BACK TO Seersana took less time and felt like it took forever. Vasiht'h spent it trying not to let his concern bleed too deeply into the mindline; that it was a futile exercise was at least interesting for what it demonstrated about how broad and full the mindline had grown. He would never have imagined the thin thing that had raveled between them spontaneously in their first years of knowing one another could evolve into this complete communion. Jahir guarded his memories—not intentionally, Vasiht'h sensed, but simply out of deeply ingrained habit—but his thoughts and feelings he shared generously, and the bedrock of his personality, his mere existence, registered in Vasiht'h's consciousness now as a constant as sure as his own breath and blood moving in him. There was no doubt their shared experience at Mercy, so soon after permanent establishment of the bond, had made the intensity of the bond possible. Vasiht'h wondered if Sehvi could tell him about it from her reading. 'Traumatic experiences lead to the strongest ties,' or something.

So he knew Jahir could tell he was worried. But the mindline also reassured him. His friend was withdrawn but still present, and if he spoke very little Vasiht'h could feel how every hour they

spent in lighter gravity worked on the persistent physical degra-
dation Jahir had been suffering.

He had instincts—new ones, or old ones given new respect—
and every one of them whispered that his friend needed space. So
as much as was possible between two mind-bonded, he granted
it. Caught up on his studies. Wrote Palland to tell him he was
returning. Sent missives to his parents, his grandmother, as many
of his cousins as he could manage. Jotted off notes to his friends
at the university; tried to figure out what to do with his schedule
now that he was once again mangling it with his return after all
the trouble he'd gone through to arrange his leave of absence.
And as he did so, he remained exquisitely aware of Jahir: sleeping on the bunk beside him, consenting to eat in silence, sitting
alongside a window, watching the stars smear past in Well. As
he'd told Sehvi, the mindline urged him to wait . . . so he did.

⊗⊗⊗

The first touch of Seersana's light on Jahir's face was bene-
diction—and shame. To have returned so swiftly, and for what
felt like so little cause, and yet so much cause. . . . Jahir looked
up at the sky, then suffered himself to be led back to where he'd
come. Once they'd reached campus, Vasiht'h said, "I thought I'd
go look for a place for us to stay, since our apartment from last
semester's been taken."

"I had forgotten," Jahir murmured. "That it would be so."

"It's not important," Vasiht'h said. "Do you want to come
with me? Or . . ."

"I should begin to make arrangements for my schooling,"
Jahir said. Something in him flexed against the ice: a gnawing
anxiety at how much he had put on Vasiht'h's shoulders. "It is
not too much trouble?"

Vasiht'h's small smile felt like the first pale hint of dawn.
"Not at all. I'll bring back some brochures, you'll see. I'll meet you
at Tea and Cinnamon in the afternoon. All right?"

"All right," Jahir said, bowing his head.

Left alone, he contemplated the sky a little longer,

acknowledged the ease of standing on the surface of a world that did not want to crush him quite so badly . . . bowed his head to the grinding ache that remained in raxed muscles and worn joints. It would pass, but for now it remained, along with his other responsibilities. He checked his data tablet for office hours and set off. To put it off would not make it easier, presenting himself to a man he admired as a failure after all that had been done on his behalf.

He had thought Kayla and Meekie's scrutiny had educated him sufficiently in the changes Selnor had wrought in him. He was wrong. KindlesFlame took one look at him and stood from behind his desk, eags flagging.

"I seem to have misplaced a little weight," he said, apologizing in response to that dismay.

KindlesFlame was silent a moment, then smiled faintly. "I suppose that's only to be expected if you're going to be a record-breaking medical hero."

"I . . . beg your pardon?" Jahir said.

The Tam-illee's brows lifted. "You *are* here, right?"

"I am," Jahir said. "Because they sent me away. For medical reasons, lest I wear myself to the fineness of tissue."

Now KindlesFlame was staring at him. "Alet. They didn't send you away. They ended your residency period. The way they're supposed to when they're done with you." Seeing no sign of understanding, the Tam-illee said, "As in 'done and can graduate.' Didn't you read the evaluation Doctor Levine wrote you? You've earned your license. They said after everything you did during the klaidopin outbreak, you've earned it several times over."

His knees quivered, and he grasped the back of the chair facing KindlesFlame's desk. And then, to his everlasting astonishment, his eyes welled and a paroxysm of grief clenched him, and he wept: for all that made sense to him, and everything that didn't, and for the strain, and for the knowing that at last he could let it all go. When the spell passed he had somehow found his way into the chair and the Tam-illee was sitting across from him, close enough that their knees nearly touched.

"All out of your system?" KindlesFlame said kindly.

"I believe so." He gathered in a shaky breath. "How did you know?"

"I was one of your faculty advisors, you'll recall." The foxine smiled. "I was keeping track of you. Besides, I told you I knew someone on the residency application board at Mercy, didn't I? And I do. Grace and I have been friends for twelve years now."

"You know Levine?" Jahir asked, startled.

"Oh yes. And the letter she wrote you is better than any letter I've seen her write," KindlesFlame said. "She was very impressed with you. And not just because she got herself in trouble with you in the break room." He smiled crookedly at Jahir's sudden stillness. "Yes, she told me. That got me a Well-pushed real-time call even. She was falling all over herself with remorse."

"It was a difficult situation," Jahir murmured.

KindlesFlame snorted. "Your talent for understatement has only grown more acute in your absence, I see."

"Did they really pass me?" he asked, his incredulity making him quiet.

"Wouldn't you have passed yourself?" KindlesFlame leaned back in his chair, hands casually linked and loose over his chest. "You get a shiny new student resident, fresh out of college where his only work was under supervision. You saddle him with Mediger's—and you have the worst case of it I've ever seen, and you're not even in the environment that caused it anymore—and then you dump him into what you just went through. He makes it through. Not only makes it through, but is cited by colleagues for his actions, and law enforcement for his aid. There's even an attached thank you from Fleet; wet is one of their particular nightmares, and they're very diligent about expressing gratitude to anyone involved in helping them clamp down on it. So. You have a student who manages all that, and you don't think he's earned his passing grade?"

"But I saved no one," Jahir said softly.

"It wasn't your job to save their lives," KindlesFlame said. "Unless you're going to switch gears completely and take my degree path. You didn't *have* a job there, alet, save maybe to minister to the families, and even then there are volunteer chaplains to do that. And yet you made yourself not just useful, but vital ... often, apparently, at grave risk to yourself." He tilted his head. "Do you know why you did that, by the way?"

Jahir said slowly, "I have some notion."

"Good. That's not something you can leave unexamined." KindlesFlame lifted his brows again. "So. Why wouldn't they have passed you?"

"A residency is two years," Jahir said. "I feel I am missing a great deal."

"Maybe you are," KindlesFlame said. "But I think you went through more in a month than most residents are going to go through in those two years. And two years on Selnor apparently wouldn't have agreed with you."

Jahir touched a hand to the hollow under his cheekbone, self-conscious. "I suppose I am become a touch gaunt."

"You look like hell," KindlesFlame corrected. "If I'd been your physician, I would have had no choice but to send you packing within a few weeks anyway."

Jahir looked up at him, startled. "Truly?"

"Truly. As it is, I want you in my office twice a week for the next few weeks ... that is, if you're staying. Are you?"

"I . . . I don't know," Jahir confessed, bewildered. "I had assumed I would have to find a new residency and resume my schooling here. If what you say is so, then ... I need not?"

"Not at all. You could kick up your heels until the end of the semester, graduate, and go find someplace to try out your new license."

"In medical xenopsychology," Jahir said.

"That is what you've been studying for almost three years," KindlesFlame observed.

Jahir shuddered. "No. No, I must go back and redo it." He felt the Tam-illee's sudden interest as he finished, "This is wrong for me. You were right, and so was Vasiht'h. I need a life with more balance than what I have just experienced."

"A hospital job's not going to be a constant illegal drug epidemic, you know."

"No. I know." He thought of the acuteness of the grief in the crisis care wards, the piercing strength of the emotions, fear and mourning and anxieties thick enough to choke. "But it's still . . . all intensity and no breath-pause. You told me once that there was virtue in a practice that was mostly headaches and sprained ankles with only occasional emergencies. That was a wisdom I should have embraced."

"Ah, well. Sometimes we have to learn things the hard way," KindlesFlame said. "I did my time in crisis care, alet. That's how I figured it out." He leaned back. "So am I hearing you want to go clinical?"

"Yes." Here at last was the relief he'd been waiting to feel since making the decision to leave Selnor. It was sweeter than honey and heady as wine, and it dizzied him.

"Shouldn't be a problem. If I'm guessing right, you won't have to run the full two years again. The residency for clinical's done here; the university has a series of clinics throughout the city it uses for that purpose, though I'm guessing you won't have to spend the full year there. They'll accept your medical residency evaluation as proof that you have what it takes." KindlesFlame cocked his head. "I'd say maybe a year at most."

"And . . . if I wanted to take a minor?" Jahir asked, feeling his way carefully around the aches in his heart.

"In what?"

"Pharmacology."

KindlesFlame said nothing, meeting his eyes. Then, "You sure you're not overreacting?"

He had not intended candor, but he said, "No," because the Tam-illee had earned that much of him: no evasions, no denials. "But I was always good at the chemistry. And . . ." Inspiration, sluggish but functioning again, provided the second reason. ". . . I may have cause to need a working knowledge of soporifics."

"Soporifics," KindlesFlame repeated.

"My roommate made a study of dream therapy," Jahir said.

"Perhaps the two of us might embark upon the application of his results."

KindlesFlame barked a laugh, slapped his knee. "Excellent! Your Glaseah, yes? Armin and I were talking about the chances of the two of you finally figuring things out."

"Armin?" Jahir asked, mystified.

"Professor Palland," the foxine said, grinning. "He's your friend's major professor. And yes, we've been discussing the two of you since before you left. So, is this your plan then? The two of you graduate and go into practice together?"

"I think so," Jahir said, because they had never discussed it, had they? That they would remain together, certainly, but to work together? He had not even told Vasiht'h of his own change in plans, and yet . . . and yet . . . "I am certain."

"Excellent," KindlesFlame repeated. "Now this is a course of action I can get behind. But first," he held up a finger. "You need to recuperate. Fall semester's already started but I think we can get you in. You can take a couple of lecture classes, just to keep from getting bored. But nothing more strenuous. And I was serious about you seeing me twice a week until I'm sure you're back to normal. Is that understood?"

"Clearly," Jahir said, sheepish.

"Good. Let's see if we can get Lasa on the line. She might not be the best choice for your faculty advisor if you're going clinical instead of medical, but if she's not up to it she'll give us some options for someone new. We'll work out a schedule and get you back on track."

Jahir nodded. And added, "You were not serious, I hope. About my being lauded."

KindlesFlame arched a brow. "You haven't been watching the news."

"No," Jahir said, fighting a sudden anxiety. "I have not, nor do I wish to. Pray tell me I have not been on it."

"Not broadly, no," the foxine said. "In the medical and law enforcement communities?" He smiled a little. "Sorry, alet. You can't control what other people make of your behavior. Like it or not you made a splash."

"God and Lady," he murmured. Resigned, he said, "So long as I need not be exposed to it."

"No one's going to rub your face in it," the foxine said. "But don't be surprised if people in the profession recognize you. For now, at least, until the next big emergency. Which . . ." A grin, "won't be your responsibility. Now, enough about your new, and painfully earned fame. Let's see if we can get you set up . . . and then you're for the clinic with me, where I can do a proper work-up and see what in all Iley's hell Selnor did to your system."

CHAPTER 23

VASIHT'H HAD NOT BEEN on campus an hour before his data tablet popped up with a message: *What are you doing here?*

He didn't need to check the tag for a message that blunt. He answered, *It's a long story,* and waited, standing beneath a tree and smelling the familiar scent of Seersana moving out of a sun-burnt summer and into autumn. Since fall semester had already started, it must have been a hot summer to linger in the air that way. He was glad: the heat on Seersana had a different quality than Selnor's, and he was savoring the difference and what it meant about where he was.

When he looked down at his tablet few moments later, he found the expected reply: *Meet me at the gazebo.*

Vasiht'h packed the tablet and headed toward the apartments where he'd spent most of his graduate career. Half an hour later he pushed open the door on the enclosed gazebo where the quad-mates had feted so many successful semesters and found Lucrezia stirring sangria, a plate of partially chopped fruit alongside.

"Come squeeze," she said. "And tell me what in battlehells you're doing back so soon." She looked up over the pitcher. "Don't tell me he sent you away."

"No," Vasiht'h said. "No, it's nothing like that." He obediently took a knife to the fruits that needed cutting and started squeezing them into the pitcher while she stirred. "We're here to finish school. The residency on Selnor didn't work out for him."

Luci flicked her ears back. "I can't imagine him failing at anything."

"He didn't," Vasiht'h said. "He just ran into some obstacles that even he couldn't surmount." Remembering her field of study, he said, "You know about Mediger's Syndrome?"

"Oh, hells." Luci's ears flattened completely. "Selnor . . . that's over halfway down the scale on the heavy side. And he had problems here . . ." She trailed off, then shook her head. "That must have been rough."

"Yes." He licked lemon juice off his fingers. It tasted like Jahir's rue, which made him both not want to taste it and to keep licking it to figure out how that worked, would work from now on.

"So you're back to stay?" she said, interrupting his thoughts.

Vasiht'h shook himself. "Until we're done. I don't know what we're doing after school, but . . . whatever it is, we're doing it together."

She put her spoon down. He felt her gaze on his face and tried not to let it heat his cheeks as he started on the pineapple. He dropped the resulting chunks into the sangria and then faced her, squaring his shoulders, head lowered.

"You're afraid I'm jealous," she said, eyes wide. "Oh no. No, arii. Never that." A swift hug, intense if not Harat-Shariin typical. "Never. The two of you were meant to be together. Anyone with a half-folded brain could see that."

Vasiht'h managed a smile. "Before either of us, apparently."

She snorted. "That's how it usually goes." Sniffing the results of their labors, she pushed the tray away and fetched two glasses. "Have the two of you got a place to stay? You can use our couch if you need it."

"We might take you up on that. I'm supposed to be looking for an apartment, but I just got here. As you apparently noticed. How did you . . . ?"

"You forget I can see your location," Luci said, handing him a glass. "I'm done with classes for the day, so it was my time to check mail." She smiled. "Anyway. You and Prince Handsome come by tonight, ah? Even if you don't need the place to bunk down. We'll have a quadmate meeting, just like old days."

"The old days of all . . . what, two, three months ago?" Vasiht'h said, laughing.

"Feels like ages," she answered, mouth quirking. She had a sip of her own and finished, "It's too bad you can't have your old place back."

Vasiht'h considered the sunlit highlights in the wine. "No. It's all right." He smiled a little. "It might only have been a few months, but things aren't the same. Living in the same place . . . I think that would have been a bad try at pretending nothing's happened when so much has."

She was looking at him again with a very peculiar expression. He said, "What?"

"You're right. You're different." She reached out and drew a fruit-scented finger down his nose. "Very different."

He restrained the urge to lick her finger and rubbed at his muzzle, smiling. "I'm still me, arii."

"You're still you, yes, but . . . different." She nodded. "I'm glad to see it. I like the difference." She leaned over and hugged him, holding her glass out of the way. "So you'll come to the quadmate meeting? I'll send you the time when I talk to everyone."

"Yes," Vasiht'h said. "And . . . Luci, thank you."

She chuckled. "For what? Getting you drunk before sending you off to your beloved?"

"For being you. And being here." He lifted the cup and drank off the entirety of it before setting it down. "And for *trying* to get me drunk before sending me off to my very non-sexual relationship."

"I could pour you the whole pitcher?" she said, grinning.

"Wouldn't be enough for me to want to hop into bed with anything." Vasiht'h laughed. "And it wouldn't be enough for you to prove you're stereotypical Harat-Shariin."

She chuckled. "I know. And that's why I'm going to say 'thank you' too. For never trying to make me be that. You know, the two of you did more for me with that talk and the nap on your couch than any therapist ever has since?"

He looked up at her sharply.

"It's true," she said. She lifted her cup. "Here's to things working out the way they should."

He refilled his glass just so he could tap it against hers.

———⊗⊗⊗———

Vasiht'h found Jahir sitting on a bench on one of the walkways leading to Tea and Cinnamon. The Eldritch had his hands folded in his lap and was leaning back, watching the shadows of leaves moving as the breeze sighed through the trees: this, Vasiht'h knew from the mindline, where the endless changing patterns intersected with the warm sun and cool air and made a meditation out of approaching autumn. Beneath it ran a trickle of ease at the familiarity of the sight, of students passing, of the taste of the air in his—their—mouths. Vasiht'h padded to him and sat beside the bench's end, wrapping his tail over his feet and looking up at the branches too.

There was a new thing in the mindline, then. A sense of frailty. Of the erosion of bone sockets, grinding, of taxed muscles and heart. Chagrin, bittersweet on the tongue, seasoned with a receding fear of what might have been. An Eldritch, who'd expected to long outlive everyone around him, to remain the sole unchangeable element in a world doomed to ephemerality, now held in cupped mental hands the waters of mortality, had looked into them and seen his own face . . . and that awareness had a soundtrack, of the healers-assist from Mercy refusing him a second try at the wet victims, of Vasiht'h's frightened exclamations, of KindlesFlame's lecture on how poorly he'd fared on Selnor.

An apology, then, wordless and humble. It filtered to Vasiht'h and became impression. *I thought I was the only one with the right to fear. But I can die here easily, too.*

It was a gift. Vasiht'h felt no need to embarrass either of them with remonstrations. He accepted it in the spirit it was offered, and gave back a warm acceptance, and made words out of it. */I think we've both learned a great deal./*

/Yes./ Jahir sighed and smiled at him, such a vulnerable, lop-sided smile to be formed from such a miniscule lift of a corner of that mouth. "Healer KindlesFlame has put me straight about a great many things."

The mindline embellished that with trailing sparks. Vasiht'h glanced at him. "That feels promising."

"The residency," Jahir said. "They terminated it because they passed me. And wanted me gone before I ground myself to powder, a fate KindlesFlame tells me I narrowly avoided."

Vasiht'h paused, stunned. "Then . . . you're done."

"I would be," Jahir agreed. "If I wanted to embark on the career I am now licensed for. But I thought . . . perhaps . . ."

The mindline was leading the words, and catching them Vasiht'h jumped. "You want to? Really?"

"Your dream therapy works," Jahir said. "And it requires esper practitioners. You are studying to become one such. I could be another. It seems a sensible course of action, if . . . you are well with it?"

"It's what I've wanted since I saw you," Vasiht'h said, and didn't know that was true until he'd said it aloud.

Jahir closed his eyes, bowing his head. Vasiht'h couldn't see his face past the fall of light hair, but he could feel the smile, small and bright and open.

"I will be back in school, then, this semester," Jahir continued. "KindlesFlame is arranging it. The semester is not so far advanced that I cannot catch up with a few lectures, which is all he will permit me to do until I am healthy again."

"A very sensible man, Healer KindlesFlame." Vasiht'h didn't try to suppress his glee, knowing it would escape him into the mindline anyway. It felt like the wind in his fur while running.

"And you?" Jahir said. "Why do you taste . . . smell . . . no, taste . . . like wine?"

"Because Luci was plying me with sangria," Vasiht'h answered, amused.

"She wanted the story out of you."

"I think she just wanted me to have an excuse to tell it if I wanted to," Vasiht'h said. "She's invited us to stay on her couch until we figure out where to live. Which is good, since I admit I haven't gotten much done on that count yet."

"I have not paid you for all you've done yet—"

"Later," Vasiht'h said. "There's time for that later. Would you like to go to Tea and Cinnamon? Luci's invited us to a quadmate meeting later, if you'd like to go—"

Welcome, like the warmth of a hearth after cold. "Yes," Jahir said. "I would."

"So we have some time between now and then. We could go look for apartments after we eat."

"We could," Jahir said.

Vasiht'h eyed him, head tilted, feeling the hesitation like a precipice. "But?"

"But I would very much like to see the children."

Vasiht'h smiled. "Me too. We can eat later."

Jahir nodded, and reached over, hand up. Vasiht'h slipped his into it, and the mindline expanded, bringing with it his friend's quiet happiness. There was nothing of winter in it: no numbness, no shock, no pain or distance. Here was the thing he'd been waiting for . . . all wrapped up in the offer of a single touch.

I'm here. I'm willing to be known.

Vasiht'h squeezed, gentle, and let go.

I'm here. I'm willing to let us grow.

Together they set out for the children's hospital, beneath familiar trees.

CHAPTER 24

W HEN THEY ARRIVED, the children were away with Berquist
for the conclusion of several medical tests, but the two of
them had been gone so briefly their credentials were still logged
with the hospital, and they had no trouble being admitted to the
proper floor. They were even recognized—or at least Vasiht'h
was. The healers-assist had become accustomed to the Glaseah
coming and going alone, and needed a moment to realize that
Jahir had returned with him this time. The fourth time someone
glanced at him, paused and hid their expression behind the rigor-
ous facades cultivated by medical personnel on every world and
in every time, Jahir suppressed a sigh and felt a flush of sympathy from the mindline.

/Tired of getting that look?/

/I had grown tired of it the first time I received it./

Vasiht'h's chuckle was just audible beneath his breath.

The corner of the room was still a neat arrangement of
pillows and blankets, and Jahir pulled a chair up to it as Vasiht'h
settled alongside him.

"We don't have to wait," Vasiht'h said, but there was nothing
behind the words but a patience: he was observing form only.

Jahir smiled and settled in.

He had drowsed off, he thought, but the sound of the door opening woke him, and the chatter of the two humans and the Seersa as their keeper herded them back into their room. A sudden, electric pause. And then squeals of delight. Jahir opened his arms for them and managed to gather them all in as Vasiht'h watched, his pleasure bright as sunshine in the mindline.

"Prince Jahir!" Amaranth exclaimed, the first to reclaim speech. "What are you doing here?"

Jahir glanced at Vasiht'h. "I believe you know that Vasiht'h left to come find me, yes?"

"He told us," Kuriel said, wide-eyed. "But he didn't say he'd be coming back!"

"I didn't know," Vasiht'h offered.

"But it was the right thing to do," Jahir said. "So I have come back, and I shall be here for another year or so. Perhaps closer to two."

"Probably closer to two," Vasiht'h said, wry. "Since I think I've got a bit longer than you."

This won him a longer embrace, the three children pressed against him so tightly he fought to breathe . . . and there was a song in him like laughter, that flowed out through the mindline, and nourished him because it was shared though he gave it no voice.

"So," Vasiht'h said, when they'd relented and he could breathe again. "Should we color? Tell stories? Make puppets?"

"All of it!" Kuriel exclaimed, throwing up her hands.

The Glaseah laughed. "Gently! We'll be back. There's no need to rush."

"That's true, isn't it," Persy said, beaming.

"Let's start with coloring," Amaranth said. "And then maybe we can have poetry."

As they repaired to the small table to collect their materials beneath Vasiht'h's watchful eye, Berquist finally stepped closer, crouched alongside the chair and looked at him. Jahir remained still for her scrutiny, and when she finally lifted her eyes to his he said, "I am under the care of a former dean of the medical school and the current director of the student clinic."

"KindlesFlame?" she said. "All right. Nothing serious?"

"Nothing being here won't solve," he said.

That made her smile. "I feel that way sometimes."

He joined the children at the table, to pick out crayons and pencils and ask them about their health, their day, whether they had had gelato lately, all the small events of childhood and all the grave ones that intruded with their illness. When they had colored their fill, they retired to the pillows in the corner, and Vasiht'h gave Jahir his data tablet, already showing the poetry volume they'd used most frequently for the purpose. The Eldritch sent a wordless gratitude through the mindline and chose one about naiads and the sea, and Kuriel sat on his lap and the two humans in front of him as he recited for them.

As they were preparing to leave, Kuriel said, "Your pretty ring . . . you're wearing it around your neck because it's too big for your finger, aren't you?"

Surprised, Jahir paused. "You noticed?"

"When you were reading and I was leaning on you," she said, flicking her ears back. "I know how you feel. I get like that too. My clothes get loose. We all do."

He gave her his full and patient attention. "Do you have any advice for me, arii?"

She nodded. "Eat more cookies."

Vasiht'h waited until they'd left before asking him about the source of his amusement, and then they shared the laugh.

"I haven't, you know. Had any cookies for some time."

Vasiht'h's huff carried through the mindline. "You haven't had any *food* in some time. At least, not enough of it."

"Because you have not baked," Jahir replied, folding his arms behind his back as he paced his companion.

Vasiht'h eyed him. "Is that an observation, a request or an accusation?"

"It is," Jahir said, savoring the words, "a psychological evaluation."

"Ohhh, is that what this is? Psychoanalysis?" Vasiht'h folded his arms in mock disgruntlement as the mindline carried the effervescence of his amusement. "You told me once I only bake when I'm upset."

"That observation lacked nuance," Jahir said. "You also bake when content."

Vasiht'h's amusement collapsed into pensiveness. "I think I cook more when I'm content and bake more when I'm upset."

"I think you cook and bake because it is a form of meditation, and it calms you." Jahir glanced at him. "I have missed your cookies."

"You could certainly use them," Vasiht'h said. And laughed, quieter. "So could I. Come on, let's go meet Luci early. We can take over her kitchen."

"That seems a fine plan."

———⊗⊗⊗———

Lucrezia opened the door on them and called, "Brett, the lost lambs have returned!"

"Great, tell them I'm hungry!" Vasiht'h covered his face with a hand. Brett appeared, peered past Luci's shoulder. "Well? It's either you cook or we starve."

Luci put her hand on his nose and pushed him back. "Don't listen to him. Mera's bringing curry and I still have half a pitcher of sangria. We'll be fine."

"Half a pitcher of sangria!" Brett complained. "That won't make Mera tipsy. It won't even make me tipsy!"

"We're barely into the semester and he's ready for winter break," Luci said dryly. She waved them inside. "Come on. I'm going to finish refreshing the pitcher here. The kitchen's all yours if in fact you want to use it." She eyed Brett. "And if you don't, that's fine too. Isn't it, arii."

Brett shot Vasiht'h a hopeful look. "But you really want to, don't you?"

Vasiht'h glanced at Jahir, found the Eldritch standing with his hands clasped behind his back, head lowered just enough to leave his face in shadow. The smile on his mouth was something

Vasiht'h felt more than saw. It made him glad that they'd come instead of finding some more impersonal and convenient place to sleep while investigating a permanent housing solution. "Yes, yes. As long as you've got something I can bake with . . ."

"If they do not, the genie can surely be convinced to produce the necessary raw materials," Jahir offered.

Vasiht'h snorted. "At three times the cost." Luci was looking at him now, too, and he laughed. "Okay, I'm not fooling anyone. Yes, I'll bake. Take me to your larder."

Brett and Luci cheered.

That night was a good night. Chopping nuts and chocolate was work within Jahir's reach, and to share a kitchen with him again was salve to Vasiht'h. He hadn't realized how much of his youth had involved making food with his sisters and brothers and parents, and how those memories had shaped his sense of family and trust, until he had his best friend beside him, forming dough with that charming meticulousness that seemed so out of place in such an otherwise regal bearing. They brought the results with them to the gazebo, where Mera and Leina were waiting, and that part—that was as if they'd never left, the ease with which their friends accepted them again. But everything was different, too, because if he concentrated, he could taste the flavors of the food and feel their foreignness through Jahir's senses. The mindline sang softly, camaraderie and comfort and gratitude. And when they returned to Luci's apartment and settled down to sleep, they did so next to one another: Jahir on the couch, Vasiht'h on a nest of spare blankets and pillows gleefully (if messily) constructed by their hosts.

/Is it good?/ he asked, not because he needed to know but because he wanted to hear the answer, wreathed as it would be in all Jahir's feelings.

/It is more than well,/ was the response, soft.

It came gentled with music, and Vasiht'h exclaimed, struck by the realization that they could, /We should go back to the concerts./

The shiver that ran Jahir's length needed no flourish in the mindline.

/Tomorrow,/ Vasiht'h said. */I'll buy tickets./*

When they slept, their shared dreams were informed by the music Jahir remembered so vividly.

CHAPTER 25

VASIHT'H BROUGHT JAHIR to several of the apartments maintained at the university's edges by its housing department for returning students, or students with families. The Eldritch trailed him, hands clasped behind his back and gaze intent, and made no comment on any of them. The mindline between them remained far too coy for Vasiht'h's taste, and after the fourth tour he waited, leaning against the side of the building, for his friend to step back outside. Jahir looked for him, found him and paused at the obvious ambush.

"What aren't you telling me?" Vasiht'h asked, torn between amusement and exasperation.

Jahir looked back at the door, tilted his head a little as if listening to some interior voice. "They are dwellings suitable for students."

"Which we are . . . ?" Vasiht'h said, now more curious than irritated.

"They are modest. . . ."

"Which you usually like," Vasiht'h pointed out.

The Eldritch cleared his throat. "Rather aggressively so. Arii, we have been coasting on your budget for some time, and you have not permitted me to pay you back. But we are not poor."

This was a new use of the word 'we.' Vasiht'h paused to savor it like he would a new flavor. He'd taken for granted that they'd live together. And then, after Jahir had made the suggestion, that they would eventually work together. That they'd also share financial fortunes wasn't something he'd at all considered. "We aren't?" he said, still deciding how he felt about it.

"No," Jahir replied, and the mindline tickled with the pressure of his gentle amusement. "I would very much like to live near campus. But would you allow me to finance someplace a little less . . ."

"Modest?" Vasiht'h said, giving in to the good humor.

Jahir glanced at the apartment and said, "Humble."

"Humble," Vasiht'h repeated, trying not to laugh.

"Aggressively so."

He did laugh then. "Fine. But you're going to have to show me what you have in mind, all right? I don't know how . . . un-humble . . . 'we' can afford."

"I would not want to be overtly un-humble," Jahir began.

"Aggressively un-humble—"

"I would not want to be in poor taste," Jahir finished, more firmly, though his mouth was twitching and the mindline was shimmering with his withheld laughter. He began walking back toward the Pad station. "But I would like something bigger."

"Is there any particular reason why?"

Images then, unexpected and brilliant in memory: cooking dinner for the winter festival, Mera slouched all over the couch and most of the floor in front of the hearth, toasting them with a glass of mulled wine, the pinpoint reflection of candlelight off dishes and silverware. Jahir said, "Because we like to entertain."

"Oh!" Vasiht'h said. Quieter. "Oh. Yes. Yes, we do." He shook himself and said, "Bigger apartment it is. But still modest in its bigness."

"Excess is gauche," Jahir agreed, satisfied.

Several days later, after a rather long afternoon in lecture, Vasiht'h returned to Luci's place to find Jahir waiting for him, seated on the step outside the door. The mindline communicated a quiet pleasure at this ability to just sit without having to hurt, and even the growing cold in the breeze didn't distress the Eldritch, compared to that ease.

"Good trade-off?" Vasiht'h asked, smiling.

"Very little compares to the ability to move freely," Jahir said. "I have something to show you."

Vasiht'h sampled the mindline, tasted the sparkles of anticipation of it like bits of mint. He re-shouldered his bag."Well, then . . . let's go."

Fifteen minutes later, Jahir unlocked a door and led him into a bright open space, flooded with autumn sunlight from the skylights. Vasiht'h's first impression was of honey-colored wood and ivory tile, and a lot of windows looking out on a courtyard with a fountain.

There was a kitchen. It was a glorious kitchen. He walked into the center of it, turned—and could! It was large enough for his centauroid body—and said, "Yes."

"Yes?" Jahir asked. "I have not shown you the rest!"

"I can sleep in the kitchen," Vasiht'h said, laughing. "But fine, go ahead. Show me around."

It was not actually much larger than their university apartment had been. But it was far and away more beautiful. The materials had not been beaten down and scuffed by generations of absent-minded students; the wood still glowed with polish, the bathroom fixtures were still brilliant. Nothing was dented or battered. There were a lot more windows, and that was saying something given the Alliance's fixation on installing them in even the most meager of shanties. And there was a fireplace.

"I didn't think you'd be able to find one," Vasiht'h said, observing it.

"It was my first criterion," Jahir admitted, standing at his back. "I didn't look unless the apartment had one."

Vasiht'h grinned. "You know these places have heaters."

"It's not the same."

"No," he said, because he'd learned that was true. "It's not." He sighed and smiled. "It's beautiful. It's probably astronomically expensive. But if we can afford it?"

"We can afford it."

That 'we' again. Vasiht'h wondered how much negotiation would be involved in the future, managing that financial 'we.' He looked forward to it. For now, though: "I'd love living here."

"Then it is perhaps fortunate that I've already paid the deposit."

Vasiht'h mimed throwing a pillow at him. "You could have waited for me to say yes!"

"Even if I knew you would?"

"Especially if you'd known I would!" he said, and laughed.

"You are only half in jest," Jahir observed, thoughtful. "I'll be more careful of such assumptions in the future."

"But only a little," Vasiht'h said. "Because sometimes, surprises like this are nice."

"I promise," the Eldritch said, solemn, and a frisson of that vow shivered the mindline and Vasiht'h's spine. "And now, since I have so cavalierly selected our apartment and deprived you of any financial stake in it, I shall say: you can decorate."

"Now that," Vasiht'h said, rubbing his palms together. "I can do." He grinned. "And it gives us another excuse for a party."

"Our first," Jahir observed.

Vasiht'h paused, tasted the emotions in the mindline, finally separated out the thoughts, or what he thought were the thoughts, anyway. He chose the greater intimacy of that communication to make sure he'd gathered the nuances. /. . . *since we have decided to stick together?*/

/*Just so.*/

He flushed and rubbed his cheek. Then chuckled. "Well, let's make it a good one, then."

⸎

Their first party involved homemade pizza and Luci's sangria set out on the floor while everyone helped unpack the two boxes Vasiht'h had put in storage before leaving: mostly kitchenware and dishes. When they were done, Leina looked around and said,

"And now we go shopping."

. . . and that was an unforgettable episode, herding a Cira-caana, a Harat-Shar, two Seersa and one mutely amused Eldritch through various boutiques in one of the fancier shopping districts of the capital. They did more window-shopping than actual purchasing—they bought all of one rug for the great room—but Vasiht'h had not laughed so hard in weeks and he found he'd needed it. Just the sight of Merishiinal ducking to fit into stores designed by the four-foot tall Seersa, craning his upper body around corners to poke at wind chimes and peer at lamps while his Seersan roommate dashed after him, trying to keep him from tipping anything over. . . .

"We're a traveling comedy routine," Vasiht'h observed to Luci when they broke for late afternoon coffee.

"Angels, yes," she answered, tail curling. Cocking her head, she added, "Why is Prince Handsome suddenly averse to drinking anything with milk in it?"

"Everything they were using to keep him from losing every pound on his body was milk-based," Vasiht'h said.

She mmmed. "Yes, I can see how that would become a bad association. Particularly since the news is all over a wet outbreak on Selnor." She glanced at him. "Know anything about that?"

Vasiht'h grimaced. "The news, huh."

"It's pretty big on the medical nets," she said, casual.

"I guess it would be."

She chuckled. "You are awful at this, you know. Take lessons from your friend, ah?"

"In?" Vasiht'h wondered.

"Gracefully side-stepping questions you don't want to answer." More seriously, she said, "No wonder you came home so quickly." She considered, then added, "Is it all milk? Brett will cry if we don't make eggnog for the holidays."

Vasiht'h snorted. "Forget Brett. *I'll* cry."

———— ❦ ————

The one thing that should have registered about the new apartment and didn't hit Vasiht'h when they prepared for bed and he stopped outside the bathroom. Jahir looked up from where he was sitting on the floor, toweling off his hair.

"This is a one-bedroom flat," Vasiht'h said.

A long pause. The mindline was tense, like a reflection of someone holding his breath.

"I did not think that would be an issue?" Jahir said, careful of the words.

"I . . . didn't think you would prefer that?" Vasiht'h said.

"I would rather much mind it more otherwise."

Vasiht'h paused, working through that. Seeing his frown, Jahir said, "I would like it, if we were in the same room." With some chagrin, "Universal is my second language."

"I forget that sometimes," Vasiht'h murmured. "You speak it well." He folded his arms. "I'd prefer it too, to be in the same room, but we've only done it because we had to, in the past. I thought once we had the space, you'd want more privacy."

Jahir hid a laugh, and in the mindline it was equal parts humor and helplessness. "Arii . . . you have seen me nearly dead. Certainly reduced to the point of uselessness. In very near to every vulnerability, and no doubt the ones you haven't yet you will someday see, if we remain together as we plan. The mindline makes everything plain. I think perhaps we should reconsider our definitions of privacy where they apply to one another."

"All right, granted," Vasiht'h said, following the amusement up the mindline until it infected him too. He padded to Jahir's side and sat next to him. "I just thought I'd leave you the illusion of it, since it's so important to Eldritch."

"I prefer to look at the truth of it," Jahir said. "And learn what I might about it." He glanced up at the Glaseah. "You as well, yes?"

"Yes." Vasiht'h watched him resume toweling his hair. "It's grown."

"It has," Jahir said, looking at it. And then, abruptly: "Would you cut it for me?"

The startlement the mindline brought him would have been funny had the matter not been serious; had not his own intensity communicated itself to his friend. He had not had the chance to cut his hair since coming to the Alliance, and it had become long enough to trouble him, even growing as slowly as it did. But he had not known how to cut it himself, and had been troubled reconciling his own traditions—of the intimacy of the master/servant relationship that made it safe for someone to touch him, to use scissors near his head—with the Alliance's impersonal customs, where grooming was a transaction to be paid for between strangers. It had never sat well with him. And though Vasiht'h was not and would never be to him what his body servant had been, he could think of no one else he trusted with that intimacy. "The length. It belongs . . . about here." He put the flat of his hand at his ribcage. "Any longer is . . ."

Vasiht'h frowned, groping through the impressions Jahir was allowing to seep into the mindline, and Jahir allowed it because he didn't know himself how to explain. The Glaseah said, slowly, "Not irritating. And not upsetting. And not an imposition, or inappropriate . . ."

"Not where I want it," Jahir finally said, because in the end, it was that simple. His first moment of childish rebellion against the things that seemed to make no sense on his world . . . the same things that had eventually driven him off of it, seeking the answers others had contrived to all the challenges of forming a healthy society.

Perhaps the Queen was wise in casting her seeds to the wind. He loved the Alliance with a passion that surprised and disarmed him. But he loved his world, too, in all its myopic stagnation, and wanted nothing more than to return one day and bring all that he'd learned to them.

But not today. And not, he thought, looking at Vasiht'h's alien face, for a long time.

"It's not where I want it," he said again. "And it would be

awkward for me to trim it myself. I could take myself somewhere
and have a stranger do it, but I would prefer otherwise, if you
were willing."

Vasiht'h reached out, hesitated. Jahir sent a wordless encour-
agement through the mindline, and the Glaseah gathered the
ends of his hair in small hands, testing the texture. Jahir sensed
his curiosity at it, so different from that of the brothers and
sisters he'd groomed growing up. "It wouldn't be hard," Vasiht'h
said. "As long as you didn't want some fancy style. For that you
really would need someone with training. But if all you want is to
take some length off of it?"

"That is all I need," Jahir said.

"Then I can do that." Vasiht'h met his eyes. "This is important
to you?"

How much to share? He was obligated to keep the Veil. The
Eldritch Queens who'd instated it had never imagined one of their
own willingly committing to the intimacy he had with an alien,
by embracing the mindline; he wondered what Liolesa would say
if he asked her where to draw the line, but his few memories of
her were of her remote beauty, and the occasional wicked sparkle
in her eye, hinting at a personality that would re-shape a world
or kill everyone trying.

"It is important to me," he said, slowly. "To be self-sufficient.
And if I am not to be so, then to be open to allowing others to
shoulder some of my burdens without . . ." Find words. What
words? "Without the armor of condescension or arrogance."

Vasiht'h shook his head. "I'll get a comb and scissors. I have
one in my kit."

Sitting on the floor with his hands in his lap, Jahir sought
any sign of regret or unease, found none. Sorrow for the boy
he'd been, perhaps, for being trapped in a system impervious to
change. But all things changed. One day, he would be part of it.

A blanket draped around his shoulders. He looked up, startled from his thoughts. /I was—/

"Cold," Vasiht'h agreed, and settled down behind him and
began to comb, little pulls at his scalp. "Besides, it'll give the

hair a place to fall so we won't have to sweep it up." The Glaseah chuckled. "I wish my sibs had had hair this straight. Would have made things a lot easier!"

"You cut it for them?"

"Oh, we all took turns," Vasiht'h said, sounding distracted. "There were a lot of us. Twelve Glaseahn kids . . . that's a lot of legs and arms and heads and wings, and all of them need some kind of grooming. Claws trimmed, hair cut, fur trimmed or thinned, wing vanes oiled—"

"You oil your wings?" Jahir asked, interested.

"If they get cracks, or it's too dry out," Vasiht'h said. A pressure against Jahir's ribcage then. "Here?"

"There, thank you."

The scissors pulled at his hair, snipped. Vasiht'h brushed and continued. "The boys all wanted short hair—it was easier to take care of—but some of my sisters preferred longer styles. I had seven sisters . . . I got pretty good at it."

Which explained the warm comfort in the mindline; this was a familial activity for his roommate, reassuring in its familiarity. Jahir basked in it, eyes closed, and let his thoughts wander until Vasiht'h stopped abruptly, his thoughts crystallizing into a single exclamation.

"Arii?" Jahir asked.

"You . . . you were going to go buy all the furniture I was looking at and liking!" Vasiht'h exclaimed.

Jahir hesitated, then said, rueful, "The mindline has its own notions of privacy, I see."

"You can't," Vasiht'h said. "Promise me you're not going to do that. And yes, I feel you feeling at me, I know how you are with promises, but I mean this. You can't . . . just . . . do all of that. And no, it's not about us making decisions about things together this time."

Jahir glanced over his shoulder at him. "What then is it about?"

Vasiht'h hesitated, scissors lax in his hands. Shaking himself a little, he said, "I'm . . . not sure. Here. Tell me."

A flush then, of embarrassment and indignation, and a little resentment. Jahir chased the latter down and found helplessness near its root, an emotion he had to unfold, and unpack, and open yet again to get to its wellspring: *Partners share everything. Responsibility too.*

No wonder, he thought, that this had risen through his mind while allowing someone else to cut his hair, brought forth by his own discomfort with the Alliance egalitarianism, not because he disagreed with it because he did not, had never, because he had always found his world's stratification unfair . . . but because he'd grown up being told he must take care of those who had less than he.

"I understand," he said. "And you are right. I have an idea."

"One I'll like?" Vasiht'h asked.

Jahir nodded. "I think so. But perhaps we should finish what we're doing first."

"All right." The gentle pressure returned, the high-pitched snips of the shears. After a moment, Vasiht'h said, "This is hard for you, isn't it. Adjusting."

"I fear it will be," Jahir said, low. "It is one thing to move through the Alliance as . . . a . . . tourist. Another to participate in it quite as fully as I now must, if I am to be a fair partner."

The gentler pressure of the comb now. "We have an advantage at least, if communication is the source of a lot of misunderstanding."

"Yes," Jahir said.

A long pause. Then, "I think that's done. How's that feel?"

Jahir straightened, felt the strands tickle his arms above the elbow. "Much better, thank you."

"Good. I'll get ready for bed, and then you tell me this idea of yours, all right?"

"Agreed," Jahir said.

While Vasiht'h used the bathroom, he looped the blanket close around his shoulders and padded into the empty great room. It took some doing to find what he needed; it had been in his bags, but someone had partially unpacked them on their arrival here. By the time Vasiht'h emerged, however, he'd used the board hung next to their pantry to good effect, and stepped back to allow his partner to see the results. Vasiht'h reached up and touched the small papers, each one bearing some item they'd seen on their excursion.

"So that we know what we still need," Jahir said. "But each is on a separate page, so we can take it down when we've decided we will go get it. We can take turns, if it pleases you better. Or do it more informally."

Vasiht'h's satisfaction welled through the mindline. He stroked the paper that read 'kitchen table.' "This one first. I know a place we can rent one for cheaper than the one we saw in the store earlier."

"And if we decide we want to keep it?" Jahir wondered.

"Then I will let you foot the bill of having a genie create one from the specs," Vasiht'h said with a grin. "This is perfect, arii. Thank you for really listening about this."

"It is my pleasure. Also . . . my responsibility. Yes?"

Vasiht'h glanced up at him. "You . . . you're going to be something else to live with."

"A good something else, I hope," Jahir said.

"I'm going to grow like a tree," Vasiht'h said, and the mindline bloomed with the image of one of Anseahla's great rainforest giants, exuberant and vital and bright, twined 'round with wildflowers. It made sense of a metaphor that would otherwise have been opaque to him . . . and gentled an anxiety in him he hadn't even known was lingering, from a memory of dreams of dying flowers, and he a helpless gardener. But it wasn't his task to be sole gardener of blooms too delicate to survive without aid, was it?

/No,/ Vasiht'h answered. /That's not how it works./

"I will learn," Jahir said. And then, his smile growing lopsided. "But grant me some forgiveness at how long it will take me to believe it."

Vasiht'h grinned. "As long as we figure it out together, we'll do fine."

———∞∞∞———

The following day, Jahir left early for his appointment with KindlesFlame, leaving Vasiht'h to sit in the kitchen and look out the windows at the birds landing on the edge of the fountain. He finished his breakfast and his coffee, cleaned and regarded the barren apartment. And then he checked the time on Anseahla and made the call he'd been avoiding, or too busy to place, for months.

His mother answered on the first alert, appearing on the apartment's wall screen. It was larger than the one in their student flat, and of far higher fidelity. He could have counted the gray hairs framing her eyes.

"Vasiht'h," she said. "My love, I've been expecting you."

"Have you?" he asked, trying not to fidget. "I know I should have called. . . ."

She shook her head. "Your sister told me you were busy with something." She held up a hand to still him. "No, she didn't say what. I knew better than to ask, anyway. She's always kept your confidences. But now that you're here, I want to know what's going on. Your letters were far too cagey."

"Dami," he began. And then, because the enormity of it was overwhelming and he couldn't get around it: "I've found a mind-bonded."

She stared at him, her ear feathers splayed. "Vasiht'h?"

"A mind-bonded," he said, shoulders slumping with relief. If he told his parents, it was real, wasn't it? Somehow it made it feel that way. "A real mindline. Like something out of stories."

"You met someone?" she asked, bewildered. "Last I heard you weren't even good friends with any Glaseah . . ."

"Not any Glaseah," Vasiht'h said, feeling calmer. "My roommate, the Eldritch? Him."

"Oh, love." She stared at him, and he could almost feel her compassion and her concern and her happiness. "Are you sure? They live a long time, don't they?"

"They can," Vasiht'h said, and saying this made it real too.

"But they can die just as easily as the rest of us. Didn't you used to say that life was too short not to live?"

"As I recall, right before you left for Seersana," she said, her mouth twitching.

"You were right," Vasiht'h said. And added, "Oh, Dami. Did you ever have to shake Tapa to keep him from paying for everything?"

She started laughing.

He told her everything: the mindline's first attempts to ravel, the advice he'd given that had sent Jahir offworld, his following, the wet epidemic, everything. She listened with all the grave attention familiar from his first memories of childhood until he'd exorcised it all, and when he was done he looked up at her. "That's it, Dami. That's everything." And then, unable to help it, "Did I do all right?"

She smiled across stars and said, "Love, you did wonderful."

Vasiht'h sighed and couldn't help a chuckle. "Twenty-four years old—more or less, given all this flying across worlds—and it still feels good to hear my mother tell me I've been good."

"Maybe so," she said. "But you're not a child anymore, Vasiht'h."

Something in her voice made him look up at her.

"You've been searching for yourself for a while," she said. "And when I looked at you, I still saw the little boy I had to take care of, to watch out for. Now I see a young man who's found his center. You crossed the threshold, heart." Her smile became merrier. "Not that I'm giving up the prerogative of worrying about you, and still thinking of you as the little boy I had to help pick burrs from between his toes. But I think I can relax a little now. You're finally on your way."

"And you can tell that from all the way over there?" he asked, teasing only a little.

"Oh love." She shook her head. "You should see yourself. If you could, you'd know how I knew." Such a tender smile. "You look happy."

After the call, Vasiht'h looked at himself in the bathroom mirror. Did he look happy? He canted his head, searching his eyes. All he saw was himself . . . and wasn't that the point. *I decided to make decisions about my own destiny*, he thought. *And become the actor in my own life, instead of floundering around until something happened. I guess that's the difference between just keeping your head above water and actually swimming for shore.*

He smiled and jogged to the kitchen, and when he left he took the "kitchen table" paper with him.

CHAPTER 26

The table came first. Then another rug. Chairs, a rack for firewood. Floor pillows for the species that found chairs difficult.

Schooling became routine. He and Vasiht'h settled into their classes. Jahir took the chemistry classes KindlesFlame okayed, enough to give Vasiht'h the odd occasional dream of molecular diagrams. Vasiht'h gave his attention fully to his ethics and legal classes, and let the material bleed back over the mindline, knowing Jahir would be sitting through those lectures himself come the following semester. And his friend gradually put back the weight he'd lost to Selnor, filled the cadaverous hollows between his ribs and the tendons on the backs of his hands, became again a sight that turned faces for better reasons.

"Is it hard?" Vasiht'h asked one day, pouring himself a freshly cooked cup of kerinne.

"What part?" was the absent reply. His partner was sitting at their kitchen table—their table, Vasiht'h thought, pleased, not Jahir's—going through the material for his approaching midterms; the mindline whispered of pharmacokinetic variability and membrane permeability and other terms that floated, accreting context.

"Any of it," Vasiht'h said. He went through the cabinets and came down with a can of black tea. Setting a kettle to boil, he continued, "I wasn't sure how you'd be doing, coming into the semester partway. You had so much trouble the first year."

"I did, didn't I?" Jahir sat back, pen loose in his hand. He still wrote as many notes long-hand as he took on tablet. Vasiht'h never tired of watching that unlikely calligraphy come from something as simple and cheap as a modern pen. "But that was before I had lived here, and lived through quite so much. I think the process the children began, Selnor finished."

Vasiht'h couldn't help his wariness; they were not so far from the experience for him to be sanguine about the memories.

Jahir lifted a hand, just a touch, his smile pained. "I know." He gathered himself, then continued. "I did not spend much time there, but what time I did was . . . very intense. And though the memories aren't clear, I know things I would have thought would not have caught. If that makes sense?"

Through the mindline, Vasiht'h saw a flash of readings gathered during triage, passing patients through. Races in all their biological idiosyncrasy, now indelibly burned into the memory of someone who'd never so much as seen an alien three years ago. An ability to glance at a halo-arch and know instantly whether the person beneath it was thriving or dying . . . and if the details were not yet socketed in place, there was a framework for them to hang on, and it was increasingly easy to add to that framework.

"It's easier," Jahir said again. And looked at the cup of tea that appeared before him with a surprise that tasted like pepper in Vasiht'h's mouth. "I . . . did not know that I wanted tea."

"You don't want coffee," Vasiht'h said. "And you don't want kerinne. But you do want a stimulant, which rules out cider and hot chocolate. I guessed."

Jahir sipped, closed his eyes. Chuckled, quiet. "You guess well."

"I know you," Vasiht'h said. "Selnor was like that for me too. Everything that went before, crystallized."

"And now you read me like I read a halo-arch?" Jahir asked, but if the mindline was right, the thought amused him, pleased him.

Vasiht'h grinned. "Oh, there are plenty of mysteries left, don't worry. But something as simple as whether you want tea or hot chocolate, that I can manage."

"Sometimes it is the simple things that are the most revealing," Jahir said. And then, thoughtful, "Shall we entertain for the holidays?"

"I thought that's why we got the big apartment?"

"I mean . . . entertain," Jahir said, and that came with the image of not just their quadmates, but teachers and staff, people from All Children's—including the girls, if they were well enough—all moving through a warmly lit scene enshrouded in evergreen garlands.

"Oh!" Vasiht'h said, heart leaping. How long had it been since he'd had a real party? His family gatherings at home were enormous. "Yes. Yes, I think that's a great idea. But let's pass our exams before we start inviting our faculty advisors to dinner . . . !"

Jahir laughed softly. "Yes. I return to my books." He glanced at the tea. "Properly fortified."

Vasiht'h grinned. "Dinner later. You're doing prep."

"Set the vegetables out. They shall meet my knife."

It was a good dinner. Good to see the Eldritch eat; good to see him relaxing. At the meal's conclusion, Vasiht'h said, "So, I wasn't sure if you'd be interested, but there's a jazz band playing at the Stringleigh Center downtown tonight. I know you probably want to keep studying but—"

Jahir was already heading for the coat hanging by the door.

———

They spent the afternoon in one of the Performing Arts Center's more intimate venues, at a table in the back listening to a performance even Vasiht'h could tell was tremendous; through the mindline it became something sublime, lent a luster by his partner's far more acute hearing and better appreciation for the subtleties. But Vasiht'h let himself acknowledge that his own heart sped to the beat, that he felt it standing his fur on end . . . that he could be moved to passion, something he would have

denied a few years ago. He hadn't been indifferent to music, as
he'd claimed; he just hadn't wanted to let it in. He hadn't wanted
to let a lot of things in, thinking that playing tourist was the
same as getting involved. This was on his mind on their trip
back, taking one of the people movers toward the nearest Pad
station, the bright lights of the city smearing against the dark
blue and black outside the floor-to-ceiling windows. Jahir's quiet
comment surprised him.

"You were right, you know."

"About what this time?" he asked, smile quirking.

A hint of amusement, fondness filing its edges. "When you
told me it was no good to throw myself so deeply into schooling that I was forced to forgo actually living here." The Eldritch
looked back toward the receding spire of the Arts Center, the
light striping his face as the passing street lamps scrolled by.
"This is a necessary thing."

Vasiht'h sampled the mindline's complex texture and said, "A
life in balance."

The Eldritch inclined his head.

Vasiht'h watched the lights go by a little longer, then said,
"You know it hasn't been all one way."

"Ah?" Jahir glanced at him, hair swinging around his throat.

"You've taught me things too." The pounding beat of the
music, the sudden syncopation making his breath skip, like his
breath had skipped so many times on Selnor. The understanding
that life was change and changeable, and that it could exhilarate
as well as terrify. The awe and joy of diving into that maelstrom
rather than standing aloof from it, clucking his tongue at all
the poor people who got so mixed up trying to make their way
through the chaos. He tried to find words to express all of that
and realized he didn't have to when Jahir's wordless, humbled
acknowledgement reached him, gentle as a breeze in spring.

/I guess words are irrelevant now./

/They have their place,/ Jahir replied. /A new way of doing
things need not supplant the old ways. It can expand your options
instead./

Vasiht'h glanced at the other passengers sharing their cab with them and hid a laugh from everyone but his partner, who looked at him quizzically.

/I think our body language indicates we're still talking, but no one can hear us anymore./

The Eldritch scanned the compartment, then looked fixedly into the dark, mouth twitching. /I can see some of what we do will take some practice./

/It will if we don't want people to know we're talking!/

Jahir did laugh then, and Vasiht'h did his best not to notice the looks they garnered as they stepped out onto the platform and headed home.

CHAPTER 27

They passed their midterms and their finals, and spent their holiday shopping, entertaining, cooking—"eating," Jahir had complained, splayed in one of their chairs by the fire, and Vasiht'h had snorted, unrepentant—and enjoying the break immensely. Over mulled wine by the fire, during one of these parties, KindlesFlame said to him, "So, settled in?"

"I think so," Jahir said, watching the flames and wondering if he should add another log. He could feel his mentor's regard. "It has not been as hard as I'd thought."

"Mmm. Well, next semester is the real test, you know."

Jahir tilted his head. "I am forewarned. What is it I should be wary of, then?"

"Unless I miss my guess, your schedule's going to involve taking your first practicals?" At Jahir's nod, KindlesFlame said, "That's when you're going to find out if you like it or not."

"I suppose I should feel more anxiety over the prospect, since this is what I reneged on my residency on Selnor to pursue."

"You didn't renege on it," KindlesFlame said dryly. "But yes, most people would be nervous. You're not?"

"No," Jahir said, surprised that it might be so. "Is that strange?"

The foxine chuckled. "No. I felt the same way about medicine. It was like coming home."

That was a touch so swift Jahir almost didn't feel the piercing pain of it, like the dagger he'd once taken to the shoulder. Not because he wanted desperately to find that feeling of belonging himself . . . but because . . . he had. This had become home, had become easy and right, had become a point of strength to move from. What did that mean for him, who one day would be recalled to the homeworld? And did it matter, when that time might be centuries from now?

KindlesFlame had been studying his face as he'd worked through the implications. The foxine said, gently, "So. Not worried, mm?"

"No," Jahir said. And then, thinking of Selnor and how critically he'd overworked himself. "Well. Perhaps a little."

"A little is normal," KindlesFlame said. "If it becomes a lot, you know where to find me."

"You have been a great helpmeet, alet."

KindlesFlame snorted. "Don't thank me 'til it's over." And lifted his glass. "Cheers."

Jahir tapped his glass to the Tam-illee's and drank.

⎯⎯⎯⎯⎯ ⊗⊗⊗ ⎯⎯⎯⎯⎯

There was one practicum class scheduled per semester; not a formal class, but a way of logging required hours toward the practical requirements for the degree. In the first week of class, the student received his assignment to any one of seven separate clinics throughout the city. It struck Jahir as an interesting coincidence that both he and Vasiht'h were assigned to the same clinic on campus. It puzzled him to discover they were scheduled for the same shift. When they compared their initial schedules and discovered the same clients on them, Vasiht'h said, "What in Her name are they doing?" And stood, dropping his data tablet in a messenger bag and slinging it over his shoulder.

"Arii?" Jahir asked, startled.

"I smell Palland's fingerprints all over this," Vasiht'h said.

"And I'm going to go have it out of him."

"Have what out of him?" Jahir asked, but he reached for his scarf and coat.

"Whatever cute thing it is he's plotting, because he's plotting something and he didn't bother to consult us," Vasiht'h growled.

Jahir knew better than to argue with his roommate in such a mood. He buttoned his coat, pulled on his gloves, and followed the Glaseah into the raw cold of Seersana's early spring.

Their arrival caused the Seersa to rise from behind his desk, giving Jahir an opportunity to evaluate him against the impressions he'd inherited from Vasiht'h but never made for himself. It fascinated him to find the Seersa shorter than he expected—Vasiht'h being barely five feet to his six and a half made sense of that—and younger; Vasiht'h saw the lines hidden by the thin fur around Palland's eyes far more easily, having grown up seeking signs of age on Pelted faces. But the merry sparkle in the professor's eyes was just the same.

"Vasiht'h, alet," Palland said agreeably. "And here at last is the source of so many of your worries. Jahir Seni Galare, I presume?"

"You have me to rights," Jahir said.

"Lefeyette's given good report of you. It's nice to finally have a chance to make your acquaintance, though I am guessing you're here for a reason?" The Seersa smiled, all innocence, ears perked.

Vasiht'h folded his arms. "You know why we're here."

"Maybe," Palland said, after a moment. He tossed a data tablet onto the desk between them. "Recognize that?"

Vasiht'h picked it up, frowned. "This is my research from last year."

"Mmm-hmm."

The Glaseah's irritation was like the seasoning on an affection Jahir could taste like curry. He hid his amusement and let his roommate handle the conversation.

"You're throwing us together so we can test my findings?"

Palland snorted. "I'm not throwing you together, alet. You're already a team. And you have been testing your findings for a year now. I'd like you to take them into the clinical environment with the person you appear to have chosen to go into practice with." He glanced at Jahir, lifted a brow. "I'm presuming that is the plan? You're a contact esper."

There was no use denying what was plainly known to half the medical school, given the issues he'd had in his first years. "I am."

"And you know about his research?"

"I do."

"And? You game?"

The colloquialism took him a moment, but he inclined his head, hiding his smile. "I am."

"So?" Palland said to Vasiht'h. "Your problem is . . . I'm guessing at your next move and arranging permission for it, and that irritates you because you really wanted to think of it yourself?"

"A little bit." Vasiht'h sighed and smiled crookedly. "Alet—"

"Vasiht'h, you would have thought of it yourself and come to me within a few weeks," Palland said, seating himself. "I'm saving you some time, that's all. Unless you're saying you're not interested?"

A question in the mindline now, tentative. Before it could develop words, Jahir answered, /Yes. Of course I will. I have been interested in your research since you advanced the idea to me. I said we should practice it together after school. The sooner we begin, the better, yes?/

Palland was watching them, leaning his face on a hand with the finger extended, pressing into his cheek. "Done conferring?"

"Is it that obvious?" Vasiht'h asked, rueful.

"If you want to hide it you need to stop looking at one another," the Seersa said with a smile. "Or talk to people more oblivious to physical cues."

"We're interested," Jahir said for his friend. "And grateful that you have made arrangements in advance."

"Excellent. We'd like to see how it works in practical application ourselves. I've gotten you placed with Healer Ravanelle. She's comfortable working outside standard rules, and you two are going to have to make up new ones as you go along. Explain to her what you're planning and accept her guidance. And keep us informed."

"Us?" Vasiht'h said.

Palland grinned. "Us, your keepers. That would be me for thee and KindlesFlame for your man there."

"I see," Vasiht'h said, folding his arms. "Got us all figured out, have you, sir."

"Not at all!" the Seersa said, cheerful, ears swiveled forward. "That's part of what's so fascinating about the two of you. So go off and prove us right."

⚬⚬⚬

Ravanelle was another Seersa, a female, black as spilled ink with brilliant orange eyes and a mannerism both relaxed and curious. Jahir liked her immediately, and some of his amusement spilled into the mindline, pricking his friend's interest.

/What?/

/Her demeanor is what we are striving to project, is it not?/

Vasiht'h studied her and smiled. /I think we'll be different, but the effect . . . yes./

"So, my newest project has arrived," Ravanelle said. "Come in, aletsen. Let's have a discussion about the scope of your practicum."

They joined her in her office, very different in character from Palland's, which had the look of something thrown together over decades of occupancy by different tenants. The furniture in Ravanelle's office matched, was comfortable, had been selected not to stress her authority but to give visitors equal footing with her, something she demonstrated by seating herself on one of the well-stuffed chairs facing the dark wood coffee table by the window. Jahir took the couch; Vasiht'h sat beside him on the floor, his shoulders near the Eldritch's knee.

/She does not miss the significance of how we sit./

/She shouldn't,/ Vasiht'h thought, amusement candying the words. /She took the assessment classes once upon a time herself./

"Can I get you something to drink?" Ravanelle asked after they'd settled. "It's cold outside. I have coffee and tea."

"We're fine," Vasiht'h said for them both, and her brows lifted.

"I see." She leaned forward, hands folded on one knee. "Professor Palland tells me the two of you would like to refine the techniques Vasiht'h was exploring in his research last year, and that this research involves direct subconscious manipulation via esper ability, performed on unconscious subjects. Is that correct?"

"It sounds a lot more menacing put that way," Vasiht'h said ruefully. "But yes. You're correct, Healer."

"Since you did a year's worth of research on the topic, I'm sure you appreciate some of the difficulties involved here, alet?"

"Some," Vasiht'h said. "I won't say I've anticipated all of the challenges, of course."

She grinned, flashing ivory teeth. "You're good with the academic jargon, I see." And laughed at Vasiht'h's chagrin. "No, don't worry. I won't hold that against you! We all have to learn it." She tapped her knee with a finger, thinking—quickly, because she continued after a breath-pause. "Here's my particular challenge, aletsen. My role at the clinic is to oversee the students working here. I do that by assigning them senior therapists, already licensed, to sit in on the sessions and make sure they're on the right track. But I don't have any esper therapists, and unless I'm mistaken, anyone I sit in a room with you is going to see all three of you sitting quietly without speaking until it's over. Yes?"

"That has been how it's worked in the past," Vasiht'h admitted.

"So you've done this before," she said, eyeing them. "Together."

"By accident." Vasith'h tucked one paw under the other, and Jahir sent him a wordless reassurance: *No need to fidget. All is well.* "A couple of friends who needed us, and it just . . . happened."

"No hard feelings?" she asked, tilting her head.

"From them?" Vasiht'h shook his head. "They were glad afterward. It's what made us think maybe there's something to this."

"So I've got two students I need to supervise through their

practicum, and no way to actually supervise them." She leaned back, lacing her hands over her solar plexus. "What would you recommend I do?"

Vasiht'h looked up at him then. */She has a point about the problems involved. And we have to do this right./*

Jahir practiced not looking at him, letting his eyes rest on the scene out the window and hoping his friend would not take offense. He sensed nothing like that through the mindline, fortunately, only a resolve that he found admirable despite the uncomfortable road it was leading them to. */You want to offer to take whomever is observing with us. Do you know if we even can?/*

/No. But we can at least try. And if it doesn't work, at least we did everything we could think of./

Jahir did glance at him then. */And if it is not safe for the observer?/*

A touch of concern, sharp as the suggestion of knives. */If it's not safe for her, then how is it safe for our patients?/*

He shook his head minutely, more to clear it than in rejection. */I don't think it's a danger to the person we are paying attention to. But we cannot pay attention to more than one person at a time./*

/Oh . . ./ Vasiht'h pursed his lips. */You're thinking we might lose track of them./* He wrinkled his nose, one eye squinting. */Is that even possible?/*

/Do you know if any of this is possible?/ Jahir answered gently, his laughter twining around the words.

"This is the most fascinating conversation I've never heard," Ravanelle observed, amused. "Care to let me in on any part of it?"

/You explain./

Jahir said, "We are debating the possibility of drawing an observer into our . . . link. When we do our assessment."

"The link," she repeated. "What's allowing you to communicate right now, you mean."

"No," Vasiht'h said. "What we have with one another is different. You can't be a part of that—"

Jahir interrupted. */Can she? Can anyone? Is there such a thing as a three-way mindline?/*

/I'm trying to concentrate here!/ "—but historically what we've done with patients is a less intimate, more transitory connection. There's a possibility we can draw a fourth party into that, but we're not sure how safe it would be for them, since we won't be able to devote any significant attention to their welfare."

/Nicely said,/ Jahir offered.

/Keep thinking at me, it makes it easier to borrow your speech patterns./

/I like how you talk./

/I like how I talk too./ Vasiht'h tried to keep the emotion that would have inspired a grin in the mindline, where it wouldn't intrigue Ravanelle. */But you have the trick of sounding like an authority by being so formal all the time. I'm not above using it if I can./*

Jahir was studying Ravanelle. */I don't think you succeeded in impressing the risks of the procedure on her./*

"Excellent," Ravanelle said. "I can't wait to listen in."

———— ∞ ————

"So what do I do?" Ravanelle asked two days later when they met her at the clinic for their first appointment.

"What do you usually do?" Vasiht'h asked for them both.

The Seersa nodded at the door. "The patient gets to state a preference. If they want the faculty observer in the room, then I stay in the room. If they don't, I wait outside and listen in remotely."

/One of us will have to touch her./ Jahir said.

Vasiht'h frowned. */Or maybe she could touch the patient?/*

Jahir hesitated. "That may work better." To the Seersa, he said politely, "If you could touch the patient when we begin, that may give you the best . . . vantage."

She chuckled, ears perked. "You haven't the first notion of the vocabulary to use either, do you."

"There has not been much literature written on the subject."

/You see?/ Vasiht'h said. */You talk her talk well./*

Jahir didn't say that the level of obfuscation available to

Universal was nothing to that which could be achieved with his native tongue. */One should speak the language one's auditor responds to best./*

A silence in the mindline, sudden and thoughtful. Jahir glanced at the Glaseah. */Did I say aught wrong?/*

/No,/ Vasiht'h said. */But that was good. I'm going to think about the implications of that for therapy while you prepare us for this./*

/While I!/

Vasiht'h grinned and said, "I'm going to go get a blanket and pillow."

"I guess that makes sense if you want them napping," Ravanelle said. She pulled up a chair beside the couch. "Here good?"

"That should do."

"And I just . . . touch the patient. After she's sleeping, I guess. And then I'll be able to watch?"

"That is the hope," Jahir said.

"Excellent," Ravanelle said, grinning. "I'm excited. Let's do some science."

———⦂⦂⦂———

Their first client was a male Seersa, a striking golden brown with stripes and hazy spots and brilliant blue eyes. From Jahir's vague assessment, Vasiht'h thought the Eldritch found him a rather handsome example of the species, and Vasiht'h agreed as they introduced themselves and took his name. */Probably has people falling all over him. Wonder why he's here?/*

"I can't stop eating," the male said when they asked.

In response to Jahir's bafflement, Vasiht'h sent, */He's probably under medical supervision—/*

"I go every week for metabolic adjustments," he continued as Ravanelle watched them and they watched the patient. Through the mindline, Vasiht'h felt Jahir's little 'ah' of revelation. "But I'd kind of like to stop doing that because it's annoying, having to schedule it all the time, and it's not free. But I just . . . I see food and I don't know how to stop myself from eating it. I tell myself 'hey, stupid. You know better.' And I really do. But I still eat it."

He grinned, a charming, crooked smile that would probably have made half a dozen people swoon. "Doesn't matter what it is, at least. I'll overeat vegetables along with cake. But I don't need the calories, you know?"

"Did you ever go without food at some point?" Vasiht'h asked.

"Oh, sure." He waved a hand, casual. "When I was about six, we went through a bad period, my family. And I had two little sisters, twin sisters, and they were weak, you know? Everyone worried about their health. And we already didn't have enough to eat, so there were weeks where the only thing I could remember was how much my stomach hurt and how light-headed and weird I felt." He spread his hands. "But, see, I know. I know that's the problem. I've been to therapists before, and it's not like this is some great mystery to me. I've talked and talked and talked about this, but talking hasn't made it go away. So I heard that the clinic was getting some new student therapists in and that they worked with the subconscious and I thought, 'well, hells. That's the one thing I haven't tried.' So here I am."

Vasiht'h said, amused, "Pretty straightforward."

The Seersa grinned again. "Hey, I try to make things easy for people. So, what do I do? Take a nap? That sounds pretty good to me too."

"Sure, if you'll just stretch out on the couch there." Vasiht'h took the blanket from Jahir. "Healer Ravanelle is our faculty oversight. Is it all right if she keeps an eye on us while we work? She'll have to keep a hand on you while you're sleeping."

"Yeah, sure, that's fine." He took the blanket. "You going to stare at me until I fall asleep? I'm not sure that will work."

Ignoring Jahir's restrained amusement, Vasiht'h said, "No, actually. We're going to leave you here, if that's all right."

"It's better than you staring at me," the Seersa said with a laugh. He took the blanket and cuddled into it, stretching his toes before tucking his legs beneath himself on the couch. "You could also . . . I don't know. Dim the lights."

"We could, at that," Jahir said, rising.

Outside the room, Vasiht'h said, "This is obviously something we need to think through a little more."

"Getting them to sleep?" Ravanelle said. "Shouldn't be too hard to arrange now that it's occurred to you that you should encourage it. There are thousands of studies on how to create a healthy sleep environment." She grinned and tapped the data tablet Vasiht'h was still holding. "Why don't the two of you get reading while your patient settles in."

⁃⁃⁃

But their patient did sleep, and they slipped back into the room and looked down at him together as Ravanelle padded around them and took her seat by the couch.

/What are you thinking?/ Vasiht'h asked. /That has you so sober?/

/The same thing you are, perhaps,/ Jahir said. /That this reminds us a little of what we have been through./

Vasiht'h drew in a slow breath, relaxing. /It does. But it also reminds me of helping Luci, and the girls./ He held out his hand, and when the Eldritch looked at it, added, /This part, though, we did learn on Selnor. And I think it's wise. To stay grounded./

Jahir smiled and slipped his fingers around Vasiht'h's palm. His skin was warm; felt like home. Vasiht'h nodded to Ravanelle, who put a gentle hand on the patient's head between the ears, and then they went into dreams. Vasiht'ht wasn't sure what he'd been expecting: something to do with the problem, maybe. But it was a very normal dream about something else, something mundane, a test, smeared together with girl troubles and a vague longing for trees and sunlight. They could ghost through it, unseen, and they did, looking for some clue . . . and did not find it until near the end, when Jahir said, /Here./

Vasiht'h drifted over to a scene where the Seersa was talking with a girl over a picnic blanket. There was a basket, and there were plates, and the two were eating . . . but there was no food.

/Strange,/ Vasiht'h said, and imagined food into the scene. Once he had, it stuck, and they retreated, puzzling.

The patient woke not long after, yawning. "So," he said as he straightened. "Am I hopeless?"

"Do you feel hopeless?" Vasiht'h asked, smiling.

"Nuh, that I don't." He grinned. "Should I come back next week?"

"Yes. And tell us how your week goes," Vasiht'h said.

After he'd gone, they looked at Ravanelle. She laughed. "Oh no. I can't tell you how you did. What do I know about this? That's why I'm here. To see."

"But you did see something," Vasiht'h said.

"I did," she said. "Like . . . imagining things, but not quite as strong. And I could tell you were talking, but not what you were saying. It was a little like . . . well, like seeing someone else's dream." She shook her head. "Amazing. But I feel like I need a cup of coffee."

Jahir said, perfectly polite—and perfectly timed—"Perhaps you should have it, then, in the five minutes we have before our next arrival."

/There's this barb to your humor,/ Vasiht'h observed as the Seersa snorted and jogged out. He was trying not to smile. /That I'm betting you're sitting on most of the time./

/I was merely making a suggestion . . ./

/You're annoyed at her intrusiveness./ Vasiht'h's mouth twitched. He hid it by flicking through the data tablet's appointment list to bring up their next client.

Jahir cleared his throat. /It is a touch tiresome, to be the subject of scrutiny./

Vasiht'h looked up at him suddenly, tasting something just a little sour . . . resignation, ruefulness, too much history. He grimaced and said, softer, "Sorry, arii."

Jahir touched him with a feather-soft sweetness. /As nothing. We continue./

/We do./

———— ✺ ————

Their second patient was a student dealing poorly with the stresses of her far too strenuous course loads on top of anxieties over disappointing her parents—she fell asleep so quickly they hadn't even closed the door when they heard her grow still, and her dreams were a clutter of breathless darting scenes that they had to slow in order to even see. The third did not show up; Ravanelle shrugged it off and said there were always a number of people who made appointments and had second thoughts.

Their last appointment of the day was a listless Asanii who stumbled to their couch and felt her way into it, curling up into herself and resting her head on her knees. Ravanelle took her seat on the chair beside her, watching with flicked back ears.

/This is . . . Esna Verelna, yes? Was there anything on the intake form?/

/No,/ Vasiht'h murmured. Aloud, he said, gentle, "Esna?"

They both felt her crumble before she started sobbing, and the dissolution of her control reminded Jahir so strongly of the wet victims that he didn't pause, and neither did Vasiht'h. They lunged for her as she collapsed, and Vasiht'h wrapped himself around her, one foreleg on the couch and his arms around her shoulders. Jahir knelt on the floor, gripping his partner's hand and pausing—a heartbeat, just long enough to brace himself— and then he rested his hand on her arm and took the brunt of her depression like a blow.

She was alone—

No, you're not.

She couldn't get through this—

Yes, she could.

She had nowhere to turn—

We're here.

She pressed her face into Vasiht'h's collarbone and cried, her back heaving with the strength of the paroxysms, and her grip on Jahir's hand was so tight her tendons stood in sharp relief against the back of her hand. But the coil of her anguish was loosening, and as abruptly as she'd begun crying, she trailed off and looked down at Jahir, eyes wide.

"We're here," he said again, soft.

She looked over at Vasiht'h, who nodded once. Slowly.

A ragged gasp, and then she relaxed, shoulders slumping. A few minutes later, she was asleep in Vasiht'h's arms.

/*Do we need to . . . ?*/ Jahir asked.

/*I don't think so,*/ Vasiht'h said. /*At least, I wouldn't want to touch her dreams yet. I don't even know what this is about. I'd like her to be able to talk about it first, if she wants.*/

/*She may not want,*/ Jahir said.

/*She may not. But this . . .*/ A sense of safety, held in someone's arms, a sense of someone understanding her needs: /*This she did.*/

Ravanelle cleared her throat and they both looked at her, surprised. That she was still there was unexpected; somehow they'd both forgotten her presence.

"Technically," she said, voice low to keep from waking a girl that they both knew wouldn't wake for anything less monumental than an emergency siren, "you're not supposed to be touching the clients. There are therapeutic modalities that do use touch, but we don't teach them here."

/*She is thinking of . . . what?*/ Jahir asked.

/*Harat-Shar, probably,*/ Vasiht'h replied. /*It's a cliché that they heal with sex, but they also do cuddle-therapy. It's a little more nuanced than most non-Harat-Shar assume.*/

Jahir thought of how much his touch had meant to the Tam-illee widower on Selnor. He said, picking the words carefully, "It is not something I would undertake lightly. But she had a need."

The Seersa was looking at the exhausted girl in Vasiht'h's arms. "Hard to argue with that," she murmured, and sat back down.

/*You think she will have complaint of us for this?*/

/*I don't think I care,*/ Vasiht'h said, and the words felt like they were leaning. Wryness? Jahir could feel the smile on his friend's face. /*I don't think you do, either.*/

/*No,*/ Jahir said after a moment, and rested his head against Vasiht'h's foreleg, still holding the girl's hand.

They stayed that way until she stirred. They listened to her emotions wake with her mind, and foremost among them was her surprise not to be immediately ambushed by her grief. She was puzzled instead: where was she? Why was she warm? Why did she feel secure? When she realized where she was, puzzlement became embarrassment until Jahir squeezed her hand. Distracted, she looked down at him and he shook his head, one of his slight movements, and there was compassion in his eyes, enough that she said, "You know. You feel it."

Neither of them interrupted her. She did not want words. She looked at the long fingers twined in hers, then at Vasiht'h . . . and set her head back down on his shoulder. "Is my time up?" she asked, hesitant.

"Just about," Vasiht'h said.

"Can I come back?" she asked, softer.

"We'll be here," the Glaseah said. "Both of us."

She was still for a moment, then she nodded, a jerk of her chin. After extricating herself from them, she slung her bag over her shoulder and hurried out, but there was something different in her bearing: a self-possession that had been missing before, something that allowed her to feel sheepish rather than so crushed she'd been unaware of her relation to the world.

Ravanelle was considering them, but she didn't share her thoughts. She rose and said, "See you two day after tomorrow."

The practicum was their only class of the day, so they walked home together through a blustery afternoon, denying spring with a cold front Jahir could feel as some undefinable pressure in his joints as it approached. He was glad of the scarf and coat, and of Vasiht'h at his side, though he suspected the warmth he derived from that presence was more mental than physical.

"Did it bother you?" Vasiht'h asked, after they'd crossed one of the small bridges and started making their way toward the Pad station that would take them off campus. The Glaseah glanced up at him, forelock blown over one eye and quivering in the breeze. "Touching."

Jahir drew in a breath, careful of the bite in it. "It remains difficult." He looked down, seeing the occasional old leaf, damp and crumpled. "It remains necessary. It helps to have you there."

"You don't have to, you know."

"Reach out to people who are in need?" Jahir asked. Not a challenge, and not an attack. An acknowledgment of what they both knew better than to deny. Vasiht'h's sigh, exasperated, affectionate, conceded the exchange.

"It is who we are," Jahir offered.

"I know," Vasiht'h said. "But I had to say it. Now that I have, though . . . I think it makes a big difference to people. From me they get . . . a lack of threat. Because everyone knows about Glaseah. A hug from one of us is assumed to be safe, non-sexual. From you they get . . . that they're worth it. Because someone for whom it's hard, bothers. Makes the effort."

Jahir didn't ask if he was sure of the ideas. He could work through the impressions from the Asanii himself, and there was truth in the observation. It didn't matter if the girl had known the typical Eldritch strictures against touching. She had known in the place under words, where body language and other cues spoke directly, that she could trust them . . . because they trusted one another.

"We do a delicate thing," Jahir said, feeling out his own impressions. "When we reach out to others."

"Good thing we do a lot of practicing, reaching out to each other."

Jahir smiled at that, looked up into the wind. And said, "Let's get gelato."

"Gelato!" Vasiht'h exclaimed, laughing. "In this weather?"

"I'll have mine with coffee," Jahir said. "Perhaps you can have one of those unholy hot drinks they make with melted ice cream."

Vasiht'h mused. "That does sound good. You're going to ruin your dinner, though."

"I have gained enough weight."

Vasiht'h snorted and trotted after him. If there was something enigmatic in the mindline about the response, Jahir did not question it. They were bonded, but they had the right to their own thoughts.

CHAPTER 28

"YOU THINK HE'S damaged?" Sehvi asked, brow wrinkled.

"Damaged is a strong word," Vasiht'h said. He sat facing the wallscreen in the main room, comfortably sprawled against the sofa. Jahir had a morning class on the last day of up-week and a habit of staying out afterward: his way of politely leaving Vasiht'h to make his calls in privacy. Most of the time, Vasiht'h wouldn't have cared if his roommate had wanted to listen, though he had no idea how Jahir would have felt about some of the gorier stories Sehvi shared about her hands-on experience with obstetrics. "I don't think he's damaged. I think the experience of being so weak was foreign to him and it's stuck with him, the way it would with any of us who had a scare about our bodies."

"Even though he was on Seersana and needed the regimen there initially," Sehvi said.

"He could walk here without getting tired," Vasiht'h said. He thought of the ring Jahir had not yet taken off the cord around his neck. "Selnor was a much different proposition." He leaned forward to fetch his cup of kerinne from the rug now that it was no longer steaming. "I'm going to see if he gets past it on his own. If not, I have some ideas."

"Some ideas, huh," his sister said, resting her cheek in her palm in a gesture they'd both gotten from their mother.

"A few. You know. Being the fancy therapist and all."

She grinned. "How's that going, anyway? It's been a couple of weeks since you started, right? Figured out how to achieve galactic peace yet?"

"I'll let you know once a galactic war breaks out," Vasiht'h said dryly. More seriously, he said, "I think it's going well."

"You think," she repeated. "Isn't this something you know? I mean, your patients aren't leaving worse off than when they come in, right?"

"No," Vasiht'h said, stroking the wall of the mug with his thumb, thinking. "I think they're getting better. But we have a faculty overseer—it's a practicum, you know how that goes, right?" At her nod, he continued, "And she's gotten . . . really quiet. Which is strange, because when we first started, she was *not* quiet. She was energetic and interested and curious. She wanted to know all about our experimental methods. So having her get so closed-mouthed about it so quickly . . ."

"Mm." Sehvi tapped her fingers on her desk, a sound he could hear clearly across the sector. "Maybe she always gets quiet? She wouldn't want to prejudice the results, right, or influence you all while working. . . ."

"That's just the thing," Vasiht'h said. "She's supposed to be doing all that. The overseeing is supposed to be part mentoring. We're still students, and this is part of the teaching process. We're not expected to fly without back-up until we're in our residencies."

"Which your partner's already completed."

"In a medical specialty, which doesn't apply to the clinical environment." Vasiht'h leaned back, shaking his head. "No, it's not normal. And I've talked to some of Ravanelle's other students. They say it's usual for her to do some conferences at the end of every week, talk out the problem cases, make suggestions. She's not doing any of that for us. She asks us questions and prompts us to discuss things, but she doesn't *say* anything. And it's making me nervous."

"But you haven't messed anything up yet, have you?"

"No," Vasiht'h said, slowly. "At least, not that we can see. From the patient perspective, anyway. The people who are seeing us have come back, when it's part of the deal with the student clinic that they can request a different therapist if they're not comfortable with the one they've been assigned. They know we're learning . . . there are safeguards built in so they can feel safe, so they can back out of situations that make them unhappy. No one's backed out. But our methods . . . they're . . . nonstandard." He shrugged, helpless. "We don't fit the mold. So I worry they're not going to know what standards to judge us by."

"You'd think they'd judge you by the standard of whether your patients are happier," Sehvi said with a snort.

"You'd think. But academia isn't results-driven. You know that. We grew up with professors for parents. It's about process."

"Maybe over there it is," Sehvi said. "For me, not so much. Maybe that's why I like repro engineering so much."

"Speaking of which, how's your semester going? Gene theory finally making more sense to you, or is that tutor too distracting?"

To his surprise, she blushed and started playing with a pen on her desk. "Um. Well . . . yes, I think I'm finally getting it."

Vasiht'h set his cup aside and leaned forward. "Finally, a good story on *your* side for a change! Come on, ariishir, let's have it."

"Well, you know I had to find the only other Glaseah on campus," she began.

⁂

"We are done?" Jahir asked as KindlesFlame withdrew from the side of the bed.

"You are, yes. Go on, get up."

The halo-arch retracted, and Jahir sat up. "It remains a form of magic, that the instruments here can discern anything without requiring someone to disrobe."

"If I wanted to do specific kinds of imagery, we'd need you to strip," KindlesFlame said absently, studying the read-outs. "But

for something this general, there's no need to make you freeze."
He shook his head. "You have some of the most mysterious
biology I've seen, alet. And I've climbed all over real alien races."

The word 'climbed' was evocative from someone not given
to hyperbole. Jahir ran through his mental catalog of aliens and
guessed, "Akubi?"

The foxine flashed a grin at him past a shoulder.

"You climbed over an Akubi? Truly?" Jahir said, interest
piqued. "What was that like?"

"Warm, musty, a little bit furry and feathery. I don't know
how to describe their integument, except maybe 'variegated.'"
KindlesFlame set his data tablet down. "You're looking good.
How are you feeling?"

"I think after Selnor anything feels better in compare," Jahir
said.

"Mmm." The foxine folded his arms. "Would you humor me
by allowing me a little granular imagery?"

"I can't allow . . ."

"Not with a machine," the Tam-illee said, smiling a little. He
tapped the corner of one eye. "The old-fashioned kind."

"I . . . suppose?"

"Take off your shirt, then."

Jahir pulled it over his head and folded it, setting it aside
and resting his hands in his lap. The metal of his ring felt suddenly cool on his chest, exposed to the air. He ignored the sensation, waiting as the Tam-illee considered him. KindlesFlame
walked around him, said, "Bend forward? Head down." Curious,
he complied. "Now sit up again and lift your arms—straight up,
yes. Like that."

Wondering what the foxine was looking for, Jahir said, "And
have you derived anything from this examination?"

A tap on his ribcage startled him for being completely without
emotional data: the foxine's stylus. "You're getting there. Not
quite as much flesh as I want to see, but your skin is finally the
right color again."

"It had changed?" Jahir asked, surprised.

"Sure. And your smell too." He chuckled, though Jahir had been certain he'd schooled his expression to something a little less incredulous. "No, you don't need to do that little infinitesimal eye widening trick at me. I'm not kidding. Part of being a healer since time out of mind is paying attention to the details. A halo-arch can tell you a great deal, but you need the instincts for the times you don't have them . . . or they fail you." He canted his head. "You had front row tickets for some of those failures, so don't tell me this surprises you."

"No," Jahir admitted slowly. He drew his shirt back on, pulling his hair out from beneath the collar, and began adjusting the cuffs.

"Mm. And now what are you thinking in that too close mind of yours?"

Jahir tried not to find the buttons he was straightening as interesting as they'd become. "That medicine remains fascinating." No, he thought. To be honest with those you have chosen to trust is important. "That it becomes more fascinating as I study it."

"Why does this bother you?" KindlesFlame wondered, leaning against the wall as he waited.

"It doesn't. Not . . . precisely." He paused, then said, "Have you ever thought of taking up another profession?"

"Me?" The foxine huffed a soft laugh. "I'm happy where I am. And even if I wasn't, I have too much invested in this one."

"And if you had more time?"

KindlesFlame hesitated, then arched a brow. "I see. So this is about confronting our mortality."

Jahir thought about his enjoyment of the chemistry classes. And the ferocity of feeling he had for what he did with Vasiht'h during their practicum. He loved them both. Knowing that he had the time to devote to both when so many people around him would not have that luxury was . . . strange. To put his life in an order—first, become a therapist until your best friend dies, then do something new—made him uncomfortable. There was despair in him, with which he had made an uneasy peace, and it made him realize that before he'd left his world he had known very little of either love or grief. He finished straightening his clothes and pushed off the bed.

"You'd make a fine healer," KindlesFlame said.

"Do you think?"

"Oh yes." The foxine smiled. "Gotta eat more first. You're underdoing it still."

Jahir grimaced. "I thought I was doing better."

"Better than you were, certainly. I'm sure trying to figure out how much fewer calories you need here than you did on Selnor's a trial. But you need to pay more attention to it." The foxine chuckled. "Eat more ice cream or something."

Jahir thought of the bizarre medical concoction Vasiht'h had fed him at Mercy and shook his head a touch.

"You really would," KindlesFlame said as he ushered him out. "Make a fine healer. Thinking about it, someday? You have time."

"I do," Jahir said. "But I'd like to make a fine therapist first."

"Convince Ravanelle of it, then." When Jahir stopped abruptly, KindlesFlame said, "I expected to hear something from her by now. She's an talkative sort. It's strange for her to be cagey."

"We wondered," Jahir murmured.

"Keep going," the foxine said. "If there's no map, there will always be people who assume you're lost. Prove them wrong."

CHAPTER 29

THEY CONTINUED FEELING their way through their patients' problems. The Seersa who couldn't stop eating cheerfully returned every week, and they went through his mundane dreams until they found the inevitable empty pantries, dinners without courses, glasses without drinks, and restocked, refilled and added in all the missing food. They talked with new patients about their anxieties about school, about starting new lives, about family problems, about relationships. Their distressed Asanii returned and did not speak—she curled up on the couch and slept, usually holding one or both of their hands.

Ravanelle watched it all, silent, until the Asanii's sixth visit. Then she said, abrupt, "Why does she keep coming back?"

"She's depressed," Vasiht'h said.

The Seersa eyed him. "I can tell that much. But she hasn't so much as said what's bothering her."

Vasiht'h looked at him, shared his vague impressions, the needs, the aching emptinesses. Jahir sorted through them, nodded and said to Ravanelle, "She lost both her parents."

"Suddenly," Vasiht'h said. "Very recently."

Their faculty advisor was staring at them. "Did she tell you that at some point? In her head or otherwise?"

"Not . . . intentionally," Jahir said. "But it is in her, nonetheless."

"And your plan for resolving this?" she prompted.

In the mindline, Vasiht'h's response tasted like hot broth and exasperation. The Glaseah said, "Grief isn't something you cure like a disease. It doesn't answer to a schedule. It doesn't necessarily want to be talked at."

"And sleeping is going to help her."

/Don't defend against it,/ Jahir said. /She is not accusing, but testing./

/I know,/ Vasiht'h replied, testy. /But she could have been saying something all along. And helping us! And now this?/

"She needs to feel safe, Healer," Jahir said before his friend could speak and prejudice their overseer against them. "She feels safe here. That is our plan."

Ravanelle nodded and headed for the door. When Vasiht'h would have stepped after her, Jahir held up a hand. /No, arii. Let her work./

/What work is she doing, precisely?/

Jahir looked after their advisor, head canted. /Questioning her own certainties, I think./

Vasiht'h sighed. /You really think she's that confused?/

Jahir chuckled softly. /Aren't we?/

"We're students," Vasiht'h pointed out. "We're supposed to be more confused than the faculty."

"We are pioneers," Jahir said. "And we are going to be late to see the children."

———— ≈≈≈ ————

They still went every week to see the girls in the hospital. On good days, they served as escorts down to the greening hospital garden so Kuriel could point out the waking fish to the two humans and all three children could look for flowers or shiny pebbles. On harder days, they stayed in; Jahir read them poetry and told them stories, and Vasiht'h played games with them. Jill drank her coffee at her station outside the room, or joined them for the jaunts down to the garden. Vasiht'h watched Jahir holding an exhausted Persy in his arms while telling her a fantastical tale about the dragons small enough to steal through her bloodstream and lend aid to the pharmaceuticals warring with the cancerous cells there—the mindline whispered textbook imagery to Vasiht'h, suggesting that at least some part of that story was being fueled by his roommate's studies, and it certainly convinced Persy, who liked the notion of having her own private dragon army.

"What girl wouldn't?" Jahir said as they made their way off the hospital grounds.

"Want a private dragon army?" Vasiht'h chuckled. "I don't know. I'm sure Amaranth would prefer a unicorn army."

"The mind boggles," Jahir said. "A unicorn army."

"They'd look strange in uniform," Vasiht'h agreed. He felt the Eldritch's enjoyment of the spring sunlight through the mindline; the weather had finally warmed up for long enough to convince the trees that spring was here for good and everywhere around them, things were blooming. The smell on the breeze was intoxicating.

Vasiht'h glanced over at his roommate, thought the time was about right. If he was wrong . . . but he trusted his instincts. He made sure the buckle on his messenger bag was secured and trotted along, affecting innocence—probably poorly—and enjoyment of the warmth, far more believably. Jahir said nothing until they stopped on the sidewalk beside one of the university's many broad fields, felted with soft new grass over which at least one butterfly was darting.

"You have a feel to you, like you have ice cream I don't know about yet," Jahir said, eyeing him.

"That tree," Vasiht'h said. "Recognize it?"

The Eldritch lifted his head, and the breeze tugged at his hair, pulled it past his throat. The mindline made it clear that Jahir never posed himself, and yet he always managed to look posed. Vasiht'h guessed that was what being photogenic was, by definition. He couldn't decide if it amused or amazed him. Mostly, he thought, he was glad the Eldritch no longer tied his hair back. That would have been a reminder of memories he was glad to forget.

"That," Jahir said suddenly, interrupting his thoughts. "Is the tree that is good for climbing."

"Or lounging under," Vasiht'h agreed. "And it is spring. A nice time for climbing or lounging."

"As I recall," Jahir began, his tone cautious, "the last time I climbed this tree, you berated me for not being more careful of my health."

"And I am about to berate you again, for the same thing," Vasiht'h said. "Arii . . . you're not frail. I know you know that in your head. But your head is going to have to teach your heart, because you can't keep going without some kind of exercise. That's part of acclimatization, and even if Seersana's not Selnor, you still have to build the muscle. You got a bit of a head start on that while you were away, but I don't want you to lose it because you're afraid."

"Am I afraid?" Jahir asked, wondering. Such a softness in the mindline. Vasiht'h found his roommate's capacity for introspection gratifying, if surprising.

"You are," he said. "A little." He patted his bag and said, "So we're going to fix it."

"We are?"

"We are."

"By . . . ?"

"By making things right," Vasiht'h said firmly. "In this case . . . by me getting to that tree first this time, because a biped beating me there is embarrassing. And that's all the warning you'll get because I'm off!" He put his head down and burst into a sprint, claws sprouting from his paws with the force of his lunge. The mindline sparked with Jahir's surprise and then overflowed with laughter. He felt more than heard his friend following, shared his own sense of his body at work: the muscles gliding under his pelt, the tattoo of his paws on the earth and the tickle of grass against bare toes. He was delighted to receive a response: the sough of breath hard in his throat, the breeze on a face unshielded by fur, the joy of a body that worked and, at the last moment, the rough scratch of bark under bare palms as Jahir swung himself up onto the branch. Vasiht'h skidded to a stop beneath him and they panted together, the sun warm on them both.

Vasiht'h said, "You're out of shape."

Jahir laughed. "I am out of condition."

"Is there a difference?" Vasiht'h dropped onto the grass where it had been cooled by the tree's shadow. "But you didn't break a bone getting here."

"That . . . I did not."

The mindline was dense with Jahir's thoughts. Vasiht'h let him have his silence and enjoyed it until he felt some of the busyness clear. Then he said, "The university has a pool, you know."

The feeling that washed back to him through the mindline gave him great satisfaction.

Later that evening, Jahir let himself into their apartment, bringing with him the smell of brine and a memory of light shimmering on bright water. Vasiht'h closed his eyes and lifted his head, letting it pour through him, and then smiled as the Eldritch sat across from him at the table. He was wearing his ring on his finger now, and not on the chain around his neck.

"You still think we should be mindful of Ravanelle," Jahir said.

Vasiht'h tilted his head, let his agreement seep between them.

The Eldritch smiled. "I'll wash up for supper."

CHAPTER 30

RAVANELLE SCHEDULED a week off for them in advance of spring break, saying they deserved the time. "Use it to catch up on your coursework," she'd said, waving it off. "We see a slow-down around the holidays, anyway. People go home, go on vacation."

"This sounds fishy to me," Vasiht'h grumbled, ignoring the faint puzzlement the mindline fed him, figuring the Eldritch would intuit the colloquialism from the context. "Why does she want us out of the office?"

"Perhaps it is just what she suggests," Jahir said. "We do have midterms."

"So does everyone else," Vasiht'h said. "You'd think the stress of it would inspire more people to show up at the student clinic, not less. And don't say something about going on vacation. That makes sense during the break, not before it. You don't go on a vacation long enough to start before spring break when you're a student. At least, not if you actually care about your education."

Jahir said nothing for so long that Vasiht'h finally eyed him. "What? The mindline is full of . . ." He paused, licked his teeth and grimaced. "What is that flavor?"

"Anise," Jahir said.

"Are you sure?" Vasiht'h said. "I'm a baker, remember? That's not the anise I know."

"I am from a different world."

Vasiht'h snorted. "You think I'm overreacting."

"I think . . . perhaps you might consider reframing the situation."

"This should be good," Vasiht'h muttered. "All right. And how exactly am I supposed to reframe this situation?"

"That perhaps Ravanelle is also one of our patients," Jahir said, and Vasiht'h could sense him feeling his way into the words. "And that by working on our student patients, we are also, slowly, working on her."

Vasiht'h's brows lifted. "You want me to believe that."

"I want you to consider that perhaps there is an inelasticity there that suggests . . . damage. Or anxiety."

Put that way . . . Vasiht'h scowled, his stride slowing. Jahir stopped walking and turned, waiting, hands folded behind his back.

"Yes?" Jahir said. "I value your opinion, arii. Am I right?"

"Maybe," Vasiht'h said. "But it doesn't make me feel any better when she's the one who has to agree to pass us for us to go forward."

"Think of it as another test."

"Another test," Vasiht'h muttered. "As if we don't have enough of them."

The message Jahir found in his queue a week later surprised him, and spreading it did not cure him of that surprise. Nor did he think his roommate likely to be glad of it. He sent a response and then busied himself in the kitchen, setting out ingredients, pondering. Should he make the cookies? Or put Vasiht'h to work making them? He let his instincts guide that impression and started a pot of black tea. When the Glaseah entered, it had already scented the apartment's great room with its astringent fragrance, and Vasiht'h paused, frowning.

"Why do I smell more-almond butter?"

"Because," Jahir said. "I am making tea, and you are making cookies."

"I am?" Vasiht'h placed his messenger bag down by the door, wary.

"You are. Come by, I have it set out for you."

There were times when Vasiht'h's body language reminded Jahir strongly of great cats; his lower body, while patterned like some other creature's, had much more in common with a pard's than it did with anything less powerful. The way his roommate was stalking toward the kitchen was one of those moments. The Glaseah rounded the corner of the island and squinted at the *mise en place*. "Okay. What's gone wrong."

"It's not so much wrong as that we will be receiving a guest tomorrow," Jahir said.

"And this guest is . . ."

"Verelna."

Vasiht'h stopped short. "Esna Verelna? As in our client from the student clinic?"

Jahir pressed a cup of tea on him, forcing his roommate to do something with his hands besides clench them. "The same. I had a message from her earlier. She found my address and asked for an appointment, as we are not otherwise available this week."

"*What?*"

"Drink," Jahir said firmly, and was gratified when Vasiht'h did so despite the turbulence in the mindline. To diffuse some of the hostility brewing in his roommate's head, he said, "Was it all right that I said she might come?"

"What? Of course! Though . . ." Vasiht'h put the tea down and grimaced. "Is it allowed for us to do that? Do you know? Can we practice after hours? Without supervision?"

"I don't know," Jahir replied, grave. He offered the spatula to Vasiht'h, who took it absently and started bouncing it against his palm. "Do you recall anything from the explanation they gave us at the beginning of the semester?"

"I don't, no," Vasiht'h said. "I guess I could ask Professor

Palland . . ."

"But?" Jahir said, feeling the hesitation as a queasiness.

"But what if he says no?" Vasiht'h said. He took the jar of more-almond butter, which Jahir had left open, and started scooping some of it into the mixing bowl. "Obviously, she wouldn't have gone through the trouble of finding you if she hadn't really wanted to see us. Our personal codes aren't listed through the student clinic, and yours in particular . . . I don't know how you do it, but it's slippery as fish in water. You'd think 'search for the call code of the only Eldritch on Seersana' would be a pretty simple task, but half the time you don't turn up."

Unlike Vasiht'h, he knew there were censors prowling the Alliance's databases, cleaning up any references to him or the few others who'd ventured off-world. They were more dedicated in their destruction of things like medical data than they were with call codes; their sweeps were probably wiping his location rather than the actual ability to contact him. No doubt the Asanii had assumed he'd be easier to locate for the same reason Vasiht'h had mentioned . . . but to pin him down, she would have had to keep trying until she caught one of the references before it was swept.

She had been trying. Very hard. Since nothing in their contact with her had suggested a lack of intelligence or subtlety, as tacit as that communication had been, he suspected that choosing to send the message to him rather than to his far easier to find friend was her way of telling them that the appointment mattered.

All he said, though, was, "I agree with you that it's important to her. It is why I told her she might come. Do you think if we told Palland he might find some reason we should avoid it? Liability, or an academic issue?"

"It's better to ask forgiveness than get permission," Vasiht'h said. His thoughts were smoothing out now that he was paying attention to the process of baking. Satisfied, Jahir withdrew to a stool to let him work. "We can always say it was just a visit."

"Would that not be a lie?"

"I don't know," Vasih'th said. "Given that Ravanelle hasn't so much as said a word to us about how we're doing . . . for all we know, she doesn't think of our methods as therapy at all. But you know what bothers me?"

"What?"

Vasiht'h pointed the spatula at him. "That she scheduled us off this week. Did we have appointments booked that she canceled?"

"I don't know," Jahir said. "Perhaps we should ask Esna when she arrives."

"Perhaps we should," Vasiht'h said, and turned his full attention to the cookie dough.

＊＊＊

The following morning, Esna arrived on their doorstep, her hands in her pockets and her head dipped, and it was strange to see her without the bag she took to school. Jahir let her in and said, "Alet."

She smiled at him, one of her brief, butterfly smiles.

"We have a couch set up," he continued. "Would you like something to drink? A tisane?"

"A cookie?" Vasiht'h called from the kitchen.

That made her look up; that he could see her pupils dilate made him realize she had light eyes. Grey, flecked with blue. She'd so rarely met their gazes without tears that he hadn't noted their color. "A . . . cookie?"

"More-almond," Jahir said.

"More-almond!" A long pause. He thought she was working through the notion of using something so expensive to make cookies. Then she smiled, and this time the smile was complicated, plucking at one corner of her mouth and leaving the other hesitant, unturned. This smile stayed for longer than a few heartbeats, and he glimpsed the personality beneath the constant grief. "Ah . . . all right."

So she sat on the couch and had a cookie and an herbal infusion, something mild, and then she curled up under one of their blankets and slept. After a while, she smiled in her sleep.

The complicated smile, the one that stayed for longer than a heartbeat.

"Do you think we should try now?" Vasiht'h asked, low. "With the dreams."

"No," Jahir said. "No, what she needs is presence. And here she doesn't have to touch us to know we are nigh. Also, your cookies are magic."

Vasiht'h, who'd been following along without much attention, started at the last sentence. He peered up at Jahir, then chuckled. "Maybe we should make it part of our therapeutic interventions from now on."

They let her sleep herself out. When she woke, she rubbed her eyes and thanked them, quiet, gathered herself to go. At the door, she said, "I'll tell the others." And then she was gone, walking down the sidewalk and leaving them staring after her.

"That implies she talks to people," Vasiht'h said, hesitant.

"Or that she knows our client list and is willing to do them a good turn," Jahir said. "I . . . think we should be prepared."

———— ∞∞∞ ————

They received their first request that evening, and another three the following day. Vasiht'h handled the scheduling, slotting the appointments around their existing classes and leaving the last two for the first day of the break, since the students weren't leaving town. After they'd sent the final one away, Vasiht'h flopped his upper body on the couch and sighed. "All right, well . . . if we're going to be damned, at least we'll be damned for going all out. Right?"

"Do you know what I think?" Jahir said.

"What?" Vasiht'h answered, reply muffled by his arms.

"I think we need a vacation."

Vasiht'h lifted his head, not trusting the sudden innocence in the mindline. It looked like a field of nodding buttercups. Smelled like spring and sunlight. He half expected some sort of fairy to come traipsing through it in a moment.

"So I have taken the liberty of arranging one."

"You . . . did what?" Vasiht'h said. "Without me noticing?"

"You have been very busy," was the sage reply.

Vasiht'h narrowed his eyes. "You realize this means we can hide things from one another."

He'd expected unease or hurt or anger. To have Jahir laugh . . . he wasn't sure whether to be exasperated or relieved. "Oh, arii. Of course we can. A mind is a complicated thing. More complicated than its surface thoughts, its reactions to the moment. You have hidden things from me before—"

"I have . . ." Vasiht'h stopped and flipped his ears back. "Okay, well, only the whole thing about you and your problem with thinking you're frail."

"Which you hid until you judged it the right time to prod me, and it was," Jahir said. "And I thank you for that." He leaned back, one arm over the back of the couch and his legs stretched in front of him. "You would know if I was hiding something significant. I would know that in you as well. But we can't know one another in entirety."

"We're just going to come closer than most people," Vasiht'h said. "All right. I can see that." He tilted his head. "You've been thinking about this."

"It is what we're doing, in part, with the clients."

"Clients or patients?" Vasiht'h wondered. "The student clinic calls them patients."

"'Patients' implies disease. The people who come to see us aren't sick. To suggest it is to inculcate that belief." Jahir smiled, a little. "You have just seen what that did to me, and I didn't even realize I had internalized that belief until you dragged it out into the light." He shook his head. "I am halfway through a historical perspectives class in the pharmaceutical track. It has been . . . enlightening."

Vasiht'h lifted his brows and let his curiosity tug at the mindline until Jahir glanced at him and repeated, "The mind is a complicated thing."

There was something lurking under there, so Vasiht'h tugged a little more until the Eldritch narrowed his eyes. "You will tip me over."

"So tell me."

"And you worried that we could hide aught from one another?"

"Tell me," Vasiht'h said, grinning this time.

"I have been doing a little research on the side on klaido-pin—that is the technical name for—"

"Wet," Vasiht'h finished, the fur on his spine fluffing up. He didn't ask why; that was obvious. "Have you learned anything worth knowing?" he asked instead.

"Only how little the Alliance still understands," Jahir said. "In a way, it is comforting to know that as advanced as you are, there are things you have yet to explain or explore."

"I never worry about that," Vasiht'h said. "I don't think we'll ever know anything. Which reminds me. Vacation?"

"You took me to the sea on Selnor," Jahir said. "I have arranged for us to go to the sea on Seersana."

The mindline twinkled: lights in fog. People's voices. Laughter. Vasiht'h frowned, puzzled. "I can't tell if that's a party or a lighthouse."

"It is a party in a lighthouse," Jahir said. "A lighthouse converted into a bed and breakfast, and I have invited the quadmates."

Vasiht'h covered his face to keep the snickers from escaping, and failed. "I can't believe you hid that from me."

"Because it's a bad idea?" Jahir asked, a touch of anxiety in the words.

"Because Brett can't keep a secret to save his life!"

"Ah!" Jahir said, smug. "Well. Now you know where half your cookies went."

CHAPTER 31

T HE VACATION WAS EVERYTHING Jahir had hoped when he'd
arranged it: a moody locale, cool and humid and mysterious, complete with a tower perched on a rocky crag and a path
down to a pebbled beach with the bones of a shipwreck perched
on it like the wooden spars of a sea creature's ribcage. From
the merry sparkle in their innkeepers' eyes, they were used to
indulging the over-active imaginations of their visitors, and even
hosted several gatherings where they told quite convincing ghost
stories, all of them improved by their nautical setting. During the
day, they hiked along the beach, picking up pretty stones, having
picnics on likely-looking buttes with commanding views of a gray
and unknowable ocean; at night, they retired to the lighthouse
for warm drinks, or followed tour guides with honest-to-good-
ness fire torches into the dark to good sites for bonfires. On the
final night, at the bonfire their hosts had built on the beach near
enough for the sea's hissing approach to threaten it, they spotted
a giant fin breaching the water, catching highlights off the fire,
a fin so monstrous several people in the gathering shrieked. In
the morning, a group of divers and one Naysha joined them at
the water's edge to demonstrate how the trick had been done;
it amused Jahir that on a world where technology could have

been used to project a solidigraphic image of just about anything imaginable, people were still making things like this work with props.

"It would be easy to do it with the projectors," the innkeeper had said while he was downstairs with his bag, waiting for Vasiht'h to join him. "The fun is making it work without all the fancy gadgets."

On the way home, Vasiht'h said to him, "You're crazy. And that was fun."

Jahir grinned.

———— ⦿ ————

They returned to their studies, their practicum, their carefully balanced schedule of nights with their friends or out to concerts, lunches with their respective advisors, mornings with the girls at the hospital. It was a busy life, but Vasiht'h observed the contentment in the mindline and was pleased. Even better, Ravanelle said nothing to them about their clandestine meetings with the students outside the clinic; either she hadn't found out or she didn't care, but either option worked for him.

Two weeks after the holiday, their hungry Seersa patient surprised them by declaring, "I've taken up sports."

"You've done what?" Vasiht'h asked, surprised.

The foxine started laughing. "You should see your faces. Well, your face, Vasiht'h." He nodded to Jahir. "I have a harder time reading yours, but I assume you're both surprised . . . otherwise, you—" pointing at Vasiht'h, "would be a little less obvious about it."

Now they were both interested, and Ravanelle's ears had twitched toward the patient as well.

"Could you explain that?" Jahir asked.

"Oh, I don't know how to say it?" He shook his head. "It's like you're emotional sinks for one another. If one of you's not something, then more of the thing the first person is can drain into it, and it sort of equalizes? That's my guess."

He and Jahir exchanged glances. /Well,/ Vasiht'h said dryly.

/I guess it's not just our body language while chatting that we have to watch./

/Control over one's deportment is not necessarily a good thing./

That with such irony that it tasted like metal filings, but Vasiht'h didn't begrudge the Eldritch it after his experiences with Professor Sheldan and that Seersa's beliefs on how control of one's body language somehow transformed a person into a liar or a manipulator or Goddess knew what.

"So, sports," Jahir said.

"Yes," their patient said, satisfied. "I've never felt comfortable doing that before. Now, I enjoy it. I'm playing soccer. Running. Can you imagine? And I don't go in for the adjustments anymore."

"So . . . you're not overeating," Vasiht'h guessed, careful.

"Not anymore." He grinned. "It's like all my pantries filled up. Or maybe like I expect them to be full? I don't crave anymore. I feel . . . I don't know. Relaxed. Did you two do all that while I was sleeping? Pretty incredible." He pursed his lips. "I guess I could relapse. I don't feel like I will. Are you worried?"

To admit that they were as mystified as to the mechanism of their success was probably not a good idea. Vasiht'h said, "Are you?"

"Nah." The Seersa grinned. "I think I'm fine." He leaned forward suddenly, one elbow on his knee, a rakish pose that fairly shouted his confidence. "Say, I don't suppose you'd be willing to see my mother? She's got the same issues. You know. Maybe you can make her picnic lunches."

"I . . . ah . . . don't know what the policy is on non-students using the student clinic," Vasiht'h said.

"Figures. Well, when you're in practice, I'll look you up." He rose. "Thanks for everything."

"Our pleasure," Vasiht'h said for them both.

After the Seersa left, he glanced over at Ravanelle to see if she would say anything, but she was reading her data tablet. When she looked up and caught him staring, she said, "Next patient's in ten minutes."

"Is that common?" Vasiht'h said, deciding to brazen it out. "Complete cures like that. A remission of psychological sickness."

She returned her attention to her tablet. "It happens."

/How can she be so opaque when she was so open when we first met her?/ Vasiht'h asked, his frustration making the words burn in the mindline.

/I wonder,/ Jahir murmured.

/Wonder what?/

But Jahir wouldn't say.

So he took his concerns to Palland, if the rant he delivered in his major professor's office could be dignified with any description as civilized as that. He finished his tirade by saying, "She's trying to sabotage our practicum. I'm sure of it!"

Palland cupped his mug in both hands and leaned back in his chair, brows lifted. "Because she cut your schedule a week prior to the break? Are you sure she really wasn't just trying to give you some time off? Maybe she thinks what you're doing takes a lot out of you."

"Do you think it takes a lot out of me?" Vasiht'h demanded, flattening his ears.

Palland's eyes dropped to his student's feet, flowed back up to his face. His regard was so thoughtful that Vasiht'h sat back, chastened. He was about to apologize when the Seersa said, "No. Actually, I'd say the opposite. I think for the first time you're doing something you love, something you're good at . . . and it's energizing you."

Vasiht'h's mouth dropped open.

"Having said that," Palland said, setting his mug on his desk, "I'm not the one on site, alet. She has to have a better idea of how this is going than I do."

"But telling all our clients we weren't available—"

"She may be testing you," Palland said. "She may be resorting to testing you in the only way she can, lacking any real insight into your methods."

"By badgering us?" Vasiht'h said, irritated.

"By measuring the responses of your students." Palland said. "Seeing if they're willing to switch to a different therapist. Students who visit the clinic are used to being rotated around if they're going to stick it out for longer than a semester."

"But why in the middle of the semester?" Vasiht'h asked. When Palland pushed a cup over to him, he watched his professor fill it and dutifully took a sip, letting it calm him. Some kind of tea. Hibiscus? No, but floral. He thought Jahir would find it cloying, wondered if that affected his reaction to it, couldn't tell. "Aren't they supposed to fill out evaluations by the end of the semester anyway? Why is she probing in the middle of the semester?"

"Because she needs to have some idea of how things are going before it's all over," Palland said dryly. "Alet . . . aren't you being a little hard on her?"

Vasiht'h stared at him. "She's supposed to be guiding us."

"And how exactly is she supposed to do that?"

Vasiht'h put the cup down. "Sir, our methods might be new, but dream interpretation is an ancient field of study. And the psychological principles are going to be the same, no matter how we're going about affecting them."

"Mmm."

That was it? Mmm? Vasiht'h narrowed his eyes at the Seersa. "What?"

"I assume you're taking case notes?"

"Yes?"

"So what makes you think she has anything to add to what you're already doing?"

Vasiht'h bared his teeth. "The fact that she's had seventeen years of experience doing this and we haven't? Sir, this is our practicum. If she fails us, she's going to put us back a semester, maybe prejudice our next overseer against us."

"Vasiht'h," Palland said, and the firmness of his voice was quelling. "Ravanelle's fair. She's not going to throw the semester if the two of you get good evaluations."

"Even if she can't tell how we're doing it?" Vasiht'h asked. "I know it sounds crazy, sir, but without being right there in our heads, she can't really tell how we're doing what we're doing. For all she knows, we're brainwashing our clients."

"Give her a little credit," Palland said. "She's a smart woman. If she can't find a way to evaluate your process, she'll figure out how to evaluate your results."

∞∞∞

"So his advice was to trust her," Vasiht'h concluded later over the remains of their dinner. The mindline brought him a whiff of cinnamon and he said, testy, "And no, I do not need to bake an apple crumble."

"You don't?" Jahir said, interest piqued. "I had not had anything specific in mind. I like the notion of an apple crumble."

Vasiht'h opened his mouth to protest but seeing the hope in his roommate's eyes made him laugh. "Aksivaht'h bless," he said. "What am I going to do with you."

"Feed me until I pop, most probably," Jahir said. "Shall I make coffee now? How long will this crumble take?"

"I'm not making—oh, fine. An hour, probably. Wait on the coffee."

Jahir managed to look abashed despite not moving much. Perhaps it was the feeling in the mindline, a faint skin flush that Vasiht'h was fairly certain wasn't his, but that he couldn't see on his friend's fair face without scrutinizing it. "I could slice something if you need it done."

"You can start by peeling. After that, you slice."

In the kitchen, plying the knife, Jahir said, "KindlesFlame shares Palland's opinion."

Vasiht'h paused, pastry cutter in hand. "That we should trust Ravanelle?"

"That we should trust the system," Jahir said, carefully shaving the top of the apple. He always did that: cut a flat surface on fruit so he could hold it steady against the cutting board. The mindline's permanence finally brought Vasiht'h a hint of his friend's concentration, and fainter, the fear that he might cut himself badly with the knife if the fruit slipped out from under him.

"They can reattach them, you know," Vasiht'h said.

Jahir looked up, startled, honey eyes wide. "I beg your pardon?"

"Fingers. If you slice them off. They can be reattached."

Jahir stared at him for several heartbeats more, then said, with commendable dignity, "I would very much prefer not to put either of us through the trouble of escorting me to a clinic with one of my fingers wrapped in a napkin."

"I think I'd prefer not to spend my evening that way too," Vasiht'h said. He went back to cutting the butter into the flour. "I still don't trust any of it."

"We shall do right by our clients," Jahir said, cutting his apple with careful strokes. "The rest will take care of itself."

CHAPTER 32

THE CHALLENGE THEY'D been expecting was visited on them two weeks before the end of the semester, when they arrived at the clinic to discover all their appointments had been canceled.

"That's weird," Vasiht'h said, ears flattened. "Why didn't they call to tell us not to come?"

"Because you still have one appointment," Ravanelle said, joining them in the hall. She folded her arms. "Me."

"You?" Jahir asked.

"Me. For the next two weeks, I am your appointment."

/We may need to sit down for this,/ Vasiht'h said, and Jahir couldn't tell if that gelatinous texture was unease or surprise or revulsion. Perhaps all three?

To banish it, he replied, /At least it is in the open now, arii./

/Maybe./

Ravanelle led them into the room they used for their patients and sat on the couch, facing them. She crossed her legs, resting her hands on her knee, and said, "I've been watching the two of you work now all semester. And I've been paying attention in this trance you pull me into, but it's really hard to interpret anything through that. It's like . . ." She trailed off, ears flicking outward as her gaze lost focus. "It's a little like trying to understand a dream.

I'm lucid enough to watch it happening, but I can't tell what part you're playing with it. Are you moving through it because the students are dreaming you in response to your presence? Or are you fixing things somehow?" She shook her head. "Sometimes I think I can hear the two of you talking, but it's not a channel I can access, if that makes sense."

"It makes sense, inasmuch as any of this does," Jahir said.

She snorted. "There you go. Diplomatic as always." She folded her arms, leaning back on the couch. "Now I know what the students tell me. And I know something from my independent evaluations of them. But that's not enough. Not for something like this, where there are no rules yet, and where we don't even know if the methods are going to be harmful."

Vasiht'h opened his mouth to protest, but Jahir sent a soothing quiet through the mindline. /Let her. This may be the only way we can convince her./

"So," Ravanelle finished. "You've got two weeks. Try this thing on me."

"Is there some problem you wish us to address?" Jahir asked.

She chuckled. "I'm tired and stressed. Is that enough?"

"I guess we'll find out," Vasiht'h said. "Can you fall asleep?"

"Sure." Ravanelle pulled her heavily jointed digitigrade legs onto the couch and fluffed the pillow. "Any excuse for a rest."

They stepped out of the room to give her some quiet. Jahir waited for the outburst and was pleased when Vasiht'h sat on it instead.

"It wouldn't be productive to be upset," the Glaseah said after a moment.

"She is giving us a chance," Jahir replied. "And as we are going into her subconscious mind, you may not want your resentment of her neglect to reach her."

Vasiht'h made a face. "Wouldn't that be a mess." And then laughed. "Don't give me that severe look. I'm not going to do anything to jeopardize our grades. I want out of this as much as you do."

"Good."

"Of course, we might still fail because she doesn't need a therapist," Vasiht'h said. "Wouldn't that be ironic."

"I would prefer not to court such ironies by mentioning them."

"Do you really think that works?" Vasiht'h wondered.

Jahir said, "This from the male whose Goddess made the world with Her thoughts?"

"Good point." Vasiht'h looked at the closed door. "Prayer might not be such a bad idea right now, at that."

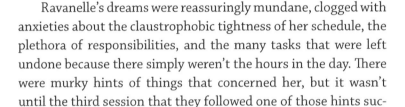

Ravanelle's dreams were reassuringly mundane, clogged with anxieties about the claustrophobic tightness of her schedule, the plethora of responsibilities, and the many tasks that were left undone because there simply weren't the hours in the day. There were murky hints of things that concerned her, but it wasn't until the third session that they followed one of those hints successfully to its source . . . and saw themselves.

They backed out of that dream so quickly Jahir almost gave himself a headache.

/Oh hells,/ Vasiht'h said as Ravanelle slept beside them, innocent of their shock. /Is this what it looks like? Is the professor who just implied that our passing grade is going to be based on whether our therapy works on her . . . having psychological issues with us?/

Jahir rubbed his forehead slowly. /Yes./

Vasiht'h covered his face; Jahir could hear him taking several long, slow breaths.

/Come. Let's step outside a moment./

In the corridor, Vasiht'h said, "Now what do we do? How can we tackle this at all? Ethically, it's covered in thorns."

"I think our only choice is to tell her," Jahir said. "We cannot assuage her concerns directly. At least, not with our therapeutic methods."

"We haven't been able to demonstrate the technique to her, though," Vasiht'h said. "How can she make her decision if we don't?"

"I don't know," Jahir replied. "But we certainly can't adjust her interior perceptions until they show us in a more favorable light."

"No." Vasiht'h looked away. "No, we can't. It's just . . ."

Unfair. Ridiculous. Frustrating. Laughable.

"Yes," Jahir said, wryly, and pushed the door back open again. They came to a halt over the couch, looking down at their professor, revealed as somewhat more careworn in her sleep than she managed to look when animated by her ferocious energy. "Do you wish to do the honors?"

"I should," Vasiht'h said, and set a hand on the Seersa's arm. "Healer Ravanelle? It's time to get up."

She cracked her eyelids, squinting. Then sat up and shook herself. "Already? It doesn't feel like it's been two hours."

"It hasn't been," Vasiht'h said. "We've . . . run into a problem."

One brow went up. "Ah?"

/Here I go,/ Vasiht'h said, sour as lemon juice. "In our first sessions, we noticed you had some anxiety about a particular issue, so we've been trying to chase it down. And today we finally isolated it."

"Oh?" she asked, straightening completely. "This should be good."

"And . . . it's us," Vasiht'h finished. "Right now, the thing that's most upsetting you is us. So we pulled back and woke you up to tell you we can't . . . well, we can't do anything more."

"Why not?" she said, brow lifted.

/Is she making a joke?/ Vasiht'h asked, incredulous.

/I think that looks more like a test to me./

"Because to fix your opinion of us is wrong," Vasiht'h finished.

"Isn't that what you've been doing with these other people?" she asked. "Fixing their opinions of things."

Vasiht'h's words came so tight with tension they made Jahir's shoulders ache. /Help. You handle this./

"It is one thing to offer someone help in battling an issue that has nothing to do with you," Jahir said. "Another to manipulate their beliefs to your own profit."

"And manipulating them to conquer their issues isn't to your profit," Ravanelle said, hands folding again on her knee.

"Only as much as it is to anyone's profit to see other people more content, more whole." Jahir replied, ignoring Vasiht'h's strain. "This is what we have gone into the profession to effect, is it not?"

"Helping people cope with their problems, their fears?" She tilted her head. "That's why most people do it, yes. You honestly think that's what you're doing? What if you hadn't figured out my problem? What if you'd spent weeks tromping around my subconscious, influencing me? What if you hadn't figured it out in time, and changed my opinion of you?"

"But we did figure it out," Vasiht'h said, quiet.

"And I daresay you have not changed your opinion of us," Jahir finished, and Vasiht'h sent a startled squeak through the mindline.

"Wow," Ravanelle said, studying him. "You're never that blunt."

"Forgive me," Jahir said. "It was not intended as insult. Merely as an observation. It is true, isn't it?"

She smiled a little then. "I think we're done here. You two can take the rest of the semester off."

"What about our patients?" Vasiht'h asked.

Ravanelle looked at them, brows lifted. "What about your patients, is it?"

"We have a responsibility—"

"Don't worry," she said. "They know the way it works at the clinic. They get a good rate, but they know the student therapists come and go. They're not going to expect to keep you."

They had to be content with that, Jahir thought, because it was all they were going to get. He opened the door for Vasiht'h by way of tacit suggestion and his roommate walked through it. They were halfway home beneath a sky gone gray and blustery when the Glaseah said, morose, "Well, that's done it."

"We did our best," Jahir said.

"If we'd just kept our mouths shut . . ." Jahir didn't have to send his disapproval through the mindline; Vasiht'h had trailed off and sighed, his mood gone leaden. "But we couldn't, of course. Not once we knew. It wouldn't have been right."

Jahir paced him, hands folded behind his back.

"You're not upset?" Vasiht'h asked.

"Yes," Jahir said. "But . . . surprised also, at the abruptness of our dismissal."

Vasiht'h frowned, and then yelped. "What? That was rain?"

"No," Jahir said, eyeing the sidewalk. "That was hail. Now we run!"

Racing for their apartment, Vasiht'h sent, /*There are not enough cookies in the world today.*/

/*Probably for the best. I'm not sure we could afford the ingredients for so many.*/

CHAPTER 33

Jahir received more mail now than he had expected he would ever, particularly given how difficult it was for people to reach him. He had distributed private keys here and there, but there were enterprising individuals who used other means, such as sending messages in care of the university, or Mercy. But he found himself glad of it. He had made his choice: he would stay. Now it was time to begin building the connections he had been leery of inviting when he'd been uncertain of his course. So he sent mail to Paga, practicing his sign, and listened with interest to the story of the Naysha's trip to the homeworld of the alien Platies, and renewed his promise to one day return to have his mindtouch with an aquatic alien. He read mail from Griffin Jiron and Radimir and Paige and Maya on how things were proceeding at the hospital, observing with amusement how different the letters were; Jiron tended toward a broad perspective, the hospital's interaction with society and with the recent drug outbreak, while Radimir's were mostly talk about hospital politics. Maya's were filled with funny—or hair-raising—anecdotes from working triage, and Paige's were commentaries on how working at the hospital differed from the expectations she'd had in school. He enjoyed them all and responded between his studies, hoping his own letters proved as interesting. He received occasional viseos from Kayla and Meekie as well, always a delight.

The one letter he'd been expecting, however, was long in coming. He spread the message from his mother, without alarm, knowing that very little changed on their world so there would be little news to prompt frequent letters. He read with interest about the various doings of his distant family members, and the tenant farmers and families that owed allegiance and received protection from his. It was not until he reached the end of the note that he paused, fingers stilling on the floating display.

The Queen informs me that you have acquitted yourself well recently, and earned the thanks of some of the Alliance's impor-tant organizations. I told her I was not at all surprised, as you have excelled at everything you have turned your hand to. I am proud of you, however, and I believe her to be also. She has sent along an increase in your stipend, saying that you will need it soon to settle yourself in your new profession—you are graduating soon, are you not? I say this so as to warn you, knowing that you have expressed misgivings about the stipend in the past. Do not argue with her about it until you know if she is right or not! I have no idea what it would cost to set oneself up as an independent in the Alliance. Perhaps you do? Either way, use the money, or let it accumulate. And tell me where you dwell, if you do not choose to stay on the world where you are being schooled.

Jahir skimmed the courtesies that ended the letter and leaned back. He had not thought as far as what he would do when he left, and it was an issue still a year away in the deciding. Did Vasiht'h have some notion? Would he want to stay? Assuming, of course, that Ravanelle did not fail them! He managed a grim smile. That would be luck. He could afford to tarry, of course, and try again at his leisure until some university gave him the license to practice. His partner did not have that luxury. He pondered putting the question to Vasiht'h, and decided there was no point until they knew when they would be done with the schooling. Composing himself to reply, he took up the stylus, wondering whether he should explain the Queen's cryptic comments. He was still trying to decide when a spark traversed the mindline in advance of Vasiht'h peeking into their bedroom. "Arii? I have news."

"Good news," Jahir guessed.

"Meekie and Kayla did so well they're done early. They're coming home this week!" Vasiht'h said. "Jill just asked if we wanted to be there for the reunion."

"Oh!" Jahir said, sitting up. "How could we miss it?"

"That's what I figured you'd say. I'll tell her." Running like a current beneath the words: *And we'll have something to look forward to.*

"Arii," Jahir said. "We will get through this."

"I know," Vasiht'h replied. "One way or the other."

⚬⚬⚬

The chosen day was a bright one, presaging summer; Jahir turned his face up to the sun as they approached the hospital and drew in the warm air, and through the mindline he felt Vasiht'h's pleasure at his pleasure.

/You don't feel it?/

/Sun on fur feels different,/ Vasiht'h replied. */Sun on skin is so much more . . ./*

/Intimate?/

/Immediate,/ Vasiht'h said after a moment as he padded into the foyer. */But that too./*

Upstairs, Berquist waved them in. "They know something's up, the rascals. Are you sure psychic powers aren't contagious?"

"I hope not," Vasiht'h said, laughing. "That sounds like a lot of trouble."

"Go on in." Berquist grinned. "Tell them we're going out. Just not where."

In the room, the three children were in soft, comfortable and shapeless outfits that reminded Jahir strongly of the first time they'd met in the parking lot, when the girls had been jumping rope. The two humans were sitting on their beds, swinging their legs, and Kuriel was leaning against one of them, playing with a plush Seersa doll. They all looked up when he and Vasiht'h entered, three eager faces, curious and young, and suddenly Jahir thought that they would all survive.

/From your thoughts to the Goddess's mind,/ Vasiht'h whispered, then said aloud, "Well, girls . . . are you ready for an adventure?"

"Me and my dragon army are always ready for an adventure!" Persy declared.

"Do we get to leave?" Kuriel asked.

"We do," Jahir replied.

"Then I'm even more ready than Persy."

"Let's go to it, then." Vasiht'h held out a hand and Kuriel took it, leaving Persy and Amaranth to follow Jahir. Berquist joined them outside and they all made their way to the lift, and from there to the lobby. How strange it was to realize that when he'd first come to All Children's he'd avoided the lifts for fear of touching strangers. The possibility still disturbed him, but he no longer allowed it to deter him either.

The gasps of their charges when they reached the world outside the hospital, and the blue summer sky and the warm air redolent of a spring nearing summer's marge . . . that was worth every effort.

"Why don't we walk this way?" Berquist said, pointing toward a field dotted with trees.

"Do you think we could climb a tree?" Persy asked, eyes shining.

"I don't even know if I can walk far enough to get to one of those trees," Kuriel muttered.

Vasiht'h snorted. "That's why you brought me along, right?" He patted his withers. "Free ride."

Kuriel stared at his back, then started giggling. "Okay. I will sit on you if I get tired."

They set off at an easy pace, letting the children explore at their leisure. Jahir followed Berquist's lead, and she seemed in no hurry.

/I could get used to this,/ Vasiht'h murmured, the sending dense with pleasure.

/We have been fortunate,/ Jahir said. /In so many ways. But in this way in particular . . . that we ran into these children, when we might never have met them./

/Or one another. I know./ Vasiht'h inhaled, nose lifted, and chuckled. /As the Goddess willed it./

Jahir smiled and ambled after Amaranth.

"Getting tired yet, girls?" Berquist was asking, and for her pains received a chorus of 'no's despite the flagging energy of her wards. "All right. Just a bit longer. Why don't you go sit on that bench for a minute, get your breath back?"

Amaranth said, serious, "Miss Jill, that bench is taken already. I see people sitting on it."

"I'm sure they'll make room," Berquist said, indulgent.

Amaranth eyed her as the other two girls padded past, then went with them. Jahir drew up alongside the healer-assist and said, "I believe good Amaranth is suspicious of you, alet."

"She would be." Berquist grinned. "You sure that psychic thing isn't wearing off on them?"

"If it is, what's about to happen isn't going to be any surprise," Vasiht'h said.

They all paused, waiting. The girls got to the bench and saw who was waiting for them there. The squeals were loud enough to be heard across the distance.

"Guess not," Vasiht'h said, grinning.

∞

Kuriel took advantage of Vasiht'h's offer on the way back, sitting astride him and resting her head on the back of his humanoid shoulders. She was heavy, but not much more than a few saddlebags full of books, so he made no complaint. Amaranth walked at Jill's side, but Persy looked up at Jahir and lifted her arms in mute appeal. Vasiht'h paused, about to say something, and stopped as the Eldritch lifted her up. The girl wrapped her arms around his neck and curled her legs around his waist, and the mindline brought a doubled impression, of the warmth and fragility of her body, and of her emotions: happiness, safety, exhaustion.

/All right?/ Vasiht'h asked, tentative.

/I am fine./ Jahir glanced at him and added, /And I thank you for your suggestion about the pool. You were right, and it has helped./

/You're welcome./

Back in the girls' room, they helped Jill tuck the children into bed, and to an instant sleep. Jill ushered them out and closed the door with satisfaction. "Now that was a good day. One of the best days they've had in a long time."

"We're glad we got to be a part of it," Vasiht'h said.

She smiled. "It wouldn't have been the same without the two of you. Which reminds me . . ." She eyed Vasiht'h. "Your residency year's coming up. When can I make my appointment?"

"I'm . . . sorry?" Vasiht'h said, ear feathers sagging. "Your appointment?"

"My appointment," she repeated. "The one I've been trying to make since you started doing research here! And you kept telling me that research psychotherapy wasn't going to prepare you to be a licensed therapist. Well, you've changed tracks, right? Which means you need to do a residency year. If you're doing it here, I want my appointment. And I want it before anyone else gets in!"

"Anyone . . . else?" Vasiht'h said weakly. He thought he found this funny—no, that was Jahir's amusement, leaking through the mindline.

"Oh yes." Jill sat on her stool and took up her cup of tepid coffee. "Everyone you did research on before can't wait to sign up. That's how I heard about it, actually. One of the students who's been seeing you in the student clinic came in to General next door with a broken leg and was talking about seeing the two of you, and it got to Healer Frendis—do you remember him? Maybe not. He was in one of your studies, anyway. Frendis told someone who told someone else and . . . you probably know how that works around here by now. Anyway, the short of it is, they're all speculating on whether you're going to be here for your residencies. I'm not. I want to make sure that if you are, I'm first this time." She folded her arms. "So consider yourself warned."

"I . . . yes. Of course." Vasiht'h said. "The moment we make our decision."

"Good."

Outside the hospital, Vasiht'h said, exasperated, "Oh, just let it out before you sprain a rib."

"You cannot sprain a bone, arii," Jahir said, somber . . . but his eyes were dancing. "So are we staying here for our residency?"

"We don't even know if we're going to pass our practicum!"

Jahir folded his arms behind his back and said nothing, strolling alongside with no evidence of concern.

"If we do—" Vasiht'h stopped, then eyed him. "You want to stay?"

The merriment in the mindline softened to something more serious. Still happy, but pensive. "Leaving was the wrong thing to do before," Jahir said.

"Right," Vasiht'h said. Staying did feel right. For now.

CHAPTER 34

T HE SEMESTER BROUGHT final exams. They immersed themselves in last minute studies, and Ravanelle did not summon
them back, not to continue her therapy, not to discuss their
grade. Vasiht'h's agitation was so extreme Jahir did not think
there was a recipe in the world that could have diffused it, so
he did not suggest any. Instead, he took his roommate for walks
long enough to tire even four legs used to Anseahla's greater
gravity, and blessed the school's swimming pool for developing
the stamina he needed to accompany his roommate.

But the semester did end, and brought with it their grades,
and Jahir knew as he entered their apartment that something
was wrong because the spike of rage that slammed into him was
so concrete he steadied himself on the wall to keep from staggering. That there was no blood involved was a shock.

Vasiht'h appeared from the door into the bedroom, radiating
his anger. "She gave us an Incomplete."

"I beg your pardon?" Jahir said, trying to think past his
roommate's wrath. He hadn't known Vasiht'h was capable of
such anger . . . not here, not absent some life or death situation
like what they'd fought on Selnor. "An Incomplete? What does
that signify? I've never been awarded one."

"It means we didn't finish the coursework to her satisfaction," Vasiht'h growled. "And to make it worse, she wants to see us about it." He lifted his data tablet, pointing at it. "We have an appointment. Today."

"Then . . . I am glad I have not taken off my boots?" Jahir said.

"How can you be so calm?" Vasiht'h stared at him. "She's holding our academic careers hostage!"

"I think I am calm because you are angry enough for us both," Jahir said. "And it is bidding fair to give me a headache. Arii, she is not holding our career hostage. There must be an appeals process, and if it fails we try again next semester. Healer Ravanelle is not the only professor overseeing the practicum."

Vasiht'h folded his arms. "This isn't another of your 'I just have to live with it' responses, like you had with Sheldan, is it? Because he was out of line, and Ravanelle is out of line, and you'd better believe we'll file a petition. We'll petition the living thoughts out of this. And then beat it for good measure."

The hyperbole was so ridiculous that Jahir paused, waiting for the Glaseah to admit to it. A resignation filtered into the mindline, feeling like an old rag to the touch. He wondered at the association but chose to say, "Are you calm enough now to see her?"

"No," Vasiht'h said with a lopsided grin that had absolutely no humor behind it. "But you're calm enough for us both."

———— ∞ ————

It wasn't a lie precisely, Vasiht'h thought as Jahir opened the clinic door. The Eldritch was calm enough for them both, and it helped make him willing to suffer through this meeting. But the Glaseah was also puzzled, and that was damping his anger now that he was thinking things through. The grade made no sense, and the meeting even less so. Why call for them if she'd already made her decision? More importantly, why wait to call for them until it was too late? He sighed as Jahir chimed for entrance to Ravanelle's office, and reminded himself that if it was too late there was no point yelling at her about it.

Then again, there was no reason not to, since it couldn't prejudice her against them anymore than she already was, apparently.

Without looking down at him, Jahir said, /*Let us not close doors without cause.*/

/*Even if slamming them is fun?*/

The corner of Jahir's mouth twitched.

/*Even if there is just cause?*/

/*Arii . . .*/

/*Fine, I'll be good.*/

/*Next time you tell me you are passionless, arii, I shall present you with the memory of this day.*/

Vasiht'h snorted. /*Being angry at Ravanelle is small business, compared to loving you.*/

Jahir glanced at him, wide-eyed, and then the door opened for them, revealing the Seersa rising from behind her desk. "Aletsen. Come in, please."

And here Jahir had been worried about him fighting to hide his anger. Vasiht'h was too busy being smug at how completely he'd shocked his roommate with a revelation that really shouldn't have been such a surprise. Being a thousand million years old didn't make someone omniscient, it seemed. Sitting in front of the desk, Vasiht'h wrapped his tail over his feet and resettled his wings, listening to Jahir take the seat alongside.

"Congratulations," Ravanelle said, putting a data tablet on their side of her desk. "On your passing the practicum this semester."

Amazing how quickly his smug satisfaction could shatter in the face of the knowledge that he could be caught just as flat-footed. Vasiht'h said, "W-what? But we had . . ."

"An Incomplete, yes," she said, nodding. "Because having you here was my way of making sure of things." She grinned. "Unlike the two of you, I don't read minds. Have to rely on my far more primitive gut instincts."

They didn't exchange glances, but it felt like they had. Vasiht'h yielded the conversational floor to Jahir, who said, "Perhaps not so primitive, as your conclusions have escaped me.

May I ask how we were tested, and what conclusions you drew from our reactions?"

"You may," Ravanelle said, leaning back in her chair. "And really, the whole semester's been the test. That's how it's supposed to work, of course, but I had to find other ways of evaluating the two of you, since I couldn't directly observe your methods. That was true, what I told you. Your evaluations were glowing—I've rarely seen such unqualified praise from the patients who come here—so there was that. When I canceled your appointments prior to the break—"

/I knew it! I knew she'd done it on purpose!/

"—it fascinated me that none of your clients were willing to switch to other therapists that week. And in fact, if I pieced together stray comments here and there correctly, they went looking for you, didn't they." She lifted a brow.

Vasiht'h cleared his throat and said, "They were just visiting."

She guffawed. "'Just visiting.' Sure. Be honest, alet. I'm not going to penalize you if the answer is—"

"Yes," Jahir said.

"Right." She continued, "So there was that. I also wanted to assess your reaction to the schedule change, not just theirs and, yes, you reacted much as I expected."

"Which was . . ." Vasiht'h said, wary.

"To help them, because they asked," Ravanelle said. "Not that I want to reward rule-breakers, but you're already breaking rules with how you're doing all this, so I'm willing to pay out the line a little. But having done that and seen that your patients came back to you, I started wondering if it was something you put in their heads. Which is when I asked for you to work on me."

"And when we found out that we were your problem," Vasiht'h began.

". . . and told me about it instead of fixing it," Ravanelle said, nodding. "That was encouraging. But I couldn't be sure of it unless I could be sure that you hadn't. That you weren't just saying that. So I canceled the remainder of my appointments and waited to see if my anxieties resolved themselves magically."

"But if they did not, then why did you pass us?" Jahir asked, bemused.

"Because I didn't," she said. "Until you walked into this door and I had a good look at your faces, and realized you're still a thorn in my side and I'm still irritated at you both for giving me no clear way to decide whether what you're doing is safe or good or not." She chuckled. "You didn't manipulate me. So I changed your grades while you were making faces at one another."

/At least that pause was good for something,/ Jahir murmured. Vasiht'h hid his smirk.

"Do you really believe us a danger?" Jahir asked, quieter.

Ravanelle hesitated, playing with her stylus. Then she set it down. "I tell you something, aletsen. You had three sessions with me, and . . . they were . . ." She frowned, looking away. "They were interesting." Shaking her head, she said, "No, that's not fair. They were sublime. Very peaceful. I felt . . . like someone was very focused on my welfare, and cared very much about not just me, but other people. Which is very much in line with your evaluations from the students. That girl who never spoke wrote that she could sense the bond between the two of you, and that assured her that there was love in the universe." The Seersa grimaced. "Which sounds like some honeyed greeting card verse. But she really believed it, and I went into those sessions skeptical of what I was going to find, and I felt it too." She sighed. "No, aletsen. I don't believe you're a danger. But the truth is I don't know how to teach you. I don't know how to critique you. And I don't even know how you accomplish anything. That makes me very uncomfortable as an educator . . . and I'm afraid I was glad to terminate those sessions, because I didn't really want to develop any deeper feelings about you both. So if I have any teaching to do, here it is." She pointed her stylus at them. "What you do is an intimacy even more profound than most therapy. You need to figure out how to disengage clients who become too engaged."

/She is not telling us . . ./

/A repeat of what I've told you before? That people like to fall in love with you?/ Vasiht'h tried not to laugh.

/*I believe she is talking about us, arii. Not just me!*/

/*You keep believing that.*/ More soberly. /*But her point about codependency is a good one. Say so.*/

/*And you cannot because . . . ?*/

/*I am too busy trying to keep a straight face, thinking of all the lovelorn men and women who are going to be collapsing in your wake.*/

"Thank you for the warning," Jahir said. "It is a good one. We will put serious thought into the matter."

"And thank you for passing us, despite us being the thorn in your side," Vasiht'h added.

"Yes, well. Get out of here," Ravanelle said. "And don't come back."

"Until next semester at least," Vasiht'h said, getting to his feet. "For the second session."

"You won't be here," Ravanelle said. "I'm recommending they advance you to your residency. Another practicum like this would be wasted; you need to be out there, flying under your own power. It's pretty evident to me you're going to be writing your own manual on this technique, aletsen. The sooner you start getting the experience in, the better."

From an Incomplete to being skipped forward a semester? Vasiht'h eyed Ravanelle, wondering if he detected a mischievous twinkle in her eye.

"We will do our best," Jahir said. "Good afternoon, Healer."

"Good luck, aletsen."

Outside the clinic, Vasiht'h stared at the brilliance of the sky and said, "Well. I think this calls for some gelato." He started trotting down the sidewalk and paused when Jahir didn't fall in alongside. "Or . . . maybe you want lunch instead?"

Quiet, Jahir said, "In sooth? You love me."

Vasiht'h shook his head. "Do you even have to ask?"

A long pause, and the mindline soaked it, like deep water and all the mysteries under it, and the currents that moved it. Jahir walked forward to join him, paced him. And after a moment said, "You know it is returned."

"I know," Vasiht'h said. And smiled, letting that settle

between them before he said, "So lunch, or ice cream?"

"Ice cream," Jahir said, grave. "Always."

EPILOGUE

"I'S THIS THE PLACE?" Vasiht'h asked. "The memory is hazy for me."

"This is it," Jahir said, and the quiet of the moment filled the mindline, twining with the shimmer of the sun on grasses bent by summer's breezes. He knelt there on the hilltop and spread his fingers through the grass until he could feel the earth, and even it was warm, radiating up through his palm. He sighed and closed his eyes. "Here."

Vasiht'h turned his face outward toward the source of the breeze, eyes narrowed against the glare.

"Do you feel her?"

Vasiht'h hesitated, then said, "Only in the memory of her blowing away on the wind here. I feel her . . . in that she's everywhere now. How the Goddess is. Everywhere, because Presence is everywhere. That puts her here," touching his breastbone, "as much as it puts her anywhere in the world."

"That is a good way of thinking of it," Jahir said, and let the words go, resting his hands on his lap and lifting his face to the sun. How long he remained there, he couldn't say; nor did the mindline suggest, for Vasiht'h seemed as ignorant of it as he. But after a time, he went into his pocket and brought forth the medical bracelet, and the chain he'd strung his ring on. He set them on the grass, smoothing the blades. The light traced the edge of the metal, glinted on silver.

After he stood, Vasiht'h said, quiet, "I had no idea you kept them."

"It is not so much that I kept them, as that I didn't throw them away," Jahir said. "They were not a thing to be thrown away." He glanced down at his offering. "They were a thing to be let go of." Like so many things in the Alliance he would one day have to give away. That he would lose. That he would have to make his peace with outliving.

A warm hand touched his wrist, startling him from his reverie. Vasiht'h waited until Jahir met his eyes, and then said, very clearly, "But not today."

"No," Jahir said. "But not today." He managed a smile. "I am decided, arii. Don't fear."

"I don't," Vasiht'h said. "Not anymore. I just don't want you to feel alone. And . . . that reminds me. Would you like to come home with me when I go back in a few days?"

"Ah?"

"My family," Vasiht'h continued. "They'd like to meet you. Now that we're done with the degrees, they very particularly want me to come home for a celebration, and Dami asked me to invite you specifically."

"I . . . I would be pleased to, and honored," Jahir said. "But I thought Anseahla was even heavier than Selnor?"

"It is. I wouldn't expect you to stay long," Vasith'h replied, beginning to walk down the hill. "I'm going to stay a couple of weeks, but you can just stop by for a day or two."

"And . . . then what?" Jahir asked, puzzled.

"Then, I thought you might check out a place," the Glaseah said, cautious.

The mindline shivered, offering flashes of images: a train ride, a busy port, a distant haze in a sky that looked real but memory told him was artificial. Not his memory. Surprised, Jahir said, "This is a place you want to live!"

"I think you might like it too," Vasiht'h said. "Which is why I'd like you to go explore it on your own for a little while."

"And this mysterious place?" Jahir sampled the images, felt the frisson of anticipation in them like wine.

"Starbase Veta. I got laid over there on my way to Selnor," Vasiht'h said. "It's . . . well. I'll let you see for yourself."

"Starbase Veta," Jahir murmured.

"You can pick out an apartment, as long as I get to buy the kitchen table."

Jahir laughed. "So sure you are of this."

"Let's just say . . . I have a hunch." Vasiht'h grinned. "Anyway, we're going to be late for our own graduation party if we don't get going. Or worse, all our guests will have drunk all the wine."

"Heaven forfend," Jahir said. "We shall make haste."

At the base of the hill, though, he turned. Looked back at what he was leaving behind. Presence was everywhere. Presence was here, and in the heart. He rested his palm on his breast.

"Jahir?"

"Coming," he called. They went down the hill together, leaving behind the stillness, the memories of ash smeared on brow, of the inevitable passing of all things . . . back to the city, to their apartment, where Jahir opened the door on the people awaiting them, the smell of fresh-baked cinnamon cake, of wine, the sound of laughter, the faces, the raised glasses welcoming them. He let Vasiht'h precede him, glanced once over his shoulder . . . and then smiled, and went inside.

His partner brought him a glass. /You're home,/ Vasiht'h said, warm as flagstones on a hearth.

/We're home,/ Jahir agreed, and took it from him. /My friend./

BRIEF GLOSSARY

Alet (ah LEHT): "friend," but formal, as one would address a stranger. Plural is *aletsen.*

Arii (ah REE): "friend," personal. An endearment. Used only for actual friends. Plural is *ariisen.* Additional forms include *ariihir* ("dear brother") and *ariishir* ("dear sister").

Dami (DAH mee): "mom," in Tam-leyan. Often used among other Pelted species.

Fin (FEEN): a unit of Alliance currency. Singular is deprecated *finca,* rarely used.

Hea (HEY ah): abbreviation for Healer-assist.

Kara (kah RAH): "child". Plural is *karasen.*

Tapa (TAH pah): "dad," in Tam-leyan. Often used among other Pelted species.

ALMOND SAUCERS

VASIHT'H'S VAULT OF COOKIE recipes would need its own cookbook (and chef) to be properly replicated. But almonds make a fair approximation of more-almond, so I'm including Vasiht'h's recipe for a nut butter cookie Jahir named for the shape of the results. Almond saucers are flat, thin cookies, but chewy, not crispy, and like their fictional counterparts are fabulously expensive due to their ingredients. They are, however, moist and modestly healthy . . . if you are suffering from high gravity syndrome.

Almond Saucers

- 1 cup and 2 tbsps almond flour
- ¼ tsp   baking soda
- ⅛ tsp   sea salt
- 1 ¼ cup   brown sugar
- ½ cup   butter (soft)
- 1 egg
- ½ cup   almond butter (or half almond and half peanut)
- 1 tsp   vanilla
- 6 oz   chocolate chips, melted (optional)

Preheat oven to 325° F. Mix flour, baking soda and sea salt in small bowl. Set aside. Cream butter and sugar in large bowl. Add egg, almond butter and vanilla and mix until smooth. Add in dry ingredients and stir. Refrigerate this dough for at least an hour (longer is better). Place tablespoon-sized dollops on parchment-paper-lined pan—leave room for spreading. Bake for 12–14 minutes.

For maximum decadence, wait until cookies cool, then dip half of the cookie in melted chocolate and allow to set. These are sweet cookies, so we recommend dark chocolate for the contrast!

Yield: 24 cookies (or so)

RETURN TO THE ALLIANCE
MORE FICTION SET IN THE PARADOX UNIVERSE

EARTHRISE, BOOK 1 OF *Her Instruments*. Reese Eddings has enough to do just keeping her rattletrap merchant vessel, the TMS *Earthrise,* profitable enough to pay food for herself and her micro-crew. So when a mysterious benefactor from her past shows up demanding she rescue a man from slavers, her first reaction is to say "NO!" And then to remember that she sort of promised to repay the loan. But she doesn't remember signing up to tangle with pirates and slavers over a space elf prince. . . .

EVEN THE WINGLESS. The Alliance has sent twelve ambassadors to the Chatcaavan Empire; all twelve returned early, defeated. None of their number have been successful at taking that brutal empire to task for their violations of the treaty. None have survived the vicious court of a race of winged shapechangers, one maintained by cruelty, savagery and torture. Lisinthir Nase Galare is the Alliance's thirteenth emissary. A duelist, an esper and a prince of his people, he has been sent to bring an empire to heel. Will it destroy him, as it has his predecessors? Or can one man teach an empire to fear . . . and love?

About the Author

DAUGHTER OF TWO CUBAN political exiles, M.C.A. Hogarth was born a foreigner in the American melting pot and has had a fascination for the gaps in cultures and the bridges that span them ever since. She has been many things—web database architect, product manager, technical writer and massage therapist—but is currently a full-time parent, artist, writer and anthropologist to aliens, both human and otherwise. She is the author of over fifty titles in the genres of science fiction, fantasy, humor and romance.

Mindline is only one of the many stories set in the Paradox Pelted universe. For more information and additional stories about Jahir and Vasiht'h, visit the "Where Do I Start?" page on the author's website.

Twitter: twitter.com/mcahogarth
Website: mcahogarth.org